BOOK 1 OF THE COVENANT OF SOULS

G.A. LUNGARO

This book is a work of fiction. Names, characters, businesses, organizations, places, events, and incidents either are the product of the author's imagination or are used fictitiously. Any resemblance to actual persons, living or dead, events, or locales is entirely coincidental.

Souls of Magic's Dawn
Copyright © 2020 by G.A. Lungaro.

All rights reserved. Printed in the United States of America. No part of this book may be used or reproduced in any manner whatsoever without written permission except in the case of brief quotations embodied in critical articles or reviews.

Published by Trinacria Press

Cover Design by 100Covers.com
Interior Design by FormattedBooks.com

For information contact :
http://www.galungaro.com

Map Art by G.A. Lungaro & Christopher Lungaro
ISBN: 978-1-7340679-1-0

First Edition: February 2020

10 9 8 7 6 5 4 3 2 1

Trinacria Press

DEDICATION

*To Jennifer
Isidora and this story would not exist if
it weren't for you and Oriana.*

ACKNOWLEDGMENT

To my children, Joseph, Chris, and Allie, you have always been my #1 fans. You have grown to amazing people, despite having me as your father.

To my wonderful and supportive life partner Amanda, you have been my rock through all my crazy projects, ideas, and endeavors.

To my editor Stacy, you elevated my writing and this story to another level. Thank you.

To Carmelo. You helped me publicize and promote this story with invaluable aid, honest sincerity, and with the motivation to want to help people succeed.

To my dogs Caramon, Leo, and Ghost… come on. They're dogs; they deserve love all the time. Also, two of them are named after characters from some of my favorite fantasy novels.

THANK YOU ~ KICKSTARTER BACKERS

Rich P.
Carmelo Chimera
Robert J. Sanchez III
Edward Angelo Reno
Christopher Lungaro
Mike Leaich
Martin C. Svendsen
Jeanne O'Connell
Richard Ohnemus
Ptahmet
Pookie
Ryan Colbeth
Josh Lucas
Jennifer Eagan
Adam Martinez
Maria Lungaro
Natale Vaniglia
Nick & Georgia Shizas
The Alaskan Greywolfe
K.R. Ruthenberg
William
Cody L. Allen

TABLE OF CONTENTS

Dedication..iii
Acknowledgment..v
Chapter 1.. 1
Chapter 2.. 7
Chapter 3..14
Chapter 4..28
Chapter 5..36
Chapter 6..42
Chapter 7..52
Chapter 8..61
Chapter 9..71
Chapter 10..75
Chapter 11..86
Chapter 12..90
Chapter 13..97
Chapter 14..110
Chapter 15..112
Chapter 16..118
Chapter 17..131
Chapter 18..139
Chapter 19..149
Chapter 20..158
Chapter 21..162

Chapter 22 175
Chapter 23 182
Chapter 24 194
Chapter 25 200
Chapter 26 207
Chapter 27 218
Chapter 28 221
Chapter 29 226
Chapter 30 234
Chapter 31 250
Chapter 32 253
Chapter 33 261
Chapter 34 268
Chapter 35 274
Chapter 36 282
Chapter 37 289
Chapter 38 298
Chapter 39 308
Chapter 40 324
Chapter 41 334
Chapter 42 337
Chapter 43 344
Epilogue 349
About the Author 355

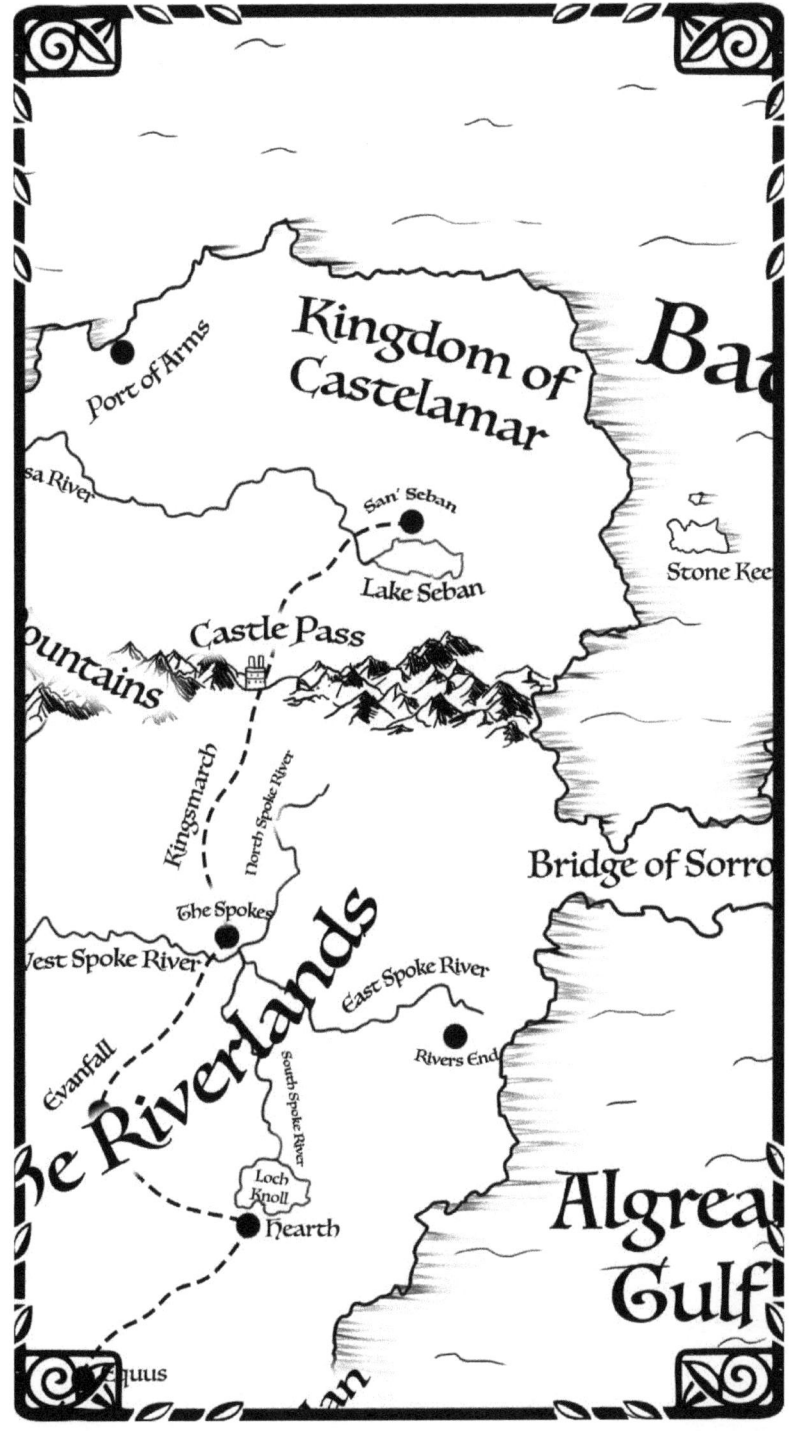

CHAPTER 1

"Would you stop squirming!" Isidora shook with irritation as she watched Gideon on his horse. The hood of her long black mage robes hid her expression.

"You know I don't travel in full plate unless headed to battle or to parley. It chafes and rubs," Gideon tugged at his breastplate in irritation. His armor was not as decadent as other knights. He saw it as a tool, not a piece of vanity. The only pride he took in its appearance was to polish it regularly, so it remained bright.

"I don't care if it cuts off the circulation to your head. Stop acting like a child," Isidora kept her head forward and urged her horse ahead. Gideon shifted once more in his saddle to adjust the chain mail hose that dug into his hindquarters before catching up with her.

"I still don't understand why I have to wear this. I could have just as easily worn a set of nice leathers. Better yet, I am a warrior-mage; I could have worn robes that would impress him more than plate," He yanked off his helm and shoved it in his pack at his side.

Isidora sighed and closed her eyes for a moment, her mind attempting to formulate a response that wouldn't offend the young man too much, "Gideon, my D'ni, my teacher is a Black Robe and a Sidhe. He would not consider what you do as true magic," Gideon did not know much of the ancient Sidhe language, but he had heard her use the words D'ni and Tra'ni enough to realize they meant teacher and student. He also knew when using those words; it went deeper than just the simple common tongue translation. Teacher and student shared a bond unlike no other when it came to the world of the Art. He shook his head. Although he knew he had her complete trust and love, he always felt a rivalry for admiration when it came to Azrael.

"My magic has saved me and my people many times, Isidora," He said casually.

Isidora's head spun around to face him and reared her horse to a halt. Her violet eyes grew narrow and bore into him, "You have not passed the Trials, Gideon. You have not spent your life in the study of the Art as Azrael, and all other true magi have! Do not compare being a mage to knowing a few battle spells!"

Her last sentence came out as an angry spit as she urged her horse forward at a slow gait. Gideon did not even attempt to mask his pained feelings as his horse trotted along beside her. He could sense her looking at him through the corner of her eye as they rode and knew Isidora immediately regretted her outburst. With a sigh, she softened her tone, "Gideon, you know I admire your poise and experience in battle. I trust my life in your hands willingly, not something I can say about many people," Isidora halted her horse and gave him a tender smile, "All I am saying is that I want my husband to make a good impression. Azrael is not easily accepting. It's bad enough I am coming to him to request his aid in becoming a Summoner. He never considered the use of Celestial Quintessence as true magic. He believes the quintessence to be a proxy between the mage and the magic."

Gideon returned her smile even though his stomach was doing somersaults. He knew much of Isidora's mentor. She never failed to remind him, disregarding that there were not many on Tinil'Gan who hadn't heard of the Archmagus Azrael. Azrael was Sidhe, a race of immortals. He was rumored to be over ten thousand years old and had been present during the creation of Tinil'Gan. Isidora had told him it was closer to four thousand years that Azrael had walked this plane, which was difficult enough for a twenty-four-year-old mind to comprehend, especially considering the shortness of human lifespans. Even shorter when you were a knight.

Isidora carried a lot of mystery around her. In a way, it was what first attracted him. It had been four years since this young, beautiful, and mystifying mage came to court. She had entered with commanding poise demanding to see the king, to offer her services as a mage. The rest of the court chuckled and murmured about what she looked like beneath the black velvet mage robes. She was beautiful without doubt. Curled, raven locks of hair spilled out from under her hood. Her eyes bright violet and wide, although he could tell she tried to make them more narrow. Her face was round, yet slim perfectly framing a fantastic smile during private times. There were times he felt dull next to her beauty. His hair was of a soft auburn with smooth waves. He was clean-shaven, unlike the style in Castellamar of mustachios. His jaw was square and definitive and his eyes of deep brown. He stood at a proper height of around six feet and a well-toned muscular build required of knights. Her beauty though was not what made him fall in love with her.

No one took her seriously because she was so young, barely twenty-two. Prevailing wisdom said that magi of any skill were of a more advanced age due to the years of study required. They had no idea this woman was trained in magic since she began to walk, by the one who was considered to be the most powerful mage on Tinil'Gan.

The first to learn what this meant was his cousin Vinnyearn. With his sword out in a relaxed manner, he had circled her, making glib remarks about how her robes did not show her shape. He paid dearly when he took it one step too far and attempted to lift the hem of her robes with the tip of his sword. With one quick murmured word from the enigmatic mage, Vinnyearn's sword began to glow red with the heat, as if it had just come out of a blacksmith's forge. With a yelp of pain, he dropped the sword and gripped his burned hand, and then found himself flung to the other end of the court, slamming against a wall. Isidora had not moved at all.

Tomfoolery soon turned to anger and distrust as the rest of the court moved in quickly to defend their injured comrade. Although not in the line of succession like Gideon who was the King's nephew, Vinnyearn was still a noble of House Montefroy, and the knighthood was akin to a brotherhood. Attack one, you attack all. Isidora made quick work of three of the five men who advanced towards her. Two of the knights were pinned against a wall by an ice spell, angrily struggling to free themselves, causing the others to look at each other in doubt. The last brave soul ran into an invisible shield wall Isidora had cast, knocking himself out at her feet just as King Diomere entered and brought the sparring to a halt. Gideon never moved a muscle but instead watched in rapt awe. Never had he failed to jump to action, but this display of courage and power enthralled him.

When the king demanded an explanation for the disruption and mayhem in his court, Gideon finally woke from his enchantment. He narrated the ordeal truthfully. His words of admiration for the young woman were felt by his uncle. The king was impressed with Isidora's boldness and apparent mastery of her Art and accepted her into his court, trusting his nephew's judgment to the dismay of Vinnyearn and his friends. Truth be told, the only thing truly injured was Vinnyearn's pride.

It didn't take Gideon long to formulate a plan to get to know the new mage. For the first few months, she rebuked him soundly and quite insultingly. Although still relatively young herself, Gideon at the time seemed like a child at twenty. Never deterred, he kept on pursuing her in his most innocent and boyish fashion. Eventually, the purity of his intentions and complete honesty of his love caught Isidora's attention. Although still rough around the edges, Gideon won her heart. Three years after her arrival in court, they married.

Now a year later he was accompanying his wife back home to begin a new chapter in her life. He chuckled softly to himself. He mused how to begin something new one typically returns to where they started.

The pair of riders crested a hill and looked down at the plains below. The late-summer breeze played upon the lush grasses and made them appear as waves upon a sea. In the distance, tiny thatched roofs of the homes dotted the landscape. These were the outskirts of the city of Arcanis; the capital city of the Isle of Winds and the home of Azrael's tower, *Il'Muni Arus*. It was just past midday, and the city proper was still at least a half day's ride away. Gideon sighed heavily and adjusted himself on the saddle once more in preparation for the last lap of the trip.

Isidora looked over, "It is not too far off now, my love. Once the proper introduction and niceties have been made, you will be able to get out of that armor. Until then, please compose yourself. I don't want Azrael's first thought of you to be that of a schoolboy picking the leggings out of his arse."

Gideon furrowed his brow and looked at Isidora questioningly, "First thought? We have been married for a year. How can the first time meeting me be his first impression?"

Isidora bit her lip. She aimed her voice to sound as innocent as possible, "Oh, didn't I mention that I haven't told him about us yet?" Grinning awkwardly Isidora spurred her horse at a gallop. Gideon remained behind as his mind pondered what Isidora had just said until finally, he realized.

"He doesn't know we're married? He doesn't even know who I am!" Paling, Gideon frantically spurred his horse forward in pursuit of his wife.

CHAPTER 2

Il'Muni Arus. In the ancient language of the Sidhe, it means the Tower of Mystics. As far as architecture goes on Ti-nil'Gan, Il'Muni Arus was a marvel; situated in the center of the temperate and serene Isle of Winds, off the western coast of the Evening Lands. When first constructed, the tower was designed to be a house of magic, as well as a fortification, thus its location at the foot of the Isle's largest mountain, Sky's Pike. Between the back of the tower and the base of the mountain's foothills was a large courtyard, which was only accessible from inside the tower. Contained in a magical barrier, this was where the tower's creator and primary resident, the Archmage Azrael, trained and practiced the more dangerous aspects of the Art.

The central spire, constructed of a seamless piece of onyx, rose to the sky in a twist formation. The tower was supported on three sides by flying buttresses. Two buttresses spanned out majestically from the east and west side and attached themselves upon two smaller towers that stood two-thirds the height of the central spire.

The tower proper soared up into the sky, where, on overcast nights, the clouds hid its upper reaches. Atop its incredible height, the building flared out into a large flat area which created a balcony. From this majestic vantage to the south was the principal city of the Isle, Arcanis.

Although the tower had many windows for the multitude of its rooms, most were dark when the sun had set and night enveloped the land. Except for a solitary light, that could be seen emanating from the uppermost window; Azrael's study. This evening, it wasn't any different.

The room itself was circular, its entire diameter taking up the top floor of the tower. Across from the door in the back of the circular room lay a large desk crafted from obsidian; and behind the desk sat Azrael. In front of him upon the desk rested a hefty tome. His finger traced the lines of text on the page as his eyes absorbed what he read.

The Archmagus was slight of build—a lifetime of study and the practice of magic does not develop a muscular physique—but he appeared to be the epitome of health and vigor. He wore the black robes as one of his order; the ones he wore today were his typical formal robes of sleek black velvet with silver embroidered runes along the hems of the sleeves. Even in the warm study, which had a pleasant fire in the hearth, he had the hood of the robes pulled up over his head. Underneath the hood, long silvery-white hair spilled out onto his shoulders. Although its color was not due to age, Azrael's hair was the only feature that gave him an aura of an older man.

His face bore no lines; it was still a relatively smooth face, olive in color, unlike the pale shades of the similar but very different Elves. His countenance was of a man in his mid-thirties, in human reckoning. The only lines that ever marred his features were slight smile lines that etched the side of his thin lips when he flashed a cynical smirk and small lines on the sides of his eyes when they narrowed—which was quite often. The immortality of a Sidhe afforded him this perk, but appearances mattered little to him. The sparkle from the fire reflected in his eyes, but it was not because they were bright. It was because his eyes were as mirrors, orbs that reflected all light. The select few fortunate enough to gain an audience with Azrael would say one could not see into Azrael's eyes, but rather only saw themselves reflected.

Although Azrael's power as a mage deterred most would-be enemies, those eyes caused fear of their own. The intense gaze of those mirrored eyes, coupled with the cunning wit and sharp mind of the Archmage, made it clear he was not a man to be trifled.

Azrael's eyes scanned the tome and the air before the desk shimmered and shifted slightly. Unperturbed, the immortal Sidhe continued his reading. The shifting air swirled for a brief moment then coalesced into a purple vortex. Out of this vortex appeared one silky feminine leg, and then another, soon followed by a voluptuous body.

The woman's clothing, what little of it there was, was a translucent red material molded to her skin. It covered just enough of her nether regions to leave little to the imagination. The top barely contained a buxom bosom and held them cupped like they were floating in water. Her hair was bright red and cropped short with a playful curl at each ear. The eyes curved upward and were completely crimson with no pupils. There was a slight hint of a point in her eye teeth. She floated slightly above the ground with her arms crossed, staring at the Archmagus with a playful grin on her face.

Without looking up or ceasing his reading Azrael addressed his visitor, "My study, Lear'Za, does not contain any nubile young boys or girls for you to play with, and I certainly hope you did not leave any of the villagers below looking for their young ones either. So to what do I owe this visit?"

Lear'Za's lips curved upward. With a wave of her finger, one of the ornate chairs in the room slid over to her and levitated off the ground. Smoothly, she sat down in the chair and crossed her legs all the while the chair remained slightly off the ground, "Oh come now *Seer'kaat*, you know I would never dream of doing that again ever since you threw a tantrum over a minor tryst. Besides, that was centuries ago."

One of Azrael's eyebrows lifted, but his eyes remained on the tome, "I would hardly call having your way with a young, newlywed couple and leaving them drained of their lives a tryst daemoness. Due to your antics, I had to feign destroying a blood-thirsty troll to calm the citizens of Arcanis."

Lear'Za chuckled slightly and stretched out seductively on the chair, "Oh, but it was so much fun *Seer'kaat*. I do so love the young ones the best, so innocent and soft. But that was a very long time ago, and I begrudgingly acquiesced that death and intercourse in this dimension are not as intertwined as in mine. If only succubi were not as misunderstood"

Slamming the tome shut, Azrael finally lifted his head and removed his hood. His mirrored eyes reflected Lear'Za's sultry smile at her, "I am beginning to regret allowing you free access to my tower, daemoness. I am a busy man, so spare me the details of your disgusting escapades and tell me why you find it necessary to disturb my studies."

Lear'Za displayed a playful pout of hurt feelings and sat upright. With a snap of her fingers, a long-stemmed crystal wine glass appeared in her hand, half-filled with red wine. She took a sip and addressed the Archmagus, "You do so hurt me, Seer'kaat. If you weren't so crusty and boring, I'd consider teaching you a few things. Alas, you are a curmudgeon, a bore, and not my type. At any rate, I heard you have a visitor arriving."

"Unfortunately I have many visitors, some invited and some not," Azrael said with pointed and impatient sarcasm.

Knowing that comment was aimed at her, Lear'Za gave another grin, "Well this visitor is also one of the selected few who has unfettered access to your humble abode. It has been a long time since I have seen her."

Lear'Za loved playing these games with him. She also understood that despite his outward display of disdain, he played the game back. On an outward glance, most would not understand their friendship. She was lost and trapped in a foreign realm when he encountered her. Tinil'Gan was so unlike her realm; she would never have made it three days, let alone three hundred years as a resident. She was, as a daemoness, incredibly powerful even on Tinil'Gan. Her power though was severely more limited than it was in her homeworld. Considering daemons on Tinil'Gan were used by magi as beasts of burden and slaves to further their ambitions; they were not people. If she had roamed Tinil'Gan alone without guidance and knowledge on how to assimilate, it wouldn't have been long before a cadre of magi would have set out to dispatch her. Azrael did not see her this way and respected her as the sentient being she was. Throughout the early years, he helped her learn this land, and in turn, her wise counsel had tempered his jaded and bitter nature. Through this adversarial turned mutual respect relationship, Lear'Za had become Azrael's most trusted confidant. She knew things about his life no one alive knew, and she knew details of his relationship with Isidora that not even the girl was aware of. She doubted the Archmage would have ever thought a daemoness, who for all intents and purposes was a succubus, would play the role of his conscious.

Sighing, Azrael rubbed his temples and sat back in his chair, "I assume you mean my Tra'ni. Yes, Isidora is expected to arrive. What matter is it to you?"

"She is more than just a student, Seer'kaat. We both know she is critical to the scheme of things to come," Lear'Za sipped her wine again, staring at him over the rim of her glass. In her mind, she counted to three, waiting for the outburst, and he did not disappoint.

Azrael stood abruptly and planted the tips of his fingers on his desk and leaned forward, "Do you think I need reminding? This has been my burden for thousands of years. Trust me, I know it far more intimately than you," He stood upright and folded his hands behind his back. Turning slightly, he gazed out the window that was behind his desk, "Events are moving quickly now. The time is approaching."

"You have not spoken to her in a few years," Lear'Za said pointedly.

"It is quite difficult for me seeing she just left my tower that night without a word," the mage said without turning.

"Do I detect a hint of hurt feelings?" Lear'Za said with a chuckle. Azrael merely snorted. She knew Isidora's departure had hurt him even though he would never admit it, "You knew that was to pass," Lear'Za whispered as she ran a finger around the rim of her wine glass.

Azrael tilted his head to the side, "Of course I did! It does not, however, make it any easier to stomach. After all I did for her."

Lear'Za placed her hand over her mouth to stop herself from laughing out loud, "After all you did? You made her life here a veritable hell, Seer'kaat. You were far from kind."

Azrael spun around, his mirrored eyes boring into the daemoness, "What do you know of kindness? You rape and maim for sadistic pleasure! I did what I had to do for her to live up to the potential that flows in her veins."

"I do not rape! They all come to me willingly. But I digress," Lear'Za took a small sip of her wine, "A kind word of encouragement and praise now and then would not have killed you."

Azrael sighed heavily, and his head dropped some, "Kind words are for infants and the sickly. Much as steel must be hardened by a hot flame, so must the soul be forged. She would not be prepared for what is to come if I coddled and babied her. Emotions cloud the mind, Lear'Za. People such as us cannot afford to have the waters muddied."

"You know I care little for other's feelings, Seer'kaat. In her case, I think there should have been an exception. At any rate, she is close and will arrive shortly," Another sly grin played on her face, and she bit her lip once more, "She has someone with her."

"She is a mage in the service of Castellamar traveling in free lands. They have been traveling for well over a week. It is only natural that she brought an escort with her."

Her grin grew wide, and she licked her lips, seductively, "I think this one is different."

Azrael's eyebrows rose questioningly. His thoughts were interrupted by a humming globe that slowly floated off his desk to hover before him. Inside the globe was a shimmering image of one of the many servants that took care of the tower.

"My lord, the Lady Isidora and her escort have arrived. Shall I send them up to your study or have them quartered and fed first?" The image of the servant in the globe said stoically.

"Their journey was long and tiring. Give them some food and drink. I am sure Isidora will also want a warm bath. Once they are rested, we can retire to the main library."

"Understood my lord," The globe flittered away, sat upon his desk, and went dark.

Lear'Za touched the rim of her glass with a finger, and it refilled itself with dark-red wine, "Do you mind if I join the party?"

Azrael's eyes narrowed, "If I said no, would you oblige?"

Lear'Za took a playful sip of her wine and smiled, "Of course not."

CHAPTER 3

Isidora took a deep breath and sighed when she stepped over the threshold of the doorway.

"I will help tend to the horses Isi, I'll catch up with you," Gideon said with a smile. Isidora smiled back and entered the foyer.

She had forgotten how grand the old place was. When she had first arrived here, she was only five years old. Then, the tower had seemed as vast as an entire city to the eyes of a child. In between studies, she had roamed for hours in the near-empty tower and still had only seen a small fraction of the rooms. She always smiled when she thought back on it. It had been her home since Azrael came to Longerbane for her.

That day, most of the people in her small village had cast wayward glances when they saw the dark-robed Archmage walk through their streets. He spoke to no one nor did anyone dare approach him. Although they were simple folk, uneducated in the ways of magic, even they could feel the power he commanded as if it were a thing tangible in the air. The man knew where he was headed and intended to make his way there as quickly as possible.

House Shadowbane was a lessor house of Castellamar for many years. In the days of the Old Kingdom, its status had been much higher but fell after the rebellion. Thus, the home of Griffon and Mara Shadowbane was modest and humble. They were an older couple, older than most parents of a five-year-old would be. They had tried for many years to have a baby and had nearly given up hope. Joyously, Mara had found herself with child after she had all but dismissed the notion. It was, indeed, a miracle.

Often times, people try to look for more common reasons for an event rather than claim miracles. It was when Isidora was about a year old that Griffon started noticing the looks and whispered conversations behind his back. It didn't take him long to realize the townsfolk thought him cuckolded by his wife, "Good old Sir Griffon," they said when they thought he couldn't hear, "couldn't be man enough to father a child, so Mara had to find herself a suitor," It didn't help that Isidora's bright violet eyes were a far cry from Griffon's dark amber eyes, or that both he and Mara were fair-haired and Isidora had raven locks. He ignored it, for the most part, and believed in Mara's honor, but he could not deny the fact that his daughter was different. Griffon often told Isidora he wasn't surprised when the black-robed man came knocking on their door that day.

He had explained to Sir Griffon and Mara that she was special. She was a child of magic born uniquely, unlike any other child. The magic that roared inside of her would quickly overwhelm the young girl as she grew if it was not harnessed and trained. The man introduced himself as Azrael and offered his services as a teacher of the magical arts to help Isidora learn to control her gifts. He assured Griffon and Mara that he would see to all of Isidora's needs and that it would cost them nothing except time with their daughter. The training process was long and arduous, and she would reside with Azrael at his tower on a far-off island. Her father objected for as long as he could, but finally, Mara convinced him to let her go with Azrael. Despite all the jabs and whispers, she felt nothing but love from her father. Mara always reminded her that he was dour until the summers when she would return home for a few months.

I should go visit Ma and Da after this trip. It has been too long. She smiled then was roused from her musings when a servant appeared and bid her follow.

Not much had changed since she was last here; indeed, not much had changed since her youth. Most of the rooms were unoccupied. Azrael was the master and sole resident, except for the small serving staff that oversaw daily operations. She followed one of the servants up the ornate wide spun spiral staircase. As she ascended, her hand brushed along the smooth varnished oak handrail—the same handrail she had held onto most of her young life. She counted the steps as she always had and smiled to herself when they stopped after twenty-six, which meant they had arrived on the third floor.

The third floor is where she lived for nearly twenty years. She went home to her parents Griffon and Mara for a month or so in the summer or during holidays like Yule and the Spring Solstice festival, but for the most part, this tower was her home. She didn't even have to look up at the servant to know the room in which he was leading her to. After the stairs, turn right, four doors on the left side. When she entered her old room, she gasped and froze.

Not one thing had changed since she left five years ago. Her elemental charts still hung on the wall. Her desk scattered with various vials and small containers. On the corner of the desk stood a stack of vellum: her poetry. Her bed was unmade, left the way it was the morning she got up and left the tower for good. She felt a hand on her shoulder, and looked over at Gideon who had found his way upstairs courtesy of another servant. She smiled wistfully and placed her hand on his.

Gideon's eyes scanned the room in awe, "So this is where you grew up. Your room was tidier than mine ever was. Except for the bed, of course."

She chuckled and lightly slapped his hand, "Stop it. Azrael valued order as a virtue as much as he values the Art. He instilled those same values in me. The bed, that last morning was a tad hectic for me," Slowly, she walked to the bed and sat down. Her hand brushed softly across the down pillow, and her teary eyes lifted to the nightstand. Almost instantly, the tears dried. Her face became dark and hard. Standing abruptly, she grabbed the envelope that sat upon the nightstand. It was the letter she had left for Azrael the morning she left. It was still unopened; the red wax seal unbroken. Gritting her teeth the letter went up in a short-lived flame in her hand and fell to the ground as ash. Gideon quickly came to her side and sat down beside her on the bed.

"What was that, Isi?" His face creased.

She sniffled and dusted off the ash on her hands, "It's nothing of concern. Like the past; dust and ash."

His face fell as he held her shoulders, "Isi, you know you can always talk to me."

An uncomfortable cough from the servant who stood at the door ended Gideon's words made them turn their heads quickly.

"Is everything in order my Lady, or do you require any more service?" The servant shuffled uneasily.

"I am afraid it is not in order," She shrugged from Gideon's embrace and stood tall, "This is the room of a foolish young girl. I am no longer that girl but a grown woman. A grown woman with a mate. We require a room large enough to accommodate a couple."

"I will have to talk to the Master to assure..."

"You will have to do no such thing. I have seen many guests ask for specific needs and rooms during the years I was here. I know the room at the end of the hall is a large suite with a large bed. Bring our things to the room and draw me a bath. Don't make me ask twice."

"Yes, yes, my Lady, without delay," The servant scampered off down the hall while shouting for his subordinates to prepare it. She turned and looked at her old room once again.

Gideon walked up behind her and placed his hand on her shoulder, "Don't you think you were a bit harsh to that man? He was just doing his job, you know."

Folding her arms, she hardened her face, "He can take it. He just needed to learn I am no longer a little girl and student."

He dropped his hand and hugged her from behind, placing his chin on her shoulder, "You sure you don't want to talk about this?"

"It is nothing of concern, Gideon. Nothing of concern at all."

The servant's voice from behind them made them turn, "Your bath is ready, my Lady."

Nodding to the man, Isidora and Gideon walked out of the room. Isidora stopped briefly to close the door behind her, "I want the room cleared of its effects and disposed of, I want nothing of it."

Gideon looked at the closed door and then at Isidora as she walked away down the hall, his face saddened and creased with worry.

There were not many on Tinil'Gan, who could claim to have been allowed access to Azrael's tower, but those that were could recount one thing for certain: the Library of Il'Muni Arus was vast. Scholars from around the realm clamored to gain access to the thousands upon thousands of ancient texts and tomes the library housed. The secret and lost pieces of history most likely could be found there. Isidora knew Azrael reveled in this. He enjoyed the knowledge that he was among a very select few who had an accurate account of the history of Tinil'Gan. Having lived for over three millennia, afforded him this pleasure. His aid was so invaluable to her ambitions for this reason. She had to convince him.

It was in the center of this vast, brightly lit room in which Lear'Za had taken a seat—a seat which hovered slightly above the ground. She lounged in the chair playing with a nearly empty wine glass, a bored expression on her face as Azrael walked along the bookshelves. His arms folded behind his back and now and then he would pause to admire a particular tome. Isidora paused outside the entryway with Gideon behind her. He gave her a look as if to ask why they are stopping. She placed a finger to her lips to indicate silence. She then quietly watched and listened.

Lear'Za sighed loudly and dropped her head in her hand, "Were you planning on ever engaging in any stimulating conversation, or would you rather make love to a book?"

Azrael cocked his head to the side and gave Lear'Za a thin-lipped smile, "I admit these books offer me more excitement than you do, daemoness. Pardon me for having a more refined taste," Isidora placed a hand over her mouth to suppress a laugh. She always enjoyed Azrael's and Lear'Za's bickering. Watching this helped ease her nervousness for the discussion that was to come.

"Do you have any idea how many men would kill to have me sitting in a room with them?" Lear'Za leaned to the side and draped a shapely leg over the arm of the chair, "You treat it like a curse."

"I would hardly call it a blessing. Pleasures of the flesh have never intrigued me. Emotions, such as lust..."

Lear'Za rolled her eyes and finished Azrael's sentence, "...cloud the mind and offer no real intellectual value, blah blah. I have heard it many times, *Seer'kaat*. Who has ever said sex had to be intellectual? I think I would curl up and die if I had to be in a constant state of mental acuteness to enjoy myself. It is called fun. Tell me, have you ever even tried it?"

Isidora had seen enough and giggled quietly. Beckoning Gideon to follow, she entered the room, "I doubt he will answer that question, Lear'Za. Even if he has tried it, he would never admit to it." Lear'Za spun her head in the direction of the voice. She wore black robes similar to Azrael's; the hood pulled down to reveal long, curly locks of raven black hair and bright violet eyes.

"Isidora! My goodness child, you have blossomed!" She rose from the chair and floated lightly over to Isidora and embraced her, "It is good to see you, my dear. You look stunning! The Archmagus over there is dour as usual. Tell me, have you reconsidered my offer?"

Isidora chuckled and smiled, "Although I am honored Lear'Za, I am sorry to say women never have and most likely never will be my fancy," The young man behind her blushed a rosy red.

Lear'Za seductively chewed her lip as she peered over Isidora's shoulder at him, "How about your strapping escort? Perhaps he might want to go play some while you and crusty over there chat?"

The young man's blush deepened, and he suppressed an audible choke. Isidora's gaze became firm, "Not unless the both of you want to be at the bad end of one of my spells."

Lear'Za's eyes flashed in excitement, "Isidora, you devil you!"

"Oh, for all that is holy, are you quite done with this foolishness?" The idle chatter irritated Azrael, and he finally turned from the shelves that lined the wall. Isidora wondered if the servant told him she called Gideon her mate. Lear'Za's enthusiasm wasn't helping either. Her fingers played with the hem of her sleeves, hoping this wasn't the case, "I assume you are here for a reason, Tra'ni. Considering you left five years ago without so much as a word, I doubt you are here to reminisce," Azrael's tone was harsh, and the use of the Sidhe word for student was intentional.

Isidora's eye's narrowed, a habit picked up unwillingly from Azrael, "Yes D'ni, I did come for a reason. I apologize for having manners and greeting an old friend. It slipped my mind that civility was not one of the things you felt were important," She said firmly, her shoulders now set back and her back straight and confident. She was not going to show any weakness; he had to know how serious she was. Thoughts of her marriage flew from her mind as she set her resolve.

"Manners are lost on the uncouth, my dear child," Azrael spat back, "I might as well have wasted my time teaching a stone to speak. Now that the oh so wonderful pleasantries have been observed, are you going to bother to introduce the poor man stuck in mute silence behind you?"

Isidora stifled an irritated groan, her previous fears about explaining their relationship began to gnaw at the edge of her consciousness; instead, she smiled and placed her arm in Gideon's, drawing him to her side, "This is Sir Gideon Stormcaller. He is the son of Sir Falco of Castellamar, fourth in line for the throne of the Kingdom," Gideon gave a broad uncomfortable smile as he shuffled his feet slightly. Azrael raised an eyebrow. Then he began to chuckle, a chuckle that grew into roaring laughter a moment later. Lear'Za smirked and shook her head.

But Isidora was not amused. Gideon looked at her, quizzically, "Pray tell, D'ni, what do you find so amusing?" Her words came out stained with venomous anger. She clenched her fists, preparing herself for the answer. *He figured it out*, she thought

Azrael's laughter lightened, and he smoothed his robes as he tried to compose himself. He flashed a thin-lipped smirk as his mirrored eyes shone sardonically, "I do apologize Tra'ni. Honestly, I do. Castellamar, you say? The same Kingdom of Castellamar that boasts of valiant knights, who do nothing except competing in tournaments every other month? The kingdom is a shadow of its former self."

"Enough!" Isidora's body shook with rage. "You have gone too far this time, Azrael! He has done nothing to you..."

"Isidora, please," Gideon had finally broken his silence and placed a hand on her shoulder, gently moving beside her. Isidora felt a wave of relief come over her. She was about to blurt out everything and that soft touch from Gideon refocused her. If Azrael's comments had injured him, she could not see it on his rugged face. It still held the youthful, innocent composure that had made Isidora fall in love with him, "Your teacher is correct. Honestly, I am ashamed of the way my family has conducted itself the past few generations. And yes, it is true Castellamar is not the mighty empire it once was. We once controlled all the lands east of the Distillar River and south to the Ironwall Ice Shelf. Now we hide behind the Castellian Mountains, reveling in stories of old. Those of us faithful to the old ways hope that King Diomere will hold true to his recent decree..."

A derisive snort from Azrael interrupted Gideon's words, "King Diomere is both a fool and a puppet of the Council of Lords, most notably Lord Sulik."

Isidora could see Gideon stiffen and clench his jaw. She patted his arm; it was now her turn to comfort him. Lord Sulik was well-known as a power-hungry man. The fact that Lord

Sulik was Sir Falco's brother and Gideon's uncle made the comment truly barbed. The only consolation was Sulik had accepted the role of Realm Regent under his father's time as king. To prevent conflicts of interest a Realm Regent, if of royal blood, gave up their rights to succession.

Azrael sat down in one of the comfortable chairs, "We are not here to discuss politics, are we? If I am not mistaken, you have come here to request something of me. Let us get on with this."

Isidora pushed down an overwhelming feeling of anger. She knew this was Azrael's way of once again getting in the last word on a subject. There was no way she could respond to that barb without appearing childish and impulsive. Swallowing her pride, she sat in a chair not far from Azrael. Gideon took a position standing behind her.

"You are correct, D'ni. I have come to request your assistance. While I know full well your opinion on such matters, I am a true mage in the ways of the Art, who has passed my Trials. This gives me the right to decide my fate and path. I have decided to become a Summoner," She noted Azrael's usually narrow and probing eyes widened. Undeterred she continued, "I know you do not consider summoning true magic. However, I have done much study on the practice. I am not making this decision with my eyes closed."

Slowly, Azrael sat forward, his hands gripping the armrests tightly, "This is a waste of your talents, Isidora."

Lear'Za sat in a hovering chair to Azrael's right. She had remained quiet during the verbal battle between teacher and student—she witnessed far too many in the past to bother interfering. Isidora was grateful when she spoke up, "Why don't you hear her out, Seer'kaat? What is the harm? She is a grown woman now, capable of making her own choices," Isidora nodded to Lear'Za in thanks, but Azrael shot the daemoness a glance she understood without words. Some choices were made for her before she was even born; a fate she cannot prevent.

"As Lear'Za has said, I am more than capable of deciding the course of my future. There are so few Summoners not because their magic is wild and unpredictable, but because it is misunderstood," Isidora was confident he knew all about this type of magic. He was always analytical; she needed him to understand using her own words, the passion she held for it, "A Summoner is not a puppet of the Celestial Quintessence, or the avatars summoned from therein. Yes, the quintessence is a powerful force of nature, but it is sentient. It feels and is conscious. Within it resides the souls of beings who selflessly sacrificed their mortal lives for a greater good — beings whose great sacrifice granted them celestial powers and a home within the quintessence. As an avatar, they can continue the battle for justice and the greater good, but this time with power and immortality. A Summoner merely guides these avatars and uses their magic to give them form upon Tinil'Gan. Something I feel not only am I completely adept at doing, but I was made to do."

Azrael sighed and sat back, looking up at the high ceiling. Isidora searched his mirrored eye for a clue of what he was thinking, but as always could not. Azrael rubbed his eyes for a moment and then turned his gaze to Isidora, "You are aware a potential Summoner must first be chosen by The Calling."

It was Isidora's turn to smile, "Of course, not only have I been given The Calling but I already have my Natural Avatar," Isidora smiled wider with pride. A person did not choose to become a Summoner. A magical invitation is given telepathically from the Quintessence, a method known as The Calling. The choice made by a person is whether or not to answer this call. Once the choice is made, the first duty of the new Summoner was to summon an avatar from the Quintessence. The task was not a simple one. Most avatars had innate power, drawn from the quintessence. To summon a Natural Avatar, a Summoner must give some of their magic, a piece of their life force, to give form to it.

She closed her eyes. A slight hum filled the room, and a violet aura began to glow around her. She raised one hand. She murmured, "Lelani hear my call and arise," A shimmering violet glyph appeared on the floor between them. The glyph wobbled slightly, and Isidora could feel a bead of sweat forming on her brow. She steeled herself and delved deep into the magic she felt in her blood. The glyph stabilized and began to spin slowly and hypnotically. A swirl of ethereal violet fog came up from the center and swirled back and forth is a sweeping fashion over the glyph. Suddenly it began to twirl like a funnel cloud, small tendrils of purple lightning highlighting it. It shot up high into the ceiling and crashed down into the glyph. When the fog cleared it revealed a translucent violet fox. The fox shook its body as if waking from sleep and came to sit beside Isidora's chair. She had put forth great effort to arrive at this point. She could only hope that Azrael would be equally impressed.

"It seems you have already committed to this path before coming here. Now you expect aid and support? Have I taught you nothing?" Azrael's voice strained. She clenched her teeth.

"I expect nothing D'ni. You taught me to rely on no one and that my only true ally was the Art. I did precisely as you have taught me. To have confidence in my power and control over the Art!" It was the loudest she had gotten since they had arrived. She once again felt Gideon's reassuring hand on her shoulder as he stood behind her chair. Lelani lifted her head slightly when Isidora yelled in concern, then nuzzled her snout into her tail when she saw her master was ok. She gave the fox an assuring pet.

She watched Azrael as he stood from the chair and paced the space between them. She did not know where this would go at this point. He stopped and faced her.

"There is no turning back now. What do you need of me, then?" He said in a defeated tone.

Her jaw dropped; she expected more resistance from Azrael. She tried to compose herself before speaking. One thing she did not want Azrael to know was the great amount of effort and concentration needed to maintain Lelani once summoned. It took so much of her energy that if she wanted to construct a simple protection spell at that moment, she would be unable to, "As you well know, a Natural Avatar is far from the only avatar a Summoner can produce; it is merely the first stage. There are more powerful avatars out there somewhere, hidden in secret places that were sacred to them in life. It is those places I must find. I have already done the research on heroes of the past that have most likely been touched by the quintessence in the afterlife. I know how well-traveled you are, not to mention the vast collection of maps, past and present, you have in your possession. Your aid in finding these places would be invaluable to me D'ni," She paused to catch her breath. The combination of her zeal and the energy sapped by Lelani was starting to affect her significantly. She could feel small beads of sweat on her forehead even though the room was cool. She looked into Azrael's mirrored eyes and could not tell if he noticed her fatigue. *The more powerful avatars would take even more of my energy to keep summoned. I will not give in to fatigue now. I am stronger than this.* She cleared her throat and continued, "All I ask is for your guidance through Tinil'Gan, to find these avatars."

Azrael steepled his fingertips under his chin, "Although I don't approve of this path you are taking, Isidora, I will assist you. If for nothing more than to further my education in this particular craft, as well as making sure you don't get yourself killed. So be it."

Lear'Za clapped her hands loudly with a broad grin on her face, "Finally some excitement! Road trip, it is my dears! There is so much to prepare! We will have to take my carriage; it has all the creature comforts. Of course, I insist you ride with me, Isidora; it's only befitting for a lady. I am sure your D'ni won't mind us bringing some of the wine he has casked in the cellar."

Isidora's mind was in a frenzy. She was beside herself, not believing this was happening. Lear'Za's excitement gave her more confidence; this was the right decision. She gripped Gideon's hand that was still on her shoulder and looked up thankfully.

Annoyed, Azrael turned to Lear'Za and raised an eyebrow, "Who said you were coming along, daemoness?"

Lear'Za curled seductively in her chair and winked, "Who's going to stop me, Seer'kaat?"

Isidora smiled at the daemoness' humor. She thanked the gods for the distraction Lear'Za provided and released Lelani. Exhausted, she slumped in her chair. The first of the two things she wanted to tell Azrael had passed successfully. The other that she was a married woman, still loomed large in her mind.

CHAPTER 4

"Are you certain, this is the one you want to try for?" Azrael asked as his eyes poured over the tome Isidora had given him.

Isidora hesitated, glancing out the library window. It looked out over the tower's garden, where beds of colorful flowers arranged in patterns around curving walkways — pink, yellow, purple — bloomed in the sunshine. She'd spent hours reading in the garden when she was young, but never bothered to learn what any of the flowers were. Now, as an adult, she recognized the peonies, hydrangeas, and larkspurs, among others. The colorful and quiet peace of those memories brought a smile to her face and calmed her.

"Yes," she said, turning her gaze back to Azrael, "Yes, I am sure. Potential avatars have the greatest possibility of manifesting from the souls of heroic sacrifice. Sir Reginald Tempest is one of the most storied figures of Castellarian history. His valiant deeds at the Battle of Rania are legendary," She stood near the table where Azrael placed the book for further inspection. Glancing around the room, she saw Lear'Za remained seated quietly. Isidora noticed her ever-inquisitive eyes intently paying attention. Since her youth, outside of her magical training, Lear'Za was never far from Azrael's side. Her magical family was indeed odd—a daemoness succubus who showed love and compassion. In a way, she felt like an aunt to her—a counterbalance to Azrael's dourer demeanor. Her eyes then went to Gideon, who was close by offering his quiet support by his presence. Everyone in the room knew this current conversation was between teacher and student.

Azrael smirked as he rubbed his forehead, "And this choice has nothing to do with that one," He tilted his head towards Gideon. Isidora rolled her eyes.

"Of course not, D'ni. Please try and grasp the fact I am a grown woman, and regardless of your animosity, I did learn from you. I have a good feeling about this and sincerely believe we will find an avatar at the place of Sir Reginald's sacrifice. The real question is where. Rania is nothing but a desert now," She looked at Gideon and could see a hint of irritation on his face. Gideon had a hard time grasping why she revered her teacher so much when he was so irritable and at times seemingly cruel. It was difficult to explain with words.

Taking his iron-handed approach was not easy, but she knew it never came from a place of malice. There was always a sense of fatherly concern in his criticisms. She always sensed there was a great sadness within the Archmage, and this always tempered her anger. There was one time, when she was around ten, that she asked Lear'Za why Azrael never looked happy. Lear'Za responded by holding her cheek and telling her a person's past can mold their lives. She was puzzled by this; to this day, she cannot fathom what trauma had befallen her teacher to mold him into a jaded and bitter man. If there was one thing she was sure of, Azrael always had her best interests in mind, even if it was overbearing.

Azrael went to a nearby shelf filled with rolled-up parchments. Thumbing through a few he stopped on one with a barely audible "Ha" and pulled it from the shelf. He brought it to the table and unrolled it, revealing what seemed to Isidora to be a very ancient map.

"This map, I acquired almost six hundred years ago from a traveling merchant. He desperately needed some paracress herb for a transaction he was making with another mage. Paracress was quite rare and expensive at the time. I so happened to have a good size cache of it. He told me he would pay any price. I don't think he realized with whom he was involved. I asked him for his collection of maps. Considering the deal a steal, seeing he had to pay no amount of currency, he gladly offered them up. Most of them were nothing out of the ordinary except for this treasure."

Isidora gaped at the map, "This looks nothing like the world today. Castellamar owns everything east of the Distillar River on the Western Continent. There is no Duminos or Kardian Empire."

"This map dates back more than two thousand years, before the splitting of the Elvan Realm, to the time when your friend's ancestors were more than the sham they are now; the Age of Power. During this period, Castellamar's chief rival for power was the Kingdom of Rania. The Luminori Elves only controlled the lands west and south of Luminos, with the Distillar as a natural buffer zone between them and the rest of the world," Azrael's hands smoothed out the map lovingly.

"Rania was not always a desert. In fact, it housed some of the most fertile lands on the Western Continent. It had a natural port to the north for trade; a large coastline for fishing, and despite its smaller size, it made Castellamar quite a foe. The Battle of Rania you spoke of is what brought about its ruin some 2,500 years ago. Most know of the cataclysmic event that brought about the kingdom's destruction, the Devastation, but many dispute the epicenter of the battle."

Isidora frowned at the map. Although Rania looked small, she had heard about the vast expanse of the Ranian Desert. Nothing remained there now except miles and miles of dunes. Whatever might remain of the battle site was certainly covered up by the endless desert now. Her hopes fell into the pit of her stomach, "How are we ever to find anything in that god-forsaken place?"

Azrael's finger traced a line through what was once the Kingdom of Rania and paused. He spun suddenly and went to another nearby bookshelf and scanned the rows of leather-bound books. He spoke out loud as he quickly searched for what he sought, "The main and obvious reason the location of the battle is questioned is that, for the most part, no one survived. It is often said that history is written by the victors, the only Castellarian to survive was an insignificant foot soldier who had been sent back by Sir Reginald. Ha! Here it is," He snatched a book that was high on a shelf. Blowing dust from its cover, he brought it back to where Isidora was still studying the map. As he thumbed through the pages, he resumed his story.

"Although he had left the battle prior to any real fighting, not to mention the devastation, he was greeted in Castellamar as a hero—the only survivor of the Battle of Rania. His family benefited from this fame by becoming wealthy gentry. Castellamar may not have had many specifics of the battle to chronicle, but they did have this one man to herald. Most of the legends of Sir Reginald and the Battle of Rania stem from his stories."

Azrael stopped speaking as he came to a page in the book he was looking for; his finger stabbed at a drawing on the page, "This is his family crest, created after his ascension to nobility."

Having heard a history of his homeland, Gideon came to the table and stood next to Isidora. They both looked at the page.

Isidora admittedly knew very little of Castellamar's history. She cared little for the nobility itself, something instilled in her by Sir Griffon due to their House's lowered status. She looked to Gideon, educated since youth on the nobility and heraldry. He seemed just as confused. Isidora was the first to speak while Gideon continued to study the crest, "I am sorry, D'ni. I do not understand how this brings us any closer to finding the location of the battle."

Azrael sighed and rubbed his forehead, "Gideon, you are of the nobility. Look at that crest. Do you notice anything odd?"

Gideon had not lifted his gaze from the page since he began inspecting it. His brows creased, "It's a customary four-partition crest. For the most part, it has standard heraldry," He paused for a moment over one quadrant of the crest, "This is a bit out of place. This position typically represents the family guardian. It's usually either some sort of animal or representation of a patron god. This crest has a goblet. As far as I know, no god has a goblet as its emblem."

"That assumption would be correct, young knight. There is no god, saint, or patron in the history of Tinil'Gan that uses a goblet as an icon. Therefore, it must represent something else. Something sacred. Something that is now considered mystical by the Castellarians. There is one artifact in existence that was captured from Rania during the war."

Sudden understanding lit Gideon's expression, his eyes widened, and a triumphant smile spread across his face, "The Chalice of Abbas! That's it, Isi! Before the fall of Rania, this artifact was brought back to Castellamar. No one knows when, though. If this soldier chose the Chalice for his crest, he must have brought it back with him," Isidora smiled and squeezed his hand. He returned her smile with a broad warm grin.

Azrael finished Gideon's enthusiastic revelation, "The Chalice was housed in only one location in Rania, the Temple of Al'

Zadal," Azrael's finger stabbed the map once again, at a spot marked Al' Zadal.

Isidora's didn't let her excitement show on her face, but in her soul, she was exuberant. The dream she had been cultivating the past five years was truly underway. She turned a warm smile to Azrael, "This is why I came to you, D'ni. I knew if there was anyone on Tinil'Gan that could aid me, it was you. Thank you."

Lear'Za, empty wine glass dangling upside down from two fingers, watched the entire exchange with sheer boredom. Quickly, she floated out of her chair and came between them before Azrael could let out what was sure to be a cynical barb, "Well, now that the destination is decided, can we finally get moving?" Isidora put a hand over her mouth to hide her smile. She knew Lear'Za was trying to shield her from any possible unneeded retort from Azrael.

"Yes, there is much to prepare," Isidora said, hoping she hid her excitement, "Although I know you want to leave immediately, Lear'Za, it's already afternoon. It is better off to make sure we have all the necessary supplies prepared and depart first thing in the morning. If you both do not mind, I will take my leave and begin my preparations now."

Gideon nodded in agreement, "I will see to our supplies if you will allow me the assistance of your tower's staff."

Azrael nodded to Gideon and Isidora gave a short bow. They both moved quickly out of the library to the stairs.

Lear'Za watched them until they had disappeared up the stairs. Once they were gone, she floated to the opposite side of the table, facing Azrael, who was still looking at the maps on the table. Folding her arms with a quirk in her lips, she spoke quietly to the Archmage, "You were alive during the Battle of Rania."

Azrael's eyes did not leave the map as he released a short sigh, "I am glad you have a grasp of rudimentary arithmetic, daemoness. What is your point?"

Lear'Za smirk grew wider as she leaned her hands on the table, "You knew all along where the battle took place."

"Of course, I knew where the battle took place. It almost killed me. I was on the western shore of Rania. The blast caused by that fool Sir Reginald and his magi blasted the entire region into a desert and me into the sea. By the time I regained consciousness, I was in the middle of the ocean floating on some crates. It took all the strength I had left to cast the small spell that helped me wash ashore to this very isle."

"Then what was the point of that little charade?" Lear'Za knew what the answer would be. She enjoyed prodding the Archmage even if it meant drawing his ire, and also understood that although his ego was large enough not to need stroking, he enjoyed displaying his intelligence and cleverness. He also knew she would ask questions that he did not need to answer. He was certain she did it to annoy him, and it usually worked. They had been playing this game of cat and mouse for a very long time, and neither was willing to stop any time soon.

"This is Isidora's quest. If she is to be prepared for future events, she needs to be able to think on her own. Gideon at least did not disappoint. And he seems competent. I was disappointed to see it was he who figured it out and not Isidora herself. I also was aware of her eyes deferring to him many times, and the look I saw was emotional. I don't know if I have done enough to prepare her, daemoness. I am beginning to worry."

The playful expression Lear'Za usually wore faded away. This discussion was a familiar, one she and Azrael had shared many times in the hundreds of years they had known each other, "You know full well where I stand on your treatment of that girl, Seer'kaat. The one thing I can say with certainty is you have done everything you could to prepare her for her destiny. The only disagreement I have is that you haven't told her about it or her past. Especially where you fit into it."

If anyone had been looking closely, they would have seen for a brief instant Azrael's composure give way, the mirrored orbs that are his eyes crack, and his teeth clench as if physically hit in the stomach. The moment was so fleeting, so quick, that if someone had seen it, they would have doubted afterward that it had happened at all. He sighed and walked away from the table and Lear'Za. He took two steps towards the stairs and stopped. Without turning his head, he said, "To be prepared for anything and everything, daemoness, means just that, not knowing. If one has to know the intricate details of what can happen to be prepared, then they are truly lost. I hope for everyone's sake I have imparted enough of that wisdom to Isidora," With that said, Azrael disappeared into the darkness of the staircase. Shaking her head, Lear'Za faded from the room.

CHAPTER 5

The sun rose over the Isle of Winds. It would prove to be another beautiful late summer day on the Isle. The timing of their journey was optimal; they would avoid the fierce winds when crossing the ocean to the mainland. It would still be incessantly hot when they reached the Ranian Desert, but not as hot as it would be at the height of summer. As Azrael watched the servants load the packhorse, his mind began to view fortune with trepidation. He could not shake the feeling of being pulled. That is to say; he felt as though what he considered free will and choice were fate and destiny. Knowing he would have more than enough time to ponder those thoughts later, Azrael shook his head and concentrated on the task at hand and inspected the load.

After a filling breakfast, Azrael and Isidora came down to the courtyard to find their horses groomed, saddled and ready as Gideon had promised. Just then, the courtyard gates opened and what Azrael could only describe as a monstrosity rode through. Four magical fiery horses, flames spouting from their nostrils, pulling a carriage of burnished gold made its way into the courtyard. Rotund and ornate, the carriage was large enough to carry a dozen passengers in comfort. Just as its owner, the horses, and carriage hovered a few inches off the ground. Noiselessly, it floated to a stop beside the group of waiting horses. The regular horses neighed and frantically hopped in fear of their magical duplicates.

With a sigh and roll of his mirrored eyes, Azrael stormed to the carriage door and ripped it open. Lear'Za gasped and stuck her head out.

"You rickety old curmudgeon!" she screamed, "What do you think you are doing?"

"What do I think I am doing?" Azrael seethed, "If you think we are taking this monstrosity with us, then you are more insane than I ever imagined."

With feline grace, Lear'Za stepped from out of the carriage, "I don't ever remember asking for your permission, nor do I remember ever needing it!"

"Just as I do not remember inviting you on this journey. If you insist on accompanying us, you will do so as lightly and efficiently as possible. I want this journey to be quiet. This thing will attract every cutthroat, thief, and rogue from the four corners of Tinil'Gan."

Lear'Za bit her lip in frustration and stomped her foot like a child. Instead of the thump sound, one would expect to hear, the air underneath her foot crackled with tendrils of crimson light, "Fine, you old bore! I was just concerned about Isidora. The gods know collecting avatars will be taxing on her, and she could use some comfort on the journey."

Isidora concealed a smile and trotted her horse up to the arguing pair, "Thank you for your concern, daemoness, but I can assure you I will be fine. Azrael is right. We will need to travel light."

"So be it," Lear'Za heaved one last loud sigh and snapped her fingers. The carriage and three of the horses disappeared, leaving only one of the flame-spouting equines behind, equipped with a saddle and bridle. Not to be completely undone, the saddle was just as ornate as the now disapparated carriage. The fine leather tooled with scenes of carnal lust. The intertwined bodies of the artwork highlighted by burnished gold accents. The bridle was also golden and bright, playing off the more subtle accents on the saddle, "There now I will be as pedestrian as the rest of you."

Azrael sighed and shook his head; this was probably the most toned down version of Lear'Za they would get. While he still held his reservations about her presence due to her loud character, it was still required. One he valued highly, regardless of their verbal sparring.

After a few minor provision checks, Gideon indicated they were all set. The quartet made their way out of Il'Muni Arus, down the road that led through Arcanis proper, and onto the road leading east. They would take a ship in Port Sirocco on the Isle of Winds eastern coast. Traveling at a fast gallop with little or no gear, one could make the trip in a single day. The group, though, was loaded down with a packhorse and there was no need to rush. Azrael had sent a courier ahead to charter passage. They would ride the full day at a leisurely pace, stopping for a brisk lunch, and then camp alongside the road for the night. After another early morning start, they would have a half day's ride to Port Sirocco and be at sea by the afternoon.

Gideon enjoyed the comfortable silence of the first leg of the trip. He was excited about this journey, excited for Isidora, but he could not shake the sense of trepidation. Not for the expected trials and tribulations expected on a quest, such as cutthroats, thieves, and general ne'er do wells. Instead, he felt like there was an underlying threat, something Azrael wasn't telling them. Perhaps no one noticed it; perhaps it was a trick of Azrael's mirrored eyes. An aura of concern emanated from the Archmage. He was also unsure what to make of the daemoness. He hadn't ever heard tales of a speaking sentient daemon let alone encountering one. Isidora seemed to trust her as much as she trusted Azrael; this was enough to calm his concerns.

He shook his mind of his musings and enjoyed the beautiful morning and scenery the Isle of Winds had to offer. They started the morning by passing through Arcanis's main road. He could smell the fragrance of the day's bread and hear the telltale bangs and pangs of a nearby blacksmith ring through the air. The citizens here lived such a simple life. Their homes were modest, tightly thatched rooves and walls of hearty oak. He smiled as children ran by whooping and hollering in delight. It was not often a party of companions, led by Azrael, came through. Gideon glanced over at Isidora who rode next to him and smiled. The happy children made him wonder what their child would look like if they had one. Isidora smiled back and chuckled.

"What, pray tell, are you staring at Sir Gideon?" She said with a playful curve to her smile.

"You know full well what my eyes are fixed upon and will always be fixed upon," He responded quietly to keep this conversation between them, "I am excited to be here with you Isi, I know how much you want this."

He could see her eyes soften, a look that always made his heart beat faster, "I couldn't have asked for a better companion and husband."

He grinned widely and looked forward, his mind wandering back to the children. They had not yet discussed having children. It was one of the very few things they had not addressed as husband and wife. Her drive was intense. He was starting to believe the bittersweet reality that she may not have the time to be a mother; it was his only secret reservation he had about supporting this dream of hers. He left his thoughts behind with the happy families of Arcanis as they exited the city gates.

By noon, they had passed most of the wheat and cornfields and crested the same hill he and Isidora had descended the previous day. Gideon looked back on Azrael's tower; the sense of trepidation crept back into his conscious. Once they had come down the other side of the hill, they came upon an expanse of prairie that would be most of the rest of the road to the port. The companions stopped here for a quick lunch under the early afternoon sun. They spoke idly of current times, and Isidora told Lear'Za of her adventures during her five-year absence. Azrael remained aloof and distant during lunch, busying himself with maps rather than join the conversation.

Knowing they still had much ground to cover, they ended their rest and mounted their horses. The sun took its inevitable trip westward as the group preceded eastward, casting long shadows before them. The sun felt good on their backs and seemed to propel them further than expected. By the time the horizon was taking on a reddish hue, they had reached the small forested region that marked the last leg of their journey. They found a proper clearing within the wood that had the remnants of previous fire pits — a much-used camp spot for those traveling to the port.

It didn't take them long to gather some wood and get a warm blaze going. Gideon had caught a few rabbits while gathering firewood so the group could have some warm meat for what would probably be a long while. Once they were settled in and eating a hearty rabbit soup, Azrael took the peaceful time to go over their itinerary.

Gideon shifted slightly and sighed. He did not want to interrupt the Archmage, but he felt it necessary, "The Luminori Elves are not known for their kindness to outsiders. Is this wise?"

Azrael continued as if Gideon had not interrupted him, "I am familiar with the Luminori Elves and the Guardian Giasis. It should not be much of a problem to pass their security and make our way through the Linian Forest towards the desert," Pausing, Azrael looked up and narrowed his eyes in the direction of the forest. Gideon followed his gaze but saw nothing in the ever-darkening woods. After a moment, Azrael continued speaking, "Between the shorter ocean passage to Luminos instead of the nearest Castellarian port and the direct route to the desert, this route will cut our trip by at least a week, if not more. Not to mention the path will be much easier."

Nodding solemnly, Gideon conceded, "It seems a good plan. I do apologize if I seemed..." Gideon's words were interrupted by a ruffle of some nearby leaves. Instantly, the group arose as one. Gideon's sword was out before he was fully standing. A murmur of a defensive spell was already playing on Isidora's lips and an offensive one on Azrael's. Lear'Za floated high above the group, prepared to strike with claws and otherworldly magic. Although the Isle of Winds was a peaceful place, nowhere on Tinil'Gan was safe from nighttime brigands looking for an easy take. But brigands would be in for quite a shock if they tried to rob this powerful group. All four faced in the direction the noise had come from, poised, and ready.

The leaves rustled again, and suddenly, there was a high-pitched, "ACHOO!" A small ball of light shot out from the tree line and hit Lear'Za square in the chest.

"In the name of your gods what is it?" yelled Lear'Za as the others turned to look in astonishment at the glowing object planted neatly between her breasts.

With a slight chuckle, Isidora stopped her chanting, "It is a pixie, daemoness."

CHAPTER 6

"And we still have the matter of the Dwarven embassy, which seeks a nominal, non-voting membership in the Conclave. This matter has been bounced around in committee for months now."

Diarmuid rubbed his forehead as the next debate raged on. The past few months had been a tiresome bore in the chambers of the Conclave of Magi. As Chief Counsel, Diarmuid knew he should pay more attention, but the trivial matters of bureaucracy and administrative functions made his headache. Because of their long lifespan, many assumed elves were creatures of infinite patience. How little did they know. It didn't help matters that Diarmuid had more pressing issues on his mind, and the empty seat on the Dais of the Nine was a constant reminder. This particular seat had been vacant for almost 30 years, now. An awarded seat is for life, and that meant that it was impossible to appoint a new occupant until its occupant dies or is banished. It had been a mistake to award that seat to an immortal Sidhe.

The Conclave of Magi had been created over three thousand years ago for the express purpose of regulating and protecting the Art. In the time before the Conclave, ill-trained magi had caused havoc across Tinil'Gan.

Eventually, the three Orders of the Art—the White Robes of the Light Arts, the Green Robes of the Neutral Arts, and the Black Robes of the Dark Arts— had come together and formed the Conclave of Magi.

Their first order of business had been to create the Trials. The Trials were a series of challenges put together to test the competency and skill of aspiring magic users. Only if one passed the grueling Trials would they be accepted into one of the Orders and be called magus. Failure was not as kind: it meant death. This test would weed out the incompetent and weak, and keep the Art pure and Tinil'Gan safe.

The Conclave's second function was to govern the magi's role in the world. Magi who aspired to conquer a nation, or the world itself, with their power, riddled Tinil'Gan's ancient past. Even those meaning to do well could cause tragic outcomes. The urge to destroy evil can lead even the righteous to despotism. The Conclave was the only power in the realm that could stand in the way of such ambitions. It was the latter that currently occupied Diarmuid's thoughts.

The empty Conclave Chair belonged to the Archmagus Azrael of the Order of Black Robes. A respected member of the Conclave, Azrael has never crossed the line into domination and world control, but he knew of Azrael's hatred for the God Leto, as well as his obsession with an ancient prophecy. A prophecy that is known to few outside of the Conclave or certain small religious zealots. Diarmuid did not fear Azrael was trying to conquer the world; he feared the Archmage sought to upset the divine balance of the gods. To many, challenging a god seemed laughable, but he knew how powerful Azrael could be. If there was any being on Tinil'Gan that could attempt it, it was Azrael.

Although Diarmuid was nearly four hundred years old, the seat had belonged to the Archmagus long before Diarmuid's time. Many felt Azrael should be Chief Counsel; they tended to forget Azrael had turned down the position numerous times. Nostalgia played a large part in the adoration. Azrael was Sidhe, known by all magic users as the most potent and attuned race when it came to the Art. The Art flowed through a Sidhe's veins like no other race. Add in their immortality, which spared them the ravages of time and age, and they were indeed the Art personified. However, the Sidhe numbered very few. Azrael was the only Sidhe known of by the Conclave, and in the public eye for that matter. Unless scrutinized, a Sidhe's appearance was not unlike that of an elf, which contributed to the mystery. Conventional wisdom demanded that, if Azrael was not the last of the Sidhe, he was indeed one of the few remaining of that mystical race. The faction of the Conclave that allied itself at least in thought with Azrael disliked Diarmuid. It was a decision he had made that caused Azrael to end all communication with the Conclave twenty-five years ago. Diarmuid grimaced at the memory. He grew tired of the meaningless debate in the Conclave and slammed his gavel until the room went silent.

"We have matters of more importance to discuss. One this Conclave fails to address time and time again. It concerns the matter of Azrael and his student," A collective groan and complaints came from all sides of the dais. Diarmuid continued, speaking louder over the protests, "This is not a matter than can be ignored any longer!"

An Archmage of the green robes, Judica, lifted her hands to quiet her comrades, "The girl's training began twenty-five years ago Diarmuid, and she has proven to be an excellent mage since she passed her trials. This is a dead issue."

Since its inception, the Conclave had supervised an apprenticeship program. It would not accept any promising young people until the age of ten. At that time, they would enter the Academy at Ti'Relan Tower, which was the Conclave's home. Here they would attend classes in both conventional education as well as that of the Art until the age of twenty. At that time, it would be apparent to both the student and the Conclave which Order they were suited to and would be assigned an apprenticeship with an established mage. At the age of twenty-five, they would be sent back to the Tower of Elizar to complete the Trials. Azrael had other plans for Isidora.

Diarmuid stood and placed his hands upon the dais, "Twenty-five years ago Azrael brought Isidora before the Conclave, a young girl of the age of five. It was apparent to all of us that the Art flowed within her, and she would be a sure candidate when she reached the prescribed age of ten. Azrael had decided he was going to take this child into his tower and train her himself. This goes against the core values of our orders and the Conclave's laws!"

Berilil, an Archmage of the black robes, pulled at a stray thread on the hem of his robes. Without looking up, he responded, "That he did. And despite our protests and reading of our laws, he trained one of the best young magi we have today. What does it matter now Diarmuid?"

When Azrael first approached them that day with Isidora, the Conclave Chairs chuckled and laughed. It was unheard of, a five-year-old child trained in the ways of the Art—and not only that but to be trained by Azrael and not through the Conclave's academy. The chuckles died when Azrael removed his hood, and all saw the seriousness in those mirrored eyes of his.

Diarmuid gritted his teeth. He knew for certain the two Archmagi who represented the black robes would defend Azrael to the very end. Berilil's comments were not unexpected. The consistent loyalty Judica and her fellow green robes held made matters that much more difficult, "Do any of you even remember what he said that day? He said, 'I know more of the ways of the Art than this entire dais combined. You dare doubt me? I did not come here for your permission.' Those were his words! If he feels he holds more knowledge and wisdom than all of combined, what is to stop him from doing it again, when the stakes are much higher?"

A murmur of discussion rose among the Archmagi once again, and this time it was Diarmuid's white-robed comrade Hestion who motioned for silence and then spoke, "My dear Diarmuid, removing our pride from this, was he wrong? Azrael is older than all of us combined and began practicing the Art before the creation of this Conclave; by the gods, he was one of the founders! Not once in his entire existence, is there any record of him causing undue turmoil or tipping the scales of power in his favor. Other than this relatively minor infraction, he has only and always put the Art before everything."

Diarmuid slammed his fist on the dais, "Which means he has all of eternity to foster plans none can even contemplate. Who knows what kind of monster, hell-bent on the destruction of Leto that Azrael has fostered and created within Isidora. Honestly, who knows what goes on behind those mirrored eyes?"

Angrily, Judica now stood. Her dark brown eyes bore into Diarmuid, "Enough, Diarmuid! Yes, Azrael indeed broke our rules and traditions when he chose to train Isidora. However, it was you, Chief Counsel, who drove him from this chamber. It was you who issued the formal decree admonishing and prohibiting the action. That decree caused Azrael to turn his back on this Conclave and to leave that chair forever empty and utter his last words," No one present that day would forget Azrael's parting words, "One day," he had said, "you will realize you need me more than I need you. When that day arrives, I will not answer your scream for aid, nor will I pity you."

Diarmuid clenched his fists, "Which only proves his loyalty is not with this Conclave or the Art."

Judica smiled and sat. She looked at Diarmuid again, her face stern, "Those parting words, my dear Chief Counsel were aimed at you, not the rest of us."

Diarmuid sneered and took his seat once again, as the Conclave moved back to other matters. Judica was correct, Azrael had aimed those words at Diarmuid. And it was indeed the last time he ever corresponded with the Conclave. Azrael and his apprentice Isidora departed the Conclave, and since that day, Azrael had never returned nor had he answered any summons. The only correspondence the Conclave received was six years ago when Isidora returned for her Trials. The Conclave went into an uproar that day. They knew they could not refuse her into the Trials; no mage that requested the Trials was turned away. This long-standing rule served two purposes. If the mage was not worthy, they were willingly walking into their own grave. If they passed, then the Conclave knew it had a new mage in their ranks capable of handling the Art. In this case, it was a matter of principle. Those on the Conclave who sided with Diarmuid knew that if Isidora passed her Trials, they were recognizing Azrael's triumph and admitting they were wrong and there was little doubt in their minds that she would succeed. Those opposed were upholding the tradition and rules of the Conclave on this matter. The only real objection Diarmuid's camp could offer was that she was too young, only twenty, not the prescribed twenty-five needed to take the Trials. The opposed countered with the argument that the age requirement of twenty-five only held to those who went through the Conclave's training program, not those trained otherwise. To no one's surprise, Isidora became the youngest mage ever to pass the Trials. She carried no word or message from Azrael and left the Tower promptly after her Trials, without a word spoken.

For these reasons, and others not confirmed but suspected by Diarmuid, he did not trust Azrael. His suspicions twisted and contorted his mind; he could not concentrate on the mundane proceedings. He sighed with relief when the meeting adjourned. He was awaiting some news about Azrael today and did not want to waste any time. Rising from his chair, he didn't stop to talk to anyone and left the chambers. With his eyes cast downward, he walked at a brisk pace down the gilded corridors of the Tower of Elizar. As he approached the door to his quarters, the door opened for him without slowing his pace and closed neatly behind him.

When viewing Diarmuid's quarters, one would not instantly think of a mage's living area; upon entry, there was a large foyer lined with crystal statues of nymphs and woodland creatures. Typical fare for those of Luminori Elvan nobility to which he belonged. The floors were of polished white marble that was always warm to bare feet. Above the main living room was a large sunroof letting in the day's sunlight that bathed the many red and yellow velvet plush pillows and low laying divans again of typical Elvan fashion. Being a mage did bring prestige to Diarmuid, but being a Luminori Elf gave him even more pride, and he was not ashamed to flaunt it.

When he entered the living room area, he stopped in a brief moment of shock. A figure in black robes was seated in one of the divans. He was slight of build and was casually drinking a glass of wine. Upon hearing Diarmuid enter the rooms, the figure turned his head and removed his hood, revealing a young, pale, Elvan man with sandy blond hair tied in a long braid. The man smirked at Diarmuid's startled look and chuckled.

"Come, Diarmuid, you should be used to this by now. You impress upon me the utmost secrecy of our meetings, then turn as pale as a ghost when you see me in your quarters," The mysterious Elf said.

With a small grunt to himself, Diarmuid adjusted his white robes and sat on the divan across from the black-robed elf, "It is not the fact you are here that disturbs me, Caiaphas. It is the fact that you make yourself at home while I am not present."

Caiaphas softly chuckled as he looked down at his glass and swirled its contents, "Considering the fact that I am an outcast and technically banned from this Tower doesn't give me many options to wait and speak with you. You demand these updates conducted in person, the Tower's home spell is the only way back from the Isle of Winds to make an immediate report. Your quarters are the only place I can be safe from sight here."

Caiaphas did not raise his eyes from his glass. He watched the red wine swirl around like blood going down a drain. Flames of disdain smoldered in the young elf's eyes. Diarmuid smirked. He knew the power he exerted over the banished black robe; Caiaphas' personal feelings towards him were irrelevant.

"Do not test my patience, Caiaphas," Diarmuid spoke in a condescending tone as if he was a child. *He needs to be reminded who is in control,* "This mission I assigned to you is a penance. I will not enter a repeal of your banishment to the Conclave if this continues," Diarmuid softened his tone and continued, "Now, to matters at hand, what news do you bring from the Isle of Winds?"

Caiaphas looked up. If the barbs he had thrown his way affected him, the black robe Elf showed no signs, "The Archmage is on the move. He left his tower early this morning with his student, a Castellarian knight, and that daemoness whore he befriends. They make for the port. One of his servants left the night prior and chartered a ship. At this time, their destination is unknown."

Diarmuid snorted in derision. Standing up quickly, he placed his hands on his hips and bore his eyes down upon Caiaphas, "You came here to inform me that they chartered a ship without knowing the destination? Of course, they chartered a ship, you fool. They are on an island! I need to know what that cursed Sidhe is up to," He leaned on the edge of the table and drummed his fingers, "Isidora has returned to him, and now they leave together. None of this bodes well," He was beginning to wonder if trusting this dark Elf with this task was a wise choice. Wise or not, he had no one else with Caiaphas' skills to employ.

Through clenched teeth, Caiaphas countered, "If you allowed me to finish, you would understand why I am here," Diarmuid smirked. The dark Elf had pride, and despite his impertinence, he wanted to prove himself, "As I was saying, the servant had not given the captain a destination, only instructions to have the ship ready the following day for the group, and that Azrael would let him know their port of choice when he arrived. Upon hearing this, I found it pertinent to discover their destination before the ship's departure. Upon dire threat to my safety, I followed the group until they made camp. From a nearby copse of trees, I was able to hear their plans. They make for Luminos."

Diarmuid's eyes went wide, and a huge grin spread across his face, "Well done, Caiaphas! This works out perfectly! I am going to visit Guardian Giasis myself," He rubbed his hands together. If there was anywhere outside the Conclave in which he had influence, it was with the Guardian of his homeland. He was one move ahead of Azrael now. He turned his attention to Caiaphas once more. "I will need you to keep an eye on the group when they arrive in Luminos. If I have my way, you will not have too much to do, but still, I want to make sure."

Upon hearing Diarmuid's wishes, Caiaphas stood up and nearly spat his words, "Do you wish death upon me? I am Duminion, which is a death wish if I enter Luminos. Aside from that, I cannot again come that close to Azrael. His power is great, Diarmuid. Dare I say, greater than you want to believe. I swear he sensed my presence and, for a moment, I felt his mirrored eyes upon me. If it wasn't for..." Caiaphas shook his head, "I cannot again get that close, Diarmuid."

Laughing, Diarmuid made his way to a nearby desk, "I never fashioned you for a coward, Caiaphas. My orders still stand. Fear not; you will not have to get too close to them again. As I said, I believe my plans will be more than enough. You can leave now."

Without saying a word, Caiaphas drew his hood over his head, chanted a few soft words of magic and became invisible to sneak his way out of the tower.

Diarmuid watched with a sneer as the black robe outcast cast his spell and disappeared. He turned his attention back to his desk and pulled out a scroll that he had received the night before. The seal, bearing the double *Rs* of the Realm Regent of Castellamar had already been broken, as he had read it numerous times. *Odd it may seem, but Lord Sulik and I have a common cause.* Sulik wished a certain knight not to return to Castellamar; the same knight that now traveled with Azrael.

CHAPTER 7

"I've had many people and things in there, but I have to say a fairy is a first," Lear'Za chuckled as she plucked the struggling creature out of her cleavage. The pixie yelled and flailed as Lear'Za held it in front of her face. Yelled was a bit of an exaggeration. Considering her diminutive stature, it sounded more like squeaks and whistles. She was about six inches high with translucent wings resembling those of a dragonfly, wearing a blue dress with torn-off sleeves and a ragged, knee-length hem. She had long, wavy locks like Isidora's but had fuller lips and round eyes. Despite her height, she would be what one would consider a shapely and attractive woman. At the moment, however, nothing in her demeanor could be classified as charming. The string of curses and downright obscenities she flung even made Lear'Za wince a few times, "My, my, she is feisty!"

The pixie's face turned bright red in anger, "Feisty? Feisty! First of all, I am not a fairy! I am a Pixie and stop staring at me like you don't know me, daemoness!" The pixie adjusted her dress as she hung from Lear'Za's fingers. "Fairies fly around the forest, picking flower petals and singing all day. Pixies, on the other hand, contribute something to the world; we assist the dead in finding their way home!" She wriggled around some, more kicking her feet in Lear'Za's direction, then settled herself with a sigh and crossed her arms. She glowed a deep red, "You may think people enjoy having their face and whatnots in between those monstrosities, but it is not a pleasant experience having your whole body in there, and the life almost smothered out of you!"

Lear'Za no longer chuckled but was full-on laughing. She placed the pixie on a nearby tree stump, "Talia? Is that you? All of you small creatures look alike to me."

Azrael eyes lingered on the spot of brush where the pixie had emerged, splitting his attention. Shaking himself out of the intense scrutiny of the area, he turned to Lear'Za and the pixie, "Yes, daemoness, it is Talia."

Gideon had a perplexed expression. Isidora laughed and patted him on the back, "Gideon, as stated, this is Talia. She is a pixie, one of the Fey Folk. They have inhabited this isle for quite a long time. In fact, they were here long before Azrael arrived. Talia and her kin were the first denizens of this Isle, and my D'ni chanced to encounter them when he came here. She has been a friend since. I first met her when I was six. I had never seen a magical creature before, and I was delighted. Is that not right, Azrael?"

Azrael's focus was still elsewhere. He waved his hand dismissively, "Yes, yes, Isidora," Azrael knelt before the stump so that he was eye level with Talia. When she noticed his closeness, she began smoothing out her clothing and hair, "What happened in the brush, Talia?"

Talia's eye twinkled, she smiled at the Archmagus' attention. Composing herself, she answered Azrael's question, "Well, I was making my way through my normal duties—there were a few lost souls wandering aimlessly that needed my aid. Suddenly, I ran into what seemed a brick wall where there was nothing but open space! Whatever I hit made me start sneezing uncontrollably and the next thing I know one monster sneeze sent me flying into those twin peaks of hell that belong to your friend over there," Lear'Za suppressed an audible chuckle and teasingly adjusted her breasts in her tight top. Talia sneered, stuck her tongue out at Lear'Za, and returned her attention to Azrael, "That's about it."

Azrael's brow creased in thought, "Can you show us where this happened?"

Talia smiled brightly and flew in circles, "Of course! Follow me!" Her bright light spun around them for a moment and darted towards the trees. Azrael followed her and beckoned the others to follow.

Talia led them to a small clearing. The air was thick with the scents of the forest, "It was right about here. I was just about to lead this poor lost soul to his final destination when I started sneezing so hard is shot me right out the trees into Lear'Za death mounds," Lear'Za folded her arms and pursed her lips at the comment. Talia stuck her tongue out at her.

Azrael walked around the clearing and stopped at a small shrub. He knelt and rubbed its leaves with his fingers. He looked at his fingers and noticed a glittery brown substance, "Do you have any allergies, Talia?"

Talia tapped her finger on her lips for a moment and then smiled in remembrance, "I do remember when I was really little, I was in our village's alchemist's hut and had the same sneezing fit. My mother told me it was due to the angelica root the alchemist was using."

Azrael's mirrored eyes narrowed, and he stood and paced for a moment. He stopped and spoke to no one in particular, "Angelica root is not native to this island. Though it is a major ingredient to an invisibility spell, which would explain the unseen wall you ran into. Some of the dust that this interloper sprinkled over him- or herself aggravated your allergies when you ran into them. Can you remember anything else, little one?"

Isidora fumed. Gideon, the only one that noticed amid the commotion, placed a hand on her shoulder and whispered in her ear, "Isi, what's the matter?"

She responded in a whisper rasped with anger, "Nothing. Leave me be, Gideon," She briskly shrugged his hand off her shoulder. Azrael displayed more gentility in five minutes then he had shown Isidora her entire childhood.

Not noticing the exchange between Isidora and Gideon, the pixie scrunched her face in thought. Scratching her head, she looked up at Azrael, "Now that I think of it, I did hear something, but I wasn't sure at all what it was. I figured it came from one of the spirits. It sounded something like 'pillows.'"

"Pealos?" Azrael's eyebrow rose as he questioned the pixie.

"That's it!" Talia jumped in excitement.

Azrael sighed and folded his arms into his sleeves, "Pealos is an Elvan curse word, loosely translated as 'damn it.' We are being followed, and I have an idea who may be behind it. For the time being, it is inconsequential, but I will require all of you to keep an extra eye out during our journey."

Just as Azrael finished speaking Talia gave a little yelp of excitement, "There he is! I thought I lost the poor soul," At the very edge of the clearing, a glowing form of a human male was hiding behind a tree, his head peeking out watching the group.

Gideon jumped back and grabbed the hilt of his sword. His eyes were wide in astonishment, "By the gods, is that a spirit? In 25 years of life, I have never seen any magical creatures. In one day, I have met a daemoness, a pixie, and now a spirit! Is it just this isle?"

Isidora's mind was still on Azrael's treatment of Talia. Azrael chuckled and spoke before she could, "This isle is indeed more magical than most locations on Tinil'Gan, but it is not the isle that is allowing us to see this spirit. A pixie's life charge is to guide lost souls home. Our proximity to her magic is allowing us this glimpse of things normally unseen."

Talia nodded in agreement and smiled, "Hold on, I have to take care of this," She flew off towards the soul still watching them.

Isidora had seen this many times in her youth, but it never failed to amaze her. The extraordinary event about to happen brought her out of her melancholy thoughts. She held Gideon by the arm and whispered, "Be calm my love; you are about to witness something not seen by the vast majority of this world."

They watched in silence as Talia flew up to the soul and caressed its translucent cheek. The man had a somber and sad look upon his face. With Talia's touch, he smiled slightly, and a shining tear ran down his face. Talia flew around him in lazy circles for a moment then flew away a few paces in front of him, hovering at eye level.

She spread her arms out and closed her eyes. The seemingly never-ending glittering, ethereal dust that flowed around her began to spin around her, forming an open circle with her in the middle. The ring of dust started to glow brightly, a small tendril reaching out and attaching itself to Talia. The center of the circle began to shimmer and swirl like a million stars in the sky, creating a magical doorway. The soul came forward and smiled. With a last look at the group of observers, he turned and walked into the doorway and disappeared.

With a flash, the doorway vanished and broke apart into the typical dust that flowed around Talia at all times. Talia opened her eyes and flew around dizzily for a few moments.

Gideon swallowed a lump in his throat. He looked at Isidora in concern, "Is she ok, Isi?"

Isidora patted his arm in assurance, "She is fine Gideon. What you just saw was Talia's innate magic that reaches across the void to celestial quintessence where all souls go. Their home. The process, while not harmful to the pixies, does take its toll on them and leaves them a bit drained afterward. They are using their magical life force to open that doorway. In a way, they are the doorway."

Once Talia steadied herself, she rejoined the group and smiled sleepily, "I think I am going to stay with you all for a bit if that's all right. I need friends around me for a while; it gets lonely out there for us pixies."

Azrael nodded to the pixie in acceptance, "We would be glad to have you with us, Talia, just mind your behavior," Azrael turned to the rest. I am going to sleep; I suggest you all do the same," Without another word, Azrael walked out of the clearing back to where they left the horses. Isidora's eyes trailed after him. The earlier thoughts of how kind he was to Talia returned. No one noticed the small tear in her eye. Shaking it off, she went to prepare her bed as well.

The next morning, the group ate quickly without much talking and began the journey to the port. The ride was quiet and uneventful, but due to the previous evening's events, all were on guard with a spell on their lips or hand on a sword pommel. Undaunted and unashamed, Talia joined the group and floated along close to Azrael's horse. None complained; a pixie was hardly a burden on a group given their small size.

By midmorning, the group arrived at Port Sirocco. The accommodations had been made by Azrael's servant before their arrival, as planned, so the boat and captain were ready for them. Azrael's reputation preceded him on the Isle of Winds, but superstitions at sea always superseded reputation. Azrael had to pay the captain extra because they were ferrying two black robe magi and the seductive yet visually unsettling daemoness. It was no surprise to Azrael that by the time their trip ended a sailor had died of an unknown illness; the daemoness had her way once again. To some, this would seem a despicable act. Azrael had a better knowledge of the daemoness; he understood a succubus did this for sustenance, not just pleasure. While distasteful, it was also unavoidable. At least over the centuries, he had taught her to limit it to her need for sustenance. Other than the 'mysterious' death, the two-day trip to Luminos was uneventful and peaceful. Being at sea during pleasant weather gives that feeling of serenity and was always an excellent way to begin a journey. The peace would soon end.

"Land ho!" A sailor shouted from the crows-nest. The companions came from below decks to see the coast of Luminos as it appeared on the horizon. Even from the sea, the sight was magnificent. Surrounding the city was a lush green forest. The vast Linian Forest contained all sorts of trees; mighty oaks with leafy canopies, shady glens where animals rested, towering evergreens with points threatening to pierce the sky. The city itself while still one with nature, contrasted all the greenery. Crafted of opaque crystal of varying colors, the buildings of Luminos were unique. A majority of the buildings were of muted red and yellow, which were the nation's colors. Besides those, one could also see crystal structures of violet, magenta, and azure. The magical craftsmanship of the elves grew the crystal quartz from the ground up. With exacting precision, they shaped the facets to catch the light perfectly and made the city shimmer without being blinding. Without much strain, one could see the top spires of the Palace of Light, the home of the Guardian of Light, located in the capital Luminori. Constructed in the same way as the rest of the buildings, it stood out from the crowd and was the elves crowning architectural achievement.

"It's breathtaking," Gideon stared in rapt amazement, "The time and effort it must have taken to create such beauty."

Azrael snorted as he made his way to the bow of the ship, his hands folded in his sleeves, and his hood pulled low even in the mild weather, "They used magic, warrior. Only the elves would be vain and frivolous enough to waste the Art on something as mundane as constructing simple buildings. I can understand the Palace, but when every home and business is constructed thus, it makes one think if they value the Art as one should."

Isidora smiled, "You still can't deny the beauty, D'ni. Using the Art or not, nowhere else on Tinil'Gan can one see such a sight."

A cynical smile played on Azrael's face, "To what end, Isidora? It is a waste of talent and a vainglorious attempt to try to demonstrate their so-called superiority as a society and as magi. All I see is vanity, not beauty," Azrael turned and walked away from the ship's rail.

Gideon leaned in and whispered in Isidora's ear, "Does he see the beauty in anything?"

Although Azrael spoke from his true feelings, Isidora knew his cursed eyes also played a part, "He literally can't Gideon. It's his eyes. Those mirrored orbs Leto cursed upon Azrael only let him see evil and reflect away good." In many ways, she felt sorry for him.

Gideon shook his head in disbelief, "Leto? A god cursed him? What could he have done to deserve such a fate?"

Isidora sighed. She wished she could answer that question, "I do not know. He never would tell me."

Gideon wrinkled his brow and fell silent. Shortly after, the crew loaded their belongings onto a rowboat as the group climbed in and made their way to the port. Their uneasiness grew as they began to see armed guards on the dock, more armed guards than a port usually had.

"Seer'kaat, I have been to Luminos many times, and I have never seen so many guards posted on the docks. What do you divine of this?" Lear'Za's tone was unusually severe. Azrael's eyes narrowed as they got closer and the crew tied off the boat to the dock, but he did not answer. The elvan guards swarmed around them the moment they disembarked. A notably medal and ribbon bedecked elf came forward; he was undoubtedly the captain.

"By order of the Guardian of the Light, you are to come with us immediately for this unauthorized docking and threat of attack. Do not resist or my men will shoot you down where you stand."

Azrael laughed, "The five of us hardly poses a threat of attack. Unless the pixie worries you so."

The elvan guards pulled back their bows in unison. The captain's stoic face did not change, "Do not force me to hold to our conviction."

Azrael raised his hands and nodded to the rest to do the same, "So much for a royal welcome. Take us to your Guardian, soldier."

CHAPTER 8

Elves are not one to cause a commotion. Elvan soldiers escorting a group of two black robe magi, a knight, a daemoness, and a pixie was enough to pique the interest of the populace of Luminori. All members of the group were a rare sight in Luminori, the daemoness made it once in a lifetime. It almost seemed a parade, as elves lined the streets to catch a glimpse of the odd procession. It made Gideon nervous, despite the stillness of it all. He was grateful that they did not restrain them, making them appear as criminals.

He distracted himself by admiring the architecture. They passed under a large crystal arch and entered the heart of the capital. The site of the crystalline structures from the port gleaming in the sunlight was tremendous, but up close it was even more breathtaking. Gideon noticed even Azrael, with his cynicism and cursed eyes, chanced a glance at the wonders, wonders he had seen before. They could see crystals of various colors embedded in the winding roads of Luminori itself. Each building was unique, in the same way that naturally-occurring crystal structures were. They passed a bakery. There were elves working dough and smoking ovens, emitting the sweet smell of fresh bread. But it was housed in an amber crystal structure that rose straight up from the ground, with shards of colored crystal branching out at angles. The windows themselves seemed seamless, made of the same amber crystal, only thin enough to be clear and transparent. Even the chimney was the top-most crystal projection that was hollowed out, releasing the pleasant smoke of the ovens.

"It is all so, timeless," He said to no one in particular.

"If the word timeless were made into a visual construct, Luminos would be it," Azrael, who was on his right, spoke nonchalantly. "Luminos, and particularly its capital Luminori, has not changed in thousands of years."

Every other building was the same fashion, yet unique in its own right. An azure blacksmith's shop with an octagonal rotunda of crystal pillars with diagonal azure crystal formations creating a wall between each post. A bank housed in a golden crystal pyramid. On and on it went, the displays and wonders dizzying to those unfamiliar with the site. Gideon welcomed the distraction of conversation. "That would make sense. One would think they would welcome change at some point."

Azrael removed his hood under the bright sun, "It is in part due to the elves long lifespan. It is not unheard of for an elf to live to a thousand years, the average age being six hundred. They do not procreate often. A typical family consists of one or at most two children. Meaning that since the founding of the nation, many of the ruling Houses of Luminos consist of four, five generations. How much changes in that many generations in Castellamar, sir knight?"

Gideon nodded. He never thought of it that way. In many ways, the knighthood itself was very rigid and unchanging since his great grandparent's time, or earlier. Another thought crossed his mind, and he had to ask, "Who were those elves we saw outside the city proper when we made our way from the port?"

Before they had entered the city gates, Gideon saw random, meager huts along the road. This scene could be seen all over Tinil'Gan from the simple farmers of the Riverlands to the Luminori elves' cousins in the east, the Duminari. All those people would have looks of peace and happiness. Content with the fact they are surviving, dependent on no one. The elves he saw outside the city did not look as happy, or as fortunate.

"The rigidity in the topography of Luminos is a reflection of its people," Azrael remarked, "Feuds between Houses never end. Grudges are passed down generation to generation as well as professions. If a House's founders were warriors in the Royal Army so was every member of that House that follows. At times there would be dissension and a particularly rebellious elf would want to follow a profession other than what was prescribed by his House—resulting in expulsion from the House and all its rights and privileges. They would be an outcast and only be able to practice their trade with other outcasts. Those are the elves you saw outside. The forgotten."

Gideon's face grew somber. He knew the pain felt by dishonored knights expelled from the order. These elves were stripped of their identity, "Now I understand their melancholy and distress. They were not just cast out of the city; they were cast out of their society."

The conversation ended as they turned onto the main thoroughfare, where they reached the full view of the Tower of Light. Positioned in the center of Luminori it rose in majestic splendor. The central spire was a solid crimson and yellow quartz crystal that spiraled high into the sky. It was designed in such a fashion to catch the daytime sun at any angle, reflecting its brilliance a great distance. In four geometric corners were smaller spires of clear crystal. Elegant golden rope bridges draped across the span between the outer spires, manned by sentries keeping watch over the city.

The grounds were no less spectacular. Perfectly manicured lawns dotted with cherry blossom trees. At perfect intervals were small gardens of a multitude of beautiful flowers. Here and there were benches made of the same clear crystal as the outer spires. The road and pathways were inlaid every few feet with a red and yellow crystal stag, the stanchion of Clan Kitharii. The small procession walked up to the main doors of the palace, where the royal guard greeted them. The guards flanking the companions escorted them inside.

"D'ni, how well do you know this king? I am beginning to worry our quest will end before it begins," Isidora said cautiously.

Azrael, nonplussed, answered her, "Giasis Kitharii has been Guardian of the Light for two hundred years. I was at his coronation. I was also at his birthing celebration when his father Somalis Kitharii was Guardian. We know each other well enough. As long as all of you keep your mouths shut and let me do the talking, we should be fine, especially Gideon. The elves and Castellamar have been enemies for centuries; the Ranian devastation heightened the hatred. Luminos knew that eventually they stood in the way of Castellarian domination of the Evening Lands, and that blast leveled part of the Linian Forest."

Isidora shook her head, "But Castellamar is hardly the force it once was and has not been an offensive force for a very long time. They do not look to expand the kingdom."

Azrael smirked, "Old hatreds die hard, Isidora, some never to be quenched."

Gideon listened to the exchange and interjected, "Well, I suppose the fact we are not in chains is a good sign."

"For now, we are treated as guests but do not let the lack of bindings fool you. We are, for all intent and purposes, prisoners until the Guardian says otherwise."

They remained in silence for the rest of the way. Gideon once again distracted himself with the architecture. The interior of the tower was no less impressive, more impressive if possible. Gideon craned his neck up into the high depths of the foyer. The ceilings of the Castle in San'Seban were indeed high, but this ceiling out measured it greatly. Sunlight filled the entire room, illuminating every corner. It was a stark contrast to the stone castles of Castellamar, where a candle was needed long before the sun had set to light the dark rooms.

The windows, strategically placed across from expertly angled facets in the crystal, allowed sunlight to fill the room at any point of the day. His eyes followed the light down from the heights to his feet. The floor was inspiring; every other white marble tile featured inlays of crystal quartz designs and images. Many of the images were of stags, but there were many more of different animals and plants.

They went down a hallway that led to the center of the tower and ushered into the throne room. It was circular colored crimson and yellow. In the center of the floor was a multicolored mosaic disk cut into many pie sections. Each section showed the stanchion of one of the major Clans of Luminos, with the stag stanchion of Clan Kitharii prominently placed in the center. The lighting of the room was similar to the foyer. The walls were cut at such angles and fitted with accompanying reflector crystals that they channeled the daytime sunlight into the throne room, so it was ablaze at any time of the day. Upon the throne of the dais sat the Guardian of Light. The dais was flanked by two of the Guardian's elite rangers as his guards. And to his right, with an arrogant smile upon his face, stood the White Robe Chief Counsel Diarmuid.

When they reached the dais, Azrael bowed, and the rest of his companions followed suit. Talia, her flapping wings keeping her several feet off the ground, attempted an in-air bow. Instead, she performed a complete summersault. She blushed and floated to Azrael to sit on his shoulder. Azrael removed his hood, revealing his mirrored eyes, and stepped forward.

"Greetings, Guardian of the Light. I hope the day's light shines upon you today, as it always has," Azrael completed the traditional Elvish greeting. He purposefully did not acknowledge Diarmuid. He managed to hide a thin-lipped smirk when he saw the red flush of anger on Diarmuid's face. The Guardian smiled and nodded his head.

"Welcome once again to Luminos, Archmagus. It has been long since we last met," The Guardian motioned to his right, "I am sure you are familiar with your fellow mage, Chief Counsel Diarmuid."

Their eyes met; Azrael locked on to Diarmuid's green eyes with his mirrored ones. His face did not waver until Diarmuid broke the stare with a cough and a nervous smile that tried to hide his frustration. Without averting his gaze, he smiled, "Yes, great Guardian, the Chief Counsel and I are quite familiar with one another. I am surprised to see him here. I know the great many duties and responsibilities he has to the Conclave of Magi," Azrael released Diarmuid from his gaze and looked again at the Guardian, "One would wonder at the serendipitous occurrence of this meeting."

Guardian Giasis smiled and adjusted his robes, "Correct question, Archmagus. However, I wonder what makes you grace our shores unannounced. Diarmuid is a Luminori elf and is welcome to his homeland whenever he pleases. You, however, are not."

Azrael smirked, the muted crimson and yellow light filtering into the room reflecting off his mirrored eyes, "With all due respect, your grace, I do not remember ever needing an invitation to enter Luminos when your father was Guardian."

Giasis' face became stern, "It is because of my respect for my father that you and your company were not cut down on-site when you entered port, Archmagus Azrael. My father honored and respected you, and one of his dying requests was to treat you in the same manner. That does not mean I am going to endanger my homeland when you bring another black robe mage, a Castellarian dog, and a demon whore with you!"

Gideon's jaw clenched, and he shifted his weight as if to step forward. A touch from Isidora on his shoulder calmed him. Lear'Za, on the other hand, had no such restraint.

"Well, I am offended your grace! I am a daemoness, not a demon," Lear'Za responded with a sarcastic gasp.

Azrael shot her a glance, and Lear'Za grinned and raised her hands in silence. He slowly turned his head back, and his gaze lingered on Diarmuid for a moment before returning to Giasis. His tone was calm and cold as always.

"My question, your grace, is not one of invitation. I question how you came upon this precise information and arrived at an erroneous conclusion before we even landed on your shores? Considering the company you keep at this moment, it does not take long a stretch of the imagination to come to a logical conclusion."

Diarmuid's rage was visible, but he kept his tone even when he responded, "Come now, Azrael. We are all friends here, are we not?"

"There are very few who I would call friend Chief Counsel," Azrael interrupted, "There are people in my own company that I do not consider friends as of yet. I would not assume if I were you, that you have that honor."

Diarmuid's hands clenched, and he stepped forward. Giasis raised his hand and stopped him, "Enough! My patience is wearing thin. Archmagus, to what purpose are you and your company in Luminos?"

Azrael folded his hands in his robes and smirked briefly at Diarmuid, "Your grace, we make for the Ranian Desert. We have no purpose in Luminos other than safe passage to our destination. We do not wish to curry any favor nor disturb your fair realm."

"The Ranian Desert?" Giasis folded his hands in his lap and sat forward, "What would anyone want in that gods' forsaken place?"

"Our council is our own, your grace. It does not involve Luminos," Azrael saw too much eagerness in Diarmuid's face and did not wish to reveal the nature of their journey.

"The safety of my realm is my council Azrael. I cannot allow you to tromp through Luminos with this collection of individuals without an explanation. You test my patience, black robe. My honored father was a wise man, but I never understood his friendship with the likes of you. It is an egregious shame that a black robe walks the halls of the Palace of Light."

Talia had heard enough. Her glow went from a faint yellowish green to deep red, and her face puffed up as she sat on Azrael's shoulders. In a whoosh of red light, she flew off and fluttered inches before the Guardian's face. The enraged pixie wagged a finger in his face as he stared in disbelief, "You should be ashamed of yourself, Giasis Kitharii! You know as well as anyone how many times Azrael helped your father! How good a friend he is to the forest folk! He treats us as equals, unlike you elves that look at us like silly little things for your amusement! Oh, and let's not forget what he has done for you! Why you wouldn't even be alive if it wasn't for this man. But you wouldn't remember that because you were only a sickly babe!" The pixie clenched her fists, "Why, I ought to..." Her last words muffled as Azrael grabbed her in his hand and shoved her into one of his many pockets.

Giasis shook with rage, "You best control your friends, Azrael, or this meeting will be at an end, and the only journey you will make will be to our prisons!"

Azrael patted his robes where Talia resided and whispered, "Thank you little one, but this is not your fight," He raised his head slowly and stared at the Elvan king, "Forgive her, your grace. If I am not mistaken, the pixies have been friends to the elves longer than I have," Azrael's mouth curled into his thin-lipped smirk.

Giasis sneered and cleared his throat, "Enough of this! State your purpose or leave my lands."

Azrael saw Diarmuid's face beam in triumph. Diarmuid knew that Azrael had no choice but to reveal what he was up to, "If it must be said, your grace, then I bow to your position as Guardian. We make for the Ruins of Al'Zadal on matters of magical significance to my student Isidora. She wishes to become a Summoner, and we believe there is an avatar to be found in the ruins."

Giasis rubbed his chin, "A Summoner, you say? I must say, I am surprised you would even partake in such a journey, Archmagus," Diarmuid beamed over Giasis' shoulder, "I will allow it on one condition," The king softened his tone. The matter with the pixie had not made him look good at all.

Diarmuid's triumphant look fell, "Your grace, you cannot possibly even be considering."

Giasis raised a hand silencing Diarmuid, "You are an honored and respected elf, Diarmuid; I will stop you before you say something that is beginning to sound like questioning the wisdom of your king. Azrael has never brought harm to Luminos, and my father trusted him. As much as the fact he is a black robe sickens me, he has helped our kingdom in the past. I will allow it on the condition that one of my rangers accompanies your group to the borders of Luminos. My trust of you does not extend to the company you keep, Azrael. He will keep in contact with me on a nightly basis through an Aeimer Orb. Should just one night pass that he does not contact me, our forces will fall upon you and your company, and they do not take prisoners."

Azrael bowed, "I cannot argue your wisdom, your grace. Your ranger will be treated as one of our own company. I vow to make our journey through your lands swift."

Giasis nodded and pounded the butt of his ceremonial staff on the dais three times. One of his guards came to his side, and Giasis murmured some words to him. The guard bowed and hurriedly exited through a door behind the throne. A few moments later, the guard returned, followed by a young elf. His expression severe, tall, and lithe in typical elf fashion and had the same silky blonde hair and cheekbones as Giasis. He wore the green jerkin and hose with deerskin boots of a ranger with a quiver of arrows, a longbow, and a slender elvan blade at his side. "This is my nephew Kethis Kitharii; he is a captain in the Luminori Rangers," Kethis gave a short bow, "Now if we are done here, I have more pressing matters to attend."

Azrael bowed. As the company departed the throne room, Kethis fell in behind them. As they walked, Azrael could feel Diarmuid's eyes boring angry holes into his back; it made him smile.

CHAPTER 9

Diarmuid stormed through the halls of the Palace of Light. Retainers and palace workers moved to the side as the enraged mage made his way to his quarters, his white robes billowing behind him. Upon reaching his room, he went in and slammed the crystal door behind him. With a snap of his fingers, the various braziers burst into flame as he paced about the room, muttering to himself. A slight chuckle came from behind him, and he stopped and spun in a fury. Sitting on a divan was Caiaphas. His hands folded in the sleeves of his black robes; the hood pulled low over his eyes. Diarmuid's rage boiled over, "How dare you enter the Palace of Light, *Dark Elf!* I should call the royal guard and watch as they burn you at the stake!"

"Come now, Diarmuid. We are all friends here, are we not?" The dark elf could not help using the words Diarmuid himself had spoken to Azrael only moments ago. As much as Caiaphas feared Azrael, he admired him greatly, "Your anger is misplaced, Diarmuid. It was not I who made a fool of you before the Guardian of the Light. Besides, you requested that I follow them to Luminos, so here I am despite the grave danger it poses me. Now that your hopes of Giasis sending Azrael away have failed, I assume you still require my services."

Diarmuid's anger ebbed. Of all his rangers, the Guardian was sending Kethis, his nephew. The Guardian favored Diarmuid, but he knew that Kethis had always been wary of him. Ridding himself of the ranger would not be a bad proposition. Caiaphas was correct; he would require his services, "It is not a complete loss. He was forced to reveal the nature of their journey, or at least the reason for his student returning. The fool girl wishes to become a Summoner. If it was not bad enough, she chose the black robes like her teacher. Now she looks towards fringe sorcery for power. That alone would not be enough to draw Azrael out. The time of that asinine prophecy is growing close, and somehow he sees a way to challenge Leto. They must be stopped."

Caiaphas casually played with the sleeves of his robes, "Why does Azrael's hatred for Leto upset you so much, Diarmuid?"

"I have no love for the god Leto, dark elf. Just like all elves, I am loyal to the goddess Astraea of the balance. It is that balance, which she personifies that I wish to maintain. Challenging Leto is madness. Who knows what insanity the chaos god will unleash at Azrael's heresy and unhinged hubris and, dare I say it, should he be successful."

Caiaphas sat forward, his eyes bright with excitement, "So you do believe Azrael has the potential to defeat a god!"

Diarmuid shook his head in frustration, "I am not saying that, dark elf. I am saying, win or lose, the mere prospect of what he plans is dangerous. His interpretation of that prophecy is that he alone can stop an Harbinger of Chaos. As I see it, it will be his actions that bring about this Harbinger and the destruction of Tinil'Gan by Leto's hand."

"Azrael is no fool, Diarmuid. It seems to me your grudge and hatred for the Sidhe influence your thoughts. If he succeeds, you will be forced to acknowledge Azrael as the greatest mage ever, superior to you and everyone else on the Conclave. A black robe!"

Diarmuid dove at the dark elf and grabbed him by the front of his robes, pulling him to his feet, "I've had enough of your mouth, dark elf! You follow them and make sure they do not reach Al' Zadal alive!"

Caiaphas calmly removed Diarmuid's hands from his robes. He smoothed the black fabric and then bowed. With a calm smile, he addressed Diarmuid, "As you wish Chief Counsel," With a flurry of black robes and a quick enchantment, Caiaphas disappeared from the room.

Diarmuid clenched his hands to calm his frustration. The proud elf looked upon a statue depicting Astraea in the corner and closed his eyes. His hands unclenched while he let out a soothing sigh. More relaxed, he poured himself some wine. Calmly, he sat upon a divan and drank deeply. *It is only a minor setback; these events can still play into my favor,* he thought to himself. Another recent message from Lord Sulik played in the back of his mind. *Strange times make strange bedfellows.* He cared little for the politics of Tinil'Gan, but this Lord Sulik was an ambitious man.

The Tower of Elizar was the last bastion of strength for the magi. It sat in a small outskirt of the Linian Forest on the east bank of the Distillar, in lands held by the Riverlords. Although the Riverlords suffered the tower's existence, they gave the magi little love. If what Lord Sulik planned came to fruition, he had promised favorable treatment of the magi as well as expanding the Tower's holdings and promises of more land for new towers. Let the sentimental fools of the Conclave pine for Azrael's return. Future generations would remember him as the greatest Chief Counsel in history, and he would make sure of it. What did it matter to him who ruled the Riverlands? He would bring the glory of the magi across the continent, with Towers in every corner, even if that meant working with Castellarians. He smiled and drank the remainder of his wine.

CHAPTER 10

It didn't take long for the group of companions—six now with the addition of Kethis—to leave behind the glistening splendor of Luminori for the winding paths of the Linian Forest. They rode quietly, their horses moving at a relaxed gait through the peaceful forest. Despite their vainglory and air of superiority, the elves did truly love nature and protected their forest at all costs. It had a mystical atmosphere. The belief that all nature spirits and beings of Tinil'Gan originated from the Linian Forest was a common one. That the lesser gods of nature resided there among its numerous oaks, birches, maples, and the giant sequoias found deep in its interior followed suit.

As they began the descent from the higher ground of the outskirts of the city to the forest floor, the companions found a clearing to camp for the night. Although not necessarily dangerous, the trek through the forest to the boundaries of the Ranian Desert would take at least a week. With a good night's sleep, they could make an early start in the morning. Kethis gathered some wood and started a fire as the rest undid their bedrolls. Gideon pulled a crossbow from his pack and started for the trees. Kethis intercepted him.

"Just where do you think you are going, Castellarian?" The elf's tone was harsh, and he stopped Gideon's movement with a hand on his mailed chest.

"It is a forest, good elf," Gideon smiled good-naturedly and placed a hand on his hip, "We will need our rations for the desert. Some fresh meat for dinner would do nicely."

"This forest is sacred to the elves, knight. No human, let alone a Castellarian, will hunt its woods. If it is dinner you seek, I shall find it for us," Kethis took out his bow and knocked an arrow, "Kindly drop your weapon before I remove it from your hands myself."

Gideon's face flushed red in anger, and he squared his shoulders, "First your uncle and now you. That is twice I have suffered insult due to my heritage. I have held my tongue, out of respect as a traveler through your lands, but I will not suffer a third."

Sighing to himself, Azrael made his way over and placed himself between the knight and the elf. Isidora also came over and placed a hand on Gideon's arm.

"As brutish as he may seem, Captain, the boy meant no harm. I suggest you let it be," Azrael said.

Kethis relaxed his grip and replaced his arrow in his quiver, "Remember your place, knight, and the lands upon which you tread." Kethis spun around with the quickness of a deer and silently made his way into the woods.

Isidora led Gideon away as he grumbled to himself. Talia watched the interaction and shrugged her shoulders. With a spark of inspiration, her eyes lit up, and her wings furiously carried her to and fro around the clearing. After a few moments, she stopped near the fire with a large handful of various berries and herbs. She placed them down and opened a small pouch on her left hip. She then proceeded to pull out a large—very large—frying pan. Although the cast iron pan was bigger than her (more massive than the pouch it came from), she hefted it as if it were a feather and placed it on the fire. She started putting berries and herbs in the pan. It was then she noticed everyone staring at her.

"What? The elf will be back soon with meat. I thought it would be nice to have some sauce to go with it. You people act as you've never seen someone cook before!" She went on her way, preparing the sauce without registering the fact why they were all staring at her.

Azrael even managed a grin and shook his head in amusement. It was then he noticed Lear'Za was sitting (well, floating) some distance from the fire. She had been unusually quiet since they left Luminori. He casually walked over and stood before her.

"Pouting does not become you, daemoness. I never expected you to be this depressed over a lack of a carriage."

"Your dour humor does not amuse me right now, Seer'kaat. This place is suffocating me," Lear'Za had an uncharacteristically distressed look upon her face.

Azrael cocked his head to the side and arched an eyebrow, "We have been in forests many times, daemoness. Panic is unlike you."

"It is not the trees. It is what flits among them. I can feel their distaste for me. I am not wanted here," Lear'Za's eyes darted around the treetops and she rubbed her arm anxiously.

Azrael had known Lear'Za for over three hundred years. He had gone into battle with her, faced unspeakable horrors, but never had he seen her in this state of mind. If there was one being he could call truly fearless, Lear'Za was it, "Lear'Za, if there is something here you fear, you can easily ride the ethers ahead of us and meet us in the desert."

Lear'Za bolted upright, her feet floating higher than usual above the ground, "It is not fear, you dolt!" Realizing her lack of control, she calmed herself and drifted lower, "I fear nothing. It is a discomfort, like being in a room that is too hot, or in an especially small closet with no room to move. No, Seer'kaat, I will not leave. I said I would accompany Isidora on this quest, and I intend to stay no matter how uncomfortable this blasted forest tries to make me. Your attempt at concern is appreciated but not needed," She turned her head to the side and watched Kethis bound back into the clearing carrying the fruits of his hunt, "Our Elvan guide has returned. If I were you, I would concern yourself more with keeping elf and knight separated for the rest of this journey than for my wellbeing."

Azrael gave her a thin-lipped smile and returned to the campfire, Lear'Za floating close behind. Kethis returned with a string of rabbits. He begrudgingly gave a few to Gideon to help skin and prep before placing them on the spit. As the sun set on the horizon they enjoyed the well-cooked rabbit with Talia's berry sauce. The earlier anger and discomfort disappeared, and they chatted idly.

"I still will never understand it," Lear'Za said as she sipped her conjured wine from a crystal goblet, as the rest drank fresh water from a nearby stream, "After hundreds of years on your world I still cannot understand its denizen's loyalty and insane behavior in the name of their gods. In my world, I and my kin were living gods, ruling over their people. We never questioned if we had creators, or even worse, a power above our own."

Kethis spat out a small bone and swallowed the last of his meat, "From what I know of you and your kind on Tinil'Gan, demons have no respect for anything save their own goals. Your lack of faith and insolence does not surprise me."

Lear'Za flashed a wicked grin, "My dear elf, I have made stronger and wiser men than you kneel before me willingly, knowing they would soon die. You can keep your faith."

Disgusted, Kethis busied himself with cleaning his dagger, "My faith keeps me grounded. It lets me know that, despite my failings and those of others, there are those watching who will guide the world to a better place."

Azrael smirked as the fire reflected off his mirrored eyes, "The gods, young elf lord, are not infallible. Even they scheme, plot, stumble, and go wrong. The story of my race is proof enough."

"I have always wondered about the Sidhe, Archmagus," Gideon said, leaning forward, "Perhaps you could regale us with some tales."

Talia's eyes became bright as she flittered around the campfire, "Yes, please, dear Azrael. Tell us a story, please, please, please!"

Azrael sighed and removed his hood, revealing the full brilliance of the fire reflecting on his mirrored eyes, "If it keeps you all quiet for a bit, then I will, if for nothing else than to retain my sanity."

Everyone sat forward, even Kethis.

"The stories of old told by your parents and priests speak of the three major gods, Astraea, Artio, and Leto, coming together to create Tinil'Gan and its inhabitants," Azrael spat out the name of the chaos god but they were all too entranced to notice the subtle hatred, "This is true, to some extent, except they did not do it alone. The ones we call the Elements also aided, some more than others. It did indeed take the combined forces of the Three to bring order, chaos, and balance together to form the world from the ethers and create a fire in the heavens that is the sun. It was an incredible task that, once completed, had tired the Three. They had created a world, but it was barren, no life and no nature, devoid of anything. It was a ball of dirt. They took leave of their creation and rested. The Elements saw more potential.

"Blancheflor, goddess of the sea was first to speak. She said it was so dry and lifeless. It brought tears to her eyes. Her tears fell to Tinil'Gan, filling its holes and craters, creating the oceans and lakes. In her joy, she jumped into the oceans and swam.

"Caillech, god of the winds, saw the oceans but the land was still dry and cracked. He breathed a heavy sigh, and in the skies of Tinil'Gan, the first clouds formed, carried by the winds. They picked up water from the seas and lakes and rained them upon the land.

"Next to look down was Cerridwen, god of nature. He saw water and moist land but still found it lacking. The god wrung his hands together in deep thought. He rubbed his hands so furiously that flakes of his divine skin fell to Tinil'Gan and became the first seeds. Wherever they landed, they sank into the soil and up sprang grasses, trees, flowers, and all forms of plant life. He smiled and was pleased with the lush greenery he created.

"Inquisitive by nature, Arduinna, goddess of the sky, walked on the other side of the world not bathed in the light of the sun. She found it pitch black and could not see a thing. She tripped and fell, and where she bumped her head against the sky, it fractured, creating the stars. She also created our three moons. The spot where she bumped her head bruised the sky, giving us the violet moon Corcra. A cut upon her brow spilled a drop of divine golden blood, creating the golden moon Oir. And in her distress, she shed a single silver tear, forming the silver moon Airgid. Arduinna lay on her back in pain, but when she opened her eyes and saw it was no longer dark, she smiled.

"It was then that the Three awoke from their rest and saw what their younger siblings had done. At first, the others' interference angered them. Their anger caused seas to roil in hurricanes, the skies to spit lightning and storms. It warped plants, changing them into dangerous versions of themselves, filled with poison and thorns. And the moons began to circle Tinil'Gan from being flung. Then wise Cerridwen came to his older siblings and pleaded with them. He showed them the wonder and beauty of the world and how they could use it. The three calmed their anger, and they accepted that the world was indeed better, but it needed more. It needed life. This ended what is known as the Age of Twilight."

"Ha!" Lear'Za shouted with a snicker, "Poor little gods, angry their siblings played with their toys. My people would have torn them limb from limb and ate their entrails."

Isidora groaned, "Lear'Za, please let him finish his tale."

Lear'Za rolled her eyes, "Uhg, fine. Please, continue."

Azrael shook his head and continued, "The Elements came together and, using the soil, water, wind, and light, they concentrated. From their efforts sprang all the creatures of the land and sea, as well as all the magical beings who govern nature. Life now teemed on Tinil'Gan. The Three saw the splendor, but their awe soon turned to jealousy. In their anger, they created a creature of their own. Using stardust, fire, ice, and lightning, they released upon Tinil'Gan the ancient dragons. At first, the dragons ran rampant upon Tinil'Gan, terrifying and destroying the life the Three had created. Once again, the ever calm and wise Cerridwen interceded. He suggested that dragons should number few, and live solitary lives in remote areas, and in exchange, they would be granted extremely long lives and intelligent awareness. They all agreed, and peace resumed. But the Three would not be outdone.

"They decided they needed to create life that was intelligent and aware as well, that would look to the gods as their creators and rejoice. They would create life in their own image. They began their task. Every time they tried, they were disappointed. Their creations were indeed aware, but they were brutish, not very intelligent, and bestial. These creations were Ogres, Goblins, Trolls, and other creatures we call monsters. The Three were vexed. It was then that the last of the divine family came forward. The youngest of the divine, they had stayed away from their quarreling siblings and watched in wonder at the world that was created. These three triplets were Malystrix, Azalan, and Lenae. They were the keepers of magic."

Kethis stood up, visibly agitated, "Ogres, Goblins, and Trolls created by the gods before the elves? I cannot stand for this heresy."

"Then perhaps you should return to your seat and sit through it like the rest of us," Gideon snorted. With an angry grunt, Kethis sat down once again and crossed his arms broodingly.

Azrael watched the exchange and spoke again as if not interrupted, "Magic in its purest form and essence is the life force of the gods. It is what binds them, gives them their power, and gave shape to them. The triplets, who understood magic better than all, had watched what had happened and told the Three that, to give life to the beings they wished, it would require some of their magic.

"The Three set about their task. Using the elements, first came Astraea, using her force of will and imagination she gave form to her creation. She imagined a race that was beautiful, long in life and loving of the world around it. Smiling the triplets blew some of their magic down, and the elves were created. Then came Artio, who craved order above all things. He imagined a stout, sturdy people, set in their ways and skilled with their hands. Smiling the triplets blew some of their magic down, and the dwarves were created. The ever impatient Leto pushed his way forward. He imagined a race that was strong and willful like him, ever ready to battle. Unwittingly in his haste, he imbued that trait on them, as well, giving them shorter lifespans. Smiling the triplets blew some of their magic down, and the race of man was created.

"The Three were very pleased; they marveled at their creations in glory. The triplets smiled and left them to awe. They did not require thanks; they were happy to be able to help their siblings, and went back to their true love, guarding the magic. The world went on, and the gods were pleased. They watched their creations form the first societies and towns. Being immortal gods, their pleasure did not last long, and old jealousies arose. They saw their creations' first use of magic. They were imbued with it, so they would, to a certain extent, be able to use it with the god's blessings. This is known as the Age of Awakening."

Gideon scratched his stubbled chin in confusion, "I have yet to hear about the Sidhe, Archmagus. I was almost certain they would have been one of the first, if not the first of the Gods' creations."

Azrael smirked, "Patience, young knight, the story is not over. As you will soon see, not everything is as it seems," He adjusted his sleeves and continued his tale, "History teaches us the Age of Awakening is followed by the Age of Power, then the first mighty nations rose. Few know that there is a short, but crucial event that occurred between them.

"The Three knew that their creations would not be possible without magic. They knew the triplets knew the secret of creating life and could if they wanted, create their own races. They did not trust this and confronted the triplets. They accused them of consorting together to create life behind their backs. The triplets denied this, for it was not true. Their only concern and love was for the magic. The Three did not listen.

"With every refusal of the triplets, the Three's resentment grew. Finally, their anger erupted, and a tragic decision was made. The Three banished Azalan and Lenae to Tinil'Gan separating the triplets. One, Malystrix, was left behind to guard their celestial magic. Since two were cast down to Tinil'Gan, they could no longer be gods thus they could not conspire to create life. There were a few things the Three could not do. They could not take away Azalan and Lenae's immortality. They would not age or become ill. But because they were a part of Tinil'Gan, their bodies could be destroyed. They could be killed. The Three also could not take away their command of the magic. The magic was their essence; it was in their blood. Unlike the creations of the gods, they did not require the gods' blessings to use the magic. They, although now beings of Tinil'Gan, were not *from* the gods but *of* the gods.

"Malystrix cried for her brother and sister. She was left alone to guard the magic. Even there, her duties were cut short. The Three gave the duty of overseeing magic on Tinil'Gan to each of their children, Myrrdin, Gwydion, and Belial—the three now known as the gods of the Orders of the Magi. She was left only to guard the celestial magic—until an incredible thing happened. Azalan and Lenae had a child on Tinil'Gan. They became the first Sidhe. Malystrix took it upon herself to become Patron Saint of the Sidhe and watch over this new race born of her kin, the only race *not* created by the gods. Thus ended the little known era; the Age of the Fallen."

With Azrael's last words the camp became eerily silent, the crackle of the fire and various sounds of forest nightlife became more audible and noticeable. Kethis broke the silence.

"That tale is heresy! You claim monsters, like ogres and trolls, were created before the elves, that Sidhe have an ancient kinship to the gods, and that Astraea required assistance to create my proud people?" Kethis stood up angrily, throwing a stick into the flames.

Azrael's facial expression did not change. He leaned back against a stump and pulled his hood low over his eyes, "I was asked for a tale of my people, elf lord. I gave one. This tale is older than Luminori itself. Make of it what you will."

Kethis snarled and spun off into the woods, his Aeimer Orb in hand to make his report to Giasis. Isidora's eyes were wide, her mind swirling with the tale Azrael told. Growing up in his tower, she had sometimes asked questions about the Sidhe, and it was dismissed as unimportant for her studies. She wasn't sure why, but she was also strangely curious about this Malystrix.

"D'ni, the tale was fascinating, but it leaves questions. What became of Malystrix? Why are stories not told of her along with the other gods? What of your people, where are they?"

"Her tale and that of my people does indeed continue, Isidora," Azrael paused and looked up at the night sky with its millions of stars, "However, that story is for another day. I suggest you all get some sleep. We rise with the sun and set off quickly thereafter," Azrael pulled up his bedroll and closed his eyes.

Kethis had returned and made his bedroll as did the others. Talia found a comfortable fold in Azrael's bedroll and curled up. Isidora laid with her eyes open to the night sky for some time in wonder, "There is more to that story, and I intend to hear it," She whispered to herself and finally closed her eyes. Another pair of eyes from the forest, hidden in a black robe, nodded and thought the same. Unfortunately, if his plan in the coming days succeeded, there would be no one left to tell that tale. Quietly, Caiaphas left for his camp. He would require much rest before he attempted his task.

CHAPTER 11

As Azrael instructed, they awoke at dawn. After a quick breakfast of left-over berries and herbal tea, they were quickly on horseback traversing the various pathways eroded into the ground by hunters and trailblazers. The Linian Forest was sacred to the elves; they did not carve roads through it. Whatever paths there were, meandered in all directions. Kethis quickly proved himself a blessing rather than a hindrance. He knew the forest better than any of the companions and promptly found the fastest and safest path northward towards the desert.

The fact that it was late summer helped as well. The weather was pleasant, and if it did rain, it was short, refreshing showers that didn't deluge the group as they made their way. Food was also in abundance, as trees and shrubs sprouted fresh spring berries, and the wildlife was buzzing all around them. They were in good cheer as they traveled in this manner for the next three days.

Unknown to them, Kethis' route also helped Caiaphas, for they traveled paths not as well-known, and without as many Luminori sentries and scouts. Casting invisibility spells to last an entire day and every day, would have been very taxing on the dark elf. He knew he had to conserve strength for the spell he was preparing to cast.

Whenever the group rested, Caiaphas would return to his spell books and preparations. He checked and double-checked the moon phases and components to ensure a successful casting. He had only one chance at it, and if he failed, his safety would be at risk. He also knew that, even if successful, he would be drained to the point of exhaustion and would need at least a day's rest before even attempting a minor spell. Tonight was the night.

The golden moon Oir, favored by the black robe's god, Belial, would be full tonight A full moon provided an additional chance at success. Unfortunately, he knew this would also aid Azrael and Isidora's spell casting. But he could not worry about that; he had to make sure his casting was flawless.

He silently followed the group the rest of the day, watching as the sun turned the sky orange in its decent and the group made camp. Now was the time. The final preparations and casting would take him three or so hours and would be complete after they went to sleep for the night. He headed east of the camp and found a suitable area with a clear view of the sky. His eyes closed as he murmured in an arcane tongue. A quiet whirlwind formed around him, clearing all the debris and leaves on the ground leaving a smooth patch of soil. Satisfied, he set to work; Oir would be overhead soon.

He removed one pouch from his belt. It contained white chalk dust. Carefully scattering the chalk on the ground, he created a large circle and then a smaller one a couple yards away. He walked both circles twice setting the chalk into the soil and checking for any breaks in the lines. Finding none, he set to creating binding runes in the larger circle and protective runes in the smaller one.

With the runes completed, he looked up and saw the sun had set entirely, and the stars were out; Oir was in its ascent.

His pulse quickened. He always felt a rush of excitement when he was about to use advanced spell casting, and tonight was even more special. He was sending his work against a being he felt was not only the most powerful of the black magi but the most powerful mage to walk Tinil'Gan. What Caiaphas had not told Diarmuid was that his desire to be accepted back into the Conclave of Magi was not his only motive in taking this task. He admired and respected Azrael. *Oh if I could have trained under him!* His mind would run with the possibilities and wonders he might have learned. Alas, save for Isidora, Azrael had not accepted an apprentice in over five hundred years. He shook his head from his reverie and continued his task.

He spread dried mugwort, a typical warding herb, in both circles. Again he checked the rings, making sure there were no breaks, and with the aid of his spellbook double-checked the accuracy and placement of the runes. Completely satisfied, he made his way to the smaller circle and knelt within it.

He placed the spellbook at his knees, opened to the appropriate page. He had studied the spell numerous times, committing it to memory, but he made all assurances he was prepared. Closing his eyes, he began his prayers to Belial. All magi (except for the Sidhe) were required to ask for their respective god's blessings before casting any significant spell; this was the gods' way of keeping Magi under their control. The prayers might be long and ornate in ritualistic spells such as the one Caiaphas had prepared. Magi needed to be quick-tongued to be proficient at their craft.

Caiaphas completed his prayers and felt the blessings of his god flow through him, as well as the telltale tingle of the Art in his veins. He was ready and basked in the golden glow of Oir. He stood and held his arms out in ecstasy.

At first, his voice came out in a low murmur as he recited the spell in the arcane tongue of the Art, every syllable, every inflection perfect as prescribed. He repeated it over and over, the volume of his voice rising with each repetition. Sweat poured from his head, and his eyes were wide as he felt the power of magic flow through him and his words. He could feel its power tearing at the fabric of his being, threatening to tear him apart. His grip on the control slipped, and his body screamed in agony. The dark elf refocused his concentration and brought the power back under control. He screamed the last incantation in frantic glory as the energy flowed out of him and around the two circles. He stood transfixed as the power bounced back and forth between him and the two circles.

A mist with a faint glow began to grow in the larger circle. Slowly, it grew and swirled into a bluish shape. The shape coalesced into a fearsome form of a wyrm: a *Nidhogg*. Although dragon-like, a Nidhogg was not one of the terrestrial dragons of Tinil'Gan. It was a demon, unthinking, unyielding; it's only reason for being to tear and destroy the target of its master's choosing. Caiaphas let out a mighty laugh and shook his fists in the air. Drained from the spell and his exuberant celebration, he stumbled. With a breathless laugh, he steadied himself. He had summoned the Nidhogg successfully, and it was trapped in its circle, thrashing, awaiting his orders.

"My mighty Nidhogg! Heed my command! Search my mind, and you will see those for you to destroy. Do not stop until they are destroyed or your essence fades from this plane!"

The Nidhogg nodded its head and turned out of the circle. Once out of the constraints of the circle, it roared and grew to its full height of fifteen feet at its shoulders, its head even higher with its neck fully extended. Without care for its surroundings, it bound through the forest knocking down ancient trees like kindling, heading towards its targets.

CHAPTER 12

Kethis was the first to wake. His keen hearing detected a disturbance immediately. In one fluid movement, the elf was on his feet with an arrow notched in his bow, eyes scanning the trees with his sensitive Elvan night vision.

It did not take the rest long to rise. Although not elves with Kethis' advantages, they were all veterans of battle. Gideon pulled his sword from its scabbard and was at alert, ready to strike. He heard Azrael and Isidora cast defensive shield spells and had the murmurs of offensive spells on their lips prepared to unleash. Lear'Za carried no visible weapons but with a flick of her wrists two flaming and wickedly curved scimitars seemed to grow from her hands. The sight shocked Gideon, but he had more significant concerns.

The group came together and was huddled back to back, giving them collectively, a view of the entire area. Talia glowed a bright orange of warning upon Azrael's shoulder.

They were deathly silent; all ears listened for any sounds, eyes darted left and right. Even their breaths were stilled. It began as a slow hollow *boom boom,* echoing through the trees, seeming to come from everywhere. As it grew louder, accompanied by the sounds of snapped branches and felled trees limbs.

"What is it?" Isidora murmured as her wide eyes darted around. The ground shook beneath their feet.

Gideon pressed closer to Isidora, "What could make the ground shake so?"

"Shh," Kethis breathed through his lips, "It's here."

There was a moment's pause, and suddenly the trees in front of Kethis exploded in a deluge of broken branches and splintered wood that showered the group. With a mighty roar, the Nidhogg entered the clearing.

"Dragon!" Kethis shouted, and a moment later, the beast unleashed a breath of fire upon them. In unison, they dove in different directions to avoid the blast. Scattered by the debris and rampage of the dragon, Gideon paired up with the closest ally, Kethis. The elf loosed his arrow as he flung himself to one side. It flew through the air and hit its mark on the Nidhogg's snout, but the Nidhogg hardly seemed to notice. The demon dragon's otherworldly blood dissolved the arrowhead and the shaft and fell away. *His arrows melt away as if wax.* He looked at the ranger in concern. Undeterred, Kethis continued to fire arrow after arrow at the beast.

Gideon's instincts told him to rush to Isidora's side, but their positioning made it impossible. It took every bit of skill and concentration he had to deflect the dragons swiping tail with his sword. He noted the blood splatter did not affect his sword as severely as the arrows. The hardened steel only showed minor etching from the caustic fluid. In between swipes, he glanced over at his wife and her teacher.

Azrael and Isidora, standing shoulder to shoulder on the far side of the creature, began their incantations. Even amid extreme danger, their faces showed their exaltation as they unleashed the force of the Art. Isidora chose ice magic. Gideon saw it flow from her fingertips, first as a cold mist, but as it made its way towards the Nidhogg, it coalesced into six two-foot-long ice spears that impaled the beast's left flank. The Nidhogg roared in response but did not stop its thrashing through the clearing. Gideon rolled to his left and grabbed Kethis on his way to avoid being trampled.

He looked up to see if they were safe and witnessed Azrael's cast his spell. The earth magic he used caused the ground under the Nidhogg to grow soft, turning it into a muddy swamp. The beast sank up to its knees in the sticky goo. With another few words and hand movements from Azrael, the goo hardened like rock momentarily immobilizing the creature. Gideon saw his chance. He ran up to the beast's tail and hacked away it, hoping to keep its attention divided; it had no effect. With each chop, he screamed, but every cut closed up immediately. Breathlessly, he looked up.

Talia had joined the battle; he marveled at her bravery. She flew toward the beast's snout and pulled from her pouch her large, very large, frying pan and swang it with vigor. The pan bounced off the Nidhogg with a clang, shaking her entire body and making her teeth chatter. She spun away dizzily, her teeth chattering from her failed attack. He could see her spin and dive into Azrael's robes. Gaining his breath, he began chopping at the beast's tail again. Lear'Za floated in from the other side of the clearing next to Gideon.

Her lips curved in a wicked smile, "It is not a dragon! It is a demon! Your physical attacks will not harm it!" Lear'Za yelled.

Gideon continued to hack and spoke between swings, "Then what should we do?" As he frantically hacked away, an idea inspired in his mind. He ceased his attack and closed his eyes instead. Although not a mage, he did employ battle wizardry. Holding his sword before him, he muttered a quick prayer and a brief incantation. His sword came aflame with magical fire. With his newly enchanted sword, he swung again at the tail. This time, when the sharp blade cut into the creature's hide, the magical fire entered the wound. The beast cried out in pain. With an excited yell, Gideon called out, "Kethis! Enchant your arrows. They will do it harm!"

All elves had some skill in magic. Kethis was not a mage, either, but he knew minor enchantment spells, just as Gideon did. Kethis did as told but shook his head, "They will slow this abomination down but will not stop it! The black robes will have more success!" Kethis fired a magically flaming arrow and dove beneath a swipe of the beast's claw that it had freed from the hardened ground.

Azrael and Isidora continued their magical assault, alternating between the different elements, "Every magical assault ebbs its life force," Azrael yelled over the roars of the Nidhogg, "It will eventually dissipate! The problem is a demon of this size can withstand constant assault all night! The quickest way would be to summon another demon, but I dare not attempt a delicate spell like that during battle!"

"There is no need to summon one, Seer'kaat," Lear'Za said, "You already have one. The rest of you keep the beast's attention divided."

Gideon stepped back further away from the beast and watched as Lear'Za casually made her way to the front of the Nidhogg and looked it in the eyes. She bowed her head and rose higher from the ground. A soft hum escaped her lips, and her body contorted. She began to grow and kept growing until she nearly matched the size of the Nidhogg. With a growl, her teeth extended from small pointed barbs to vicious fangs. Horns sprouted from her forehead as her hands became threatening claws. She let out a sickly growl and spat at the beast in a guttural language. A faint reddish glow enveloped her.

The surprises never end! This daemoness possesses a power I never imagined. Gideon's mind attempted to grasp what was happening, but he could only watch in rapt awe.

The Nidhogg slowed and acknowledged Lear'Za, "Yes, Nidhogg! You recognize me now! I am a *Hakkai Lord*! In the outer realms, we keep your race as pets and beasts of burden! Bow before me or face your destruction!"

The beast hesitated for a moment. The glow around Lear'Za began to fade and flicker some. As Isidora had told Gideon, there were limits to Lear'Za's power as a daemoness on Ti-nil'Gan than on her home realm. It was showing. He just hoped she could intimidate the unintelligent Nidhogg enough with her stature in the outer realms. It worked for a moment, but the beast recognized the flickering aura as weakness and roared in defiance. It lunged for Lear'Za's neck. She had anticipated the attack and blocked it with her twin flaming scimitars. The battle of demons had begun.

The two demons locked in a battle embrace. Claws and teeth snapped and raked, neither gaining an advantage. With the beast distracted and engaged with Lear'Za, Gideon was finally able to make it to Isidora's side.

"Will this be enough? He shouted as Isidora sent off another blast of ice spikes.

"I do not know. Lear'Za is weakening; I do not know how much longer she can maintain that form," A look of determination and concentration remained on her face, but Gideon sensed the apprehension in her voice. He looked up at Lear'Za and watched the aura around her fizzle. Her body started to shrink down. Gideon screamed as the Nidhogg opened its maw to bite down upon the failing daemoness. Suddenly, something flashed brightly just outside the clearing, and he shielded his eyes. The light dimmed some, and the knight blinked away the spots until his vision cleared.

An enormous white stag with a massive crown of antlers stepped lightly into the clearing. It nodded its head, and what seemed to be hundreds of satyrs erupted from all around. Many of them came with arrows of light that they fired at the Nidhogg, enraging the beast. Other goat men jumped and leaped at incredible heights as they surrounded the Nidhogg with a net, dragging it down. The creature fought and struggled but could not move as the white stag cantered casually to its snout. The Nidhogg opened its jaws and flames erupted, engulfing it. But when the smoke cleared, the stag still stood there, serene and untouched. It lowered its head and touched the Nidhogg's snout with its antlers. The beast let out a fearful cry and exploded into a cloud of sparkling blue dust that flew into the air and twinkled away like dying stars. The net fell empty to the ground.

Unsure what to make of it, the companions had come together in astonishment. Just as the blue dust dissipated, the assembled satyrs turned their bows towards the huddled companions in unison, surrounding them.

A pathway opened through them, and the white stag approached. It glowed an eerie white, and all felt the immense power that it emanated. Talia flew out from her hiding place within the robes in wonder and awe. She flung herself to the ground and knelt low. All heard its profound and musical voice, but its mouth did not move.

"I have dispatched the demon. They are not allowed in my domain. This is my forest. I sense a threat in your company, as well. State your purpose."

Kethis stepped forward, Gideon noted the confused look on the elf lord's face, "This forest belongs to Luminos, yet you claim dominion. Who are you?"

The stag kicked the dirt under its hooves and raised its mighty head, "The elves of Luminos help guard this forest, Kethis Kitharii, but it is undoubtedly mine. As is every forest on Tinil'Gan. As to who I am; I am known by many names. To the elves, I am Shin Shalaa. To the dwarves, I am Uluuk. But I am most commonly known as Cerridwen, God of Nature."

CHAPTER 13

An appearance by a god was not unheard of; throughout history, the gods had visited certain people of Ti‑nil'Gan, but it was not a common occurrence. With minimal precedence, not many knew precisely how to react. Kethis, being Elvan and faithful, fell to his knees beside Talia before the stag. Isidora and Gideon gave low bows and lowered their heads. Azrael had his reservations with anything concerning the gods—all Cerridwen received from the Archmagus was a nod of the head. Lear'Za, on the other hand, did nothing. The look on her face was one of complete indifference as if Cerridwen was merely another stag. The silence hung in the air for tense moments. Azrael broke the awkwardness.

"We are honored by your presence, wise Cerridwen. To what end do we owe your aid and counsel?"

The stag snorted and shook its antlered head, "I never expected a Sidhe to show reverence to the gods, Lord Azrael, but I accept the humility nonetheless. I think you know why, at least in part, your quest might hold a particular interest to me. At the moment there is a more pressing matter that has cap‑

tured my attention," The great stag swiveled its head towards Lear'Za, "There is one in your party that is as foreign and blasphemous to this realm as was the beast I dispatched. It is yet to be determined if this being should be allowed to leave my forest peacefully or if it should be dispatched in the same manner as the Nidhogg."

Lear'Za gave her usual curved smile, the sharp points of her eyeteeth showing. The uncomfortable sensation she had experienced since entering the forest intensified, but she did not let it show on her face, "So, you are one of the vaunted gods of Tinil'Gan. I can't say that I'm impressed. You have no dominion over me."

The stag extended to its full height, its antlers held high, "I have dominion over the forests of Tinil'Gan and as a god over this realm, demon. You do not belong here."

"I did not ask to be on this realm godling! It was one of your misguided creations that dragged me here and, due to his stupidity, trapped me!" Lear'Za sneered.

"I can gladly right that wrong, demon spawn," The stag's eyes glowed.

Azrael, sensing the danger, interceded, "Mighty Cerridwen, of all the gods you are known for your wisdom and patience. Let us not rush to judgment without explanation. Let this be adjudicated in the way of the forest," Azrael walked forward slowly towards the stag, "I call for the wisdom of the Fae Conclave."

Isidora listened to the exchange with bated breath. She had heard of the Fae Conclave from both Azrael and Talia. They stand judge, jury, and if needed, the executioner of all who stands before it. She went to open her mouth, but the stag god interrupted her.

The stag snorted and stomped, "Lord Azrael, you are clever as you are intelligent. You invoke a Tribunal of the Woods, and I am duty-bound to oblige. I assume you shall be the accused's counsel?"

"I will," Azrael bowed his head.

"So, it shall be. You also understand that as counsel, your fate shall be the same as that of the one you defend, as prescribed by forest law?" Cerridwen said.

The companion's eyes grew wide and looked at the Archmagus.

"Azrael," Isidora finally was able to stammer out some words.

He flashed her a look she knew well. It was telling her to remain silent, "I understand, and accept the time-honored terms, Lord of the Forests."

Isidora feared what could happen. She looked at Lear'Za, who did not display the same fear. Instead, rage permeated the visage of the daemoness. She watched her glide over to Azrael.

"I did not ask for a defender, Seer'kaat!" She raged.

"But you do expect my friendship, do you not?" Azrael said flatly.

"Well, yes," Lear'Za faltered," But I..."

"But nothing. It is this or instant death for you. What do you say?" Azrael's last words were more pleading.

Isidora placed a hand over her mouth as she saw Lear'Za nod slowly in agreement.

"Wonderful!" The stag said after all fell silent, "I have not had this type of entertainment in ages. Let us not waste any time," The stag nodded its head and ropes of magical energy, ethereal bonds, wrapped around Lear'Za. Enraged, she wrestled with them to no avail. Azrael placed a hand on her shoulder to calm her. The stag shook its antlers, and everyone in the clearing disappeared with a flash of white light.

They all reappeared in a more extensive clearing, surrounded by giant redwoods. They ringed the clearing in a perfect circle, surrounding it like ancient colonnades that rose hundreds of feet into the air. An even carpet of green grass coated the, perfectly manicured area. The companions, save for Azrael and Lear'Za, found themselves in seats made of stone that lined one end of the clearing. The stones did not appear to be crafted by mortal hands but naturally formed by nature. Talia, being smaller, was seated upon a large mushroom nearby. At each end of the row of seats stood a satyr guard.

Azrael and Lear'Za found themselves in similar seats, but they were in the center of the clearing. Lear'Za still bound, her jaw clenched in a snarl. At the other end of the glade, facing Azrael and Lear'Za, stood a large rectangular stone dais about four feet high. In the center of the dais stood Cerridwen in his stag persona. He was flanked on each side by two beings. To Cerridwen's left seated in stone thrones, were an old, fat satyr and an attractive young woman with long auburn hair. The woman wore a short dress made of multicolored leaves, and her head adorned with a crown of maple leaves. From Azrael's teachings of ancient lore, Isidora recognized them as Silenus the Satyr Lord and Eupiphine, Matriarch of the Dryads. *His lessons on the Conclave did not do them justice.* Her mind and soul were overcome by the serenity they exuded, despite the dire circumstances upon which they convened.

To Cerridwen's right stood a centaur and a short, slim fairy. The centaur was regal in appearance, his horse body a light brown and his bare human torso well-muscled. His face was bearded, and his hair of deep black came down in a long braid. The fairy had slightly pointed ears and gossamer wings. Her silvery hair was short-cropped, and she wore a silky green gown. They could only be Droxsis, King of the Centaurs, and Tilene, High Princess of Pixies and Fairies. Isidora glanced over as Talia. The small pixie's eyes were wide, and her face content. She could only imagine the overwhelming joy Talia felt being in the presence of her people's Princess. Tilene sat in a stone throne as well, Droxsis stood on his equine legs. Singularly, they each represented the leadership of the major forest denizens; collectively, they were the Fae Conclave under the eye of their god Cerridwen.

Isidora took a moment to gauge the feelings of her companions. Gideon sat to her right, and she placed her hand in his. *He is confused and does not know what to make of all this.* Her quest had taken some unexpected turns, turns she was certain Gideon never even imagined. He was strong; she knew he could handle whatever they faced. She still worried about the deluge of magical and otherworldly beings they had already encountered would overcome him. What he had experienced in just a few days was more than most humans would ever experience in a lifetime, if ever at all.

To her left sat Kethis. The elf lord was difficult to read. His demeanor since joining their group was stoic. Other than his distaste for accompanying humans, he showed very little else. She noticed he was different; there was reverence upon his smooth, youthful features. Elves revere the gods unlike any of Tinil'Gan's races. The guardians of the forests held equal esteem.

She looked to the middle of the clearing. Azrael, as always, remained calm and passive in his visage. Lear'Za, in contrast, emanated rage. Isidora noticed her gritted teeth, the points of her eye teeth showing. The demoness's hands clenched and unclenched at her side where the bonds held them firm. *Where will this lead?* Azrael had prepared her for many things, but this was not one of them.

"Before us, we have Lear'Za, a demon living freely upon Tinil'Gan," Cerridwen's voice boomed through the clearing. "As it is prescribed by our ancient laws, demons are permitted temporary entry into our realm when under the control of a mage and, once its service is completed, banished forthwith to its home realm. The Sidhe Lord Azrael, Archmagus of the black robes stands as counsel. Lord Azrael, you may begin your plea for exemption."

Azrael stood from his seat and removed his hood. He paced before the assembled forest powers; his mirrored eyes looked at them each unyieldingly, "In order for me to make my argument, I must explain the origins Lear'Za's presence in this realm. It began some three hundred years ago, in my tower. At the time, I allowed students to study and practice there. I never enjoyed the task, but as a guardian of the Art and member of the Conclave, it was my duty.

"Under normal circumstances, my tower has precautions and wards in place that prevent apprentices from preforming any spells that are considered too advanced and or are otherwise unauthorized. To this day, I do not understand how one of my apprentices was able to circumvent the wards, or how Belial answered his prayer, allowing it. At any rate, this young one's part of the story begins and ends here, for the spell he cast was his last."

"So it was a black robe that performed the summons?" Silenus inquired in a raspy voice as he scratched his whiskered chin.

"Yes, that is correct. As it is known, only black magi possess the knowledge and spells of demon summoning. And only those of high skill and training should attempt it. Even then, there are only certain demons from certain realms that are allowed to be brought forth. This fool performed the summoning ritual in an unused room. There was a blast that shook the tower. Immediately, I ordered all visitors to their rooms and went to investigate. When I arrived, there was nothing left of him but a pile of ash in his protective circle. He had not summoned just any demon. He had summoned a *Hakkai Lord*."

Isidora saw Tilene raise a hand. The Princess' movements were fluid and beautiful, "Are there not wards put in place to prevent this during spell casting Archmagus?" Her voice was melodic. Her tone high pitched; it flowed from her tongue like a song.

"Yes, there are wards and runes drawn into the summoning circle to prevent such an occurrence. I did inspect the circle afterward. The particular rune to avoid summoning a Hakkai was rubbed away. I first thought he simply missed placing the rune, being far too inexperienced. The fact it was rubbed out meant it was there originally. To this day, I still have not ascertained why it was removed.

"Apparently, he was also unaware that his protective circle would not shield him from a demon of such power. Immediately after summoning, Lear'Za had reduced him to cinders. After that, this incident becomes even more unique. The nature and rules of summoning state that, if the mage is killed, the demon returns to its realm. However inconceivable it was, in the summoning circle stood Lear'Za. My only theory is that the missing rune that was to prevent summoning her also prevented her return to her realm.

"She attempted to dispatch me in the same manner as she had the young black robe. Luckily, I had already cast a shield spell. I was doubly lucky that he had done at least one thing right—the summoning circle was sufficient to bind Lear'Za to the spot, restricting her movements. I placed a shield barrier over the summoning circle to stop any further attacks."

Droxsis stomped one his hooves, "So then you claim the demon was stranded on our realm. I feel you would have been duty-bound to dispatch the demon as an abomination and an anomaly. Yet you did not. Why is this so?" The centaur snorted. Isidora observed Lear'Za's hands clench harder. The daemoness's face was contorted in bestial anger.

Azrael nodded and placed his hands behind his back, "I found myself in unique and interesting circumstances. Somehow, despite all precautions, this mage was allowed to summon a Hakkai Lord. And the demon had also not been released upon his death. The portal to her world was closed behind her. If there is one thing I have learned in my lifetime, there is no such thing as a coincidence. Never in the history of Tinil'Gan was a Hakkai Lord summoned and contained. The caster was always destroyed and the demon released back to its realm. Something allowed this to happen."

Isidora felt a slight breeze, almost a whisper. She looked down at the grass. They waved back and forth slightly, like ripples on a placid lake. Eupiphine's voice rang out. It was deep and reverberating; the sound seemed strange coming from the female figure, "I can assure you that the gods did not allow this. Belial may have blessed the spell but whatever events transpired to cause the error in the runes are what allowed it. You should have known this was not a part of the natural ways of our world, yet you find providence in abomination?" I find the hubris of mortals disturbing at times."

Azrael sighed, "The scholar in me could not pass this opportunity for study to pass. I knew that, for the time being, I had no way of opening a portal to an outer realm, let alone the correct one. I could have called upon the Conclave to dispatch the demon; that would have required combined efforts, the destruction of my tower, and the potential loss of knowledge. I opted to keep her contained and learn what I could.

"At first she would only respond to my queries with growls and curses in her demon language. But I saw intelligence there. Hakkai Lords are not just beasts; they are sentient beings. It took many years, but eventually, we learned to communicate. I repeatedly introduced myself, telling her my name. One day she told me her name. Or so I thought."

"Lear'Za," Tilene spoke with an airy tone, "That is your name in reverse."

"Correct, High Princess. After a few moments, I realized she had not responded with her name but instead repeated back to me what I had said in reverse. Intrigued, I spoke a few other words and realized she was repeating them back to me, only backward. I had found a way to communicate."

Isidora held back a gasp. Azrael had given her plenty of stories about Lear'Za and how their friendship grew. She was learning new details she never heard before. *Why is he always hiding something, always holding back?* The notion that, despite having spent just about all her life with Azrael, she knew nothing about him was taking a firmer hold on her. She listened intently as he continued.

"I began reversing my words. It was unnatural for me at first, but I soon mastered it. For the first time in history, a Hakkai Lord and a denizen of Tinil'Gan conversed. In the beginning, all she spoke were threats about how she would kill me if she escaped her prison, but in time, all sentient beings require conversation. She did eventually tell me her real name, but it cannot be said by our tongues, so the name Lear'Za stuck.

"Over time, I expanded her constraints. At first, I expanded the shield barrier to encompass the room so she could move around. She had use of a bed, chairs; I even helped her learn to read so she could make use of books. She began speaking of her home realm and its many wonders and horrors. As I surmised, Hakkai Lords were not simple beasts; they have a society. In time, we reached an understanding: she would aid me in learning more about demons and the outer realms, and I would search for a way to open a portal that could return to her home realm. Thus a friendship was born."

Droxis laughed loudly, "Friends? With a demon? My how the Sidhe have fallen," The centaur shook his head and snorted in derision. Your arrogance holds no bounds! You trusted her? How did it come to her walking freely on Tinil'Gan?"

Lear'Za stood up from her seat despite her bindings. Isidora also stood in fear; fear Lear'Za would act rashly. The daemoness barred her teeth and hissed at the centaur. "Rather he befriends a glorified ass like you horseman? How long must I suffer these insults!" She roared. Azrael whipped his head around and focused his eyes on her. Lear'Za calmed down and sat grudgingly. Relieved, Isidora let out a sigh of relief and took her seat. Gideon gave her a comforting squeeze of her shoulders.

Azrael turned back to Conclave and flashed a thin-lipped smile, "She raises a valid point; somehow, the people of Tinil'Gan trusted horsemen to walk freely without hunting them down to extinction."

Droxsis stomped his hooves and turned red with anger, "Outrage! How dare you, mage! Why do we amuse this insolent creature?"

Cerridwen looked to Droxsis. Although as a stag he gave no facial expression, the centaur knew the look was to calm him, "His tongue is indeed sharp Droxsis, but I am sure he has a point to make. Your objection is noted. Please continue Lord Azrael. Mind your words and control your charge."

Azrael nodded, "My comment was not meant to insult. Instead, it was to prove a point. Although their ways seem perverse and strange to us, Hakkai Lords are a societal community. This is not an assumption; these are things I alone was able to learn over centuries from my association and friendship with Lear'Za. They are no different than us. Just as some customs and traditions of the centaur differ from the other races of Tinil'Gan does not mean they are any less meaningful and should be destroyed. Even bloodthirsty beasts such as Ogres and Trolls are allowed their place on our world, however distressing it is."

The old satyr Silenus leaned forward. For most of the proceedings, it seemed as if the ancient goatman had been sleeping. "Your tale is indeed intriguing and worth merit, Lord Azrael. I still do not see the defense. Creatures like Ogres, no matter how vile, are native to Tinil'Gan. Thus we suffer them. Why should we extend this same courtesy to a demon from another realm?"

Azrael's mirrored eyes narrowed, "The defense, ancient Silenus, is that Lear'Za poses no threat to nature upon Tinil'Gan. She is a sentient being whose only true desire is to return to her realm. The judgment this court seeks will bring destruction to her. So are we murderers, then? This vaunted court that values nature and life is prepared to sentence her to death?"

Tilene sat forward, her leaf-adorned dress rippled. She smiled and folded her hands, "Dear Lord Azrael, we are not murderers. We only seek to remove the demon from Tinil'Gan."

"How do you plan to do that Matriarch? All demons enter this world, tethered to their realm through a portal. Once released or banished, their energy returns to their realm. Through some unknown influence, Lear'Za's portal was closed behind her, making her a refugee on Tinil'Gan. Any attempt at banishing Lear'Za would scatter her life force to the ethers, ending her life."

"Certainly Cerridwen, with his power and wisdom, can return her to her realm," Tilene replied.

Cerridwen bowed his head for a moment, then looked up, "The Archmagus is correct, Matriarch Tilene. My influence and power, like that of all the gods, extend only to Tinil'Gan. I fear banishment with the effect of death is our only option."

Azrael folded his hands into the sleeves of his robes, "So then, are we to be told Lear'Za is to be given a death sentence without presentation of guilt other than her very presence?"

"Are you saying the demon is innocent, Lord Azrael?" asked Cerridwen.

"As far as this court is concerned, she is innocent. She has neither brought harm to your forest or nature, nor does she intend to. To my knowledge, this is all your court has the authority to judge. However, to answer your question, she is no more innocent than any of us. We all make decisions that can affect the lives of others negatively. Even the gods are not innocent. They allow natural disasters to take place, killing their faithful," Azrael paused and narrowed his eyes, "Some even intervene personally, destroying lives with no cause but their own pettiness!"

The court around Cerridwen erupted in shouts of *heresy* and *blasphemy*. Cerridwen pounded a hoof that shook the clearing, silencing all.

"You are far too clever for your own good, Lord Azrael. I now see your motives. I do not doubt your sincerity and care for this friend, nor do I doubt your scholarly pursuits. There are underlying motives that drive you and have driven you for over a millennium. I know the curse Leto placed on your eyes, and I know why. I know of the Prophecy, Sidhe Lord, and I know where it is leading you. This demon gives you an unseen advantage and is a wild card in your endeavors. I cannot predict where this road will lead you or Tinil'Gan. But I know it must be allowed to follow its course. I am uncertain if vengeance or the pull of prophecy places you on this path, but I must stress its folly."

Isidora blinked. *A prophecy? What prophecy and what does that have to do with Azrael's eyes and Lear'Za's implied role? One way or another, I will find a time to confront him once and for all on all this mystery.*

Azrael bowed his head for a moment. When he raised it again, his mirrored eyes bore into Cerridwen's, "Be it true or untrue, that is not on trial here today and has no bearing on the decision before you."

Cerridwen matched Azrael's gaze undaunted, "A decision I feel we are ready to make. Make your beds for the night. The court will reconvene at dawn and render our decision. Fear no danger here. No harm can come to any of you in my forest. Sleep well."

Without another word, Cerridwen and his court vanished.

CHAPTER 14

Caiaphas collapsed in his circle shortly after the beast rampaged its way towards Azrael and his companions. He was exhausted beyond measure; just breathing, was labor in and of itself. At the same time, he was in ecstasy. He felt the lingering after-effects of the Art coursing through his veins. It caused small spasms, making limbs twitch and jump, and he enjoyed every minute of it. Many compare it to the feeling after lovemaking. Caiaphas would disagree; It was better.

The sense of self-preservation lingered in the back of his mind. He was defenseless. He knew if attacked, he would barely be able to lift his arm, let alone cast a defense spell. He could do nothing about it. It was the deathly game of chance he played when he decided upon summoning the Nidhogg. Caiaphas chose to close his eyes and listen to the sounds of the battle in the distance.

He heard the roars of the Nidhogg, the crashing of the trees. The unmistakable sounds of magical bolts rang through the night air. Then it happened. He felt the summoning bond he had with the Nidhogg severed; someone banished it from

Tinil'Gan. It struck him like a whip, and he sat upright with a stifled shout. His eyes were wide as his mind raced through the many possibilities. He respected Azrael and knew there was a chance the Archmagus would find a way to dispatch the Nidhogg, but he could not have done it this quickly. Something was wrong. He felt it in the air and had a distinct feeling the trees themselves were crowding in on him. His breath escaped in quick gasps as he scrambled on his hands and knees out of the clearing.

He fought his exhaustion and forced himself upright against the trunk of a tree. He attempted to slow his breath some, then proceeded to stumble through the forest, leaning on one tree after another for support. He did not know where he was going; all he knew was to get away as quickly as possible. He trudged on for a good part of the night until his exhaustion caught up with him and he stumbled and fell to the ground. He looked up and saw before him a large white stag. Caiaphas froze in terror when he realized he could hear the stag speaking to him.

"There is no escape, usurper of my forest. I should scatter your essence to the four corners of Tinil'Gan for the unspeakable horror you unleashed in these woods. However, Belial answered your prayers to summon that abomination, so thus I may not interfere. His reasons I intend to discover in due time. Consider this a rare reprieve, dark elf. Know this, though. If you to step one foot into the Linian Forest again, the outcome will not be as pleasant. This I can promise."

Caiaphas covered his eyes as a blinding white light filled the forest. When he was able to focus his eyes and blink out the stars, he found he was no longer in the forest. Instead, he was lying on a riverbank in the mud. With a sigh, his eyes closed as he lost consciousness from the fatigue, unaware his life had just been spared by a god.

CHAPTER 15

The night passed quietly for the companions. Although the previous events held many questions, Gideon found himself too tired even to speak. Sleep overtook him as if they had not slept for nights on end. As Cerridwen had said, they were safe and had the most comfortable and uninterrupted rest they could remember. Gideon was sure there was some divine magic at play.

The mid-morning sun greeted him when he awoke. Not even the break of dawn had been able to rouse him from his supernatural sleep. After a life in the knighthood and its training, Gideon rarely woke after sunrise, let alone mid-morning. He sat up and yawned. Kethis stirred awake shortly after; the elf rubbed his arms to draw away the morning chill. Gideon noticed the dying embers of a campfire none of them remember starting and quickly stirred a fire back to life. Even their horses had been returned mysteriously overnight and tethered to the trees.

They gathered around the fire, removing the last remnants of the night's slight chill. The clearing was uncomfortably quiet, as were they. No one knew how to begin speaking of the unexpected and unperceivable events of the previous night. Only Azrael seemed unmoved as he sat quietly, the hood of his black robes pulled low. Gideon threw a stick he was fiddling with into the fire and opened his mouth to put an end to the silence. But the words died in his throat as the booming voice of Cerridwen demanded their attention.

"Good morning, travelers. I hope my forest made a good bed for you all," Cerridwen had resumed his former position on the dais flanked by his forest lords, "After much deliberation, we have come to a decision. We all agree that Lear'Za is an abomination and unnatural to Tinil'Gan. To allow her to roam as she does poses many dangers and unknown risks to the denizens of Tinil'Gan."

The companions except for Azrael lowered their heads, worried and unsure of the outcome. He kept his gaze on the dais and Cerridwen.

"Lord Azrael made a compelling argument. I admire your cleverness, Lord Azrael. There are very few who know of, let alone dare to ask for a woodland trial. Although I am a god, you knew I would be bound by the rules and precedents that have been in place for eons. Once we were bound to this court, the ultimate decision had to be based on the imminent danger and threat to the woods.

"The decision was split among the forest lords, and it was I who had to cast the deciding vote. Upon the evidence provided, we find Lear'Za not a threat to the woods and creatures therein. When the demon beast attacked, Lear'Za fought back to remove it from this world. She did this of her volition, without summons or command, something unheard of amongst demons. Her actions were not even motivated by self-preservation; she could have exited the forest at any time. What this shows is an unprecedented display of friendship and caring from a demon towards denizens of Tinil'Gan. She was helping her friends. To me, this warrants further examination, and perhaps a shift in our view of demons. At least a select few.

"Also, there are other extenuating reasons for my decision. I see the winds of change flowing across Tinil'Gan. The world may not be the same once they have passed. I am unable to see if they will be for good or for ill, but my wisdom speaks to me and informs me not to stand in the way of prophecy. You and your friends, Lord Azrael, are set to play a major role in the events to come, and I anxiously await to see what shall unfold. The people of Tinil'Gan can do amazing and wonderful things when their hearts are true, despite the will of the gods. While some in my divine family disagree with that notion, I relish seeing our children attempt great feats in the name of what is good and pure."

Gideon scratched his head. *After all this, now I am a part of some significant events to come? None of this is adding up.* Gideon tore his mind away from his thoughts and glanced at Isidora. The look on her eyes complimented his feelings. *Does she know what this is about?* His eyes returned to the stag god.

"What role Lear'Za is to play is unknown to me. It also means it is unknown to the forces that stand against you, mortal or divine. In each of you I see the desire to do what is right and to act for the betterment of all. Let us all pray that the wisdom I am lauded for does not fail me, for if it has the consequences will be disastrous."

The great stag paused for a moment, and his gaze wandered to each of the companions. His piercing gaze memorized them. Gideon knew he was scanning them, attempting to judge the purity of their hearts. If it was possible, he was sure he saw the stag smile. Its gaze stopped on Lear'Za, and it shook its crown of antlers. Lear'Za's ethereal bonds disappeared. The daemoness cursed and rubbed her arms where the bonds had previously dug in.

"This court is adjourned, and you may make your way freely through this forest. You do not need to worry about who summoned the demon that attacked you. I took care of that personally. I do have one request before you depart. I will speak to the elf lord alone for a few moments. Kethis Kitharii, if you will please come with me."

Kethis' eyes were wide, and his jaw went slack in amazement, "Of...of course, Mighty Cerridwen. Your will is my command," Gideon watched as Kethis and Cerridwen walked off alone to a far side of the clearing, away from prying ears. Tilene stepped forward and, with a smile, she called Talia to her. Delighted the pixie flew in excited circles and loops to her High Princess.

Gideon pulled Isidora off to the side as well. He hadn't had many opportunities to talk to her alone since their journey began, "Isi, do you know anything about this prophecy Cerridwen was mentioning?"

She frowned, "I am afraid I know as little as you do. I have many questions of my own regarding that and other things mentioned during the trial."

"As do I. We will find the right time. For now, let's agree to not let this lie for too long. Something doesn't feel right. I feel like we are being told a small part of a story. We met a god, Isi. Whatever it is, it is something of extreme importance," Isidora nodded at him. Gideon turned his attention to the others in the distance. Although what was spoken between Cerridwen and Kethis and between Tilene and Talia was unknown, their body language showed their reactions were markedly different.

Kethis stood before the stag god in reverence. There was little movement of his mouth, which meant Cerridwen was doing most of the talking. It was not difficult to see the glowing awe on Kethis' face, and when he fell on his knees before Cerridwen, it was in subservience and humility.

The conversation between Tilene and Talia, on the other hand, didn't seem to be going as well. At first, the pixie's exuberance and excitement were evident from how brightly she glowed and the frantic loops and circles she flew before her High Princess. But as Tilene spoke, one could see the sorrow in her face. Soon Talia's glow grew dimmer, and her flying slowed until finally dropped to the ground at Tilene's feet. The Princess knelt before her servant and gently caressed her. Talia wiped her tear-streaked face a few times and nodded at Tilene. With a soft smile and a gentle pat, she sent Talia on her way back to the group just as Kethis was also making his way back with a dumbstruck look on his face.

No one pried. The conversations were kept private for a reason. While Gideon was not as devout as the elf lord, he could not deny the rare and unique event all of this was. Without a word, the Forest God and his host of woodland lords disappeared. He turned and stared at Azrael, who was in a heated, yet muted discussion with Lear'Za. While the daemoness appeared relieved it was all over, she was venting her frustrations on the Archmage. The events of the court's judgment and the private councils that occurred kept at bay the multitude of questions Gideon and Isidora had. *We will find out soon enough Archmagus. While you may be trustworthy, you are not forthcoming.*

As the companions gathered their belongings and packed their horses, Cerridwen and Tilene watched unseen. The great stag snorted and shook his head. With a smile, the High Princess and life mate of the god rubbed her hand on his short white fur.

"Rarely have you ever made an unwise choice, my love," Tilene said.

"For the sake of this world, I hope you are correct, Tilene. Never would I have imagined I would put my trust in the hands of a black robe mage and his demon friend."

"You know as well as I that this particular black robe is unlike any other who has walked Tinil'Gan. He is, and always will be, the only Sidhe ever to take the black robes. The nature of the path he chose was only an end to a means. He is still Sidhe."

"The prophecy does not discriminate. If there is anyone who can restore the balance, it is him. My other siblings can remain silent and inactive as Leto plots and schemes to upset the balance. I cannot, I dare not, interfere with it directly. But that does not mean I cannot give a gentle nudge in the right direction."

Tilene laid her head on Cerridwen's soft fur, "He has good friends. He cannot undertake this alone, and they will help him. They all play a role in the final outcome."

"I just hope they are ready for the sacrifices they each must make, and that those sacrifices do not destroy them."

Cerridwen gently nudged Tilene with his snout. The pair looked after the companions one final time as they rode out from the clearing.

CHAPTER 16

The sun rose in the east over Lake Seban in majestic splendor. Hummingbirds and finches twittered outside in the flower garden below Sparta's Sanctum. *Another beautiful day,* Sulik mused as he broke his fast on poached eggs, blackened bacon, and mulled summer ale. He enjoyed mornings like this. He ate with deliberate casualness as the sun rose over the gardens, listening to the sounds of birds and the changing of the Knight's Guard, protectors of Castle Mount. Autumn was coming, and soon, the bright summer colors of magenta, azure, and cerise would fade to the auburns and siennas of fall. Autumn meant the harvest, and the harvest meant the Fall Festival. Soon, the Sanctum would be a beehive of activity. Sulik took a deep drag of his ale.

Sparta's Sanctum stood to the west of the center courtyard of Castle Mount. Through the western windows, he could view the splendor of the Sana Valley, as Sulik did during his breakfast. Through its eastern windows, the Sanctum's position gave its resident a panoramic view of the entire interior courtyard, Holdfast's Gate, the armory, the stables, and the entryway to

Kings Keep, where the king and his family resided. Lord Sparta picked well when he chose the Sanctum as his seat; it gave the Realm Regent full view of all who entered and left Castle Mount through Holdfast's Gate. To a prudent and astute Realm Regent, this information was paramount.

The Sanctum has housed the Realm Regent for over two hundred years since its namesake Lord Sparta Stormcaller was Realm Regent to King Marteen the Mighty, the last of the Montefroy dynasty. Lord Sparta's son Gillean went on to become the first Stormcaller monarch when Marteen the Mighty passed on, and his only heir and daughter was married to Lord Sparta. In noble fashion, Lord Sparta abdicated his rights to the throne as husband to the sole heir so his son could begin the new dynasty. Some say it was for selfless reasons. Others say it was because Sparta knew he wielded more power as the Realm Regent, handling the day to day affairs of the Kingdom of Castellamar. The latter was the more accurate answer. The Realm Regent was the most powerful post in the kingdom, especially if the king was more interested in sport and games rather than politics. Lord Sulik understood this more than anyone.

It had been five years since his father had met his untimely end in a hunting accident. Those had been the most productive years for the Kingdom of Castellamar in a generation. The late king had been a beast of a man, over six and a half feet tall, all brawn and glory, a shining symbol of the Castellarian Knights from whence he came. Sulik's brother, Sir Falco, took after their father in size and appearance, followed his footsteps into the knighthood. Their eldest brother Diomere, the current king, had been sickly since his childhood. He was doted on and protected his entire life. Sulik, on the other hand, was shorter and slimmer than Falco, not a suitable form for the rigors of knighthood. But he was in excellent health and vitality, unlike Diomere. But what he lacked in muscle and prowess he made up for in intelligence and cunning. While Falco may have been King Dradius' favorite son, Sulik thanked the gods for giving him his mother's Condrite blood. At least the late king had recognized his middle son's skill in matters of state.

Sulik had been Realm Regent for his father, and for the most part, King Dradius had let Sulik handle matters of the kingdom as he went hunting, jousting, or drinking. But of Sulik's true passion, to expand the kingdom, Dradius would hear no part. *Leave the Riverlands to the sullen Riverlords and the blasted trees to the elves. We have our valleys, our wine, and our iron,* Sulik would nod his head at his father's short-sightedness and try another day. What his father did not understand was that power did not rest on iron and wine alone.

While Sana Valley was sun-drenched and had fertile soil for summer fruits and vineyards, the kingdom had to use trade and commerce for most of its grain and livestock needs. The fertile flatlands of the river lords south of the Castellian Mountains grew most of the Evening Continent's grains and had ample pasture lands for livestock. While the Castellamar's vast iron mines provided a good income, most of it was spent purchasing grain and meat from the south. There was a reason why the kings of old had expanded the kingdom's borders, and resources were chief among them. Sulik's ambitions did not end there.

Too many in the Evening Continent ignored the growing threat across the seas on the Morning Continent. The Kardian Empire had been in power there for centuries, and word from travelers and merchants told of increased militarism from the Empire. Their armies grew every year, and their shipwrights had been busy building galleys along the coast. Conventional wisdom in the Evening lands was that it meant nothing. Morningstars have never invaded the west, but Sulik did not trust it. *The kingdom needs ships.* He mulled as he crunched on his bacon.

While Castellamar did have a navy, it was a weak one at best. Its only coast was on the Battle Sea. The only place they could travel was east to the other continent or west around the entire continent to get to Luminos. The southern passage was cut off by the Bridge of Sorrows, the small land bridge connecting the two continents. The only way to travel south was by foot along the main roadway, the KingsMarch, and the rivers. The kingdom had abandoned its river fleet long ago when the Riverlords won their war of independence from Castellamar. To control the waterways and protect the seacoast, he needed ships and to build ships required wood. The elves had the lion's share of the continent's oaks, cedars, and redwoods in the Linian Forest, but the elves had cut off trade with Castellamar eons ago. Ever since the destruction of Rania, the elves hated the Kingdom. They never forgave the devastation that destroyed the northern portion of the Linian Forest. When the Riverlord Rebellion occurred five hundred years ago, Castellamar lost its power. The elves did not fear them. Sulik lost his appetite and pushed his plate away. There was a glimmer of hope in his disgust. Now that his father was gone and his sickly and malleable brother Diomere was king, his plans were beginning to take shape.

His first "suggestion" to his King Brother was to name Falco Captain of the Knights. Falco was not as quick-minded as he was, but he wasn't a dunce either. He needed to keep Falco occupied. Something the honorable knight loved so he would not interfere. Also, the Captain of the Knights was honor-bound to follow his King's will without question. While granting Falco his greatest wish and ambition, he also castrated him from any influence over the governance of the realm. After that, Sulik had nudged Diomere to make beneficial appointments to the Council of Lords. The previous council was full of Cardigans and Montefroys, full of chivalry and honor. *My father's people, the same people who whisper behind my back.*

He knew his lady wife's family, the Tempests and their feal houses Firenza and Medici, were eager for more power and favor, which made them fervent allies to expansion. Lord Humboldt Tempest, brother of Sulik's Lady Wife, was appointed Vaultkeeper and Lord Filobane Medici was appointed Whisper Master of the Realm. Sulik's young daughters were married off to the Houses Firenza and Medici in kind. Sulik had even rid himself of his nephew Gideon without even trying.

The young man was much like his father, Sir Falco, except he was more opinionated. Sir Gideon was beginning to become a thorn in his side, voicing his views in court and begging an audience with his King Uncle on matters of state. Luckily enough, the fool of a boy fell in love with a girl mage the king allowed to be under service to the kingdom. Sulik almost laughed out loud when he had requested permission from Sir Falco to marry the black robe mage. While she was not low born, she was heir to some minor house in the Riverlands, far beneath the station that Sir Gideon held as part of House Stormcaller. As it stood, he was fourth in line to the throne and could have commanded a wife from houses of esteem, such as Tempest, Cardigan, or Montefroy. But this girl was different and vital. It wasn't soon after that Sir Gideon had followed the bride in black on some quest. He chuckled at the astounding serendipity.

The only post he had dared not replace was Lord Mallister Montefroy, Royal Sergeant at Arms. Lord Mallister was his staunchest dissident and had been his father's best friend from their days in the knighthood. He was also married to Sulik's sister, Lady Honera. Although a pain in the arse, removing him would only foster more distrust from the smallfolk and make more enemies he didn't need. As long as Lord Mallister's voice was overpowered by the council, he was a toothless lion.

Everything was in place now. The proper allies had been solidified on the council, and his brother the King did as Sulik suggested. *Today is as good as any.* He crossed the room and washed up at the water basin. From the armoire, he chose a sleek woolen doublet of black and gold, the colors of House Stormcaller, with a falcon embroidered on the chest and gold filigree buttons. He completed his dress with black leather trousers and black leather riding boots. He finished it off by putting the large gold signet ring with the double *Rs*, the mark of his position as Realm Regent, on his finger, and on his hip a sheath holding a dagger with a golden falcon in flight serving as the hilt. His salt and pepper hair was cropped short, and his face hairless save for the thin goatee he had worn for years. He may not have ever been a famed Castellarian Knight, bedecked in polished and enameled plate armor, or unhorsed a fellow knight at a joust, but he was a Lord, and no one could take that away from him.

He made his way down the steps of the Sanctum and out to the courtyard. He nodded and smiled at various court residents and made a slight right towards Kings Keep, the first floor of which housed the Council Chambers. Usually, the Council of Lords convened without the appearance of the King. *Let him tend to his gardens and watch the knights train.* Sulik had expressed that notion many times; today was to be different. What he was to propose needed the King's approval and blessing and he had already coached Diomere on what to say. The knights at the entrance to Kings Keep nodded to Lord Sulik and uncrossed their halberds from the doorway to allow him passage. The two knights wore a silver phoenix clasp on their cloaks, the stanchion of House Firenza. If he remembered correctly, they were his son-in-law Hommen Firenza's nephews.

Sulik entered the chamber, smiling; he was the last to arrive as usual. They lined the table across from the king. At the far left end sat Lord Tempest. Even though graying, the fiery red hair of the Tempests was still present. He wore a silken tunic of Tempest azure and silver and a white cloak with silver embroidery of the House Tempest tiger. Next to him sat the Whisper Master Lord Medici. Medici was old, fat, and bald and, so it seemed to Sulik, always sweating. He wore loose-fitting robes of chartreuse and carmine and a necklace sporting the Medici hummingbird. Medici grinned at him as he wiped the sweat of his brow with a handkerchief. On the right, Lord Mallister Montefroy. His stern face lined with age and his hair and beard were stark white, but his blue eyes still shone with the vigor of youth. Sulik also noted a hint of hatred and contempt in those blue orbs beneath the bushy white eyebrows. Ever the knight, Lord Montefroy was bedecked in full plate armor of shining silver and enameled in crimson and indigo with a roaring bear across the chest. His sword and scabbard were on his hip, always ready for battle. He didn't nod or smile, just stared.

Across from them on a throne sat his brother King Diomere. Although Diomere was only a few years older than Sulik, childhood illness and adult weariness made him appear much older. His hair had already completely grayed, and his beard and mustache were patchy. His skin already began to have the translucency of old age, marked with liver spots, and it seemed he was all skin and bones. It was no surprise, though; the King ate like a bird, and even then he made a finch seem gluttonous. In a way, Sulik pitied his brother. Diomere had always admired his father and wished to be a knight, but he could barely mount a horse let alone ride one, and anything heavier than a dagger to cut his meat he couldn't lift. But Diomere always had a happy smile upon his face, as if to say, *At least I live, what more can we ask of the Gods?* Finally, standing on the king's left, was their youngest brother, Sir Falco. The Captain of the Knights also stood as King Diomere's personal guard. Age had not seemed to touch Falco; at first glance, no one would guess he was father to a son of twenty-four. His long chestnut hair had not streaked gray, and it fell about his shoulders upon his black and gold enameled armor. His face was clean-shaven except for the long mustachios that hung down the sides of his mouth to his jawline. Ever stern, Falco didn't turn away nor acknowledge Sulik's entrance.

Sulik smiled and made his way to his seat on the king's right, "I have not missed anything of import, have I?"

Lord Mallister harrumphed, "You know full well, Lord Sulik, the Council of Lords cannot convene until the Realm Regent is in attendance. You keep us waiting like some maidens at a ball for a dance," Sulik noted the sneer on Mallister's face. As usual, he ignored it with all grace.

Diomere smiled and waved a weary hand, "I am sure the Lord Regent has a good excuse for his late arrival. Many are his duties. There are enough battles in this world, let us not quibble amongst ourselves," Mallister grumbled into his beard and adjusted his sword belt to sit more comfortably. Filobane nodded his bloated head in agreement.

"Thank you, my Grace, and I was indeed preparing for this council, which accounts for my lateness. I would like to also thank your Grace for attending this day's council, as well. We have some important matters to discuss. The harvest is upon us, and we must fill our stores before the winter. It is well known our grain fields are barely enough to supply all of Castellamar. It's barely enough to supply San'Seban."

"If our Lords and Ladies didn't eat thrice that of the smallfolk, it might suffice," Mallister pronounced.

"Yes, my Lord Montefroy, I have seen how robust the tables are after many a tourney the crown provides for the entertainment of the knighthood, and the Lords' pleasure. With that being said, I fear tightening our belts will not feed a kingdom."

Medici wobbled his head, sweat glistening on his smooth dome, "I fear our Lord Sulik is correct. My agents have informed me how uneasy the smallfolk are this season. They fear many of their young ones will die from starvation, Artio help them."

He smirked, "Prayers to Artio the Just may help speed them along to his heavenly kingdom, but it won't put food in their bellies. That is our job. We will once again have to purchase grain and livestock from the southern Riverlords. Lord Firenza, how sits our vaults?"

The flame-haired lord had remained quiet and uninterested during the conversation so far, picking his nails with a dagger. Without looking up from his finger pruning, he replied, "Empty."

The king furrowed his brow, "Empty, you say? How can that be?"

Lord Firenza sheathed his dagger, sat forward, and steepled his fingers. His eyes darted back and forth for a moment before he spoke, "Yes, Your Grace, empty. Most of our stores were spent this summer on fitting out the knights with newer armor and swords. Not to mention the restoration work on Castle Pass."

Mallister shook with anger, "Don't lay your woes at the feet of the knighthood, Vaultkeeper. The arms and armor were sorely needed. A knight is not a knight without it. As for Castle Pass, it is the inroad to the kingdom and must be defended from our enemies. In its previous condition, a herd of sheep could have found their way up the KingsMarch right to the very gates of Castle Mount! The defense of the realm is paramount!"

Sulik hid his excitement. Now was the time to plant the seeds, "Our Lord Sergeant is correct. While there has been peace with the Riverlands, the threat is ever-present. If the Riverlords were ever of one mind, they could overrun Castellamar in a fortnight. They hold the largest expanse of fertile land and control the waterways, and they defend it with our gold. We have been fortunate that old rivalries still run hot in the south, causing them to look at each other more than us."

Mallister stood, knocking his chair over, "I am insulted by your lack of faith in the knighthood, Lord Sulik! We can hold the pass from any invader, especially southern chattel! We are knights, trained, and disciplined!"

"And green," Sulik smiled at Mallister sardonically, "The Castellarian Knights have not known battle outside the lists for generations, save the occasional goblin raid. Those southern chattels, as you call them, are knights as well, who are battle-hardened from years of infighting amongst the Riverlords. I do not doubt the honor and courage of our knights, but courage does not win battles. It just bloodies the battlefield with our men and their dreams of glory."

"The Spokes control the Riverlands," Lord Firenza said heatedly, "They lie at the head of the KingsMarch, just past the Castellian Mountains and the convergence of the main rivers. When Lord Hollister calls his feal houses, he commands a force to rival our own. Even if the other river lords did not join him, he is dangerous."

"If I may, my Lords, there is a way to solve our problems," Medici piped in. It seemed he sweat more when speaking, "The south is not as solid as it may seem."

"What have you heard, Whispermaster?" Sulik leaned back. The first domino fell, now the rest should fall in kind.

"There are still many in the south that yearn for the days of the Castellarian rule. They had greater prosperity back then and, might I add, a few still feel slighted by the way the Riverlands was divided up after the rebellion. There has also been word of increased activity in The Spokes. Increased training and ranging. The other Riverlords nervous, as well. I do know that Hardhall and Evanfall feel The Spokes took the lion's share of land. House Bargeman and House Condrite were always loyal to the Crown in days past."

"My Queen Mother is a Condrite. She told me as much in my youth," Diomere said, shaking his head.

"Are you saying that Hardhall and Evanfall could be persuaded to join like cause?" Sulik questioned.

"I am saying, Lord Regent, that there is no love lost between them and The Spokes. Every day, they fear attack and suspect Lord Hollister wants to expand his dominion. I can send whispers to Lord Condrite and Lord Bargeman."

Mallister's eyebrows furrowed, "What you are proposing is open war and the destruction of a peace that has lasted for hundreds of years. If the Spokes are attacked, be certain Hearth, the horsemen of Equus and the Snowlord of Icewall with rally their banners."

Sulik smiled, "What is being proposed is a better realm for all. The southrons were never in want when under the banner of our Kingdom. The rebellion was caused by politics and pride. Pride can be assuaged by even portioning of land claims. Yes, The Spokes present a mighty challenge, but if Hardhall and Evanfall are behind us, The Spokes could be overrun quickly and unawares. By the time news reached Hearth, we would be upon their gates. News travels even slower in the far south. By that time, the Riverlands would be solidly under Kingdom rule. Equus and Icewall will have no choice but to bend a knee for the sake of peace. The horsemen are staunch and the Vicors of Icewall hardheaded, but even they will see the folly in opposition."

"Your father always opposed expansion," Mallister grumbled with reverence for his lost friend.

"My father is dead. I see no reason to send loyal subjects to him in the afterlife due to starvation," Sulik said caustically.

Mallister's heavy eyebrows furrowed together and his jaw clenched, "The gods save me, I promised your father I would keep the peace. I will not acquiesce to outright aggression. Unless a good reason is shown that any southron is a threat to the Kingdom, House Montefroy will not partake in this. I see no point of any further talk on the matter," Lord Montefroy turned to the king and bowed, "Your Grace, if you will excuse me," The King nodded, and Mallister turned and stomped out of the chambers.

Sulik smiled. *And with you go the Cardigans and Brightons.* Sulik cleared his throat, "Well, it seems we must delve further into the subject in other ways. Your Grace, do we have your leave to gather further information and to make contact with Rivers End and Evanfall? "

"For the good of our people, I see no better way. For the good of all men living in the Evening, let it be so, Lord Regent," Diomere nodded his head approvingly.

"I will send whispers to Hardhall and Evanfall at once," Medici ponderously stood and began collecting his parchments and various effects from the table, "It seems there is no time to waste! If you will excuse me, my Lords."

"By all means, my Lord. I do believe there is nothing left to discuss and we all have our respective jobs to do in preparation," Sulik stood as well. It was then he noticed his brother Sir Falco glowering at him. He had not said a word the entire time, but Sulik noted his displeasure. *It matters not, dear brother. You are as useless as a gelded bull in this matter. All you can do is follow as commanded,* "Good day, brother," Sulik nodded to Falco.

Falco did not respond. Instead, he turned his head to his other brother, "Does my Grace require some refreshment? I can call upon your cupbearers."

Diomere smiled, unaware of the unspoken words between his brothers, "No, no, good sir. If you can, though, I would appreciate some help back to my suite for a nap."

"Certainly, my Grace," Falco gave Sulik one last fleeting scowl and helped Diomere from the throne and out of the council chambers.

Smiling, Sulik made his exit back to the Sanctum. Once comfortable back in his quarters, he unbuttoned his doublet and poured a cup of mulled ale, downing it in one gulp. With a sigh of satisfaction, the Realm Regent walked over to a bookshelf in the back of the quarters. A slight push on a specific book and it slid back to reveal a secret alcove.

The alcove hid a small altar with golden candles and golden trappings, a shrine to Leto. Sulik knelt before the altar and bowed his head, "My Lord Leto, God of Chaos and Freedom, the works in your name move ever forward. Soon chaos will spread across the Evening Continent and bring many to your name. Ever your faithful servant am I, and I await the glory that will surely come when you reign supreme," Sulik stood and lit the candles and bowed his head. Satisfied, he returned to his writing desk and began drafting orders of commission of the major Houses of Castellamar for fealty and commitment of arms.

CHAPTER 17

The heat was stifling. *How do these people survive in this gods' forsaken realm?* Caiaphas took a drag from the tepid wine he had brought up. Since he had arrived in Tunai and rented the room, he had stripped off his heavy black mage robes and spent the day in his small clothes, and he still could not escape the heat. His trek north following the Distillar had been plagued by a summer storm that rolled through and soaked him to the bone. As miserable and wet as he had been, he would rather be there again than in the inferno that was Tunai.

He was still weak from his failed attempt to stop Azrael and his companions, more vulnerable than he had ever been. He had not anticipated how much energy summoning the Nidhogg would take. He remembered scrambling through the forest, drained and disorientated with what felt like the very forest itself chasing him. He remembered a stag — after that, his next memory was waking up on the banks of a river, cold, wet, and feverish. When he saw distant mountain peaks to the north and the width of the river next to him, he knew then it was the Distillar. He did not know how long he had been unconscious, or how far ahead of him Azrael had gotten. But he knew his destination.

He began to lose hope of reaching Tunai before Azrael until he chanced upon a caravan traveling in the same direction. At first, they balked at assisting a black robe mage, an Elvan one at that. They changed their minds when he produced gold coins for their inconvenience. The horse-drawn cart was not speedy, but it was an improvement over his two feet.

The caravan rolled along happily, and they made good time. Thankfully the weather warmed each day, removing the chill that had set in. He did not realize how warm it was becoming until they crossed the Distillar. Then, he began to curse his heavy mage robes. Somewhere in the histories the reason for the materials used for mage robes was lost. Black robes were made of heavy velvet or wool, while white and green robes of dyed wool; all three typically warm, heavy fabrics.

He started envying these simple desert folk. Before the devastation of Rania, the desert was not as vast as it is now. Rania was a sparkling jewel and large oasis surrounded by wadis and regs. Back then, the ergs were small. But even then the nation of Rania maintained a large population of Bedouin nomads. Experts of the desert. After the devastation, all that survived were those nomads far from the city and oasis who now populated the vast sand sea known as the Ranian Desert.

Most of them sported light linen bishts and sirwals. Linen was light and airy, in pale colors that reflected the sun's rays. The more affluent merchants preferred expensive silken damask robes of various colors. To keep the heat off their heads, they all wore cotton ghutras held in place by a corded iqal.

In an attempt to shade his face and head, Caiaphas lifted the hood of his robes only to find it produced a suffocating sauna effect rather than cool him. He thanked the gods when he saw

Tunai approaching on the fourth day. *A cool room with some chilled wine.* To his dismay, Tunai had offered little relief.

Caiaphas never traveled without gold. Before he had left Duminos in exile, he made sure he was not empty-handed. His family was wealthy, so he had taken enough gold for a man to live comfortably for the rest of his life. Caiaphas was part of this aristocracy, and when he chose to become a mage, it did not sit well. Nobles did not become magi in Duminos. That was one rule, carried over from the past, they kept. Magi were rife among the Luminori nobility; Duminos was determined not to duplicate that. So Caiaphas had chosen exile to practice the Art. Exiled as he was, he could be a mage and use his gold to provide the creature comforts of life. So after his trials on the road, the first thing he did was to rent the most expensive room offered in the oasis town and purchased some lighter clothing. He had found more comfort in dirty roadside inns along the KingsMarch.

The rooms were spacious; he would give them that, and sported many windows to let in air. Unfortunately, hot desert air did not a breeze make. Also, every room was furnished with a cot with a lumpy straw mattress. Locals said straw was cooler to sleep in than down bedding. He found it hard to believe. There were no mountains close enough to transport ice from, and even if there were it would melt before long before there was a chance to store it in cold cellars. Even the wine wasn't appropriately stored in a cellar. Apparently to desert folk, tepid was as cold as a mountain spring. The only consolation was there had been no word or sight of Azrael and his company.

When Caiaphas could no longer stand sweating in his room, he donned the much lighter apparel he had purchased, he walked the streets of Tunai hoping to get information. Tunai was at the very southern edge of the desert and the only inhabited city between the Riverlands and Luminos. It remained an important hub of trade between the elves and humans. Although Tunai was a merchant town and saw many travelers, even here a company of two black robes, a daemoness, an elf, and a knight was not commonplace. Thankfully many spoke the common tongue; one could not trade and barter if they did not speak the language most of the Evening lands did. No one had seen the group, but that did not stop them from trying to sell Caiaphas silks, carpets, or fruit. He turned down most, but he did buy some cactus fruit. The blood-red pulpy fruit helped him with his thirst, and it reminded him of the sweet melons he enjoyed at the Tower of Elizar.

The one thing he noted about Tunai was that it had no real government. It had no ruler, no king, or a monarch. Thus it had no formal army or guard. What it did have was sell-swords and plenty of them. If there was a place where mercenaries were born, it was Tunai. They were of all shapes and races. He saw exiled elves, disgraced knights, and local Tunoshi, even a dwarf. Although Lords and their hosts of knights ruled the Evening Lands every army needed additional troops for extensive campaigns. With the constant strife in the Riverlands causing skirmishes or short wars, the mercenaries of Tunai always found work. It wasn't unheard of for some rich Lord to hire them in secret to attack lands of his enemies, in the guise of raiders. A large part of their payment came from the looting afterward. Caiaphas had an idea.

He used his magic during his first attempt to stop the party, and it had failed miserably. He should have known it would have failed with the likes of Azrael and his one-time apprentice. The addition of a daemoness did not help matters. It was difficult to admit to himself that he was not powerful enough in the Art, but he took some consolation in the fact this was Azrael, not some mere ordinary mage. He also realized it had drawn too much attention. Another magical attack would severely raise Azrael's suspicions. *There was also that matter in the forest...that stag.* Caiaphas shook his head; he still could not remember what had happened. What he did know was he did not plan to ever set foot in the Linian Forest again.

Determined in his new course of action, Caiaphas began scouring the taverns and inns of Tunai. The first few taverns didn't prove fruitful. One man, a disgraced Rivers End knight from the looks of him, boasted of his company's skill and guaranteed success with full payment in advance. Caiaphas noted the man's dinted, mismatched armor and rusted sword and doubted he was worth it. He also smelled as if he hadn't been sober since Caiaphas was a youth in Duminos. Caiaphas pleasantly told the man he would consider his offer and would contact him should he require his services, and made his way to the next inn.

When the sun began to set, Caiaphas decided to retire to his room in Tokar's Sword in defeat. He made his way across the common room to the stairs that led up to his chambers.

"*Elab shallah,* master magi," A voice offered the customary Ranian greeting.

Caiaphas stopped and turned slowly. Seated in a corner table alone, he spotted and slender but muscular Tunoshi. His skin was dark as most Tunoshi; dressed in a lavish thobe of red silk and golden damask designs. His ghutra was of red and white checked cotton with a golden iqal holding it in place. His nose was sharp; the small goatee that framed his mouth was short and neatly trimmed. He sported two gold hoop earrings in both ears matched by the many golden rings on his fingers. Caiaphas also noted the jeweled scimitar that hung in a scabbard on the man's hip. He sat casually with his legs crossed taking deep puffs out of the scented hookah on the table before him. Smiling Caiaphas gave a slight bow of his head.

"*Elab shallah,* fine sir," Caiaphas returned the greeting. "I'm afraid I have not had the pleasure of your acquaintance, yet you speak as if you know of me."

The man smiled and flashed his pearly white teeth, "Not many enter or leave Tunai without my knowing," he said with a slight accent, though his common was excellent, "Let us say I make it my business to know. However, in the interest of honesty, I know little of you save your profession, and that is as plain as the robes you wear. To be more honest, to show my sincerity, I also know you are an elf on the wrong continent and that you enquire about a motley group that may or may not have passed through. It is so?"

Caiaphas folded his hands in his robes and smirked, "It is so good sir."

The man pushed aside a chair and beckoned Caiaphas over, "Then if it pleases you, master magi, please sit and share spirits with me and talk we shall. As to acquaintance, I shall begin. My name is Jozef Shaddam of the Silver Sword."

Caiaphas cocked an eyebrow. He was no mere sell-sword; he possessed an air of nobility. The Silver Sword were not ordinary mercenaries, well known across the Evening Lands. They did not take on meager assignments or raid for a petty Lord's vengeance. They were skilled warriors who filled whole regiments of armies and were well counted upon in battle, mostly in the vanguard. They first came into prominence during the southron rebellion and played a substantial role in the successful separation of the Old Kingdom. Since then, their notoriety and reputation had grown, "It is a pleasure master Shaddam. I am Caiaphas of the Order of Black Robes. You mentioned the individuals I seek. By chance do you have information? And please forgive me if I also ask why the Silver Sword would take interest."

Jozef took a deep drag of the hookah and exhaled the sweet berry-and-mint-scented smoke. The bubbling of the water in the hookah basin accentuated the pause, "As I have said, magi, knowing is my business. I can tell you this group you seek has not yet reached Tunai, but I have friends between the realm of the elves and the desert. They have seen such a group. From what I am told, they should make their arrival in Tunai by morning's light. I also know your interest in this group goes beyond information."

This one knows too much already, "I must confess you are correct. I also must confess that my efforts have been for naught."

The Tunoshi leaned forward, "A mercenary you have sitting before you magi."

"I do believe this assignment is far below your pay grade, Master Shaddam. From what I know of the Silver Sword, they find such work beneath them."

Shaddam chuckled, "Let Jozef worry about the Silver Sword, magi. It is I that command them. Worry not why I should take interest in this. Only know you have a willing suitor."

This is too easy, "I am honored, and knowing the reputation of the Silver Sword, I don't doubt the outcome. Forgive me again if, because of your reputation, I must insist on knowing where this interest comes from."

Shaddam took another deep drag of the hookah, "In Tunai, the appearance of magi is considered *haikmar*, bad luck. Three in less than a sun's turn..." Shaddam spread his hands, "Our seers have seen strange times to come in their scented braziers. They pray to Caillech, the master of winds who moves the sands, for wisdom. The god has been silent. Chaos rises, magi of the black robes. Leto is on the ascent. It is not known what to make of this. Chaos is the way of the desert. The sands ever change; great monuments are devoured and later uncovered by the dunes. Is it a blessing or omen? Those of this realm know the greatest thing about the desert is that it has an end, as does chaos. But never-ending chaos, a never-ending desert is death. I make it my business to know. The unknown is my enemy."

"Fair enough. Then let us talk, Jozef Shaddam."

CHAPTER 18

"I did not need your help, Seer'kaat! That was humiliating and degrading. I would rather have sunk my teeth into that so-called god's hide and risk destruction than what I had to endure!" Lear'Za spat.

It had been much of the same the past two days since the forest tribunal. Lear'Za would not let it go. *Her pride was hurt, but it was necessary,* Azrael thought quietly. He had spoken the same thought multiple times since they had set out again, but Lear'Za would hear none of it. So Azrael rolled his mirrored eyes and endured her latest rant. He could see Isidora staring at him across the small campfire as Lear'Za ended her lasted rant. He knew she had questions.

Chief among them was Cerridwen's revelation of a prophecy. When Isidora and Gideon stood and walked over to him, he already knew what it was about, "We need to discuss some things, D'ni," Isidora stood firmly before him with her arms crossed. The young knight was at her side, and his serious countenance supported her words.

Azrael knew he had to tread carefully; say too little, and he would lose their trust, say too much, and all could be in jeopardy, "How can I be of service?" He replied flatly.

"We are extremely grateful for your assistance in my quest. No one certainly expected the events that have occurred and the dangers we have already encountered. The god brought up a couple of things that require an explanation," She kept her voice even. Azrael could tell she was deeply concerned but was trying not to make it apparent.

"Namely, something about a prophecy. I am not one to believe in myths, legends, and children's tales. This came from the mouth of a god. It tends to make one take notice," Gideon added. Azrael had casually ignored the bond he saw between them. Lear'Za had mentioned on the day of their arrival there could be more to this partnership than an escort. It could complicate things. He stood with a sigh and led them further away from the others. Once satisfied with their privacy, he replied to both of them.

"Gods speak in riddles and prophecies are just as murky. The one he speaks of involves the god, Leto. It is a matter I had dealt with long before either of you were ever born. It is my burden to bear," One wrong word could spur the prophecy forward at a faster pace, destroying all hopes Azrael had of thwarting it. *How long have I pondered and planned? Is it all for naught? Am I playing a fool's game, attempting to change destiny?* Those thoughts had haunted Azrael for centuries. He always came to the same conclusion. Nothing was impossible, nor were the gods infallible. Leto could make mistakes — as slim a chance as that was, it was still possible.

"That is hardly an answer D'ni!"

Gideon placed a hand on her shoulder, calming her, "What she means is the god mentioned that we all would play a role in events to come. While you may believe it is your burden, it is apparent it involves us all now. Does your wisdom not tell you that or has pride completely overtaken you?" Azrael smiled. *With great power and wisdom also comes great hubris and arrogance. Some would say I possess hubris and arrogance.* He knew how it appeared, but he also understood the fine line between confidence and hubris. Azrael never considered himself infallible; he merely knew how to increase the odds of his accuracy and success. So he answered their questions carefully.

"The thing about prophecy is they are not unlike boats and currents. You cannot stop the current from taking you down the river. All you can do is steer the boat clear of the dangers and obstacles you approach as it carries you. That is my role in this; to make sure everyone is safe. Giving you the long and convoluted details of the prophecy will not clear anything up or make it easier for any of you. What I am demanding is your trust."

The Nidhogg was no mere coincidence. Only a black robe of considerable power could have conjured that up, and then only with preparation. Someone was watching them. Someone was following them. Whoever it was had been trailing them since the Isle of Winds. He had enough enemies in the orders of the magi, but few if any were black robes. It smelled of a lackey. Someone else had given orders to that black robe but without enough proof as of yet to confirm his suspicions. Now was not a time for disharmony.

Isidora gave a sarcastic chuckle and shook her head, "Your secrets never end. A lifetime I have spent as your student. I've looked up to you as a mentor and have always trusted you," Her voice wavered for a moment, and he saw her lips quiver. She took a deep breath and firmed her resolve, "This is not about my trust for you, D'ni. This is about the apparent lack of trust and faith you have in me, in us. For now, let's get to Tunai and complete this quest. I have much to prepare myself for and must concentrate on that, but this is not over," Isidora turned and stormed off.

Azrael watched her retreat and turned back to Gideon who was eyeing him sternly, "She trusts you Archmage. More than I think you even believe. She deserves your trust and honesty. Your evasions are eroding her trust. I hope you see that before it is too late," Gideon gave him a curt bow of his head and walked off towards Isidora. Azrael observed him walk away and join Isidora by the camp. *Lear'Za was right. There is more there with those two. I hope that he is ready to understand the sacrifices to come.*

When Gideon had caught up to Isidora and hugged her, he could feel the tension in her body. He wanted nothing more than to take all of this away for her, "His secrets will see the light of day Isi. They must," He whispered.

She buried her face in his chest and sighed, "But when Gideon? After someone gets hurt or killed? We could have lost Lear'Za in those woods."

Gideon's mind flashed with the possible dangers ahead. The possibility he could lose her. Worse yet, lose her due to Azrael's secrets, "Azrael's lack of caring for the safety of others disturbs me, regardless of what he tells us".

Isidora groaned and lifted her face at him, "He does care Gideon. It was apparent in his defense of Lear'Za. My concern is not that. No matter what I do, he never seems to trust me, to confide in me. He is carrying something. Something heavy."

Gideon grew irritated. He saw something different, "All I could see was a man so arrogant he thinks no one is strong enough, or smart enough, to handle whatever he is hiding. As for Lear'Za, how do we know his defense was more for his selfish reasons rather than due to care for her?"

Isidora pulled away from him and crossed her arms, "This is what you think? You don't understand. You don't know him as I do."

Gideon crossed his arms as well. *Why is she always defending him?* "Do you, Isi? Isn't the whole issue because you don't seem to know him like you once thought? Why do you continue to believe he cares about you and tolerate him treating you like shite!" Isidora glared at him through narrowed eyes, and he instantly regretted his outburst.

"I think I've heard enough from both of you today," She spat. She turned and walked away, "Isi! Wait! I didn't mean..." It was too late. She needed time to process it, and he did not help matters. He watched her sit at the edge of the campfire with Talia. Dejectedly, Gideon sat down and picked at the grass, his eyes still on Isidora who was talking to Talia.

Gideon noticed the others were also different; changed since their encounter with the gods. Talia had grown melancholy. He did not know what Tilene had said to the pixie but her normally chatty and energetic demeanor had all but vanished. She sat and talked with Isidora, but her head was hanging low, and she glowed a sullen and muted green. He could not imagine what insight could have caused that.

The biggest surprise was Kethis. Gideon had noted the elf had been cheerier; his discussion with Cerridwen had had the opposite effect of Talia's. The elf lord sauntered over and sat down beside Gideon.

"I know Castellarian knights are typically sullen and brooding, but you seem to be taking it farther than most. If you are trying to change my opinion of men and knights, you are doing a poor job," The elf chided.

Gideon gave a halfhearted laugh, "Your sudden foray into the lands of cheer and goodwill with men seems more out of place. What has you so chipper?"

Kethis closed his eyes and took a deep breath of the forest air, "Elves appreciate providence and destiny more than men I suppose. My faith is also strong, and meeting a god has only strengthened it. There are times we have to place our ambitions and biases aside to answer a higher calling. I am not saying I love and trust the world of men; I realize there are times I have to suffer them. That includes you, Castellarian."

The elf was being evasive and not giving any details of his discussion with Cerridwen. There was no doubt that it had softened him, "Perhaps you are right," His eyes wandered off to Isidora once more, "There is one thing I have extreme faith in, I just have a horrible way of showing it."

Kethis' gaze followed Gideon's. The elf smiled, "You care for the woman, don't you? Is there a bond?" The elf smirked.

"That is none of your business, elf," Gideon smiled. His eyes caught sight of Azrael, and his tone became more serious, "We all have our secrets, I suppose."

Kethis stood up and brushed the grass off his hands. We all need faith in something Sir knight. Be it gods, magic, or love," He paused and looked to the distance, "I have decided to continue accompanying your party to Al'Zadal."

Kethis had become introspective, and his newfound motivation comforted Gideon, "I, for one, would be happy to have another sword to keep those I care about safe," He responded honestly.

Kethis nodded, "I will do my best. I shall inform the others of my decision. Pray for good fortune Sir knight," The elf jogged back to the camp.

Shortly after they packed up and continued their journey north, it was about a day's ride out of the forest when the grass began to die away, giving way to drier, harder earth and sparse shrubbery. They also felt an increase in temperature. They were close to the desert and Tunai. Gideon removed his plate armor and instead wore a leather tunic covered in chainmail with a light cloak clasped with a golden falcon. Not apropos gear for the desert but better than the stifling plate mail. They would arrive in Tunai soon and could acquire appropriate clothing if needed, and arrive they did. By mid-morning the following day they made their way towards an inn, hoping to resupply and prepare for the ascent into the desert. It didn't take long for them to notice the stares as they rode down the main street.

"They stare as if we lead an invading army into their midst," Gideon stated.

"An invading army they understand, knight, and to be quite honest it wouldn't be as surprising as what they are looking at now," Azrael replied without turning his head, "Keep your eyes forward and don't let them linger too long on anyone."

"What could disconcert them so? The daemoness perhaps?" Kethis questioned as he made sure his bow was within reach should he need it.

"They stare at the black robes, Isidora and I wear. Magi are not trusted in these parts," Despite the heat, Azrael raised his hood over his silvery-white hair.

"Our robes?" Isidora spat in a hoarse whisper, "Magi are revered across Tinil'Gan and well respected. Perhaps they need a lesson in humility."

"Mind your tongue, Tra'ni," Azrael's head snapped in Isidora's direction, "Magic is what caused the desolation of Rania and created this desert. It is said the Castellamar had employed especially power-hungry magi. They expected lordships in return for their service and eyed the plains of Rania. They prepared an especially devastating spell that would kill as many Castellarians on the battlefield as it would Ranians. As legend tells it,

Sir Reginald discovered this during the battle and led a small battalion to stop his magi from completing the spell. They arrived too late to stop it, but valiantly drove forward, causing the spell to backfire and lay waste to the whole of Rania. Thus Sir Reginald's 'grand sacrifice' even though his efforts were in vain. It was folly, and the Art suffered for it for many years after. We were mistrusted and despised across the continent. Thankfully, most of the resentment has dissipated, save for here. This is a tale I choose not to believe, but it is thought by many, so my opinion on the matter is a moot point."

"My grandsires told tales of those days. Every pixie felt the deaths of their kin in the Linian Forest," Talia said from her perch upon Azrael's shoulders. Her wings fluttered nervously. Her green glow began to shift into a warning hue of orange.

Lear'Za spurred her steed to Azrael's right, "I fear that local resentment is growing, Seer'kaat. I do believe their curiosity has grown past stares," Lear'Za's assessment was correct. The group found themselves forced to slow their pace as a crowd formed around them from all sides. The crowd thickened, and they had no choice but to stop.

Gideon trotted forward as far as he could while calming his nervous horse, "Good people of Tunai. We come to your city in peace. We are weary travelers that stop only for a day on our way through. Let us pass in the same peace we offer you."

A tall, skinny Tunoshi spat on the dry ground and fingered the hilt of his scimitar, "Peace? This from a knight with two magi in tow. All here remember the last time a knight passed through here with pet magi."

Gideon's jaw was set firm, "Those were knights of a different age, good sir, and they led an army. We are but six travelers. Certainly, we can cause no harm."

An elf came forward next; his face was scarred and marked with an *X*, branded on his cheek, "We have no reason to trust the likes of you. Whatever honor knights held was lost long ago," The elf pulled his sword from his scabbard.

In a blink of an eye, Kethis' horse was beside the man. The elf lord had an arrow notched and ready a foot from the other elf's head, "We are to take this from the mouth of one so marked? What honor do you have, outcast of the Realm of Light? What treason did you commit that you dare condemn us?"

"Does it matter? My own kind, nobles like you branded me and made me an outcast. Here I am not. It is you who is the stranger here. Who are you to aim your bow at me and further condemn me with your words?" The elf spat. Kethis lowered his bow and his brow furrowed.

The crowd broke out in an uproar. Swords were unsheathed and clattered. Gideon and Lear'Za had also drawn their swords, and the horses whinnied and bucked. Calmly, Azrael raised his head, and his lips began to move silently. Blue tendrils of lightning flashed across his mirrored eyes, and the power of the Art flowed through him. The wind kicked up and tossed sand around. The lightening in his eyes reached out and began to touch the ground around them. It twisted and turned, writhing like snakes in the sand and crackling which each flash. The circle of arcane electricity grew, pushing the crowd back away from them. The crowd hushed, some in awe, some in fear. But no one sheathed their swords. Azrael ended his chanting, but the electrical circle remained. He removed his hood and looked over the crowd.

"As the knight, said we come in peace. True, you have no reason to trust us, just as we have no reason to trust you. We did not ride into your city, brandishing our power and weapons. We do not wish to harm any of you, but we will defend ourselves. I can promise you the outcome will not be pleasant for you. The choice is yours."

There was silence. Gideon was not satisfied that Azrael's display and words would quell the impending battle; he worried it would intensify the threat. He prepared himself, anticipating the tide of humanity that would fall on them when from behind came the sound of heavy footsteps.

A score of fighting men surrounded the mob, all well-armed, which pushed them further back. When the crowd saw the mercenaries, they seemed to inspire more fear than Azrael's display, and many sheathed their weapons and ran.

Out of the ring of men stepped a richly dressed Tunoshi in a silken damask thobe. He stopped, put his hands on his hips, and addressed the remaining mob, "No harm shall come to these travelers in our city unless you wish to displease the Silver Sword," No one answered, and the crowd dispersed quickly, mumbling and groaning to themselves as they went. The Tunoshi turned to Azrael and his companions and smiled, "Forgive my fellow Tunoshi. Although misguided, they mean well. Let me welcome you to Tunai. I am Jozef Shaddam," He placed a hand on his chest and gave a slight bow, "Please let us find some drink and food so I can show you a proper Tunoshi welcome," The man flashed a white-toothed smile and gestured towards a nearby inn.

CHAPTER 19

"The deep desert is a dangerous place, magi." Jozef Shaddam leaned back and spoke between puffs of his hookah.

Azrael had to admit that, if nothing else, Jozef was a gracious host. They had dined on roasted quail imported from the forest of the elves, freshly baked flatbread smothered in garlic with an olive oil dip, olives, sharp cheese, and chilled wine. Chilled anything came at a premium in Tunai. Surprisingly the inn was pleasant; the common room was airy and wide. Most of the furnishings were plush pillows strewn upon the floor around a low sitting table or comfortable divans. At every table were servants with large palm fans to cool the patrons. Where there were no pillows, colorful rugs depicting scenes from the histories of Tinil'Gan covered the flooring. One carpet showed the three gods looking upon their world. It also appeared to Azrael that this particular inn was exclusive, judging by the two burly Tunoshi guards at the entrance. *We would have never been allowed to enter this place without this Jozef Shaddam.* Considering the reputation of the Silver Sword, Azrael was sure Jozef could afford it. His clothing was testament enough.

Through the centuries, Azrael had seen the Silver Sword's ascent as a mercenary company. They had played a large part in many battles throughout the Evening Lands, though the history texts rarely spoke of them. Mercenaries took away the glory of knights upon the field of battle, so they conveniently left out the assistance of hired swords. A knight's honor was more dependent on the bard than his deeds. The founders of the Silver Sword had been surviving Ranian knights who no longer had a kingdom to fight for or a home. Its ranks soon swelled to accept any man with fighting skill, of any race or nation—the one thing they did not employ: magi. Azrael understood the hatred they faced in the streets of Tunai.

They had been speaking for a few hours. Usually a good judge of character, this Shaddam puzzled even Azrael. Why the Silver Sword would take an interest in his companions, let alone come to their aid in the streets of Tunai did not add up in the Archmage's mind. But despite his usual cynicism and mistrust, Azrael noted something of sincerity in the lavish Tunoshi. He was an enigma, one Azrael planned on unraveling. The rest of his company was not as comfortable.

He could see how stiffly Gideon sat. Although he ate, the knight always kept his eyes upon Shaddam, and a hand was still near his sword. The knight's trust was tenuous at best, and this situation did not help. Isidora was not as stiff, but her keen eyes darted back and forth as he spoke. She would glance at Azrael, as well, to judge his reaction. Her anger with him was still there, but he taught her well. The current situation took precedence. No doubt his Tra'ni was trying to dissect the mystery that was Jozef Shaddam, but the firm set of her lips did not buoy a favorable impression. Lear'Za was aloof as usual. He did not even want to think about what was going through her mind.

Her anger over the tribunal had not yet wholly dissipated. He turned his attention back to Jozef. The mercenary popped an olive in his mouth.

"Many who enter do not return," Jozef said as he licked the oils off his fingers.

"We are well aware of the dangers, Master Shaddam. I've faced worse," Azrael said coolly.

Jozef laughed and took another deep drag of the hookah. The sweetly scented smoke had been pleasant at first, but now its cloying fumes were beginning to make Azrael gag, "This may be so, magi. However, the desert has humbled the mightiest of men. You have still have not told Jozef why you want to enter this place of death."

"As you have yet to tell me what interest the Silver Sword has with us," Azrael retorted.

Jozef flashed a smile, "This is so, and you are correct. An unknown for an unknown. Very well, magi, as it is my job to know so, I must ask. There is a prophecy among the sages of Tunai. It speaks of the return of the magi to our realm. It foretells of a great war and many conflicts. It speaks of change. Chaos."

Azrael's eyes flashed. *Prophecy. Chaos. Does he speak of the same prophecy?* Isidora and Gideon instantly stiffened, "And the word of some old crones interests a band of mercenaries why?" Azrael said, making sure his student and the knight did not deem to make this moment a time to bring up old quarrels.

"It interests *me*, magi. As I said, it is my job to know, and when prophecies begin to come to life, what greater mystery is there that can unravel before these eyes? As for the Silver Sword, whispers of war turn into screams of gold. We stand to profit much if it is so."

Azrael nodded, "A small group entering a desert does not start a war, prophecy or no."

"A grain of sand upon a dune is merely a grain of sand. It does not move the dune; it does not change its direction. That same grain of sand picked up by an errant wind can catch in your eye, blinding you, endangering your life. In a wound, it can fester and kill. If it blinds or kills the right man it can affect a multitude," Jozef spread his hands, "Either way, magi, I would like to know."

There is no place to hide in the desert, and Josef knows this. Even if I do not tell him, he will find out our destination if he so wished, "We seek the Temple of Al'Zadal."

Jozef's eyebrows furrowed, "Al'Zadal? It is ruins. Destroyed long ago, most likely devoured by the desert. Whatever treasure the temple once secreted has been looted long ago. Only the dead reside there now."

Isidora steadied her gaze on Jozef, "It is the dead we seek, Master Shaddam," Her tone was icy. Azrael noticed Talia, again on his shoulder, shaking. He did not have time to see what was bothering her. Perhaps he would talk to the pixie after this meeting.

Jozef was taken aback and flopped back into the cushions of the divan they sat upon, "Certainly you jest."

Isidora's violet eyes narrowed, "I am capable of many things, Master Shaddam. Jesting is not one I am known for."

Jozef smiled widely and clapped his hands, "Ah-ha, Jozef likes this one! She is fiery."

Gideon's eye twitched and sat a little closer to Isidora. She merely curled her lip, "I don't think you'd like to see how fiery I can be."

Lear'Za rolled her eyes, "Of course he notices the ice queen, and a taken one at that! I swear to your gods, Seer'kaat, that damn stag did something to me!"

Jozef cocked an eyebrow, confused. Azrael spoke before the discussion went somewhere he did not wish nor want to hear, "Ignore our friend, Master Shaddam. Back to the topic at hand, Isidora is not too far off in her statement. I do not want to burden you with long explanations of our craft you would not understand. In short, there are certain aspects of the magic she practices that require contact with the spirits that reside in Al'Zadal."

Jozef crossed his arms, "Two magi, a knight, an elf, a daemoness, and a pixie seek the center of our realm's ruin. A grain of sand, master magi," Jozef shook his head, "But I must know. The Silver Sword shall guide you."

Gideon ground his teeth, "We did not ask for any assistance, sir."

No one trusts him. I don't blame them, but still, "The good knight is correct, Master Shaddam. We did not ask for any assistance. Nor do we carry enough coin to employ the services of a company as renowned as the Silver Sword."

Jozef emphatically waved his hands, "Let Jozef worry about the Silver Sword. They follow my commands, and I pay them well enough. My men and I know the desert, unlike any other. It would be my pleasure, magi," He smiled and bowed his head.

Azrael noticed a marking, a tattoo, on Jozef's arm. *What is this? Can it be? If I am correct, then I am sure we can trust this man,* "Who am I to rebuke such a generous offer?" *The others, however will not understand.*

All their heads turned towards Azrael.

"D'ni, you are not seriously considering this?" Isidora said.

"Not to insult your council, Lord Azrael, but I believe Isidora is correct," rebuked Gideon.

"I do find this most unwise as well, Archmagus," The quiet Kethis found a reason to speak.

Azrael narrowed his eyes and raised a hand to silence them, "Isidora, you came to me because you trust my judgment and guidance, and Gideon you trust hers. As for you, elf lord, if it troubles you, you are free to return to Luminos."

That silenced the objections. *I hope my judgment is as sound as it usually is,* "If the Silver Sword offers its services I humbly accept."

Jozef clapped his hands again and smiled, "Ah-ha, yes, yes. This is good, no? We must celebrate," Jozef snapped his fingers at a servant girl, "More food for our friends, something sweet. Fetch some plump cactus fruit and melons and more wine."

Azrael waved a hand, "Thank you, Master Shaddam, but we really must prepare."

Jozef shook a finger, "Nonsense, we have time, yes? Trust Jozef. The winds are heavy in the desert at the moment," the Tunoshi slid more comfortably onto his seat, "In two days' time most of the sand storms shall have passed. And enough of this 'Master Shaddam' business. You shall call me Jozef. We have broken bread and shared wine. We are friends now," He flashed a smile, "Besides, I have heard news that may interest your sir knight friend, here."

Gideon's head popped up, "Me? What news could you have that would interest me?"

Jozef chuckled as he poured the fresh wine the servant girl had brought over, "As well as the elf lord," He picked up a cactus fruit and took a bite.

Kethis frowned, "Play no games, sell-sword. Speak your words."

Jozef spread his hands, "Apologies, I mean not to insult," Jozef wiped his hands of the sticky red juice of the fruit, "As you must know, the Silver Sword travels far and wide, and learns a great many things happening upon our continent. Some even bring news from the Morning Lands. It is my job to know, so I do. The news comes from a village upon the foot of the mountains. Just north of the Silver River."

Gideon sat forward now, interested in what the mercenary had to say, "Granary?"

"As you say, Sir knight. It seems the knights of The Spokes has laid claim upon it."

"What? We have had peace with the Riverlords for centuries. There is no cause," Gideon said, shocked.

Jozef spread his hands, "Who knows what reason men hold in their hearts and minds? That is a thing I shall never know for certain. What I do know is the Riverlords now control those lands."

Gideon shook his head, "But the Markens...Lord Sethus..."

Jozef popped a piece of melon in his mouth and wiped his hands together, "Dead. To a man. Even the children and womenfolk. This Lord and his heirs are no more. The banners of the owl fly above its keep as we speak."

Gideon rose abruptly and paced the floor, "This cannot be! This will lead to war! I must return to..." Gideon looked over to Isidora. His usual hardened look softened, "Isidora."

Isidora rose and placed her hand upon his, "If you must leave, I will not stop you."

Gideon ran a hand through his hair and grunted, "I vowed I would aid you in this. I cannot break that vow. We must make haste."

Jozef offered Gideon his wine cup, "There is time, sir knight. These events occurred early this morning. One of my men returned from the area in haste to give me the news shortly before your arrival. I only know because a rider nearly killed his mount to bring the news. No townsfolk have been allowed to leave; therefore, no news has reached your kingdom as of yet. Even then, there will be emissaries before your knights take to horse. Is this not the way of your knights?"

Gideon downed the wine in one gulp and sighed, "Yes. Yes, it is."

Talia broke from her melancholy and glowed a hopeful yellow. She flew down and landed on the table, "We don't have to go to the desert. This is more important! We should turn back," Talia's orange glow intensified, and she wrung her hands.

Azrael cocked an eyebrow, "Let us worry about this, little one. Others can deal with Tinil'Gan's problem at present. We are here for Isidora."

Talia stomped her foot, "I don't care about some stupid dead avatar in the desert! Your place is back on the Isle of Winds! Back with...Isidora can do her stupid quest by herself!" Talia was near to tears, and her glow shifted to a mourning purple.

Isidora leaned forward in concern, "Talia? Love, is everything all right?" She reached a hand forward.

Talia glowed a bright crimson and shot in the air away from Isidora, "No, I'm not all right! You and this quest will ruin everything! Leave me alone!" The pixie flew off in a stumble as if drunk. Azrael and Isidora looked at each in confusion.

Ignoring the exchange, Kethis leaned over and grabbed Jozef's arm tightly, "What news do you bring from the Realm of Light?"

Jozef smiled and patted Kethis' hand before gently removing it, "Another group of owl men is making their way west. The only thing that lies in their path is the elves," The mercenary spread his hands.

Kethis jumped up and threw his napkin on the table, "I must inform the Guardian of Light. Please excuse me," He stormed from the inn to fetch his scrying orb from his saddle pack.

Jozef popped another chunk of melon into his mouth and smiled, "Grains of sand, magi. Grains of sand."

Azrael bowed his head, and his mouth closed so tightly his teeth ground. *The river of time flows ever on; its twists and turns change the view; however, not the course it bears.* The verse of the song he had learned in his youth, hundreds upon hundreds of years ago, played in his mind. *It has begun, and this impending war could very well be Leto's clarion call. Which also means it is the least of Tinil'Gan's worries.*

CHAPTER 20

"This is an outrage!" The Guardian of Light was visibly infuriated as his thin hands shook. Diarmuid stood by, his own hands tucked calmly into the sleeves of his white robe, as Giasis listened to Kethis' report, "Has the world gone mad? First, a Castellarian and two black robes tread upon the Realm of Light, then my nephew decides to accompany them into a desert. Now, this? Riverlords marching towards our lands?"

Diarmuid kept his face composed. He had to be careful, too much was at stake. Giasis was trusting but also had a strong will. *I must only counsel, not appear to give commands,* "The Riverlords have become bold of late, Your Grace. I fear this may only be the beginning."

"We have the means of defending ourselves, even from The Spokes. If it is war they want, we can match them sword for sword, arrow for arrow. I would also dare to assume we have the might of magic behind us as well."

The might of magic you know I control, "Of course, Your Grace, ever has the Conclave been friends with our people. Our numbers are not as great as they once were, yet our magic is just as strong as it ever was. The Spokes may not be our only enemy."

"The Knights of Castellamar? The wretched kingdom has always been a worry for me. Not that I fear them, either. Their might may even be weaker than that of The Spokes."

Diarmuid moved closer and took a seat next to the throne. He removed his hood, his green eyes flashing, "It is not the Kingdom I speak of, Your Grace. There is as much animosity between the Kingdom and The Spokes as with the elves. It is the Hollisters who first stirred the Riverlords to rebel those many years ago. Other Riverlords still trust in House Hollister."

"You think the other Riverlords would unite in this madness against us?"

Diarmuid smiled, "I am saying, Your Grace, that it is not out of the realm of possibility. I do not see the Hollisters making this kind of move unless they knew they had some support."

"I hope you are wrong, Magus Diarmuid. We cannot hold long against the entirety of the Riverlands. If they are of like mind, it could be the ruin of our people," Giasis lowered a wearied head into his hand.

"There is an option. As the old phrase says, the enemy of my enemy is my friend. Perhaps we may not stand alone against this assault."

Giasis raised his head, "The only power is the Kingdom, and I will not stomach elves fighting alongside them. It cannot be."

"Your nephew reported that The Spokes has also raised their banner over Castellarian lands. The Kingdom will not stand idly by. War is upon the Evening Lands, Your Grace. The fragile peace we have enjoyed has been shattered," Diarmuid replied calmly.

"My nephew. Kethis' place is here, not with Azrael and his ilk. I am going to have to dispatch archers and defenders to the border to meet these invaders. Kethis should be leading them, not stumbling through a desert. He didn't even give me a good reason other than 'the gods bid me as such.' Why must this tragedy happen at the twilight of my reign? Could it not wait until a younger, more virile Guardian takes my place?"

Diarmuid nodded, "I understand your frustration, but perhaps this is fortuitous. The knight with whom Kethis travels is a Stormcaller of the royal family. Their association could strengthen bonds long ago severed. The tragedy of Rania was centuries ago. This is not the same Kingdom of old. They are more humble since being trapped behind the mountains."

Giasis sighed, "I am old even by elvan standards, Diarmuid. There was a time I thought I would be breaking bread with the Guardian of the Dark of Duminos before entertaining the wretched Kingdom. I must deal with matters at hand for the moment. The defense of Elvan lands is paramount. I will deal with these interlopers first, then decide where the next course of action takes us. Should they proceed further, I will bid Kethis speak with the Kingdom on my behalf, after his foray into the desert."

"As always, Your Grace is wise."

"I thank you for your advice, Diarmuid. My old bones scream for rest so I will retire for a nap," Giasis rose from the dais.

"Of course. May the Light of day shine upon you today as it always has," Diarmuid gave a curt bow and left the throne room for his chambers.

Every time Diarmuid had a well-laid plan, something had thrown it off. First Giasis allowed Azrael passage, and then something had interfered with Caiaphas' ambush of the group in the Linian Forest. Now, in the wastes of the desert, Kethis had learned what should have been well-kept secrets.

The ranger's interference had slowed things down. Now Giasis was preparing a defense instead of planning retaliation. Diarmuid did not wish to see elves harmed, but it was necessary to advance this cause. The defense force was certain to be in place before the hostile forces arrived. It would be a slaughter. What he had to prevent were any Elvan emissaries being sent to The Spokes, giving House Hollister warning. *This is why I hate politics, too messy.*

Diarmuid rounded a corner and arrived at his chambers. He had work to do. First, he penned a missive to Lord Sulik, letting him know of the current events. He was uncertain what Sulik could do with this information, but better he had it than not. *Somehow Azrael and that group are causing more problems without even trying to, and it seems everyone wants them gone.* Diarmuid rolled the parchment and sealed it in wax with his signet.

Next, he needed to save himself any headache with the Conclave of Magi. He penned a missive to them, as well, informing them of the events that had occurred while he had been in Luminori and that there may be a need for the magi to take action. When the time came, he would have to present his arguments in person, but better to get them thinking about it first.

The last thing he needed to do was contact Caiaphas. He had the scrying orb, twin to the one he had given the black robe, in a drawer of his desk. He would make contact later that night. For now, he called in a servant to take the missives and have them sent via pigeon to their respective destinations. All he could do now was sit and wait.

CHAPTER 21

The true extent of the living hell that is the desert could not be appreciated until one experienced it. The companions received a full dose of reality shortly into their trek. As Jozef had advised, they waited out a sandstorm for two days in Tunai. Once the winds subsided, Jozef said they could depart.

"Then let us be on our way," Gideon exclaimed.

Jozef laughed, "You wish to die, then?" They all looked at each other in confusion. With another laugh, Jozef explained that they would not depart with the same clothes they came in. Heavy black mage robes and leather armor would not do. He handed them all light linen bishts. Azrael and Isidora balked when they saw the white color of the linen smocks. It took much convincing before they finally conceded to don the bishts, "In black, you would not survive a day," consoled Jozef.

After the clothing debacle, Jozef also explained that their horses would remain behind. A horse was no desert animal. They would travel by camel. More suited for the desert, they would get much farther. There would be a chance that not even all the camels would survive the trip. The Temple was in the deepest part of the desert, a place that not many dares to reach and return alive. There was not much argument there. Kethis was a bit saddened; he had had his horse for years and always traveled with him. Jozef swore the mare would be safe in the stables.

Finally, Jozef ushered everyone back into the inn. Confused again, they questioned him, "One does not trek the desert during the day, my friends. We travel by night. It is cooler without the sun, and we can rest by day in whatever shade we can find if any. This is the way," Begrudgingly they went back inside, ate a small lunch. Despite the sense of urgency, the short respite was enjoyed. They sat around the table together and ate a good meal of roasted goat, dry cheese, and wine.

Jozef licked his fingers and sat back with a sigh, "I understand you hold this quest in secrecy, but as your guide, it would be wise to let me know more details on this. It could prove the difference between life and death if I am missing something."

Isidora looked at Azrael of reassurance, and he nodded in confirmation. She ordered her thoughts and looked up at the sellsword, "The particular aspect of magic I am aspiring for is called summoning. One of the tasks a summoner must undertake is finding locations of importance to deceased heroes in an attempt to draw their essence into an avatar form. The hopes are to earn their trust and pledge as a loyal avatar to be summoned when needed," She paused and took a drink of her wine, "The one we are searching for in Al'Zadal is that of Sir Reginald from the legends of the Chalice of Abbas."

Jozef nodded and sat forward, "I know of him from the histories, yes. So we must head to the temple's courtyard then. This is where the histories state the chalice was housed. This is deep within the ruins, and I will tell you is an arduous journey."

Gideon crossed his arms, "We are prepared. Whatever dangers we encounter, we shall do so together."

Jozef laughed, "Spoken like a true knight of Castellamar! Tell me, young knight, do you have any stories of Sir Reginald and the Chalice of Abbas?"

"The tale is one of the most honored and mythical legends in Castellamar and told to children as a story of tragedy and triumph. Most only remember Sir Reginald himself as the leader of the legendary Knights of the Golden Lance. While not as revered as Sir Reginald, it consisted of honored and storied men. Sir Ihon the Maneater. Sir Quintus the Hammer. Sir Eudon the Cunning. There were many."

Jozef cut a slice of goat with his dagger and popped it in his mouth. He tapped the pommel of his blade on the table, "Which one was your favorite?"

Gideon smiled, "I always had an affinity to Sir Jeph of the South. He was never a main character in the tales. But when he was mentioned, his deeds always struck a chord with me as the epitome of what a knight should be. He carried a legendary sword. Winterborn, Glaive of Pride's Fall."

"I, for one, find someone with the moniker of Maneater to sound more appealing. Set's the imagination ablaze," Lear'Za said with a wink.

The group broke out in laughter. Isidora smiled. *I hope this good cheer lasts. They are all here for me. I cannot fail them.* They finished their meal and retired to their rooms to rest. The night journey would be one of many out in the desert. Jozef woke them at dusk.

The company, accompanied by Jozef and four of his Silver Swords, made its way out of Tunai just as the sun winked out. The night was cooler but the heat of the day lingered long into the night. The night went by quietly as warm winds whispered through the dunes. When the sun rose, they made their first camp under some nearby boulders that jutted out from the sand. They rested fitfully in the blistering heat. Every few hours Jozef would wake them, to ensure they moved or turned as not to overheat themselves.

At night, they mounted their camels again and rode. Hot winds still blew over the dunes, and when they died down in the early hours before dawn, a sudden chill would fall. Just as they would warm their bodies, the sun's heat would make them wish for the return of night. Onward they trudged.

The idle chatter and japes disappeared by the third day of their trip. Gone were the smiles replaced with cracked lips and thirst; the wetness of their mouths replaced by the constant grit of sand. They began to question if they had even made any progress. Every dune looked like another; there was nothing to denote any distance traveled.

The desert began to play tricks with their minds as well. Mirages were constant. It seemed there was always an oasis just over the next dune, only to reveal more sand. Kethis even fired an arrow into the emptiness, swearing he saw something move. The water skins they had rationed began to run out. Jozef calmed them by showing them they could slake their thirst by eating the bulbous cactus fruit they passed. Some were bitter, but at least it moistened their mouths.

At the end of the fourth night, they made camp just as the last of the stars twinkled out of sight. Thankfully, they found a rocky outcropping that had a small cave. The group began unpacking their gear for the long, hot day ahead. Isidora saw Talia flitter off Azrael's shoulder and land on top of an outcropping, a little way away from everyone and facing the east, towards the oncoming sunrise. *What has happened to her?* After unpacking, Isidora made her way up the outcropping and sat next to the small fairy. Neither spoke for some time and merely watched the horizon as it began to change colors. Talia's glow was a muted violet-purple of mourning, a shade not much different from Isidora's eyes. Every once in a while, her wings would twitch and flutter as she gazed off, her chin resting in her hands.

Talia broke the silence without looking over, "I'm sorry I yelled at you back at the inn."

Isidora glanced over and smiled lightly. She adjusted her bisht and made herself more comfortable on the rocks, "I never asked for an apology, my friend. I'm more concerned about you. This is unlike you; not like the happy pixie who kept me company at night while I studied in Azrael's tower."

Talia crossed her legs and leaned her elbow on one knee, resting her chin on her fist. With her other hand, she flicked at little pebbles and watched them cascade to the sands below, "Life does that to us sometimes, you know. Can't always be happy."

Isidora chuckled, "Except for pixies. Never once have you been this melancholy, love. You deal with the dead, Talia, and still manage to keep your cheer."

Talia sighed, "Well, things change, I guess. Even things that aren't supposed to, and the things you hope will change never do."

"Azrael," Isidora nodded in understanding.

Talia pulled on her wings and played with its edge, "You don't understand, Isi."

"Try me."

Talia heaved a heavy sigh, "It's silly anyway. I'm just a stupid pixie."

Isidora brushed away a strand of hair that had fallen into Talia's face, "A wonderful, beautiful, and caring pixie that is loyal and dear to her friends. One that is like a sister to me. Trust me. I've tried drawing something, anything from that man. It is hopeless."

Talia made a 'pfft' sound with her lips, "You don't even realize how much he cares for you."

Isidora raised an eyebrow, "He shows you far more caring than he has ever shown me,"

Talia shook her head, "You just don't get it or see it. Every minute of his life since you came into it has revolved around you. I knew Azrael before you came along, remember. Never has he taken an interest in anyone as he did for you."

I never thought it that way. Azrael was an enigma. She could never reliably read him or his emotions. It was as if every conversation she had with him came from reading his words on parchment without any context of body language, tone, or facial expressions, "Perhaps you are right. I am certain though that he is also concerned for your wellbeing."

Talia was silent for a moment. She turned and faced Isidora, "I love him, Isi," She blushed. Her glow matching the rosy hue on her cheeks.

"Of course you do, and you do nothing but show it every day to him. But you cannot destroy the wonderful happiness of your soul because he doesn't recognize it."

Talia's lip quivered. The sun broke the horizon, its first rays shining upon her face, "It's more than that. I'm used to him not loving me back in that way. But at least he was always there…"

Isidora raised an eyebrow, "Azrael's not going anywhere, Talia."

Tears flowed freely from Talia's eyes, "I can't…I can't talk about this anymore, Isi. The sun's up now. It's going to get hot," Talia fluttered away to the shade of the cave. Isidora watched her go and then studied the sunrise for a moment. *Why do I fear what is to come? This was supposed to be a simple journey: unseen assassins, petulant monarchs, unlikely sell-swords. Even gods are taking an interest in us.* Isidora pursed her lips and rose from her perch, following Talia into the cave and hopefully some rest.

Although the cave was rocky and uncomfortable, the day passed better than the preceding days had. The heat crept in, but they did not have the sun's unmerciful rays beating down upon them. Jozef roused them all as dusk began to approach. They supped on dried rations and awaited the darkness to fall before mounting their camels. Kethis had walked out and scanned the dimming horizon with his keen elvan vision as he had every night. Gideon walked over and stood beside him.

"What do you seek, Kethis?" Gideon asked.

The elf did not stop his intense stare out into the desert, "I seek some relief, some sign we are nearing our destination. Even if it is still far off, some hint of our journey's end will give comfort," Kethis' narrowed his eyes and stiffened, "I fear I see the opposite."

Gideon stared as far as his human eyes would allow and squinted, "All I see is sand and dust."

"Even your eyes, knight, should be able to see the sand and dust are floating above the horizon line."

Gideon's eyes widened, "You are right," Gideon turned his head and shouted back, "Jozef, what do you make of this!"

The mercenary looked up from where he was packing his gear and sauntered over to the two, "What is it you see, friends?" He turned his head to the horizon.

Kethis pointed, "It looks as if a sandstorm approaches. I thought you said we should be past the winds during our journey."

Jozef eyed the horizon carefully, and his lips turned downward, "I was not incorrect about the weather, elf lord. That is no sandstorm. Riders approach. Desert raiders, they will descend upon us shortly."

Gideon unsheathed his sword, "A cloud seen at this distance…"

Jozef drew his scimitar and began giving it a few strokes of his whetstone, "Means they number many," he finished. He turned to his men, "*Khelak debar wheera ala seehoor. Eda nahir sabeen*," he said in Tunoshi, motioning to them. His men slithered away and hid behind the rock formations. Azrael and the rest came over to join the others.

"Danger approaches. We must handle this carefully. Isidora, you are with me. We take cover on the parapet of the outcropping to cast. Lear'Za and Kethis, into the cave," Azrael said calmly.

"The knight and I shall remain here by the camels to greet our visitors. Perhaps if they see we have nothing to raid I can convince them to make their way to other, richer bounty," Jozef replied.

Everyone nodded and made their way to their positions. Gideon and Jozef made as if tending the camels and gear as the raiders edged ever closer. When they arrived, it was as bad as they had first suspected. They numbered about twenty-five, more than twice the number of their group—wiry but strong Tunoshi, sporting scimitars and riding small but quick desert boars. Many were scarred and leathery, a testament of their life in the deep desert. Their leader appeared more fearsome than his fellows; a thick line ran from his left temple across his face to the right side of his chin. All of them wore the light linen bisht of desert folk, but they were dusty and dirty. He reared his boar before Jozef and Gideon and unsheathed his scimitar.

Jozef turned and smiled, placing his hands on his hips, "*Elab shallah!*" He gave the traditional Tunoshi greeting.

The raider's leader sneered at Jozef and noticed the many rings and jewelry he wore, "*Elab shallah*. What brings one so richly dressed to our desert?"

Jozef waved his hand towards Gideon, "This good man is a pilgrim; he wishes to view the ruin of Al'Zadal," There was no point in lying about their destination; there weren't many places in the desert to visit, "I am his humble guide," Jozef placed his hand on his chest and gave a slight bow.

The raiders drew slightly closer, forming a semi-circle around them that pinned them against the cave mouth. Gideon fingered the pommel of his sword.

"Such a humble man has no need for jewels," the leader said as he smiled wickedly. The raider next to him had already brought his sword down towards Gideon before his leader finished speaking. Before the blade could connect the thief gurgled, an Elvan arrow protruding from his throat.

Jozef's men ran from behind the outcropping to protect their leader, cutting down the closest raiders in swift strokes. Kethis and Lear'Za also emerged. The elf flung arrow after arrow, felling three raiders in swift succession as Lear'Za leaped with a howl into the foray, her blazing blade cleaving one of the invaders in two. Gideon had his sword drawn an instant after Kethis' arrow took out the would-be assassin. Gideon's training was apparent, and although not in his heavy plate armor he was still comfortable in his parries and blows. For knights, sword duels were akin to a chess match. Both start equally matched. With each swing, each block, a knight learns of his opponent's strengths and weaknesses. Gideon was an apt disciple in this form of swordplay. The knight fought off two raiders alone with his broadsword, each ending with a well-placed parry and deft up handed swipe removing their heads from the necks.

Jozef also was prepared and pulled his thin scimitar from its scabbard. The Tunoshi was a quick and adept swordsman. His style differed from that of the knights of the Evening Lands. His form was not stiff and governed by strength, where swords would clang together in a slow give and take of ground. Instead, the Tunoshi was like a sand devil, whirling and twirling around in a dizzying array of slashes and parries. His blade would flash in one direction, deflecting a cut from and opponent, and in one swift motion come back around, putting wounds in arms and legs. A raider came from behind, and Jozef raised his scimitar over his head, blocking a swing then fell to a crouch swinging back across his attacker's ankles removing him from his feet. The slice that cut off one man's feet kept moving upwards in an arc slicing across his first opponent's belly disemboweling him spewing his innards into the sand.

The rest of the raiders pressed in from the sides, attempting to trap them. Azrael and Isidora were chanting from atop the outcropping. Magical arrows shot forward from their fingertips, felling four men who were about to overrun Gideon and Kethis. They fell, clutching their chests as the bolts crackled and dug deeper into their flesh, leaving behind black scorch marks behind as they killed them. One raider separated himself from the attack and crawled up the side of the outcropping towards the magi. He arrived at the top and was about to bring his sword down on Azrael back. But the sword fell from his fingers when a large, very large, frying pan smashed him upside the head and sent him tumbling from the outcropping. Talia looked down at him and stuck out her tongue.

Kethis kept leaping to the outskirts of the battle, giving him the better range to unleash his arrows. When his quiver emptied, he had felled six raiders. Then he pulled out his slender elvan blade and fought beside Gideon. His motions were fluid and crisp, dodging and parrying deftly. He finished off another foe with a sword thrust through the chest, just as another attacker made a lucky slash at the elf's leg and sent him sprawling to the ground. His sword fell from his hand and rolled to his back, looking up to see his attacker prepared to drive his scimitar into his chest. Eyes wide, and he whispered a quick prayer to Astraea in preparation for his death. But the scimitar never fell. The raider stopped with a choke, and the point of a long broadsword erupted from his chest. He slid off the blade to fall beside Kethis. Gideon smiled at the elf and reached out a blood-soaked hand to him, "No one dies this day, elf, save for them,"

Kethis reached up and clasped Gideon's forearm and was hefted up. He stood before Gideon, hands still clasped

"I owe you my life, knight. My sword and arrows will protect you and yours as well," Kethis said solemnly. Gideon smiled at him briefly. They both turned and faced the remainder of the enemies that fell on them. The tide was turning.

Isidora had just finished dispatching one of the raiders who had been attempting to stab Lear'Za in the back, an icicle through his midsection impaling him to the sand. She looked up and saw more dust, and her eyes grew wide. She placed a hand on Azrael's arm, "D'ni, look," With her other hand she pointed.

The raiders were not alone. At least a hundred raiders were bearing down upon them, riding their bestial desert boars. In a few moments, they would overwhelm the small group.

Azrael clenched his teeth, and his mirrored eyes flashed with blue tendrils of lightening, "No. Not like this. It does not end like this. Enough!" He removed Isidora's hand from his arm, "Go down there now! Have everyone retreat into the cave and barricade the entrance with a shield spell," Isidora looked at him, "Now!" He yelled. She did not hesitate this time. With a small levitation spell, she leaped from the outcropping and landed gently amidst her friends below. Azrael watched as she ordered them into the cave. They looked up at him, confused for a moment, but ran after Isidora. Lear'Za was the last to enter. Looking up at Azrael, she smiled wickedly, winked, and then dove into the cave.

Azrael closed his eyes once he saw they were all safe. His lips barely moved as he murmured. He stepped from the outcropping just as Isidora had and floated slowly to the ground before the cave entrance. His chanting continued as he descended. The raiders balked and were confused at first as they saw the lone mage float down before them. Of the original twenty-five, only five remained. They saw the shield spell around Azrael as he landed and laughed, knowing they did not need to attack. In less than a minute, a hundred of their fellow raiders would swarm the area, kicking up sand as they charged in behind them. No mage's shield could withstand a hundred swords battering it.

Azrael, lost in the Art, hummed arcane words from his lips and blue lightning crackled around him. He could feel its energy course through him. The corner of his mouth turned up in sheer ecstasy at the power. His chanting increased, and a slight wind began to blow. The remaining five raiders backed up, uncertain, but once their brothers had arrived, courage returned. A swarm of swine, snarls, and screams washed over Azrael.

The mage gave one final shout of command in the arcane tongue of the Sidhe and the wind whipped into a frenzy sending his flowing white hair swirling around him in a halo. Just as the first mounted raiders were about to bring their swords down upon the Archmage, he erupted into a ball of flame, incinerating the nearest invaders and their mounts in screams of agony. The rest veered off to avoid the fate of their comrades, but in moments were doubling back for another assault.

Azrael's companions watched in awe from the cave. They could still see Azrael within the ball of flame, untouched, his hair whipping around, his arms outstretched. It was then they noticed the dark clouds that had formed overhead. A raider began to shout for retreat even as the first bolt of lightning hit him and turned him to ash. They began to scream and turned to flee.

The bolts shot out in quick succession with sudden *booms* and *cracks;* the deadly magical lighting turned all they touched into ash. Bolts began to chain between the raiders, electric currents jumping from one to another. The sky had become as dark as night, but the ground below was alight in blue lightening. It danced to and fro, sparing none. Sand scorched and turned to glass beneath them. The screams of the dying filled the desert as the lightening consumed them.

It only took a few minutes; the show of light waned and crackled in short bursts of static. It finally quieted; nothing remained save for sand, glass, and ash. The sky cleared as quickly as it clouded over, and the ball of flame around Azrael sputtered out. He stood in a circle of blackened sand. His arms still outstretched. Long silver-white hair clung wetly about him stuck to his face with sweat. He breathed heavily as the last of the flames died, then slowly lowered his arms. The Archmage's shoulders slumped, and he fell to one knee.

His friends came running out of the cave, Isidora having dropped the shield. Jozef ambled out, his jaw-dropping in awe at the carnage Azrael alone had wrought. His eyes steadied on the mage. Isidora reached her teacher first and fell next to him, "D'ni!" she screamed.

Azrael lifted a hand and spoke through heavy breaths, "Rest."

CHAPTER 22

The temple was a frenzy of activity. Acolytes ran to and fro in their golden spun robes, sandals flapping on the marble tiles. Today was to be a momentous occasion. Marcum was excited, and his smile as he went about his duties echoed it. He had been a priest in the service of Leto for just under a year. He was relatively new to the order in comparison to most of his brothers. The order rarely took on new acolytes and when they did it was in unexpected flurries, much along the lines of the chaotic nature of their god.

That was not to say there was absolutely no order. Even chaos had its orderly functions. The philosophy of chaos was not about unadulterated anarchy. It was about not conforming to rigidity, remaining fluid, constantly changing, and evolving. *Expect the unexpected.* He had always been comfortable with this philosophy. He had never enjoyed the same, mundane life day in, day out. He didn't like rigid structure. He had felt trapped in that life, so when he heard the order was taking on new acolytes, he jumped at the chance. It had been almost a decade since the last recruitment. It came suddenly, in preparation for something, but no one would say why. *Keep us always guessing, such is the way of chaos.* That was fine with Marcum; it made the anticipation grow daily.

He felt he brought much to the order. He was not young and green, nor was he old. At thirty, he had been schooled sufficiently in many fields, the product of privileged youth. He had learned reading, writing, history, geography and cartography, mathematics, and of course theology. His father had hopes of him becoming a knight, but he refused. It was not that he was not brave, nor was it because of the physical rigors. The knighthood was structured and ordered. He would have suffocated as a knight. No, this was much better.

Naturally, his family had disowned him. He lost all privileges and rights to any family holdings, lands, titles, and income. He did not weep over this loss. Once he arrived at the temple, he realized everything he needed in life was there. No longer bound by the rigidity of noble life, he exulted in the ever-changing (if sometimes menial) tasks appointed to him.

His routine would change weekly. Last week, he had been in charge of changing out the golden beeswax candles that burned on the altars through the night and then lighting them again at dark. The week before that he had been on kitchen duty, aiding the cooks in the preparation of the temple meals. This week he was assisting the Grand Bishop during the nightly rites. He was especially pleased with this assignment because that meant he would be front and center during the *event* that night.

He shivered with anticipation. He wiped the sweat off his bald pate with his hand and busied himself in the main altar room. The benches had all been polished, and the incense burners were full of myrrh. All that was left was the altar itself. He removed the gold silken coverlet and replaced it with a fresh, clean one. He polished the golden goblets, so they reflected like mirrors. He would make sure everything was perfect for tonight. He gave it one last look, checking that all was in order, and smiled in satisfaction.

Marcum looked up at the sun and saw it was just past midday and sighed. He had completed all his duties, and there was still much daylight left before the night's services. The portly monk returned to his modest chambers and busied himself with sincere prayer. By the time he woke from his deep meditation, the sun was low on the horizon, and his face broke into a wide smile. He changed his robes and quickly made his way out into the corridors. He found himself caught up in a wave of acolytes all making their way to the altar room. He shuffled amongst his brothers and pushed forward as much as he could. He wanted to get to the altar room before it got too crowded so he could have a choice spot upfront.

The murmuring when he arrived was thick in the air. It carried a vibratory tone that made it seem alive, a tangible thing he could grasp in his hands. He could feel the tingle run up his spine in anticipation. Luckily when he arrived, a bench to the right of the altar had an open seat, and he took it quickly.

The acolytes settled into their seats, and the murmur quieted into a low buzz. A set of gongs peeled out and the buzz died instantly. Every candle in the altar room was snuffed out save the three large candles on the altar itself. This was Marcum's cue. Along with two other acolytes he made his way to the altar and stood behind one of the candles. The curtains behind the altar parted, and the Grand Bishop entered.

Unlike the acolytes, the bishop was richly dressed. He wore robes of spun gold that shimmered in the candlelight. About his waist hung a rope made of pure gold crafted so delicately that at first glance one would think it was made of hemp, not gold. Every finger had a ring on it, each one signifying the eight rites of passage an acolyte must accomplish before becoming a Grand Bishop. A heavy pendant hung from his neck, also of pure gold. It depicted a compass with no needle, the ancient icon of chaos. He carried a walking staff of dark oak that stood taller than himself. The man himself was nothing extraordinary. He was well-aged, wrinkled, his skin translucent and full of liver spots. He walked with a bit of a stoop, but his strides were sure and true. His eyes, though, spoke volumes. They were deep amber and burned with the passion and vigor of youth, and a deep devotion to his faith. When he arrived at the altar the gong sounded three times again. As the echo of the last gong died, the bishop raised his hands to the air suddenly, and his strong voice rang out.

"My fellow acolytes of Leto, rejoice! I welcome you to our nightly service once again, to honor our Lord Leto and further the causes of chaos and freedom! Tonight, however, is a special night! We have always done our best to interpret our Lord's wishes and carry them out, but every once in a while, our Lord grants us with his presence and direct commands! Tonight is one of those nights!"

The room exploded in murmur. Marcum shivered in anticipation. *I knew it! I knew this was going to be something special!* It took all of his will to maintain his composure. The gongs sounded again, and the murmurs ceased. The bishop once again spoke.

"Tonight you will witness an event to be sung in song! Leto comes to us with direct commands! The time is nigh, and I shall waste no more time. Unveil the Mouth of the Gods!" Behind the altar, over the door through which the bishop had entered, hung a massive tapestry depicting scenes of the gods and creation. An acolyte pulled a rope, and the fabric fell to the side, revealing a large, circular mirror encased in a thin frame of gold. The glass seemed hazy from his perspective as if it had not been cleaned in hundreds of years. The more he looked at it, the more Marcum saw how the haze moved, like dark gray storm clouds across the sky. A tiny bell rang, and Marcum knew this was his cue. He snuffed out his candle, along with the other two acolytes.

The room fell into deep darkness. The windowless altar room was designed as such for a purpose. When communing with chaos and its God, one must be in the darkest of dark, as it was before order and uniformity brought the light. Along with the darkness came a still silence. He stared in the direction of the Mouth of the Gods waiting. At first, all he saw were swirls and mirages caused by his eyes trying to adjust to the darkness. Slowly but surely, he began to make out the dull gray haze in the mirror as it swirled and shifted. The gongs sounded three more times, and the swirl moved faster. With a sudden burst of energy, golden light erupted into the room. It sprang from the Mouth of the Gods like snaky tendrils darting across the room, dipping and diving between, around, and through the acolytes. Probing, sensing, and feeling.

Marcum found himself frozen at first by the light, his eyes wide open. For the first time, he truly felt his god's presence as it caught his breath and left him dumbstruck. The light flashed once more, and the presence intensified. In unison, the acolytes—even the bishop—all fell to their knees. He could not remember consciously going to the floor. It was as if the awesome power of Leto made his muscles do his bidding of their own accord; it was as if even the very tissues of his body recognized the greatness and commanded his body to move without waiting for orders from his mind.

Marcum was in ecstasy. He cared not that he was on his knees with his face in the dirt floor; feeling the presence of his God that very few had ever felt, or might feel again for years to come. Just as he thought it could not get any better, he heard *His* voice. It pierced his mind like a dagger reverberating through his brain. The voice did not enter through his ears; instead, it spoke to him, as it did to all assembled, inside their minds like their own thoughts. What Leto said was brief but precise.

"The Archmagus Azrael. The Ruins of Al'Zadal. No harm shall come to his apprentice. Destroy the Sidhe..."

As the last syllable echoed in his mind, the gold light retreated back into the mirror with such a force it felt like a hurricane wind slammed through the doors, and the room fell into utter darkness once again. The silence was deafening. After a moment, acolytes began lighting the candles, and the murmurs and shouts began. The bishop called for the gong. It rang out and silenced the crowd. He raised his hands, "Leto has spoken! We must act quickly and heed his words! Suggestions my brothers?"

Many shouted out offerings and thoughts: hiring mercenaries, enlisting other magi, even consulting nations. All knew none of the suggestions would work. The Ranian desert was a world away; none of the options presented were viable. Marcum searched his mind, and finally, it came to him. Slowly, he stepped forward.

"I have an idea."

The bishop turned his head and smiled, "Please, Brother Marcum share your idea."

He cleared his throat, "There is no way for us to reach the Ranian Desert in time. Any kind of large scale magical assault could also bring harm to Azrael's pupil, which our Lord has specifically warned us against. The only option we have is to strike from within."

The bishop smiled again, "It is a desert brother, Marcum. Except for a few nomads, no one resides near Al'Zadal."

He smiled broadly now; a thin sheen of sweat on his bald head reflected the candlelight, "Oh, there are still denizens at Al'Zadal. Those who we could order to do our express bidding. They are just not of the conventional sort."

The bishop raised an eyebrow, "And who would that be Brother Marcum?"

He knew he had them now. His face gleamed brightly, "The undead."

CHAPTER 23

The cave had become their home for two days and nights. They remained there as Azrael slept like one of the dead. Jozef had questioned it; it seemed the Archmage was indeed dead at times. Isidora ensured him Azrael was merely resting. Those not of magic did not understand.

The Art was more than just incantations and components. It was more than blessings of power from the gods. The magic came from within. The wielder controlled it with his willpower and fueled its intensity with his own life-force. Isidora understood the strain that the magic put on a person's body. The minor spells she used during the attack had left her sleepy and drained. The magnitude of the spell Azrael had cast was incalculable. In all the years training under the Archmage, she had never seen him or anyone for that matter display power such as that. She wasn't even sure if anyone but a Sidhe could have the force of will to keep the formidable power of that spell in check.

She never left his side as he slept, taking care to wet his lips from a water skin and wipe sweat from his brow. He never so much as twitched. The only sign that he still lived was the slight movement of his chest as he breathed and the rapid movement beneath his eyelids. Somehow even in sleep, his mind was still active. Planning, disseminating and probing.

The only one that kept her company the entire time was Talia. Lear'Za and Jozef kept watch at the cave mouth. Gideon had been brooding since their argument before they reached Tunai. Her eyes found him on the other side of the cave. He busied himself by sharpening his sword and conversations with Kethis. A weak smile came to her lips, she was happy that he had at least found a comrade on this trip. The elf had definitely changed. It wasn't any surprise; Gideon has a way with people.

Her attention turned back to her resting mentor. Talia laid on the bedroll beside the Archmage, her small head cradled in his elbow as he slept. The pixie seemed distraught. Isidora thought back on their conversation before the attack; the pixie's feelings for Azrael outmatched even her own. Although she had grown to resent him, she still looked upon him as a father figure and not just a teacher. Talia, though, seemed to love him just for the sake of loving him. Isidora glanced over her shoulder at Gideon again; she understood how Talia felt.

Gideon's face broadened when he saw her looking his way. Isidora stretched and made her way over to the others. Sitting down next to them she let out a sigh and rubbed her eyes.

"How is he?" Gideon asked softly. He was trying to win back her graces. He could never lose them, regardless of the argument, something he still hadn't learned.

"He rests. He will continue to rest, and without warning or a hint will suddenly rise. Such is the way of magic. What were you discussing?"

His back stiffened, "The attacks by the Hollisters, it makes no sense. Despite our deep rivalry with the Spokes, I know they are honorable. This does not feel like an action Lord Hollister would take."

Kethis frowned, "Nothing the world of men surprises me," Gideon's jaw clenched, "I do not mean to insult, my friend. We elves are long-lived and have seen many of the atrocities by man and knights. You'd be surprised how quickly honor is replaced by greed and power lust."

Gideon shook his head, "Still, something isn't right about this. There are other forces at play. Either way, it seems for the first time in a very long time, the Kingdom and Luminos have a common enemy."

Kethis cocked his head to the side, "Are you proposing an alliance, Sir knight?"

"Do we have many choices, my friend? Once we exit this desert, we both have a good amount of influence in our respective lands to foster this partnership. The seeds of trust begin with us," Gideon glanced out the cave opening at Jozef, who was idly speaking to his men outside, "Has your opinion changed of that one?"

Kethis narrowed his eyes, "I still do not trust him. That attack seemed too coincidental to me. How do a hundred desert swordsmen just happen to come upon a small party at this remote location? A scouting party yes, but a whole contingent reeks of an ambush."

Gideon scratched his chin and nodded, "But why all that? Jozef and his men could have easily slit our throats while we slept. He could have simply lost us in the desert to die from the elements. Just like the Hollister attack, something about all this is off. Blast it all, why can't things be simple black and white instead of shifting shades of gray?"

"Perhaps he fears the magic, like the rest of his people," They turned their heads as Lear'Za approached and joined the conversation, "The Tunoshi, as we quickly found out, have a deep-seated fear, hatred, and mistrust of anything magical. Our party consists of two magi, a daemoness, and a pixie. Slitting throats may be too risky of an undertaking against such powers they misunderstand."

Gideon raised an eyebrow, "So, you still do not trust him either."

"I do not trust anyone who can gaze upon all this and not give it even a second glance!" Lear'Za flourished a hand at her body, "A few words with Isidora at the inn and he was smitten, yet I stand here in all my sensual glory and not so much as a sideways look!"

Gideon laughed, "Is that all you think about, daemoness? Sex and pleasures of the flesh?"

Lear'Za gave a wicked smirk, "Listen, pretty boy, even you, with your stiff honor and puppy dog adoration of Isidora, glanced my way a few times," Gideon blushed deeply, "Oh, relax. I am a living embodiment of lust. It's unavoidable. Let me give you a brief education on my people.

"My realm is far different than Tinil'Gan. It is ruled by the Hakkai Lords. We are the kings, rulers, and gods of the realm. We are born, such as you see me, fully grown and aware. We do not have childhoods. Every day is a constant battle for territory and influence. I killed 8 of my brothers after our sires passed on to secure my station."

Gideon blanched, "You killed your own kin?"

"It was kill or be killed, young knight. It is the way of my world. And we are like gods there. You can imagine the hardship the mortal denizens of my realm live with. They are like cattle to us. This is the main reason you do not understand me," Her face was somber.

"Cattle? You are right, I don't think I will ever understand how life can be so unvalued." Kethis spat with a crinkled nose.

Lear'Za's head shot up, and she hissed at the elf, "Undervalued? Is that what you think? You all use the word demon as a catch-all for anything from my realm. Tell me, elf lord, since being in our company have you seen me partake in any meals with you? Have you seen me eat at all?"

His eyes went back and forth, and he shook his head, "Now that you mention it. I...no," He stammered.

Lear'Za nodded, "Precisely. But that does not mean I have not fed. Hakkai Lords are what you describe in your lore as succubi. The only way we get nourishment is from the energy produced during copulation. Without it, we eventually perish. Our powers of seduction are similar to the calming venom of a spider. We exude a scent that is irresistible to most, and while we can limit its strength, we cannot shut it off completely. It is how we are designed. The fortunate side effect of this is my prey die peacefully and in ecstasy. They feel no pain. They only feel pain unless I want them to. Until now, only one person I have come across is completely unaffected, and that's the Archmage, and I know why. This is why the Tunoshi makes me wonder."

Kethis sighed heavily and kicked a rock in the sand, "I seem to have misjudged you. While I cannot say I am completely comfortable with your needs, I can at least be understanding," Everyone fell silent. Isidora knew most of this already, but hearing it explained in this manner made her feel for the daemoness. In many ways, she was a surrogate mother while she lived in Azrael's tower.

Gideon cleared his throat, "I am sure with how long you have known Azrael you have witnessed similar situations, Lear'Za. How much longer will the mage sleep?"

Lear'Za chuckled, "Fear not, Seer'kaat will be up and around in no time. If you had tried casting a spell like that, you wouldn't just be tired. It would have torn you apart. Give the man some credit not only for his power but for saving all our arses," A loud high pitched yelp came from the back of the cave, Lear'Za smirked, "From the sound coming from the pixie I do believe he has woken."

The three made their way to the back. Jozef also heard the sound and followed suit. They found Azrael sitting up, the pixie flying around him, displaying various colors in joy. Isidora handed him a waterskin to drink. After taking a sip he looked up at everyone, "Honestly, I was not on my deathbed. You all converge like mother hens."

Jozef smiled and cocked an eyebrow, "An impressive display, magi; Jozef thinks one unseen upon Tinil'Gan for many ages, yes?"

Azrael narrowed his mirrored eyes, "There are matters I will freely discuss with you, Master Shaddam, when it comes to our journey. Upon matters of the Art, my council is my own. If we are done with this nonsense, can we please continue our journey? We have wasted enough time due to distractions," Azrael eyed Jozef for a moment and stood up.

Jozef flashed a smile and a short bow, "Of course, magi. Jozef is here to serve, yes? Let us be on our way," With a flourish, Jozef made his way out and barked orders at his men, who quickly began loading the camels.

Without another word, the companions packed up and made their way out into the desert once more. The next few days passed by uneventfully. The only constant was the heat and the sand. Near the end of the second day, Jozef halted the small caravan and called everyone together. Gideon and Kethis shared a look of suspicion.

Jozef climbed off his camel, placed his hands on his hips, and smiled, "My friends, our destination draws near. Just over this rise, there is an outcropping that supports a tiny desert village. There are elders there I wish to consult and receive blessings from before we venture into the accursed place. As well, we may replenish our water stores."

Gideon placed his hand on his sword pommel and stared down at Jozef, "What elders do you speak of, Tunoshi, and why now? Why were we not consulted of this earlier in our journey?"

Jozef smiled once more and spread his hands, "One does not know along which path the desert dunes will lead him. Just as the dunes shift, so does the path. It just so happens the desert has given us the great fortune of placing this village in our path."

Gideon gripped his pommel harder, "I suppose these elders also happen to be nothing more than a desert coincidence as well."

Jozef flashed another smile, "The desert is a place of unpredictability, good knight. Anything that occurs here is random chance, even the actions of people."

Azrael flashed a thin-lipped smirk, "We shall go to this village. Jozef is correct. We do need to replenish our water stores."

Kethis' mouth twisted, "Lord Azrael, why do you continue to trust this man?"

"One does not live to be as old as I by making bad decisions, elf lord. Unlike the elves, I was not coddled by the safety of Luminos and its surrounding forest to keep me safe," Azrael responded over his shoulder.

Kethis snarled and spun back around towards his own camel. Gideon stood and watched the exchange and rubbed the nape of his neck. Isidora stopped over by him and placed a hand on his shoulder. Gideon looked down at her with furrowed brows, "I don't understand any of this, Isi."

Isidora looked over at Azrael and smirked. She turned back to Gideon and placed a hand on his cheek, "Although he does not speak about it, my D'ni knows something, my love. He is never rash, nor is he stupid. As infuriating as it is, we must follow his lead and trust his judgment."

Gideon nodded hesitantly, "I hope you are right, for all our sakes," Isidora walked off to her camel and Gideon watched her, smiled, and went and mounted his own camel.

The caravan headed over the dune ridge and down to the outcropping. They could see the simple dwellings made of mud bricks hardened by the sun. A village was not the right word, it seemed more of an encampment. The outcropping only supported about eight meager dwellings. In the center was a fire pit with a decent fire crackling to keep the night time chill away until the morning's blazing sun scorched the ground. Three Tunoshi desert folk sat around the fire finishing their dinner. They eyed the caravan suspiciously as it approached, their hands never far from their curved scimitars. Jozef signaled for them to halt when they arrived at a more substantial dwelling, and he dismounted, "Feel free to make yourselves at home by the fire, my friends, while I consult with the village elders and give them my greetings," Jozef entered the hut and the rest made their way to the fire.

The Tunoshi quickly muttered in their own language and departed when the group arrived. Gideon sat uncomfortably, his eyes darted around, his hand almost cramping from his tight grip on his sword pommel. Isidora sat beside him. She could feel his tenseness match her own. Talia, more and more frequently, made herself at home on Azrael's shoulder and rarely left. Isidora was so distracted by her mistrust of the encampment that she cocked an eyebrow when she realized Lear'Za was no longer among them at the fire. Jozef's men were also curiously absent. She was about to question when the beads at the entrance of the hut Jozef had entered clinked apart.

Jozef exited, smiling, as usual, followed by a very old woman. She was hunched over from visible bone deformity due to age and what seemed like a case of gout. Her hair hung about her in grayish-yellow strands that were unkempt and unclean. She lurched forward supported by a crooked walking stick that was topped with a rattle from a desert snake. It made the distinctive rattle with every step she took. As she came closer, it was apparent she was also blind; her eyes were clouded over with a severe case of cataract. The crone hobbled over to the group and shook her rattle fiercely, "Strangers in our desert! Magi! Magi!"

Jozef laughed and helped her sit, "Please sit, *Shoshana*. My friends, this is Salwai, a Shoshana or seer of the desert. She has come to bless our journey."

Kethis snorted, "That did not sound like a blessing of any sort."

Salwai shook her rattle staff forward, "Quiet, elf lord! Oh, yes. Even blind, I know who you are. All of you!" She pointed her staff at each of them, "You! Ranger you are, and nephew to the Guardian of Light! You! A knight of Castellamar! Noble blood you are! You!" Her staff stopped upon Isidora, her sightless eyes narrowed, "You are an enigma. The divines are clouded about you. An unknown quality about you there is! But magi you are! You! A pixie of the forest! What fate brings one such as you to such an arid place as this! And you! Oh yes, you, ancient Sidhe. Powerful, vain, and tragic! Oh, I know you, Lord Azrael, Thane of Qui'llah and Sircko Asacorto O'Neciel!"

Isidora stiffened. *This is wrong. This does not feel right. Where is Lear'Za?*

Azrael narrowed his eyes and leaned forward, "What do you know about Sircko Asacorto O'Neciel, crone?"

Salwai shook her rattle once more, "This I know, Sidhe. Sircko Asacorto O'Neciel, the Souls of Magic's Dawn, is no more, save for you. I know you are a bearer of the Prophecy. Our time has arrived!" Isidora's breath quickened. *What is she talking about? Someone else mentions this prophecy again. And what is this Sircko Asacorto O'Neciel?* She looked to Gideon and Kethis, their stiff postures mirrored her feelings. A look between the three confirmed it. Tension filled the air, hands near weapons, spell on lips. They eyed Azrael and waited for some kind of cue, but the Archmage sat motionless and completely calm. But they did notice Jozef standing near the crone with his hand on his scimitar.

Azrael's smirk grew wider. He removed his hood, and the fire reflected off his mirrored eyes, "Well, then. You are a real Shoshana. Do what you feel you must. Stand by the courage of your conviction!" Azrael remained calm and loose, his hands folded in his sleeves.

The crone laughed a wild cackling octave, "You think you will succeed, Sidhe? You think you can stand before the might of a god! The Prophecy will devour you! Leto's will shall come to pass! What has become of your kind, Thane of Qui'llah? Where has their power gone? You are a relic, a lingering memory of a dead race!" The crone paused for a moment; her eyes darted around, and her head tilted, "How can this be? There is another?" The crone shook her head and steadied her eyes on Azrael, "It matters not! The time has come for you to join them!"

As one, they all stood weapons ready, except for Azrael. In a blink of an eye, Kethis notched his bow just as Isidora cast a firebolt spell.

The crone shrieked—not in pain but instead in laughter. A glowing golden aura surrounded her. The firebolt withered and died as it came in contact with the aura, "Aha! *Allom shellak ak ber!*"

Time froze. They were all conscious and aware but could not move. Gideon stood as if frozen in ice, sword in hand. Kethis' bow still pointed at his target. Isidora was immobile, mouth open, hand outstretched for another spell. Even Talia froze on Azrael's shoulder, stuck in an orange panic glow. All were frozen in place except for Azrael.

"Your magi spells have no effect on me fools! My god protects me!" said the crone.

Azrael laughed, "Leto does give his acolytes interesting prayer spells. Come now, Shoshana. Freezing my companions in place is certainly not all you intend. Do it!"

"Arrogant Sidhe! Vile Sidhe! Now you die!" The crone raised her staff, at the bottom was revealed a wickedly sharp blade that she swung in an arc towards the Archmage. Azrael sat calmly as it approached his neck. An instant before it appeared to be about to remove his head a blade shot out and blocked its descent with a clang. The curved blade whirled around at a dramatic speed and removed the crone's head from her body. Azrael lifted his chin, "Perhaps your god should also protect you from blades."

Jozef wiped his scimitar on the crone's tattered clothing as her head rolled near the fire.

The containing prayer spell broke with her death and Isidora, Gideon, Kethis, and Talia sprung to life once again. They began to fall on Jozef. With a shout, Azrael stopped them.

"So, *Beduiin*, you knew?" Jozef smiled, using the old Tunoshi word for magi.

"That I did, Master Shaddam."

"You realize then I had to be sure, no?" Jozef spread his hands.

"Certainly. As did I."

Jozef rubbed his chin, "And my men?"

Azrael cocked his head over Jozef's shoulder. The sell-sword turned around as Lear'Za floated out of the shadows, "They were...indisposed," The daemoness gave a wicked grin, "I really needed that. Oh, and so there isn't any confusion, indisposed means I had my fun, and they are dead. I was even able to convince them to take care of the few Tunoshi guards the crone had around before we enjoyed ourselves."

Jozef waved a hand dismissively then crossed his arms, "It is a shame. They were good men, but men nonetheless, and replaceable."

Everyone watched the exchange in confusion and disbelief. Gideon stood, his mouth agape, "What in the abyss is going on here?"

Azrael replaced his hood upon his head, "Forgive me for the secrecy, but it was necessary. We were brought into this desert to die."

CHAPTER 24

Gideon's face reddened, "What! This is an outrage! I can't believe what I am hearing! You knew and intentionally kept us in the dark?"

Isidora grabbed Gideon's arm. Her words were icy but calm, "I am sure Azrael had his reasons, Gideon. Let him explain. There is a reason, D'ni, is there not?"

"Of course, there is a reason. We are quite alive and well. I knew the moment Jozef approached us with the Silver Sword's offer we were not meant to leave the desert alive."

Kethis shook his head, "I do not mean to insult, Archmage, but why take his offer?"

"In truth, I suspected Jozef had his own motives as well; motives that went beyond the Silver Sword and Tunoshi superstition."

Jozef cocked an eyebrow, "This I have yet to figure out, Beduiin. How did you come to know this?"

"If you must know, it was completely by chance. Back at the inn when you made your proposal, I caught a glimpse of the tattoo on your arm."

Jozef laughed and clapped his hands, "Aha! You indeed are an observant one, Beduiin."

Gideon sat down and placed his head in his hands, "A tattoo? You risked all our lives based on a tattoo?"

Jozef gave a slight smile and patted Gideon on the shoulder before sitting himself, "It is what the tattoo represents, young knight. As you all have known, we Tunoshi were at one time Ranian. We had a kingdom, power, might, friends, and enemies. One of the reasons the Tunoshi distrust the magi as much as they do is because they were once our greatest allies; specifically the Sidhe. The Sidhe had great power but numbered few. The Ranian royal family was the Sidhe's sworn protectors. They defended them when magic could not. They were the Shaidaheen."

Gideon raised his head, and his eyes grew wide, "Wait. Then that means Jozef…Jozef is…"

The corner of Azrael's lip curled upward as he finished Gideon's sentence, "Shaidaheen. The tattoo he has represents one of the order. That also means he is Prince Shaddam, descendant and last of the Royal House of Rania."

Jozef gave a slight bow, "Everything Beduiin speaks is true. After his amazing display of power, I already believed. I just needed the confirmation of the Shoshana. As for my men, they were an unfortunate loss. The Silver Sword honors itself on keeping its contracts. The fact I am breaking a contract by not killing you all would not sit well with my subordinates. I could not allow the men that came here to inform the rest. Lear'Za saved me the trouble."

Isidora paced furiously, "This is more than once now I have heard mention of a prophecy, D'ni. What are you not telling us? What of this Sircko Asacorto O'Neciel she mentioned?"

Azrael nodded, "Indeed, and she was correct. I was a member of Sircko Asacorto O'Neciel. In the language of the Sidhe; Souls of Magic's Dawn. Jozef's tattoo is made of Sidhe runes representing it. The Sidhe swore fealty to Rania and provided the kingdom with magical might in its endeavors. I am presently the last and only surviving member."

Isidora crossed her arms, "And the prophecy?"

Lear'Za looked over at Azrael and stared at him. Azrael sighed, "Isidora, there are forces at play that have been in motion for eons. I can tell you this much. Yes, there is a prophecy; one that despite my best efforts is beginning to involve more people than I had wished. I suppose I should not be surprised. The sole intent of a prophecy is to play out regardless of anyone's efforts. Sircko Asacorto O'Neciel is more than just the Sidhe who pledged to Rania. It has a far more important and ancient history. They preserved the balance. The balance of power between the gods. The Sidhe understood this balance more than any other race, and this purpose is more important now than ever. That time has returned."

Kethis shook his head wearily, "This prophecy includes the God Leto, as well. Am I correct, Lord Azrael? This crone was a priestess?"

Azrael's mirrored eyes narrowed to mere slits, "Unfortunately it does, which is why we must tread carefully. The prophecy speaks of the eventual rise of an Harbinger of Chaos. A powerful pawn to spread Leto's word and dominion over the realm. Leto has eyes and ears all across Tinil'Gan. Events are moving much too quickly. It began with our delay in Luminos, then the Nidhogg, Cerridwen's involvement and now this crone, not to mention the fortuitous meeting with the last Shaidaheen in all of Tinil'Gan. I would not be surprised if the recent news of impending war is a side effect of Leto's plans. The world we know is changing," Azrael paused and sighed, "This is why I must ask this of you all now. Despite my grasping for control, it is going to involve you all regardless of my endeavors to prevent it. A new day for the Souls of Magic's Dawn begins here. It requires your oaths to preserve the balance. I do not ask this lightly. Do you all accept?"

Jozef smiled. Solemnly he dropped to one knee before Azrael and held out his scimitar before him, "This should be of no surprise. Beduiin ack Sircko Asacorto O'Neciel, I Jozef Shaddam, prince of a dead kingdom and sole remnant of the Shaidaheen, pledge my life and sword to your service and protection."

Lear'Za chuckled, "I've been by your side in this before any of them were even born; you know where I stand. Not like I have anything better to do with my time."

Talia's glow was muted on Azrael's shoulder. Her eyes were cast low, and she spoke softly, "I think we should all go home and forget this place. But what do I know, I am just a silly pixie anyway. I will go wherever you lead us Azrael. Even if it means continuing to travel with dumb-dumb over there," Talia looked over at Lear'Za and stuck her tongue out at her.

Kethis was looking down in thought. When he lifted his head, his face was solemn, "The purpose given to me by Cerridwen and this one are intimately joined. Providence has brought me here, I cannot refuse its call."

Gideon and Isidora looked at each other.

"You know how I feel. I will be wherever you need me to be. Even if I have my reservations. But this sounds serious," Gideon said to her.

Isidora shook her head and then looked up at Azrael, "I still feel we are not being told everything. Secretive you may be, but a liar and exaggerator you are not. We are with you D'ni."

"Very well, then. Hold out your right arms."

They all positioned themselves in a circle and placed their arms in the middle. Talia remained on his shoulder but stuck out her tiny arm as well. Azrael murmured arcane words in the language of the Sidhe, and his eyes shone brightly. A glowing ember of magic materialized on each of their forearms. It zigzagged back and forth across their skin with a sizzle that caused no pain. After a moment it ceased and disappeared. In its place were duplicate markings of the three runes Jozef had on his arm.

Azrael ended his chanting and looked around at each of them, "This is not an oath to me. It is not an oath to any kingdom. Even if it is not apparent now, even if faith is lost in the future, the truth will eventually reveal itself for each of your greater purposes. It is an oath you may not realize until the final moment. It will be one that is undeniable and irrefutable. Welcome to the order of Sircko Asacorto O'Neciel. Welcome to the Souls of Magic's Dawn."

"Do not let us down D'ni," Isidora said firmly.

Jozef cut the tension of the impromptu ceremony, "There is another matter I need to bring up. Our meeting is not as coincidental as it seems, Beduiin. My contract to end your little quest was with another mage."

Azrael arched an eyebrow, "Was this mage of the black robes as well?" Jozef nodded affirmatively, "It seems the mage Talia bumped into on the Isle of Winds, the perpetrator of the Nidhogg, has also found his way to the desert. This stinks of Diarmuid. Everything is starting to piece together."

Kethis frowned, "I fear you may be correct, Lord Azrael. Diarmuid holds much sway in my uncle's court."

"That he does, Kethis," Azrael said, "Far too much for my liking. I'm not yet certain, but I am beginning to see a pattern here than bodes ill for not just us, but the rest of the Evening Lands. However, presently, our only concern is reaching Al' Zadal. We have wasted enough time. We should continue on our way."

Everyone nodded and made their way back to their camels. Gideon remained behind and approached Azrael.

"I know I have been argumentative Archmagus. I will not make any bones about it, I do not know if I can completely trust you. Isidora still does. That is why I am here. Break her trust, and you lose mine, regardless of this tattoo," The knight's voice was stern.

"As I said, the oath is not to me. You owe me no allegiance. The only allegiance that mark holds you to is your own conscious of what is right."

"Let us hope that is the case." Gideon started to turn away but remembered one more thing, "Oh, the crone called you a Thane. Thane of Qui'llah. What of this?"

"A long-dead place Sir knight. One you will not find in any tome or histories told by man."

Gideon shook his head and walked away. Azrael's mirrored eyes looked up at the clear night sky at the constellations of the gods overhead. They fixed on the needleless compass formation of Leto. *You have your schemes and your multitude doing your bidding. But I have providence on my side. How could you, Lord of Chaos, have overlooked a Shaidaheen? You err, which means my machinations are not in vain.* A static storm raged suddenly in the sky, lightning arcing from one small cloud to the next, then died out slowly.

CHAPTER 25

The castle was a buzz of activity. Sulik calmly walked through the courtyard at a leisurely pace as pages, squires, and servants ran to and fro at the behest of their lords. The news had reached San'Seban of the taking of Granary and the inglorious end of Lord Marken. The whole of the capital knew of the Hollister's treachery and the open act of war perpetrated by the Spokes.

He made his way to the council chambers; of course, an emergency meeting had been called. When he arrived, fashionably late, as usual, all were present. The mood in the room was somber considering the circumstances of the meeting. Sulik had to muster every bit of willpower he had to stop from smiling. He sat in his seat and waited for others to begin the conversation.

Sir Mallister snorted, "Thank you for gracing us with your presence, Realm Regent. It is not like we are in a state of emergency!"

Sulik nodded his head and spread his hands on the table, "I do apologize for the delay. When I heard the news, the first thing I did was to stop at the temple to offer a prayer for the late Lord Marken and his family," Sir Mallister snorted once again. Sulik ignored it, "However, I did warn this council of the impending treachery of the Riverlords. Correct me if I err, Sir Mallister, but I do believe it was you who cautioned against any preventative action and asked us to trust our southron neighbors. That does not look well. It could appear to some, almost complicit."

Sir Mallister's face grew an angry shade of plum, "Do not place these atrocities at my feet, Sulik! Regardless of your maneuvering, my honest loyalty has always been and always shall be to this Kingdom and its people! Regardless of my own personal ambitions!"

King Diomere coughed slightly to end the outburst, "My friends, we are in a time of peril. Now is not the time for petty bickering amongst ourselves. Although we may disagree, I am sure all of our intents are for the protection and betterment of the realm. Sir Mallister, the Regent is correct in one thing: he warned us," Sir Mallister gritted his teeth, "Now, now, Mallister. This does not mean you did anything wrong. I agreed with your sentiment, so if you are a traitor so is the King! No, if anything Lord Sulik just had a better intuition on the matter, which is the primary reason he is Realm Regent. He tends to look at things pragmatically as opposed to sentimentally. Now we must decide on a course of action. What do we know?"

Sulik gave a slight smile; he was afforded this at the moment, and took advantage of it. He cleared his throat and unfurled the stack of papers he had brought, "What we do know as far as facts are this: the stygian owl of House Hollister flies above the keep at Granary. Lord Marken, his kin, and his household have been murdered, and Lord Marken's head sits atop a pike upon the keep walls. As for the attack itself, we have little information. They came at dawn, and within an hour Granary was overrun. Since then, they have barred the keep walls, and no one from Granary has been allowed out. We have received no emissary for Lord Hollister on the matter."

King Diomere shook his head and dropped his weary head in his hand, "Lord Marken and I used to play together as children. He was an old friend and a good ally. The realm will be a lesser place without him and his house."

Sulik bowed his head in mock remembrance, then turned to Lord Medici to prompt him. The fat lord, sweating as usual, leaned forward.

"If I may, my Lord, there is good news as well. As we decided previously, I have sent word to Hardhall and Evanfall. Both have returned fruitful. Both Lords are receptive to talks, and certainly, this heinous act by their fellow Riverlord will only bolster their conviction. It is safe to say we have the Condrites and Bargemans on our side. Also as a side note, Lord Hollister's ambitions seem to be broader than even we imagined. There is word that they also march towards Luminos."

Sulik's head jerked up. He stared down the fat Whisper Master, "This is indeed remarkable and interesting news, Lord Medici."

Filobar smiled broadly. He gave Sulik a quick wink to assure him all was under control, "Yes. Apparently, by some miraculous means, the Guardian's nephew Kethis alerted him of the attack. It is still unknown how he came by this information, as he is all the way out in the Ranian desert, but it came in time for the elves to mobilize to meet them."

Sulik suppressed the rage seething inside. *Kethis? This means Gideon knows as well. Why are they not dead yet?* "Fortunate indeed," He managed a smile.

"Kethis is the one traveling with my nephew Sir Gideon, is he not?" Diomere chimed in, "In this time of tragedy, at least I can take solace in the fact he is well. What do the elves think of this?"

Filobar leaned back and placed his hands on his belly, "I have word that, in the face of this heinous act, the elves are receptive to working in cooperation with the Kingdom. The list of our allies grows, my Lord," Filobar managed a sly grin at Sulik.

Sulik sighed in some relief, "It is evident we must take immediate action. The houses of Castellamar must raise their banners and face this threat."

Mallister adjusted his armor and grunted, "As much as I hate this, the Realm Regent is correct."

"Then, Sir Montefroy, I trust your feal houses will be contacted."

"They already have Sulik. They prepare as we speak. However, we shall not forget our honor and knightly oaths. Before any blood is spilled, we shall parlay with Lord Hollister," Mallister smiled broadly.

Lord Tempest, who had remained quiet the entire time playing with his dagger, sat forward, "You wish to parlay with those dishonorable and barbaric southrons? They don't deserve the courtesy. They placed Marken's head on a pike for gods' sake!"

Sulik leaned forward to speak but was cut short by the King, "Our knights are the Saoirse Le Vey, the Stars' Honor. Just because the Riverlord chooses to forget his oaths and measures does not mean we should, Lord Tempest. I believe Sir Montefroy is correct. Let us mourn our friend Lord Marken for the required three days. After that time the banners will be officially rallied. In a week's time, we will find a suitable envoy to send to Lord Hollister and pray the Riverlord sees the error in his folly."

"As always, my King Brother is wise. I shall make the necessary plans for the mourning period as well as the envoy team." Sulik pressed his lips.

Diomere smiled wearily, "Then we are in agreement. I will take my leave of you, my Lords. Pending any new developments, we shall meet in a week," Diomere rose, and the ever quiet and vigilant Sir Falco escorted him out without a glance at his other brother or the rest of the council.

With a grunt, Mallister followed suit and left in a clank of armor. Once the King and Mallister had departed the chambers, Sulik's smile fell to a snarl. He stood and slammed his fist on the table, "What in the name of the gods were you thinking, Filobar? Why did you not bring me the information about the Elves and Kethis immediately?"

The Whisper Master smiled and lifted his considerable girth from his seat to stand before Sulik eye to eye, "I do believe the good Lord forgets his tone. I only received the missive sent for you from Diarmuid this morning. You were indisposed at the time, and I felt this could be important news, as it was," He took a moment to catch his breath. Sulik also noticed the fat man's attempt to be intimidating, "We may be on the same side in this endeavor, but do not forget that I am a Lord of a great house, not one of your servants."

Sulik's lip quivered. He composed himself and adjusted his tunic, "I apologize if I have offended you, Lord Medici. Sometimes my passion for organization is mistaken for arrogance. However, you are correct, my good Lord. You are not one of my servants," Sulik's face grew hard, and he slowly stepped forward, making Filobar take a few steps back, "My servants do my bidding without hope of reward. They do it without question because they know they have something to lose. They know I hold their lives in my hand. You see, when you have nothing left to lose but your life, you treasure that last remaining thing and become grateful you have it. However, when you have more to lose, when you are comfortable with your station, you tend to grow complacent and forget who gave you those comforts," Filobar was pushed back by Sulik's advance step by step, until the fat man stumbled backward on the steps of the dais and fell unceremoniously onto his arse. He looked up at Sulik from the ground. Sulik placed his hands behind his back and tilted his head down at Filobar, "Your great house is great because of me, Filobar. Do not forget that. I made you Whisper Master; I gave my daughter to your brother, Sir Lorance. With a word, it can all be gone. Your position, your house's new esteem in the realm, even my dear daughter could sadly become a young widow, should some unfortunate accident happen to your brother. A widow who would be highly valued by some other house, more grateful for the chance you had been given," Filobar visibly paled, "Now, if there is anything else I should know about the Elvan situation, speak it now."

The chastised Whisper Master cleared his throat and unevenly lifted himself from the dais steps. As he wobbled to his feet, he smoothed his robes, "The situation is well under control, Realm Regent. I have assurances from Diarmuid that the Guardian is indeed receptive to an alliance with the Kingdom. If anything, the elves learning about the force headed its way has helped our cause. If attacked unawares, the elves most likely would have moved against the Spokes before we were prepared and without an alliance offer. They could have even moved against our own men on the battlefield, considering us no better than the Riverlords. Giasis hopes to send his nephew Kethis here to Castellamar when he returns from his foray in the desert with your nephew and his wife."

Sulik snorted, "My nephew. I thought Diarmuid had that situation underhand as well? Should they not be long from the living by now?"

Filobar shrugged, "What do I know of the way of magi, my Lord Regent? He assures me that the group of travelers, including your nephew, will not make it out of the desert alive."

"For your sake, I hope they do not, Whisper Master. It was you who brokered this alliance with Diarmuid, and I will hold you responsible if he does not produce results. If Kethis knows about the taking of Granary and the march on Elvan lands that means Sir Gideon does as well. If he returns to Castellamar alive, he will prove to be a thorn in my side and could disrupt our endeavors. If that comes to pass, more than just your pride and your arse will be bruised," Without another word Sulik turned and left the council chambers.

Lord Tempest let out a little laugh, and Filobar scowled at him, "What is so funny, Humboldt?"

The flame-haired lord stood and gathered his things, "For the life of me, I do not know why you wish to challenge that man. The blood in his veins is colder than the stores of wine in the Medici cellars. Mules should not aspire to be fine riding horses. Be content with being the mule he prizes over the rest of the asses," With a snicker Lord Tempest made his way out, leaving Filobar alone in the silence of the council chambers.

CHAPTER 26

"Amazing," Gideon said with a whistle, "To think there used to be a thriving, bustling city here," All around stretched the vast desert, but before them, reaching out of the sands, stood broken monuments, pillars of ancient buildings; the ruins of Al'Zadal. There was even a statue's head sitting upon the sands. Isidora approached the large statue head and knelt on one knee to study it; closer inspection revealed it was not sitting on the sands but rather the statue was buried up to the neck.

The craftsmanship was remarkably exquisite; beautiful marble brought to life. The statue was female and attractive; the curve of the full lips, the slight nose, and the sad eyes. It was as if the figure knew the tragic fate that had befallen its city. Isidora turned her head to call the others' attention to it when she spotted Azrael. The mage was standing before a crooked, half-buried obelisk carved from hard black basalt. He seemed transfixed, his mirrored eyes scanning the ancient marking and hieroglyphs etched into the stone. The rest of the group also noticed and congregated around him. Isidora stood and brushed the sand off her knees and made her way over as well.

Talia flittered over and landed on his shoulder, "What does it say, Azrael?"

The Archmage said nothing for a few moments then his voice came out almost in a whisper, "It is a hymn in archaic Ranian. It reads, "Shining Rania, blessed Rania, favorite of our God Leto. Let chaos bring peace and may His enemies whither and perish. Woe to any who defy the will of the Golden God," He stopped again, then shook his head, "The rest is buried in the sand."

Talia frowned and her glow was a muted, mourning purple, "We do not have to do this. We should leave. I'm sure Isidora can find an avatar somewhere else!"

Jozef laughed heartily, "Nonsense, small one. Jozef did not lead you all across this desert to merely turn away when we have arrived at our destination. Enter, we shall. Anything that has ever roamed these halls has been dead for centuries. The worst we have to fear is scorpions and desert snakes."

"You don't understand. None of you do!" Talia shot into the air and fluttered around angrily. Isidora frowned at Talia's display. She had sensed her uneasiness since her encounter with Cerridwen's court in the forest and still could not make anything of it, even after their talk.

"Let us not waste away in this heat. Lead the way, Master Shaddam, and let us be done with this," Azrael said.

"Certainly, Beduiin. Right up ahead is the temple itself. Centuries ago, fortune hunters carved an entrance into what was once a high wall of the temple. What we are actually looking at would have been many stories above the ground floor. All of it buried in the sands now. There is a tunnel that winds its way down into the temple proper passing through a few alcoves and chambers. Follow Jozef."

After a short walk, they arrived at what was once the magnificent Temple of Al'Zadal. Even centuries after its devastation and regular wear from sandstorms, the partial wall that jutted up from the sands appeared new. The massive limestone bricks were perfectly aligned. The seams were perfectly fit, one could not even slip a sheet of parchment between them.

Kethis approached the wall and ran a hand across it, "This is remarkable. Ranian architecture and mason skill must rival that of the reclusive dwarves."

Jozef beamed, "That is because it does, elf lord. Dwarves were not always as reclusive as they are now. Ranian masons once studied under dwarven masters. Legends state this city was at one time a sight to behold. The main thoroughfare was a walled processional that led into the city. A visitor would pass by wonderful statues and murals depicting the gods and legendary events. It led up to one of the wonders of Al'Zadal, the Al'Galad Gate. The legends say it stood five stories tall, constructed from colored limestone and bedecked with inlays of lapis lazuli and pearl. And this was just the entrance! But, alas, all good things must come to an end, no? Ah, here is the entrance. The sands have almost buried it."

Jozef dropped to his knees and dug away some of the sand, revealing an entrance. It was nothing more than a man-sized opening created by knocking away loose bricks. Between the rubble and fallen sands, a natural ramp was formed, "We can easily walk down to the first chambers. Torches were packed in your camel bags. Let us light them and walk into the past," Jozef said.

They each grabbed a torch and, one by one, lit them and crawled through the dark, ragged hole into the Temple of Al'Zadal. Jozef was correct. A somewhat steep but walkable mound of debris and sand made a natural ramp from what was a hole in a higher part of the outside wall. It appeared where they currently walked was not yet a room but rather the interior of a wall. After a few minutes, they reached another broken hole in the stone which led into the first of the chambers Jozef spoke about.

The first thing Isidora noted was the utter silence of the place. The only the sound was the soft scraping of their boots on the sand as it echoed around them. Other than that, the site seemed a tomb. She noted to herself that it had, indeed, become a tomb. The chamber itself was circular. Through openings in the sifting sand on the floor, mosaic tile could be seen. The walls had rusted sconces where torches once lit the room. On one section of the wall, a tattered tapestry hung from one hook, and in the center of the room stood a bare pedestal with broken fragments of pottery upon it. Kethis looked around solemnly and picked at the pottery fragments, "This must have been an offering room for the priests to leave their alms."

Jozef was studying the tapestry and smiled, "Correct you are, elf lord. They would come to this room throughout the day, bearing herbs and sacrifices to their god. The pedestal there held a bowl filled with their sacrifices."

Gideon grimaced and threw down a pottery shard he had picked up and wiped his hands together, "Leto was the primary god the Ranians prayed to?"

Lear'Za glanced over at Azrael. Azrael shot her back a look of silence, "It matters not. Let's continue."

Gideon looked at Isidora questioningly. She shrugged her shoulders and followed Azrael and Jozef out into another corridor. For a good amount of time, it was repetitive. A passage, another chamber, more corridors, more chambers, each slightly different. Kethis sneezed from some dust that drifted and groaned, "Do we even know where we are headed?"

Jozef chuckled and spoke over his shoulder as they approached a new chamber, "Our magi friends here have told me they seek the avatar of this so-called Castellarian hero. The epicenter of the tragedy that happened here took place in the center courtyard of the temple. That would be deep inside, on what was once the ground floor."

"Pray the gods we get there soon, before we all suffocate from this dust and stagnant air," Kethis' face was noticeably pale. Elves were accustomed to outdoor life. Places like a buried temple left him uneasy. But even his eyes opened in awe when they entered the next chamber.

Unlike the rest of the rooms that had standard ceilings, if this one had a ceiling, it was so high it could not be made out in the darkness. The room was octagonal, and each of the eight walls featured alcoves that encompassed the room and continued upwards into the darkness. How far, Isidora was unable to tell. It was high enough that wherever the ceiling was, it was shrouded in shadow. Azrael looked up and frowned, "Burial crypts, hundreds if not thousands of them."

Jozef gave a quick murmur of prayer and made some solemn hand gestures. The usual smile on his face was gone, replaced by a more somber look, "Correct you are, Beduiin. These crypts house the remains of every priest and temple guard since it was built. It is indeed a wonder."

"Perhaps you may want to rephrase that, Jozef," Lear'Za said with a slight edge of warning in her voice, "I do not think the word 'remains' is appropriate. Remains should remain where they are. These do not."

Isidora turned towards Lear'Za, "What in the god's name are you talking about..." The rest of her sentence was cut short by a quick gasp. There was indeed stirring in the crypts. Isidora watched in horror as, slowly, a bony foot emerged. It was soon followed by skeletal fingers. The companions huddled together in the middle of the room with their backs to each other, frozen in terror. It started with just a few, but quickly every single crypt came to life, the skeletons of the dead rising and crawling out.

They began to spill out even from the vaults high overhead, the skeletons falling to the ground in a clank of bones, and then rising once again.

Gideon unsheathed his sword, his gaze fixed on the fearful sight, "What in the name of the gods are they?"

Azrael's mirrored eyes reflected the torchlight, "Liches," With that one word, all the companions drew their weapons and readied spells to defend themselves from what was now a skeletal horde, armed with rusted swords and broken staves.

The fleshless faces of the liches stared at them with empty eye sockets and slack, gaping jaws, their probing, skinny white fingers reaching out for their warm flesh. Talia erupted in screams and flew around the room, flashing an orange warning glow, "No! No! She was right! This is not fair!"

They approached slowly but steadily. As one, the companions struck out in defense. Gideon's sword flashed out and smashed across the bones of the closest lich, shattering it into a clanking mess. He followed his slash with another and another, felling lich after lich. He yelled over the din of clattering bones, "Why are there liches here? In a temple of all places! We did nothing to disturb them, and I am sure we are not the first to venture into this chamber!"

He stopped slashing for a moment to catch his breath, and his eyes grew wide when the pile of bones he had just dismembered clanked back together and rose up again. It pointed its boney finger, and a disembodied voice erupted from its open jaw.

YOU WILL DIE URSURPERS AND HERETICS! OUR GOD LETO DEMANDS IT! DEATH TO THE SIDHE! DEATH TO THE SIDHE!

Lear'Za's flaming sword smashed through her closest enemy, "Does that answer your question?"

Isidora cast as many spells as she could in quick succession. Glancing over, she saw Azrael, his eyes widened as he cast his spells, destroying lich after lich. Although they attacked the group as a whole, their efforts seemed to converge on him, and they steered clear of her. She brought herself near him to assist as best she could. As they drew closer and closer she could hear their ethereal voices whispering. *You will never be good enough. You will never be strong enough. Give up. Give up.*

For the first time in her life, Isidora could see Azrael panic. His spells never faltered; he remained in control of his power and kept blasting away, but his eyes were wide and his breathing heavy.

Talia flew around in a frenzy. Lost and confused, tears streaked her face. *What can I do?* Through sobs, all she could muster was one shout, "Run!"

Outnumbered and surrounded, they saw the wisdom in Talia's scream. Kethis slashed a path to the next corridor. They ran for it, out of the chamber down the corridor. Isidora scanned the passage as they ran noticing chunks of debris and broken statues. She stopped, "Everyone, stand back," They all walked by her and stood a few feet away.

Once everyone had passed, she concentrated and murmured the same incantation she did in Azrael's library. A violet summoning circle appeared and, as before, Lelani materialized. The translucent fox shook itself and hopped around cheerily. Isidora smiled, "Lelani, we need this blocked off. Use the power of whirlwind," The fox bounced around happily, then it began to run across the corridor widthwise. Its trajectory carried it up the wall, across the ceiling, down the other wall and back to the floor. Its trot sped up dramatically, and the fox became a violet blur, creating a violent wind tossing sand and dust all around. The wind coalesced and began dragging up and throwing more massive boulders and debris into the center of the vortex. When the dust settled, the entire corridor behind them was walled off by rubble. Isidora gave Lelani a pet, and with a wave of her hand dismissed the summoned avatar.

Lear'Za laughed, "And here I thought it was nothing more than a pretty pet."

Kethis walked away from them a little further down the corridor. He shook his head. The long and straight passage ended at a blank wall, "We have stopped them, but we also may have created our own tomb," The elf said somberly.

Isidora's shoulders slumped, and she sighed. *I hadn't even thought of what could lie ahead. I just needed to stop the liches.*

"Um, we have bigger problems," Gideon said, interrupting her thoughts.

Isidora spoke through heavy breaths, "Now what?" The wall of debris created by Lelani began to shake. Dust and pebbles ran down it to the floor. Suddenly a skeletal arm broke through the center of the debris wall, and then another, "You have to be kidding," she said dejectedly.

Jozef's eyes scanned the wall at the end of the passage quickly and frantically. He ran his hands over the smooth stone and narrowed his eyes. He slowly probed the wall until he reached the center and pushed on the brick. With a scraping sound, a hidden door slid open, revealing another chamber. They ran into the other end of the room and caught their breath. The liches were slow, but they could hear them breaking through the debris wall.

Gideon leaned his back against a wall and tilted his head back, catching his breath, "There are too many of them. It does not help that they reanimate after you destroy them. We may have found this room, but we can't seal the door from inside."

Kethis was stooped over his hands resting on his knees, breathing heavily, "Nothing to fear you said, Shaddam? You have led us to our doom!"

Jozef seethed, "I have led you where you have asked to go!"

Azrael gritted his teeth and gave a shout, silencing them, "Kethis, this is not Jozef's fault. We are where we set out to be. We all accepted the dangers and came here, regardless."

Kethis sneered, "Yet none of us brought down the ire of a god except for you! You heard them. Death to the Sidhe! What have you done, Lord Azrael, to have a god hate you so?"

They all began to bicker and yell. Talia floated overhead and watched in tears. None could hear her tiny sobs over their shouts. She glanced back down the corridor and saw the liches knock the last of the debris wall down and start clanking and clamoring through. Her face fell into her hands for one final sob. *She tried to prepare me. She told me this would happen. I tried to warn them, Tilene! They wouldn't listen!* Then, slowly, she lifted her head and dried her tears with her arm and sniffed. She knew what she had to do. She took a deep shuddering breath and flittered out into the corridor towards the liches.

Isidora shook her head in frustration as the others argued. She turned around in disgust and noticed Talia. With a gasp, she shouted, "Talia! What are you doing!" The rest of the companions heard Isidora's shout and, argument forgotten, ran towards the opening.

Azrael removed his hood and stepped forward. It all became clear. With all his powers of deduction and wit, this had escaped him. It had escaped everyone. Talia's sadness after speaking to Tilene in the forest court and her growing melancholy the remainder of the trip. It never occurred to anyone what could make a pixie so sad, but Talia was not like other pixies. This particular pixie was in love. Azrael did not scream or shout, but his voice was firm, "Talia."

The pixie stopped her progress and turned around, facing them in the chamber. She no longer cried yet her face still had reminders of her tears. Her eyes were red and swollen, but she smiled, "its ok Azrael. This is how it has to be," She looked down at the tattoo on her small arm and smiled. "As you said, when we see it we'll know what the right thing to do is."

"No, it isn't, Talia. You don't have to do this. Come back," Azrael said

But I do. There is no other way. Talia smiled again and held back a sob, "No, my love. Tilene warned me that this would come to pass. She told me you would die here. This is where your mission would come to an end. Unless I made a choice," She floated forward, just to the entrance of the corridor. She closed her eyes and shimmered. Slowly, she grew and stood before them as a full-grown woman with wings. The cuteness Talia always possessed in her minute size had been transformed. When they saw her in their size, her beauty shone. Isidora placed her hand over her mouth and held back tears. Talia brought her hand up and put it on Azrael's cheek, "No, my love, it has to be this way. This is the only way to save you, and Tilene knew I was the only one capable of it."

Azrael bowed his head and shook it, "There are too many. Their essence will consume you."

Talia smiled once again, and a tear ran down her cheek, "She knew that, as a pixie, I can absorb all these souls. Yes, there are many, far too many for me to contain and take to their final resting place. But I have enough power to remove them from *this* place. She also knew how much I love you and that I would be willing to make this sacrifice," She looked over her shoulder at the approaching horde and sighed. "I've always loved you, Azrael. I know I never had your heart, but that doesn't matter. I love you enough for both of us. Goodbye, my darling," Talia leaned forward and gave Azrael a small kiss on the cheek.

She turned and walked back into the corridor. The liches were mere feet away. She turned to the companions one final time and began to glow radiantly. With a smile and a wink, she reached forward and pressed the brick closing the secret door. As the door started to close, they saw her light grow brighter, and the liches close around her whispering, *yesssss, take us home. Take us home.*

Azrael shouted out, his voice shattered, "Talia no!"

The door slammed shut. Her light went out.

CHAPTER 27

There are things in life that terrify men, rouse them from their sleep in a cold sweat, make their hearts beat too fast and, with eyes wide open in the dark, inspire them to whisper a small prayer to the gods, thankful that it was just a nightmare. Once the terror fades, they lay their head back down to rest. But what happens when nightmares become real? Where does one turn when terror no longer becomes a thing of dreams but a living, a palpable presence that grips you and will not let go until, finally, your life passes from you just to escape from the mind-numbing fear? Where does one turn when the gods have damned you? Where does one turn when you have angered your god?

Loyal Marcum, quick-witted Marcum, pious and faithful Marcum learned this quicker than he ever thought. It began shortly after he went to sleep. It started as a cold, crawling feeling on his skin. It worked its way up in a frightening tingle, completely immobilizing his muscles. It numbed him so much he could not even scream out. It became more apparent when the room shifted from complete darkness to a glorious and alarming golden glow that blinded him. But also let him see more clearly than he had ever seen before.

He knew then his plan had failed. The Sidhe had not perished as planned. The horde of undead the acolytes had called from their slumber in Al'Zadal did not do as instructed. Unable to speak, he screamed out in his mind: *Why? No one could have escaped that! The liches always do as commanded when raised by the faithful! I did my best, my Lord! How? How!*

His mind quieted, and he heard the voice of the god as if it were his own thoughts.

YOU FAILED ME, MARCUM. YOU ASK HOW? A PIXIE! A DAMNABLE PIXIE! ARE MY ACOLYTES SO INCOMPETENT THAT THEY ALLOW A PIXIE TO THWART MY PLANS?

The voice of the god Leto slowed into a low murmur and rumble that made him feel like his skull was exploding. Unable to cry out, he just stared wide-eyed with tears streaming down his face.

THE SIDHE LIVES. ALL BECAUSE OF A PIXIE! I REWARD MY ACOLYTES GREATLY FOR SUCCESS, BUT THE PRICE FOR FAILURE IS GREATER STILL.

A terror unlike no other he had ever felt gripped him. He cried in his mind: *No, my Lord! Please, I beg of you, I tried my best! The plan was better than any other in these circumstances! We could not have anticipated the pixie's interference! I beseech you, great Leto, give me one more chance! One more chance to prove my loyalty and worth! I will not disappoint you again! Do not forsake me, my Lord!*

He heard nothing for a few moments. Then the pressure in his skull grew. His eyes bulged, his tongue hung limply from his mouth.

NO, MARCUM. YOU HAD YOUR CHANCE. YOUR TIME ENDS NOW.

Marcum screamed a soundless scream as the pressure grew into immeasurable pain. Blood began to seep out of his eyes and ears, and he bit his own tongue clean off in convulsions. His body shook in the simple bed and, finally, ceased moving altogether. What was once a bright and quick brain, turned to mush inside his skull and oozed out of his ears and nose. The last thought he had before all went dark was: *I'm sorry.*

No one in the temple heard his death throws. Shortly after Marcum expired, all were awoken by an unimaginable scream that reverberated throughout the temple. A cry so powerful it shattered windows, imploded vases and woke every last acolyte from their slumber with their hands over their ears. The anger of a god was like no other.

Chapter 28

The scream woke Caiaphas from his sleep. He bolted upright, breathing heavily, sweating profusely in the dank, hot, and still air of Tunai. He rose quickly and lit a candle. He took a sip of tepid water and went to the window. The night below in the desert city was quiet and still.

He had stayed in the city awaiting word that the Silver Sword had completed their task and removed Azrael and his companions from existence. It was a bittersweet notion. Yes, he had been given this task by Diarmuid with the promise of reinstatement into the Conclave of Magi and intended to do so. Magic was his life he would do anything to hold on to that. The Conclave will hunt down, try, and most likely execute any ex-communicated mage for using magic. It had been hiding, secrecy, and good fortune that had prevented his capture. He did not know how much longer he could keep that up. But removing one such as Azrael from the face of Tinil'Gan seemed a travesty and a great loss. What he would give to study under one such as he. The secrets and knowledge that would be lost with the Archmage's passing were immeasurable.

Either way, all he could do for the time being was wait, and that is what he had done, day in and day out, with no change to the monotony of this small town — until the scream woke him.

He knew it was no natural scream. He had a greater and greater sense that it was no mortal scream. Someone was angry, furious. He mulled the thought until he was interrupted by another scream. This time, though, it was a scream from a person, and when he moved to look out the window for its source, he saw an old woman staggering down the street.

"The time has come! The time of our god's ascension to complete power is nigh! Woe all who deny him! The sign has come!" she shouted.

Caiaphas cocked an eyebrow. He hurriedly donned his robes, he rushed down to the street. He strode to the tottering old woman and confronted her, "What are you rambling about, crone?"

The crone cackled and pointed at Caiaphas, "Fool! Unbeliever! Worse yet, Magi! Your kind will be the first to fall! Know the words that spell your doom!"

He instantly regretted that he grabbed his robes on instinct, instead of the lighter linens he had been wearing since his arrival. Caiaphas shook the old woman in frustration. Something strange was amiss; something broad and encompassing. Behind him, he began to hear a ruckus forming. People woke from their sleep and entered the streets. He ignored some shouts and focused on her, "Speak woman! Plainly!"

She cackled again, then froze in place. Her eyes glossed over, and a guttural moan escaped from her parched lips. The voice that emerged was not her own.

"Hark the coming times I define
A Harbinger of Chaos
Blood of Magic and the Divine.

With this power Chaos consumes
The Holy Trinity becomes One
The Order of life no longer resumes.
A forest child's great sacrifice
Souls of the undead she calls to her
One tiny soul to begin the fall is all to suffice.
With this act, the herald's trumpet blows
In the voice of a God comes
Shaking all to their souls..."

Before she could finish, something struck Caiaphas in the head. He released the old woman, and she fell to the ground. He heard a sickening snap and saw the woman neck in an unnatural position. He cursed under his breath. He turned to find the source of the attack and saw the street flooded with people, shouting and cursing, making their way towards him.

"Death to magi! The time has come! "

The town had erupted into chaos. Caiaphas looked around, trying to understand the cause of the uproar. His simple presence could not have caused this. A few people were fleeing away on camels, visiting merchants from the looks of them, not natives. He hollered at one as he passed, "Good sir, what is happening?"

The merchant reared his camel and looked down at Caiaphas, "Something has occurred in the deep desert. A seer was murdered, magi were involved. Word is, the leader of the Silver Sword is either held captive or has cast in with the lot of them. The tales are unsure. Either way, the city is no longer safe for outsiders, especially one such as you, magi. I suggest you leave immediately," Without a second glance the merchant yanked the reins of the camel and shot down the road out of town.

The mob was getting closer. *This is madness! Did Jozef also fail? Did he join them? What was this woman talking about? It sounds oddly familiar. And that scream...* Caiaphas shook the thoughts from his head. The merchant was right; mission or no he had to leave Tunai and quickly.

He ran up to his room and gathered his essential items. He always had one means of quick escape if needed. A warp spell that linked him to his small dwelling and study, safe in the countryside near Hearth. He rarely used it unless in dire need, due to the distance it took him from his important duties, but it was called an emergency spell for a reason. He heard voices from outside, coming up the stairs to his room. Concentrating, he uttered a quick prayer to Belial and spoke the words. He shimmered and disappeared just as the mob broke down the door. As the raging Tunoshi poured in, murder in their eyes, they found nothing but an empty room.

While the Tunoshi searched for the mage, Caiaphas re-emerged, with a shimmer and shift, in the safety of his familiar cottage home, a thousand leagues away. As he solidified, he stumbled forward, sweaty and tired from the exertion, but he forced himself to his study and his small but valuable collection of tomes.

The words of the old woman rang through his head like a temple bell. There was a connection somewhere; something old and forgotten that bound everything together. Azrael. Diarmuid's hatred of the Archmage. The events in Tunai and the strange occurrence in the forest after he had summoned the Nidhogg. The current political upheaval on the continent. And lastly, and most disturbingly, the scream that had woken him.

Feverishly, he scanned the bindings of the books on his shelves. Here and there he would pull one out, flip through a few pages, then shake his head and discard it, only to snatch up another. *It is here somewhere! I know it!*

After a few more books and a growing pile on the floor, he grabbed a red, leather-bound book. He looked at the cover and smiled. The title on the faded leather binding read, *Heralds and*

Prophecies of the Ancient World. He flipped through some pages, and let out a short yip when he found the pages he was looking for. Running to his desk, he lit a candle for better illumination and sat down with the tome before him.

The chapter he stopped on was entitled *"Prophecies Concerning the Gods and the Probability of the End Times: Ti'Relian Lore,"* What was known as Ti'Relian was nothing more than a grove of trees and ancient ruins, in the far southeastern corner of the Evening Lands. It was said the greatest seers had resided there and carried out archaic and dubious ceremonies, hidden deep within their groves and monuments. From their divinations came some of the most thought-provoking and puzzling prophecies in all of Tinil'Gan. The Ti'Relian Oracles were no more, however, and nothing remained of them except a few ruins—and their predictions.

He skipped through the sections concerning the history of the seers and their habits and ceremonies and slowed his progress when he arrived at the parts containing the prophecies. When he found the one he was looking for, he placed his finger on the page and leaned closer to read.

The prophecy concerned the God Leto and the supposed eventual and inevitable spreading of chaos across the world, solidifying Leto as the one and only God above all. His jaw dropped as he read. The words the woman spoke where the opening tercets of the prophecy. He continued reading and gasped. It became clear now to Caiaphas. He sat back his mouth agape. *This goes deeper than I had ever imagined. It all makes sense. What I don't understand is what role I play in this.*

CHAPTER 29

The chamber was deathly quiet for a few moments. The silence was broken by Isidora's sobs. Gideon held her close and let her rest her head on his shoulder as she wept. No one knew what to say. They merely stood at stared at the stone wall that had shut off the lovable pixie on the other side, alone to face to her doom. A doom she willingly took upon herself to save them, to save Azrael.

Gideon looked down at his grieving wife and shook his head. He gently released her and moved to the wall to inspect its edges. From what they knew the only way to open the secret stone slab was from the hidden button on the other side, the one that Talia had used to seal them in. He ran his hands over the door, frantically, "We must find a way through! We cannot allow Talia to die in there alone!"

Azrael stood unmoving. Silently he put his hood back over his head and turned, "There is nothing we can do, Gideon. She is gone."

He ground his teeth, "Nothing? I saw you destroy an entire regiment of Tunoshi in the desert and you cannot open a door?"

"It is not the door that is the problem. Talia is gone, along with the liches. Even if we expend our energies to get through that doorway, we will find nothing but an empty corridor. That was the point of what she did; to take them all away. All we can do now is find a way out of this locked room we now find ourselves in," Azrael began to walk around the vast, empty room looking for some way out.

Isidora raised her tear-streaked face and grabbed Azrael by the arm, twisting him around, "Do you have no heart, D'ni? She loved you! Yet here you stand with no remorse, no guilt, not even a tear! You truly care for no one!"

Azrael narrowed his eyes, "I care more than you know, Isidora. Do not believe for one moment that because you were raised in my tower, you understand me. I have lived for millennia! What time has taught me is that it is futile to mourn the dead and waste energy on something you cannot change. Talia is gone. That is the end of it. The only thing you or any of us can do is make sure her sacrifice was not for naught. Now, it is best we find a way out of here. Either help or remain quiet."

Isidora angrily dried her face and turned away from Azrael. He remained behind for a moment and looked towards the sealed off corridor. Lear'Za came up to him and placed a hand on his shoulder.

"Seer'kaat, I have known you for a long while, and I have learned something of your ways. Perhaps it would be easier for Isidora if she knew the whole truth."

"Daemoness, even after all these years, I still remember what it is to see the world from the eyes of a child. Ignorance is bliss. I, unfortunately, was forced to make an uneven trade of my heart for the real world. Those long lost feelings are clouded by what I know now. It would be a blessing to return to believing in everything and knowing nothing at all; sometimes, I believe not knowing is the better way. I do not wish Isidora to lose her heart as I have. If that means she reviles me, so be it." Lear'Za sighed and threw her hands up in resignation, "You think I cannot see through those mirrored eyes of yours, Seer'kaat? You have taken the weight of the future on your shoulders because you believe only you are capable of fixing it. You play the role of all you want to be, the stalwart defender against Leto and his plans. But I know who you really are. Where will you go when there's no one left to save you from yourself? You do not have to do this alone. Remember that," Azrael looked at the sealed doorway once more, and sighed.

"I think I found something," Gideon shouted, "Look up there," They followed his finger above their heads. The ceiling was mostly gone; a big hole had been torn through it, revealing the upper level. In the corner where Gideon pointed, a shadowy alcove that looked like a doorway could be made out, "It looks like there is a passageway right there. Now, how do we get up there?"

"I think I can help with this," Lear'Za grinned. She walked up to Gideon and hugged him around the waist. She suddenly leaped with Gideon in her arms, and the knight let out a yell. She jumped high enough to drop Gideon gently on the edge of what remained of the ceiling in front of the passageway they saw and then she landed back on the floor below with the others. Gideon looked down at the rest of them with a sheepish grin, "I guess that works. You could have warned me though," He said, breathing heavily from the surprise.

Lear'Za merely winked. One by one, she brought the rest of the group to the exit. Isidora was the last to be brought up, as the rest began walking down the new passageway, she stopped and looked down at the sealed doorway where Talia had left. She bowed her head and followed after the others.

The rest of their passage through the temple was made in somber silence, each contemplating the hole Talia had left behind. They missed the soft glow she radiated, her small interjections and quips. It weighed heavily on each of them. It was some time before the solemn silence was broken by Jozef.

"This corridor is the last; ahead lies the central courtyard of the Temple of Al'Zadal. The temple was the center of the religion in the Evening Lands. Pilgrims came from all over the continent, some even traveled from the Morning Lands just to see it. It was housed in the center of the city and held even more prominence than the palace. The king gave the temple his elite troops to join the Temple Guards.

"In its day it was a wonder of engineering, in many ways it still is. It was designed as an indoor courtyard. With assistance from the elves, Ranian architects learned the secrets of light reflection using crystals. Ventilation channels were carved down from the upper stories of the temple walls all the way to this chamber. Crystals on the parapets reflected sunlight into the channels into this courtyard aimed at a large central crystal that hung from the high ceiling. It reflected all the targeted sunlight, filling this courtyard as if it were outdoors. Now those channels are blocked with debris and sand.

"Here is where Sir Reginald made his sacrifice. This I know from our history. On that day of the final battle, Sir Reginald led Castellarian Knights into the temple to recover the chalice. Most accounts are hazy, and they vary on each side; however, what is consistent is that Sir Reginald had magi in his employ. As we all know, history is written by the victor. And so, it is written that Ranian priests would rather destroy the city than allow the Castellarians to leave with their sacred treasure.

"As the priests chanted their final spell, Sir Reginald gave the chalice to a knight and ordered him to flee, while he, in his moment of glory, stayed behind to stop the priests and save Rania from destruction, even though he was there as a conqueror. Of course, Ranian tales say that the priests were casting a protection spell and it was interference from the mercenary Castellarian magi that caused the explosion. Either way, Sir Reginald died in this courtyard. Considering what happened, I think you will be surprised at its appearance when we enter," Jozef smiled and waved them through the passageway that led to the courtyard.

They were greeted by a blast of cold, moist air that hit their faces. The courtyard was a wonder; a veritable oasis in the desert. After the explosion, a crater was created in the center which had, over the centuries, filled with water creating a lake. From a crack on a high wall, a waterfall cascaded down into the lake, most likely from a deep underground well. The walls were covered entirely in long ivy and vines that draped down majestically. The elegant flagstone that was once the floor was now a plush carpet of green grasses. It was a mixture of broken ruins and fresh, new life. Shattered marble columns leaned against walls or lay on the ground, overgrown with moss and vegetation. Pieces of ancient statues missing heads and limbs were surrounded by beautifully colored flowers.

Kethis took a deep breath and sighed, "Whoever would have thought that such a paradise could reside under the ground, buried away from the sun? This is the first peace I have felt since entering this accursed desert."

Gideon walked up and clapped Kethis on the back, "It is beautiful, isn't it? One could get lost here for a long time. How could it have survived the blast that turned a whole realm into a desert?"

Jozef smiled, "Some say it was the remnants of the priest's protection spell that saved the temple from complete destruction and preserved this courtyard. Others say it was divine intervention from the gods. Whatever the case may be, the blast began here and radiated outward. It destroyed everything in its path except the epicenter itself. Thus we have one of the Great

Wonders of Tinil'Gan: the Secret Gardens of Al'Zadal. It has been a well-kept secret that few know beyond the confines of our desert and the Tunoshi people."

Isidora looked around then closed her eyes and smiled, "I wish Talia could have seen this. She would have loved it."

"The magic still lingers. While Jozef is correct and the architecture is solid, the remnants of the shield spell have kept this courtyard intact," Azrael stated.

"I still don't understand how a spell could cause that much devastation or how this room was spared its wrath," Gideon questioned.

Azrael looked around a bit then focused on Gideon, "The laymen term to describe what happened here is to call it an explosion; for all intents and purposes, it was just that. But magic is not that simple. The spell attempted was to break a priest holy protection spell, one blessed by the gods. An ill-advised practice. The first thing the shield did was absorb all the magic thrown at it until it reached a critical mass and could not absorb more. This did not destroy the shield; all it did was force the shield to purge the massive amount of mana that was poured into it. The first purge caused the destruction you see here within the courtyard and killed all within. After that, the subsequent purges expelled with resonant pulses, each one larger and exponentially more destructive than the last. With each pulse, the wild magic tore the flesh from the bones of any living creature, ripped trees and plants from their roots, and finally ravaged the soil, rivers, and lakes. It was left a wasteland. The small surrounding desert eventually encroached in on what was left as the topsoil was blown away. What was once a thriving, flourishing land became the large sand sea we know today," He paused for a moment then walked past and made his way to the far end of the courtyard, "We are here for a specific purpose. Let us be done with it,"

Azrael stopped at a large marble slab fashioned into a dais with a single four-foot-tall pedestal on top of it. At one time, there might have been a gate surrounding it, but all that was left were a few posts and pieces of rusted iron, twisted beyond recognition, "I believe you have an incantation to perform, Isidora, to call the potential avatar. This dais is where the chalice was housed. It would be as good a place as any to perform your ritual."

Isidora clenched her hands and seemed about to speak. Gideon placed an arm around her shoulder to calm her and gave a look as if to say, *It matters not. We are here, and this is what you were waiting for, my love.* Isidora's muscles loosened. She walked forward confidently to the dais, "As always your instincts are infallible D'ni."

Isidora climbed the dais and sat cross-legged upon the soft grass in front of the pedestal. She looked at everyone gathered, "Drawing a hero from the quintessence is not the same as summoning a natural avatar or one that has already pledged to me. I will fall deep into concentration. Once the hero awakens, it will call to me, and I shall awaken from my meditation. At that point, depending on the hero, they may challenge me, and the rest of you by extension, to prove myself worthy of their service. The battles are not life-threatening. If we lose, the hero will retreat to the quintessence, finding me lacking as a worthy summoner. With Sir Reginald, I am uncertain if he will present a challenge to us or not, but that will become apparent when he wakens me with his call."

She closed her eyes and relaxed. The companions stood in a semi-circle around her, waiting in silence as she devoted her complete concentration to her task. Gradually, they began to hear her repetitive chant, growing louder with each repetition. A glowing, translucent summoning circle materialized under her. No one other than Azrael understood the words, for it was in the spidery arcane language of the Art.

After several minutes, her chant reached a fevered pitch and, suddenly, her head shot up. Her eyes were open but glowing a deep violet and in the air before her appeared a glowing purple ethereal glyph. It began to spin furiously and tip on its axis, bumping the ground. *Keep it together, woman.* Isidora doubled her concentration to keep the glyph in control. If she fails here, this was all for naught. Its colors shifted along the spectrum, changing from violet to a deep crimson.

Azrael narrowed his eyes. Something was wrong, "Everyone, get back. Back now!" Everyone did as commanded, Gideon more hesitant than the rest, "If you value your life knight you will move quicker!" Azrael shouted.

Gideon scampered back a few yards, taking shelter behind a fallen column. Fear for his wife was evident in his wide eyes, "Is she going to be all right? We can't just leave her!"

Azrael sighed, "I am not sure, yet, but we cannot help her if we get injured by whatever happens next."

Gideon's hands clenched and unclenched, his teeth gritted together so fiercely he thought they might shatter. He reached for his sword and unsheathed it in readiness. *Please, my love, remain calm.* She wished she could shout the words instead of thinking them. She could not risk the loss of concentration. The quintessence never intended this to be easy. A mage had to earn its heroes.

The glyph continued to spin, still a bloody crimson. A low pitched hum emanated from it. Isidora remained still before it, her chanting monotone and distant. *I feel it. He's here.* Her head dropped as she fell into her subconscious.

CHAPTER 30

The glyph spun frantically emanating a loud hum which made everyone cover their ears. Then it suddenly fell silent and stopped spinning. A fraction of a second after, a figure burst from the center. It was translucent, much like Isidora's natural avatar Lelani, except its glow was crimson instead of violet. However, this one was in the shape of a man, a huge man. It stood nearly seven feet tall and wore the armor of a knight. The visor was pulled down, concealing its face. In its hands, he held an immense war hammer. The figure shook itself and cracked its neck as if it had just awoken from a long slumber. Its head tilted down towards Isidora and cocked to one side. Then, without warning, it raised the massive war hammer high overhead, aimed at the meditating Isidora. Deep in her concentration, she no longer could sense anything on the outside.

Gideon shouted. With lightning speed, he leaped a column and charged towards the towering figure. He swung his sword around just in time to block the downward swing of the translucent war hammer. Although it appeared ethereal with no substance, the clang of the hammer meeting sword resounded through the chamber and shook Gideon to his core. With a raw gasp, he stumbled and nearly fell over, but quickly was able to regain his footing, "What is happening, Azrael!" He shouted. Undeterred, he stood straight, his sword before him, to meet the challenge.

The others did not sit idly by. As Gideon ran forward, they sprang into action. Kethis prepared his bow and Lear'Za and Jozef pulled their swords and advanced. Azrael made his way quickly towards Isidora and knelt next to her, "She is deep in her meditation, she is physically unaware of what is happening," He placed his hands on her shoulders and leaned his face close to her ear to rouse her. He knew more than anyone that giving her a surprise start could cause her to lose control of the delicate forces she wielded in her trance. Isidora began to come around, the glow of her eyes faded and she blinked. She looked up in confusion at Azrael, "What happened?"

Azrael shook his head and helped her stand, "No time, move!" They dove to the side as the others engaged the beast of a man.

From various places of its glowing crimson armor, Kethis' arrows stuck out ineffectively. Gideon, Lear'Za, and Jozef rained blows upon it, but it blocked each deftly with the massive war hammer. Gideon shouted out, "This cannot be Sir Reginald! For a supposed hero he seems pretty confrontational for no reason!"

Isidora shook her head, "I don't understand. I did my research. The battle itself is not a surprise; most avatars engage those who summon them, but not so suddenly, without warning. It is also quite obvious this is not Sir Reginald!"

Azrael narrowed his eyes in thought, "You are right. He is not Sir Reginald. That can only mean Sir Reginald is not the hero you seek. In your chanting, I heard you call Reginald's name, correct?"

Isidora shook her head quickly, "Yes, yes, of course. It is part of the ritual."

Lear'Za dodged a blow and nearly fell to the ground, "A little quicker over there please!" The summoned avatar was relentless and seemed not to tire at all. She parried a swing of the massive war hammer and gave a small shout as it knocked her flaming scimitar from her hands. He swung again, and the daemoness ducked, the mighty hammer whizzed over her head. It crashed into a column, causing it to crumble and topple over. The courtyard shook. She floated quickly to one side as Gideon and Jozef closed in to protect her.

Azrael stared at the large man in thought, "This thing is angry, furious."

Gideon raised his sword to block another hammer swing and deflected it to the side. There was something familiar about this thing. Gideon's eyes went wide, "I know who this is! The story I told you about the Knights of the Golden Lance; this is Sir Quintus Berralis. The Hammer!" Gideon narrowly dodged to his left as the mighty hammer crashed on the ground where he once stood.

Azrael's eyes narrowed, ". Repeat the lines, Isidora, quickly this time, using his name!"

Isidora nodded, wide-eyed, and concentrated. She began to hum out her chant once again. Her voice cracked and strained.

Azrael gritted his teeth in frustration, "Calm yourself, Tra'ni! You can do this!"

The Hammer began to wear down his opponents. A wild backswing of his hammer caught Jozef in the leg and knocked him to the ground with a crunch of bone. Kethis' arrows did not affect it. The giant avatar had a dozen sticking out of him and was showing no sign of injury. Kethis leaped in desperation onto its back hoping to drive his dagger into its throat. The

Hammer reached around and grabbed the elf by his head and tossed him aside like a doll.

The others closed in, and with a wide arcing swing the avatar knocked all three of them away, sending them flying in different directions. Gideon slammed against a wall, slid down, and landed with a thump. He sat there, dazed, a trickle of blood running down the side of his face. The Hammer stalked towards him.

Isidora took another deep breath and concentrated. This time her words were clear and steady. Seeing Gideon in danger caused a profound reaction in her. She chanted the words using Sir Berralis' name.

The large man approached Gideon and raised his hammer high above him for a killing blow. Just as it began to arc down, he froze, his war hammer only inches from Gideon's head. Isidora's chants worked.

The large man stood frozen in place for a moment, then slung his hammer onto his back strap and turned towards Isidora. His crimson glow softened, and swirls of violet could be seen floating within. He ambled forward and looked down at the mage. Dropping to one knee before her, he raised a sizeable ethereal hand and placed it on her forehead. Time seemed to stop, and all the air drawn out of the room with a low-pitched whoosh. They were all transported to another time, at least in their minds. The scene opened up before them like they were present when it occurred. They were in the same courtyard, but it was obviously before its transformation; before the blast. The lake was gone, the waterfall, the lush fauna. Instead, it was a manicured courtyard, as in many palaces and temples. They were in the Temple of Al'Zadal before its destruction.

Priests and visitors walked through the garden in muted conversations and contemplations. It was the busy season; the time of year when the temple hosted hundreds, if not thousands, of pilgrims. The grass was freshly cut; the courtyard brightly lit by the channels aiming the sunlight from outside the center crystal high above their heads. The brilliance of it made it appear like a miniature sun held in thrall in the temple. The scene was peaceful, but only for a moment. With a sudden burst, the gateway entry to the courtyard was torn asunder by magic. The gate flew end-over-end and slammed up against the far wall with a crash, causing panic and screams. People ran helter-skelter as a small stream of knights flowed into the courtyard, led by two mailed men and three magi. One of the mailed men was of medium height and build; Sir Reginald. He had short but flowing blond hair and a clean-shaven face. He was handsome, full of youthful vigor. His armor was resplendent, sporting a sterling silver tiger and silver accents on blue enamel, the stanchion of House Tempest.

Next to him stood a towering, hulk of a man; Sir Quintus Berralis. He removed his visor to reveal the polar opposite of Reginald. The man was shaved bald, and his polished scalp reflected the sunlight. His face was not handsome; it was pockmarked and scarred. He had a broad square chin that jutted out, giving him the look of an ever-present scowl. His armor was not new and polished, but bore dents and tarnish. It sported no stanchion; he was of no great house. In his hands, he carried an enormous war hammer.

The three magi, one of each order, black, white, and green, all human and apparently young, could have been long from the Trials.

Sir Quintus pointed to the other end of the courtyard with his hammer, "The chalice is there. Let us retrieve it and be done with this nonsense."

Sir Reginald laughed, "Patience, Quintus. Our mission is to retrieve the chalice, true, but we are also in a war of conquest. If there is a possibility of ending this war here and now, I plan on taking it. House Tempest deserves the glory."

Quintus glowered and grunted, "I tire of nobles. This is war; there is nothing glorious about it. You play with lives for the sake of House glory and politics," He was cut short by a shout and the patter of slippered feet coming from the other end of the courtyard. They were confronted by a gang of unarmed temple priests. The one in the front was old and tired, but he had a spark in his eyes.

"How dare you enter this sacred place with arms and blood lust!" Said the old priest, "The Gods will not stand for this. We will stop you with our dying breaths if need be!"

Sir Reginald doubled over in laughter. He composed himself and smiled, "You plan to do this how old man? We have an entire regiment here, as well as magi. We will take the chalice and burn this temple down if need be. Castellamar will rule Rania."

The old priest sighed, his sad eyes blinking, "You doubt the power of the Gods, sir knight. That shall be your undoing," He nodded to the other priests. The old man and two acolytes stepped back, and the rest stepped forward with only wooden staves in their hands. They stood in a line protecting the entry-way to the chalice.

Sir Reginald shook his head, "Are you serious? This is a foolish way to die," He waved his hand, "Kill them."

Sir Quintus turned his head in outrage, "I will not order these knights to slay defenseless priests, Reginald. You speak of glory but forget your honor."

Reginald's face contorted in anger, "You forget your place, Sir Quintus. I command here, not you. Refuse me, and you are relieved of your duty, sir knight!" Reginald looked toward the chalice and saw the old priest and his two acolytes surrounding it, chanting a prayer, "We have little time. Knights, kill these priests. You magi, stop those three now!"

Chaos erupted around them and the knights dove into the line of priests. Although unarmed save for wooden staves, the priests fought back, parrying blows and using their opponent's strength and weight against them. The magi made their way towards the old priest and began their arcane chants. Quintus watched in mute disgust, unsure what to do.

The old priest and his acolytes created a holy barrier around the chalice, and the young magi began to batter against it with spells. Quintus felt the ground shake slightly. His mind raced, torn between his duty and his honor. *What is the right and just thing to do?* He looked up and saw two priests fall to Castellarian swords. Their blood soaked the ground and ran in rivulets into the joints of the elegant flagstone tile. He held his hammer at his waist, the weight of it more apparent than in the past. *There can only be one choice. There is no honor in this.*

He stalked towards the battle. With a resigned look, he raised his mighty hammer and brought it down with a crash. A shocked priest looked at him in wonder as the hammer crushed the head of the knight he was battling. His hammer swung through the ranks as he made his way forward, towards the shining azure armor. He watched as Sir Reginald made his way to the magi. *I must stop him.*

Sir Reginald grabbed the black robe by the arm and shook him, "What is taking so long? Bring down that barrier!"

The black robe turned to Sir Reginald, "My lord, the spell they used is strong, infused with the power of the gods. We can only do so much against it."

Sir Reginald railed at the mage, "I don't care if you have to tear down this whole temple! Use whatever means necessary!"

The white robe mage came forward, "My lord, using magic against a god shield such as this can cause unexpected and unforeseen consequences. We dare not do more. Those higher in our orders would know more."

"You were not paid to give me excuses! You have power, use it!" Reginald screamed.

The magi looked at each other in worry and conferred. They turned to Reginald as one, "We will do our best, my lord. Just know that we cannot foresee the possible outcome of the spell we are about to cast. It is dangerous."

"Just do it! Quickly!" Sir Reginald sheathed his sword and crossed his arms. The magi turned toward the barrier and chanted as one in the arcane language of the Art. Tendrils of energy flowed from their hands toward the barrier, crackling with power. The ground shook harder, and Sir Reginald lost his footing.

Quintus made his way towards him, battering aside knight after knight. *I am killing my brothers. Knights. You have brought this shame upon me, you self-righteous bastard.* Blood coated his dented armor, and he breathed heavily. In the distance, he saw the magi attacking the barrier with Sir Reginald watching. The ground shuddered; he was running out of time. He broke free from the battle and ran towards the dais, hammer in hand.

The magic coursed around the barrier and hummed wildly. The barrier began to shudder and flicker. Suddenly it imploded with a whoosh and then blew outward knocking everyone down, including Sir Quintus, just as he neared Sir Reginald. Quintus shook his head and sat up. In the center of the dais was a blue, glowing orb that pulsed and hummed. He saw the magi bodies, bloodied and broken, thrown yards away. The priests on the dais faired no better. Shakily, he rose and made his way there.

The old priest laid on the ground, his breath coming in gasps. Sir Quintus knelt before him and raised his head.

"What happened, priest? What is that, the orb?" Quintus questioned.

The old priest spoke wearily, "The fools, in their attempt to bring down the shield they created a mana battery. It has been absorbing all the magic aimed at it. Now it can absorb no more," The priest coughed up some blood, "It must release it. God spells are not to be trifled with. I fear we are all doomed, and perhaps all of Rania. If we are lucky, it will not reverberate throughout the whole of the Evening Lands," The old priest coughed up some more blood and grasped Sir Quintus' wrist, "You must save it. Rania is doomed, but you can at least do that."

Reginald had awoken, hearing the old priest's words, his eyes grew wide in fear. Shakily, he rose and staggered towards the exit of the courtyard. Quintus looked up and saw him, frowning. He looked back down at the priest.

"I have one last task to attend. I cannot carry the chalice from here, but I will make sure it is taken to safety. I give you my word."

The old priest smiled, "Take this," He handed him a brass pendant with a crimson ruby in the center, "It is a port key created by magi. This particular one will transport the user to our temple in Tunai. Just press the ruby firmly to activate it. While it is not incredibly far, it can buy you time to escape the blast and save the chalice," The priest smiled one last smile and expired in his arms. *I cannot leave this place. Sir Reginald deserves justice brought down on him. We will die together.* He looked around and spotted one of the surviving knights rising unsteadily to his feet. He was a young man of no great house, just as Quintus was. *So young, his knighting only a short while ago.* Warily he rose and approached the pedestal. The orb hummed and glowed a few feet above it. Stealing his courage, he took a deep breath and grasped the golden chalice from the stand; the ground shook again, more violently. He hastened towards the knight and grabbed him.

"Are you well?" Quintus said urgently. Dazed but aware, the knight shook his head affirmatively. He handed him the chalice and the pendant, "Take the chalice and flee this place. The pendant will send you to Tunai by pressing on the ruby," Quintus and the knight steadied themselves as a stronger quake shook the temple, "Return it to Castellamar," Quintus struggled with his next words. He wanted to tell the knight to reveal Sir Reginald's betrayal and dishonor. He pursed his lips. It would do no good to tarnish the name of any knight, even ones as dishonorable as Sir Reginald. It would only disgrace the Knighthood and the Kingdom. Better they did not know, "Tell them we succeeded, with great loss and sacrifice, but we succeeded. Leave now. You have little time. Make haste, and do not look back. Go!"

The knight took the chalice and nodded. He took a few steps back and saluted Quintus by slamming his fist against his breastplate. Quintus saluted and the knight disappeared by activating the pendant. He turned his attention to the retreating Sir Reginald. An apparent leg injury made the treacherous knight's progress slow; Sir Quintus closed the gap quickly. He grabbed Sir Reginald's gorget and spun him around. "Have you no shred of honor left?"

Sir Reginald paled in Quintus' grasp. He tore away and straightened himself, "Are you mad? This place is falling around our ears, and you stop to bandy words with me?"

"Your vanity and lust for power have condemned an entire kingdom to death," Quintus spat out in disgust, "You killed innocents. You deserve to die in this place with everyone else."

Sir Reginald chuckled then took on a pleading expression, "We still have some time. We can escape this disaster. I will speak of your heroism; your family will be raised to a Great House. Aid me to leave this place, and we can both live."

Quintus sighed, "I planned to leave your treachery unknown to the world, to spare the knighthood. If I aid you and we can survive, I will turn that decision. You will be brought forth to answer for your crimes," The temple shook once more, and a few columns fell, raising clouds of dust. The blue orb grew brighter and pulsed with magnificent energy, "I vow this as a knight and on my honor."

Sir Reginald sighed and nodded, "Fine. I understand, Quintus. You do what you have to do, just get the horses so we can flee this place!"

Quintus nodded and left the courtyard to where the horses were tied off. Grabbing the reins of two, he brought them back to where he had left Sir Reginald. Upon his return, the disgraced knight was no longer present. Confused he called out to Sir Reginald but his shout ended in a gurgle. His bulging eyes looked down; a sword point protruded from his chest plate. Violently it was pulled out, and he fell to his knees. Grunting, with each breath a struggle, he looked up at his murderer. Sir Reginald smiled wickedly.

"Did you really think I would allow you to destroy my family name and honor? Thank you for the horse. I will speak great things of your deeds, Sir Quintus of the Hammer," With a laugh, Sir Reginald mounted the horse and spurred it out of the courtyard. Quintus' vision blurred, not only from oncoming death but with tears of regret. He had failed. Hundreds of thousands would die while their murderer lived, and free to bask in undeserved glory. He looked over at the pulsing blue orb that would bring about the carnage.

He screwed his eyebrows in determination and forced himself to rise, using his hammer to help him stand. Blood flowed freely from his mortal wound, staining the front of his armor, but onward he pushed. He had to, at the very least, try. With the hammer as a crutch, he hobbled towards the orb; panting and grimacing he stood before it. He took a deep breath, gathering the last of his strength, then raised his hammer one final time above his head. He gave a quick prayer to the gods. He only hoped the knight with the chalice was far enough away and that Sir Reginald was still close enough. Doom was inevitable, but he decided with his last breath that he would make sure Reginald shared the same fate as those he had condemned.

With a mighty roar, all the force he had left his body, he brought the mighty hammer crashing down upon the orb.

The enormous flash of the blast ended his life in an instant and radiated outward from the temple. Within a couple of hours, the force of it had carried through the whole of Rania, ending lives before they could even cry out. Sir Reginald met his end not too far from the temple as the blast took him as well. Justice was served.

On a hilltop outside of Tunai, the lone survivor of the battle of Rania was knocked from his horse as the blast radiated out and then retreated. He had made it just far enough. The knight climbed to his feet and looked out at the horizon. A giant plume of smoke rose in the distance. What was once the Kingdom of Rania was no more. He clutched the chalice and mounted his horse. With a final glance at the devastation, he turned and galloped away towards Castellamar.

With a start, the companions awoke back in the present. Gideon pulled himself up painfully, "Did everyone see and witness all that?" The companions all nodded wearily, and they each tended to their injuries. The avatar of The Hammer stood solemnly before Isidora and looked down upon her. She was unable to control the tears in her eyes; the reality of the destruction was far worse than she had known.

Wiping her face, she rose before the true hero of the Battle of Rania, "It is a shame the world did not know of your sacrifice, Sir Quintus. I fear that even with this knowledge you have shared with us, history cannot be changed. I can offer you this. Become my avatar. Fight beside me in the name of justice and honor in the way Sir Reginald did not. Be the true Hammer of Justice. What say you, Sir Quintus?" Isidora locked her gaze on the giant apparition.

The Hammer shimmered and looked up towards the sky. The courtyard shook once again, more violently this time, as if history was repeating itself. The shifting colors inside the figure turned wholly violet in acceptance. A small rune with the symbol of a hammer shot forward and tattooed itself on Isidora's arm. She had gained her first hero avatar.

The courtyard shook steadily, now, enough to make everyone stumble. The column The Hammer had knocked down during the fight had been the last physical support holding roof from collapsing into the courtyard. The danger of being buried alive was imminent.

Azrael looked up. Dust and sand began drifting down from the ceiling, "We must flee. Between the last pillar being knocked out and Isidora's summoning magic, the last of the old magic that aided in holding this together is gone. This place is meeting its final end," His words were cut off as a mighty rumble caused tons of rock and sand to fall in front of the passage from which they had come.

"By the Gods! We are trapped!" Kethis shouted.

Jozef spoke up as Lear'Za helped him stand with his broken leg, "There is another way. Look up there. One of the channels has opened up from the impending collapse," True enough, they saw sunlight beaming into the courtyard for the first time in centuries. The last of the sand and debris that had clogged the channel filtered out, "If I am correct, this one leads up to a cliff's edge behind the temple on the opposite side from where we entered. It may be too high for us to descend, but for the moment it is better than being buried alive."

Isidora nodded to her new avatar and dismissed him with a wave of her hand. He returned to the quintessence and would return when summoned again. Along with the others, she looked towards Azrael for guidance. The Archmage had his eyes closed, and his lips were moving silently. After a few tense moments, his mirrored orbs opened, "Lead the way, Master Shaddam."

She turned and ran with the others, dodging debris and rubble that fell from overhead. Jozef led them up the fallen debris and tipped columns. It brought them most of the way, close to the channel. Lear'Za leaped while carrying each of them to the channel's opening. They began the slow climb up as it gently sloped upwards. Now and then someone would gasp as the shaft shook from the vibrations. After what seemed like an eternity, they could see the end of the tunnel. They emerged from the shaft at the top of the temple, high on a rocky embankment above the desert. They stopped abruptly and looked down.

Gideon groaned, "We can never climb down in time, and we can't jump. It's too high."

A terrifying shriek from the sky drew everyone's attention. Overhead, a large shadow passed over the crumbling temple ruins. "By the Gods, what terrible fate do they wish upon us now?" Kethis gasped.

Jozef paled and pointed up, "A dragon! My gods, a dragon!"

Indeed, Jozef was correct. Circling above them was a monstrous golden dragon. Its maw gaped, revealing rows of razor-sharp teeth. It gave another roar to the heavens as it swooped closer. Dragons were known in Tinil'Gan but seldom seen, so rarely that most believed them to be extinct. This one was extraordinarily large; its golden scales glinted in the sunlight. It lowered its massive frame and brought its head even with them, primarily Azrael, and roared. The usually brave group braced in fear — except for Lear'Za, who began laughing.

Azrael rolled his eyes and stepped forward, "Was that necessary, Cirrah?"

The mighty dragon snorted, blowing Azrael's hood off. To everyone's surprise, the dragon spoke in a low booming baritone, "Was waking me from an especially comfortable slumber necessary, Archmage?" The temple shook and their precarious perch crumbled around the edges, "I see you still keep dubious company. Greetings, daemoness."

Through laughter, Lear'Za managed an extravagant bow, "Dragon."

Azrael shook his head, "You know as well as I, I couldn't get rid of her if I tried. And considering this place is about to fall any minute, I believe it more than necessary. Besides Cirrah, you have slept nearly a century this time. It is about time you woke again."

Gideon looked back and forth between the dragon, the Archmage, and the giggling Lear'Za, his eyes wide in disbelief, "Are you kidding me? He is friends with a dragon?! Maybe telling us would have been appropriate!" Lear'Za's laughter increased. Isidora rubbed Gideon's hand and also chuckled as his face grew beet red. The dragon snorted once more and shook its massive head, "You are lucky I like you, Archmage," The temple shook again, and everyone stumbled. Cirrah looked around, "I suppose then you would like me to spirit you and your companions away from this place."

Azrael regained his footing and sighed, "That would be greatly appreciated. Less talk and more flying, perhaps?"

The dragon laughed a roaring laugh, "Climb aboard then, friends. I cannot guarantee a comfortable ride, but a ride it will be. Grab hold of my scales. Yes, like that."

They all clambered aboard Cirrah's scaly hide, straddling the smooth scales at the base of his neck and grabbed hold where they could. Once settled, Cirrah pumped his leathery wings harder, lifting them away from the doomed temple as it imploded upon itself. Isidora looked down, and she could see the last remaining parapets and walls sink into the gaping hole in the desert. For the second time, the Temple of Al'Zadal has met its end. This time, forever buried beneath the sands along with a friend she would miss dearly.

Cirrah rose into the clouds. He tilted his head back to his riders, "So to where are we headed, Archmage?"

Azrael squinted against the roaring wind and smirked, "To Castellamar, my good dragon."

Cirrah roared and flew eastward.

CHAPTER 31

Caiaphas slept fitfully that night. He tossed and turned, awoken continuously by one nightmare or another. He could not get the revelations of the previous night out of his mind. It was as if he had been blind his whole life and granted sight. It was driving him mad; he had no idea where to turn or what to do next. He certainly could not go back to Diarmuid at this point.

The white robe would be furious that Caiaphas' latest attempt to remove Azrael had failed. The merchant had said Jozef had either been subdued or turned sides by joining the Archmage. If he had to guess Caiaphas, chose subdued. But he couldn't deny there had been something off about that Tunoshi.

Caiaphas shook his head in frustration. The loyalty of the Tunoshi sell-sword was inconsequential at this point. The fate of the world was apparently in the balance and other than Azrael, Caiaphas was the only one conscious of the peril. *What can I do? I am just one mage.* He considered contacting the Conclave but dismissed the notion as quickly as he thought of it. His status as a banished mage placed him in a precarious and untrustworthy position; once Diarmuid caught wind of it, he would undoubtedly quash it.

The worst part of it all was Caiaphas had no idea where he stood. A world controlled by chaos could benefit a banished black robe mage. Then again, who knew what restrictions the God Leto might impose? It was so mind-numbing he pulled at his hair in frustration. He sat back down at his desk and read the prophecy over again, making sure he had not missed something vital.

His reading was interrupted by the pulse of his scrying orb; Diarmuid. He squeezed his eyes shut and rubbed his temples. He reached over to his small travel sack, pulled out the sphere and placed it on a small tripod on his desk.

"Yes, Diarmuid?" Caiaphas spoke evenly.

"So you are alive, wretch," Caiaphas could hear the venom in the mage's voice, "I know Azrael still lives, Caiaphas. I am disappointed."

"There were complications, Diarmuid," Caiaphas pleaded.

"Oh, spare me the excuses!" Diarmuid spat, "I had little hope of you succeeding, anyway. At any rate, events have escalated. I will have to deal with Azrael myself. I have a new mission for you."

Caiaphas cocked an eyebrow. He was surprised at Diarmuid's lack of anger, that he was still trusting him with another duty. He found this a blessing; it was best if Diarmuid believed Caiaphas was still under his employ, "It would be my honor, Diarmuid. What would you have of me?"

"I need you to travel to Evanfall and meet with Lord Condrite. I have already assured him I would send a mage to him to aid him in what is to come. Go there and offer your services to him."

"Evanfall? Why, Evanfall?"

Diarmuid sighed heavily, "Why do you find it necessary to question me, Caiaphas? If you must know, Evanfall plays an important role in the sphere of politics at the moment. Lord Condrite will fill you in on the rest, or as much as he feels you need to know. Make haste. He awaits your arrival."

Evanfall? This makes no sense. With a shrug, Caiaphas responded, "As you wish, Diarmuid. I will make leave for Evanfall immediately. It should only take me a few days to arrive. I will notify you when I have been admitted."

"Good. I have matters to attend to," The scrying orb went dark and silent. Caiaphas scratched his forehead. In resignation, he began to pack for his trip to Evanfall. If anything, being near the center of the continent wouldn't hurt in his investigations.

CHAPTER 32

For those unaccustomed to it, the flight was frightful at first. The ride was almost more comfortable than a horse. The dragon's magical aura protected them from cold winds and temperature changes, and Cirrah would periodically stop to let his riders take a nap, drink, or have a quick meal. But after the initial shock wore off, the sights that only creatures of the air can witness were marvelous.

The beginning of their journey took them over the eastern portion of the desert, and they only saw dune after dune on the ground below. Eventually, the sands lessened and gave way to grasses and shrubs as they passed over the foothills of the western range of the Castellian Mountains which grew into majestic mountain peaks capped with snow. In the center of the range stood Castle Pass, a fortified gate and bastion that was built to protect and fill the only gap in the mountains, and single land entry into the kingdom.

Cirrah took lazy circles around a few of the peaks to give them all a better view. When the mountains fell behind, they could see the Sana Valley spread out before them. Gideon smiled as he knew they had entered the Kingdom.

The dragon dove low and followed the course of the Sana River as it lazed its way through the valley, finally emptying into the crystal blue shores of Lake Seban where San'Seban sits. The bright sun reflected off his scales as he swooped low enough for a wingtip to skim the surface of the river. Isidora yelped in delight as they watched wild bison scatter across the valley at the sight of the massive dragon overhead. The flight was a welcome distraction and pleasure after the miserable desert trip and all of its dangers, not to mention the loss of Talia.

Cirrah swiveled up to a higher altitude as they approached the lake and the city. San'Seban sprawled out from the lake upon rolling hills and vibrant vineyards. Homes and buildings of sturdy stone and brick filled the majority of the city proper and more modest homes of wood and thatch lined along the vineyards and orchards of the sunlit and fertile land on the outskirts. The more affluent built large villas among the fields.

In the center of the city proper on the highest hill stood Castle Mount. Arranged in a hexagon, the curtain walls of the castle ran around the outside with a tower and battlements at each corner. It was built using white granite that was radiant in the valley's sunlight. Gideon shouted and pointed when he spotted Castle Mount. Cirrah roared and veered north away from the city.

All in all, the trip that would have taken a fortnight on horseback took them two days on dragonback. Finding an open stretch of the valley without any sign of life, Cirrah landed with a thump on the ground and stretched out a wing for his passengers to dismount. He snorted and craned his neck towards Azrael.

"I fear this is as close as I dare come lest I cause civil panic."

Azrael smirked and patted the dragon on its neck, "You have done more than needed, my friend. I am in your debt."

"Archmage, I have been in yours for eons. A small flight hardly makes up for it," The dragon opened its maw in a yawn, "Besides like you said, it was about time I awoke. I am simply ravished! Those bison we saw a while back looked tasty enough."

"Then enjoy your meal, Cirrah. I fear this may not be the last time I call upon you. We are in precarious times," Azrael gave him one last pat.

Cirrah roared to the sky, "And I will answer your call, Archmage, and meet whatever challenge awaits us together. Goodbye for now, my friend," Cirrah bowed his head to the companions and took to the sky once more, circled and headed west.

Gideon shaded his eyes as he watched the dragon fly off, "I thought them extinct and never had I imagined them intelligent."

Azrael's gaze followed Cirrah as the gold dragon disappeared in the distance, "Most believe as you do, Gideon. Dragons are reclusive and yes, as you have seen, quite intelligent; Cirrah even more than most. Don't be fooled, however. Not all of his kind are of the same temperament."

Gideon shook his head. "How a dragon came to be indebted to a mage must be some tale."

Lear'Za covered her mouth, chuckling, "It's the only beast in this world that can tolerate him."

Azrael rolled his mirrored eyes, "How very droll, daemoness. It is quite a simple tale but a tale for another day. I believe you have your concerns in San'Seban you wish to be updated on, do you not, Sir Gideon? Jozef also needs to see a healer for his leg as soon as possible. We could all use some rest. I have a nagging feeling things are about to become quite tumultuous."

Isidora tilted her head, "I assume this is all leading back to the prophecy. I am safe in the Kingdom."

Azrael narrowed his eyes, "I don't believe any of us are safe anywhere. Even here," Without another word, Azrael began walking south towards San'Seban.

The walk was quiet and not long. Before the companions reached the gates of the Castle Mount, a pair of armored riders met them. When they saw Gideon, they let out a whoop of revelry and jumped down to greet him. After a few pleasantries, one knight escorted the companions to San'Seban as the other raced ahead to inform the Kingdom of Sir Gideon's return.

By the time they entered the gates an honor guard had assembled, and a chorus of applause erupted. The Kingdom was in peril, and the return of one of its honored sons brought relief to many. His brothers in arms yelped and hollered joyously and placed a wreath around Isidora's neck. She beamed at the respect shown to her and the love expressed for her husband. A glance over to Azrael, who was staring at her, brought her back to reality. After all they had been through, she had still not informed him that Gideon was her husband. Someone was bound to mention that fact, and Azrael would find out in a manner she had not intended.

She pulled Gideon away from the throng of knights who had come to welcome him and leaned in close, "I will take my leave, my love, as you greet your friends. I will take Azrael with me. There are still certain things we have not told him."

Gideon paled slightly and coughed, "Ah yes, I understand," Gideon waved over a squire, "The Lady Isidora and her teacher require lodging immediately. See to it, and please bring our friend here to the temple to see a healer for his leg."

The squire nodded and got to work immediately. Isidora beckoned Azrael over, and the Archmage smirked and followed. The squire led them through a labyrinth of corridors, going deeper into the castle until they arrived at a hall of staterooms reserved for royal visitors. Azrael did not say a word as he entered his chambers and did not turn when Isidora followed and then closed the door behind her.

The Sidhe walked over to a window and looked down at the courtyard, watching the hubbub surrounding Gideon. Without turning, he spoke, "Apparently, you need to speak to me, Tra'ni."

Isidora paced the room and wrung her hands together, "Yes, D'ni. There is something I wish to speak to you about."

Azrael chuckled and turned, "Is it about you being Sir Gideon's wife?"

Isidora halted with a start, and her eyes were wide as she stammered, "Why...why, yes, it is. Wait. How?"

"How did I know is what you are asking? Quite simply, Isidora, to one who observes. I had my first inklings when you arrived together at my tower. Normally a knight escort would walk a few paces behind his charge, not at her side. Now, this could easily be explained if he was merely courting you. However, in Castellarian customs, a courting knight must still show chivalry in his duty and stand at the same distance as if you were merely his charge. Only a married knight would stand beside a woman in such a fashion. There were other clues as well. During our trip to the desert, before we retired one night he called you *ficclium,* an ancient Castellarian term of endearment used between spouses. I also could see the faint tan line of a wedding band upon his left hand that was recently removed, most likely just before your arrival at my tower. Now, all this evidence was damning enough in itself. But just now when we entered the castle, one of the knights placed a laurel wreath around your neck. Such wreaths are reserved for only noble lady wives," Azrael sighed, "Honestly, Isidora, if it were any more transparent it would have been laughable. Now the real question is, why in the abyss did you marry? And then, more confounding, feel the need to hide the fact from me?"

Isidora stood for a moment, her mouth agape. Angrily, she turned her back to him and grunted, "Of course you knew, D'ni. You always know everything, don't you? You relish knowing something you are not intended to know, then laugh at another's dismay when revealed. You disgust me, yet still amaze me," She shook her head, then cleared her throat, "I had a speech all planned out and prepared, but there is no point to that now, is there?

"All I can do now is answer your questions. Why? I know this is completely foreign to you, Azrael, but I love Gideon. I love him, and he loves me. Is there any other real reason for marriage? As for not telling you, I knew your reaction would not be pleasant. I was expecting enough resistance simply to ask for your help to become a summoner. I did not wish to make things more complicated with this fact until later."

Azrael sat on a divan and smoothed his robes, "Magi do not marry Isidora, at least not serious ones."

Isidora crossed her arms, "This is exactly what I meant. You know how serious I am about Art, D'ni. My marriage to Gideon does not change that!"

"It changes everything, girl! Your attention is now divided. You will no longer focus your entire thought and being upon your skill," Azrael turned his head away from her.

"I am sorry if I want more from life, Azrael!" Isidora shouted, "I love the Art; I live and breathe it as much as you."

Azrael narrowed his eyes, and his tone dropped to a cold whisper, "Never compare your dedication to the magic to my own. You have proven how much less dedicated you are."

Isidora spoke through clenched teeth, "Magic gives me purpose, D'ni, but it does not keep me warm at night. While you may find solace in your empty tower with your books and spells, most people in this world need more! You will never understand love, and I am done trying to make you understand!" Isidora turned and stormed out of the room. The door slammed shut behind her.

Azrael closed his eyes and bowed his head, and the silence broken by slow clapping. With a grunt Azrael, raised his head and saw Lear'Za sitting across from him.

"You are a complete arse, Seer'kaat, do you know that? And they call me a monster."

"I should have banished you in that circle when I first saw you, you ignorant sot," Azrael shot back.

Lear'Za laughed, "And that would have changed the discussion you just had how?"

"It wouldn't have, but it would have spared me having to discuss it with someone who was not invited to it in the first place." Azrael placed his head in his hands, "What do you want, Lear'Za?"

"I want you to care for the girl, Seer'kaat! Care for her as she deserves. Is that so damn hard?"

"I care for her in the ways that are the most important, daemoness! By training her, I have given her a gift no one could have. I have given her the tools to prepare for her future. A future she is apparently not ready for because she has now placed the entire world at peril."

Lear'Za sighed, "All I am saying is a little understanding wouldn't hurt."

Azrael narrowed his mirrored eyes, "You know I understand more than anyone. You know how wrong she is about my understanding of love."

"Just because you and I know, that doesn't mean she does. All you have shown is how completely devoid you are of it. You should tell her. Explain everything. All of it."

"Now is not the time, Lear'Za. She is not ready; far from ready. All my preparations have been for naught. It seems," Azrael sighed.

Lear'Za stood and made her way out of the room, "Then prepare to lose her, Seer'kaat. And if the threat of losing her is not enough, at least see how your inaction on the matter could jeopardize everything as well," Lear'Za walked out and left Azrael alone in the room, staring out the window at the celebration below.

Across the courtyard, from another high window, someone else looked down. He had been awake for a few nights, without sleep ever since the shout of his god. It had moved him and at the same time terrified him. He could not fail and what he saw below put his efforts in jeopardy. Sulik sat at his window motionless for a time, watching. Then, with a spontaneous snarl, he flung the tankard he held across the room and shattered the mirror in the corner.

CHAPTER 33

The companions received the treatment of royal guests. Jozef was quickly spirited away to the temple and spent the day resting as the healers completed their task. The others cleaned up and relaxed after their long journey and, in the evening, everyone was summoned to the audience hall for a feast with the king.

In the more relaxed atmosphere and confines of San'Seban, their attire became more formal. Azrael once again donned his formal black robes with the silver rune embroidered on the sleeves. Isidora's were quite similar save for a different pattern of runes. Kethis had traded his ranger's traveling garb for a more formal Elvan tunic and leggings with golden embroidery depicting the regal stag of his family lineage. Although he did not wear full plate armor, Gideon did wear his formal armor that was shined and polished. Jozef, walking with a slight limp, was resplendent in his traditional garb of flowing multi-colored silk bisht, voluminous sirwals, and sparkling rings on every finger topped off with a white ghutra and a golden iqal. Lear'Za's clothing was never made of tangible material but instead a construct of her magic and imagination. Instead of her usual very skimpy molded coverings, she decided upon something a little more formal for the occasion. She had on an ethereal dress that was quite majestic in cut and style. However, it was also transparent and revealed her undergarments as well that just so happened to be of lace and in very bright red. Gideon spent most of the time before the feast calming his fellow knights and nobles of her "distasteful" attire. It was something they were going to have to accept.

Joining the companions at the feast were King Diomere, Sir Falco, Lord Sulik, and Sir Montefroy. Although considered a state dinner, it was also a family event, and King Diomere did not invite Lord Medici and Lord Tempest to the feast, much to Sulik's dismay. The feast itself was extravagant, as per Kingdom standards. There were three main courses of roasted quail, boar, and swordfish. Fresh fruit from around Tinil'Gan was in abundance, warm bread right from the ovens, side dishes of steamed vegetables, and of course fine chilled wine.

Although thoroughly outnumbered, Sulik kept his wits about him with a smile and stood with a goblet in hand, "I propose a toast. To Sir Gideon and his wife the Lady Isidora: Castellamar is grateful for your return from your successful quest. I would also like to thank these companions who have kept my nephew safe from harm. In these dire times, we would not have liked to add the death of a loved one to the tragedies," Sulik lifted his goblet and drank deeply. Everyone else followed suit.

Gideon wiped his mouth and spoke, "Speaking of dire times, uncle, we wish to hear more of the news concerning the Spokes. We heard word of it through our friend, Jozef, but more details would be appreciated."

King Diomere gave a weak smile, "My good nephew; currently, we are in mourning for our late friend, Lord Marken and his family. In a few days' time, we shall take action. Let us enjoy our time together at present."

Gideon sighed, "My King Uncle, I understand your observance of our hallowed traditions, but it cannot distract us from the potential disaster that this might lead to."

Sulik gave a crooked smile, "The decimation of House Marken and the occupation of Granary is not a disaster in of itself, nephew?"

Gideon squared his jaw, "Of course it is, uncle. I only hope cool heads will prevail and that we shall do our due diligence before any rash action."

Sir Montefroy smiled, "It is indeed good to have you home, Sir Gideon. Your insight has been sorely missed."

Sulik snorted, "Lord Marken's head sits upon a pike alongside a Hollister banner, picked at by carrion birds as we dine in your honor, nephew. There is not much left to say."

Gideon leaned forward and pushed his plate away, "Something about this does not feel right, Lord Uncle. We've had peace. The Riverlands are plump with harvest as usual. Why now?"

Jozef took a sip of his wine and gave a loud *ahh*, "The boy speaks truth."

Everyone's head turned toward the Tunoshi. Sulik gave an audible chuckle, "And what does a Tunoshi sell-sword who has been in the desert for weeks know of the Riverlands?"

Jozef spread his hands and smiled, "Desert folk I may be, but blind and deaf I am not. As the good Sir Gideon informed you, it was I that brought news of this attack. The men wore Hollister colors and carried a Hollister banner, but of House Hollister, they are not."

Sulik's eyes narrowed, "You know this how?"

Jozef smiled broader, "It is my job to know. However, questions you have, so answers I shall provide. I have agents far and wide across the Evening Lands. I even have some in the Morning Lands across the seas. They bring me information, for as a desert proverb says, to the opportunist, information is more valuable than gold. Such a network of spies sees things that the casual or provincial person might not. One of these things is marching formations. These men did not march like Rivermen. I would also like to add another proverb if I may?"

Sulik spread his hands out, mockingly, "Please Master Shaddam. Enlighten us with your wisdom since you feel you are now an expert on Castellarian foreign affairs."

A couple of knights chuckled, and Sulik smiled in satisfaction. Jozef smiled back.

"Better a thousand enemies outside the tent than one within," Jozef said evenly, leaving out his usual cheerful tone.

The two men stared at each other, and the room fell silent. After a moment, Sulik grinned and raised his glass, "Then let us be glad our tent today is filled with friends," The knights and nobles in attendance raised their glasses with hearty cheers. Sulik found the man deplorable, but he knew he had to diffuse the tension.

King Diomere's interest was piqued, "If they were not Rivermen, who were they?"

Jozef sighed and spread his hands, "This I cannot say, good King. My agents told me only so much. Their true identity they could not decipher. However, they were convinced they were not Rivermen despite their trappings."

Kethis, who had sat silently listening, and found his moment to speak, "I fear this goes along with my reports from Luminos. I communicated with the Guardian upon my arrival in San'Seban, to brief him on our journey, and learn what had become of the contingent of these supposed Rivermen that were headed towards Elvan lands. A few nights ago, well-prepared elvan archers defended our borders from these attackers where Granary could not. They were driven off successfully. Over the centuries we have had our skirmishes with the Riverlords. Many of our veteran troops have experience fighting them. Many said these invaders did not fight like Rivermen."

Sulik's mouth twitched, "There are many possible reasons for this. They could be green troops or changes in training procedures. It is not our job to dissect their protocols. It is our job to protect the Kingdom at any cost."

Sir Mallister harrumphed, "In light of this news, I feel it is safe to say we should not ride upon the Spokes, engulfing the land in war, without speaking first with Lord Hollister. For all we know, someone might be attacking his people in our trappings, as well. This needs to be illuminated and discussed."

King Diomere sighed, "So much confusion and chaos. Sir Mallister is correct. Let us consider my nephew's return a blessing from the gods, bringing us news that could prevent an even greater tragedy. Kethis, what else did your uncle the Guardian have to say on the matter?"

"My uncle sends word that Luminos is willing to work together with the Kingdom against this threat," Kethis said, "But only under one condition."

"What condition is that, good elf?" King Diomere responded.

"The condition is that if elvan troops are to fight beside Kingdom knights, they will only do so if under the joint command of Sir Gideon and myself. I have spoken to my uncle of Sir Gideon's valor and bravery. He trusts my judgment and considers my words here as if spoken by himself," Gideon looked over at Kethis and smiled. Kethis nodded.

King Diomere nodded, "That is one condition I am happy to accommodate. Now then, since this dinner has become an impromptu council, what should we do about contacting the Spokes?"

Sulik cleared his throat, "My Lord, I feel this is something to be considered before the actual Council, with all your trusted advisors. I am sure we can come up with a logical course of action…"

"I'll go," Azrael's whispering words cut off Lord Sulik's. All eyes turned to the Archmage, who had been silent until now; his food sat before him untouched, "I will meet with Lord Hollister."

"D'ni, do you not think these are matters best handled by the Castellian royal family?" Isidora interjected.

Sulik did not waste a second in his response, "The Lady is correct, Archmagus. The Council of Lords is well equipped to handle this situation. A mage is hardly suited for affairs of state."

Azrael gave Isidora a quick sharp glance and once again cut off Sulik's words, "As a guest of this house, I will kindly ask you once, Lord Sulik, not to insult my intelligence again. I have served as envoy and ambassador in state affairs since before your great-great-grandparents were born. I have watched the decline of this Kingdom decade by decade, and it has not improved itself since you took the helm, Realm Regent. If I can be quite frank, I do not trust you as far as I can throw you and honestly cannot comprehend why anyone else trusts you."

Sir Mallister spat out his drink and laughed. Azrael looked over at the interruption then continued.

"Considering that we are unsure of the identity of these invaders, unsure about what role, if any, Lord Hollister is playing, it would serve both sides best if an independent third party served as an emissary. Time is of the essence. As I am, at the moment, the only outsider readily available, with considerable experience in these matters, it only makes sense to take my offer graciously."

Lord Sulik ground his teeth behind his smile, "And what motives are we to thank for your gracious offer, Archmagus?"

Azrael narrowed his mirrored eyes, "My council is my own to keep, Lord Sulik. I rule no kingdom and swear loyalty to none; I stand nothing to gain and nothing to lose in this matter. My motives are pure."

Sulik slammed down his tankard, and his nostrils flared. King Diomere patted his arm and interjected, "Archmagus Azrael, we do indeed thank you for your offer. Although my brother does not appear to be so, he is also thankful. He is a loyal servant to the Kingdom, and sometimes his passion gets the better of him. I know of you and some of your exploits from my youthful education. Your name is known across Tinil'Gan. On behalf of the Kingdom of Castellamar, I accept your offer."

How is this happening? His eyes darted back and forth as he went over plans upon plans in his mind in an attempt to correct for these recent developments. Then it came to him, and he smiled, "As always, I must defer to the wisdom of my King. I did not mean to insult, Archmagus, and I am indeed grateful for your offer. All I ask is that you allow a knight to escort you to the Spokes. Should Lord Hollister indeed be treacherous, we would be accountable should any harm befall you. I am sure you would like Sir Gideon to accompany you, however, if he and Kethis are to be in joint command of our defensive and possible offensive forces, they have much to prepare. I have just the person in mind, and it should be someone you trust, I am sure."

Azrael cocked an eyebrow, "And who do you suggest, Lord Sulik?"

Sulik smiled broadly, showing his teeth, "Why none other than Lady Isidora's father, Sir Griffon Shadowbane."

CHAPTER 34

Diarmuid's thoughts voraciously ate at his soul as he prepared to leave Luminos. *How did you survive, Azrael?* He had packed a few papers and items in his satchel and checked the portal for readiness.

The Windows of Time are permanently enchanted portals that led from the Tower of Elizar, the Conclave's main facility on Stone's Keep, to strategic locations across Tinil'Gan. With the permission of the leaders of nations, their capitals and keeps held one of the devices. One such window was in Luminos. Of course, this was a dangerous and possibly subversive device, so only those of the highest order in the Conclave were allowed the use of the Windows. Diarmuid, as the head of the Conclave, had such rights. Right now, Diarmuid had to return to the Tower of Elizar to speak with the Conclave immediately. The hour was late; the sun had already set. But like many across the world, he had also heard Leto's shout. The prophecy was at hand, and that meant Azrael's scheme was going to be accelerated. Discussion with his fellow magi and elicit their support against the Sidhe was crucial. He knew it would be an uphill battle, but a struggle he had to attempt nonetheless.

He made his way up the winding stairs to one of the uppermost floors of the tower. When he reached the room where the Windows of Time were kept, he placed his hand on the runes and murmured the phrase known only to the Conclave. The wards released, and the door opened. The room itself was empty other than the Windows of Time. To the untrained eye, it would seem nothing more than an expensive mirror. Made of ornately engraved silver, it was beautiful. The engravings depicted runes and scenes of magi casting spells. Three crystal orbs were embedded around the perimeter of the Window.

He touched the crystal orbs and murmured arcane words for each. Each, in turn, began to glow in the colors of the three orders of magi; white, black, and green. The opaque Window began to hum, and multiple colors began to swirl within, at first slow and then more rapidly. When they coalesced into one solid color, Diarmuid stepped through with a short flash, and the portal in Luminos went dark.

The Window of Time in the Hall of Transference within the Tower of Elizar began to glow in the same manner, and from its swirl stepped Diarmuid. The white mage made his way to his chamber to prepare for the calling of the Conclave. Somehow, someway, Azrael had survived it all. A Nidhogg summoned by Caiaphas and a hundred Tunoshi swordsman that just happened to fall on them. An Elvan priest of Astraea even informed him that, on good word, the Temple of Leto had sent a horde of liches. He had survived, along with Kethis Kitharii and Sir Gideon Stormcaller. He still could not understand how an insignificant band of companions could cause so much trouble, but that was precisely what they were doing.

Now Azrael was to act as an emissary to the Spokes, but Diarmuid's biggest concern was Azrael's delusions of grandeur and his role in the little known Ti'Relan Prophecy. Sulik had briefed him in his missive on his revised plan for Azrael and his mission of peace. The idea seemed sound, but to solidify it, he had to garner the support of the Conclave. If he could not sway them to a firm belief in Azrael's madness, he might at least foster enough doubt to prompt some investigation.

After a brief meditation, Diarmuid sighed a cleansing breath and rang a bell-rope for a servant. He instructed him to call the Conclave to meet. He watched the servant scurry out, closed his eyes, and sighed. A moment later he opened his eyes and strode to the Conclave Chambers.

It took a little less than an hour, but eventually, all of the Conclave members gathered, only one chair of the nine was empty. That infernally, eternally empty seat meant for Azrael. Diarmuid stood patiently at his position on the dais as the magi settled in. When the room quieted, Berilil spoke out.

"Well, Diarmuid, we are here. I certainly hope this is of dire importance to call us together at this hour."

"It most definitely is, Berilil. I do wish to extend my gratitude to all of you for making it here with such expediency."

"Then let us get on with it, shall we?" Berilil said sleepily.

Diarmuid smiled and nodded, "Of course. First, I would like to update you all on current affairs in the world since we are all here last. As we all were aware, there was some strife between Castellamar and the Spokes. Last we heard, a contingent of House Hollister bannermen had taken control of the town of Granary and executed all of House Marken in the process. We also knew of another force headed towards Luminos. As we suspected, Castellamar is preparing for war. The elves, warned by an elf-lord named Kethis Kitharii, were able to fend off the attack and have extended an alliance offer to the Kingdom. The Kingdom has accepted this offer."

"So there shall be war upon the Evening Lands once again?" said a female black robe.

"At the moment, we are at a point of limbo. Due to the warning from Kethis as well as the return of Sir Gideon Stormcaller, some doubt as to the identity of the invaders has been brought to light. Because of this, an envoy is being sent to House Hollister to divulge the intent and perpetrators of these attacks."

Berilil scratched his patchy white beard, "Well then, there is hope for peace after all."

Diarmuid smirked, "So one might think, and hope. However, this brings me to the main point of the meeting. The one heading this envoy is none other than Archmagus Azrael."

"Azrael? What does the Archmagus have to do with this political strife?" questioned a white robe.

"Everyone here knew of his quest with his student, Isidora. Kethis and Sir Gideon were a part of this quest, and they arrived together in San'Seban. It was there Azrael volunteered for the mission," Diarmuid said evenly.

Berilil's face screwed up in confusion, "This still explains nothing, Diarmuid. Get on with it. Why did Azrael volunteer and why should we care?"

Diarmuid took a breath and spoke, "I am sure I am not the only one who heard the shout the two nights past," The assembly began to murmur. A few shouts of *I did,* and *as did I* rose up. Diarmuid raised his hand to quiet them, "I regret this is the soonest we were able to meet to discuss these events. This was the soonest all could be available," He unrolled an old parchment and read aloud: "' With this act, the herald's trumpet blows in the voice of a God it comes shaking many to their souls.' Many of you should be familiar with the Ti'Relan Prophecies by now. Azrael's mad quest, which I have warned you about often, is being set into motion."

Berilil harrumphed, "Diarmuid, we have heard this old complaint of yours for years. What makes now any different? Yes, many heard the shout, and it may portend many things, perhaps even this prophecy. But it does not implicate Azrael with any guilt or as a possible threat to the world, let alone the Art which is what we are, first and foremost, concerned with."

Diarmuid looked down at the parchment and read another line, "'great war ensues encompassing all Old foes of East, West, North, and South battle.' Azrael is meddling in political affairs because of this! He believes this prophecy to his very core, and at this point, so should we all. He intends to stop this prophecy from happening."

"Is that necessarily a bad thing, Diarmuid? As magi, I am sure none of us would be happy with a world ruled by Leto and his impending chaos," Hestion said.

Diarmuid sighed, "It is not his intention to subvert the prophecy that I fear. It is his methods that frighten me to my core. My fellow magi, Azrael intends to stop this prophecy by challenging the god himself!"

The assembly broke out in shouts and jeers. Diarmuid leaned back and crossed his arms and let the arguments ensue for some time. A cry from Berilil calmed the magi. Once it quieted, he turned to Diarmuid, "Even if this were true, Leto would crush him. He is a god!"

"I thought by now, with all the reverence given to the Archmagus by this Conclave, you would give him the credit he is due. Azrael is not a stupid man, nor is he impulsive. Do you believe he would even consider this course of action if he did not feel he stood some chance of victory? The man is a Sidhe! Even with this Conclave's collective knowledge and extensive familiarity with history, we are still uncertain of the full extent and power of the Sidhe, especially considering what we know of some creation stories. All of us have trained and studied our entire lives to attain the power we hold in the Art. Sidhe are the Art! And of the Sidhe, it can easily be said Azrael has ever been the most gifted of their kind. As slight as his chances are, I do not believe I have to explain the consequences of Azrael succeeding. Even his failure could bring about catastrophic consequences upon magi and their use of the Art by an angry Leto!"

The assembly erupted again in a much more raucous argument. It took many shouts of *order* and gavel banging by Berilil before the assembled magi quieted. The old black robe sighed, "Diarmuid, the charges you bring are outrageous and, if true, grievous. I, for one, do not believe them," Berilil heaved another heavy sigh, "However, I believe we can all agree that we should investigate the matter at the very least, to clear Azrael of these accusations."

"Azrael leaves for the Spokes in the morning. He should arrive there in no more than three days. Choose from among you who shall be in the investigation committee. If my intuition is correct, I believe Azrael will show his true motives then and there."

Discussion and argument rose up once again as Diarmuid left the chambers. He smiled in satisfaction.

CHAPTER 35

"What are you thinking, D'ni?" Isidora burst out as soon as they had exited the dining hall and entered the sitting room where the companions were alone. The raven-haired mage was in a frenzy, pacing back and forth. Azrael walked over to a divan and sat, his arms folded in his sleeves. For the moment the others remained quiet as Isidora vented, "The gall, the utter gall! D'ni, I have always respected you and your wisdom. I have always given way to your better judgment, usually without question. But this...this is utter madness!"

Azrael gave a thin-lipped smirk from the shadowy depths of his hood, "This time should be no different, Isidora."

"You were in the royal dining hall of the King of Castellamar, insulting, no downright degrading the kingdom's Realm Regent! Barring any intervention from the King, the man could have had you fettered and chained with a wave of his hand!"

Azrael remained calm, "It would never have come to that. The man knows better."

"You had no right or place to intervene in the politics of this realm the way you did. Gideon was handling it just fine."

Azrael's mirrored eyes shone, and his hands gripped the arms of the divan, "Gideon is still a boy! He handled himself well, I admit, but he is a boy nonetheless, who is still not aware of the powers he is facing not only on the surface but behind the scenes. When have I ever steered you wrong, or anyone for that matter, Isidora? Hrmm?"

Isidora's face hardened, "I suppose Talia was led in the correct direction as well."

Azrael rose deftly; his thin hand shot out and slapped her. "Don't you dare!"

Gideon clenched his jaw and stepped forward. Lear'Za shook her head and stopped him with a light hand upon his chest. He was angry and with just cause. With a growl, Gideon stormed from the room. Lear'Za looked over at Kethis and Jozef and nodded her head in the direction Gideon had gone, and they followed their comrade without question. When they were gone, she leaned back against the wall and folded her arms, watching.

Isidora eyed Azrael with a hand over her cheek. Her low words spilled from her lips, "You have never struck me, D'ni. Not even as a child in your tower."

Azrael turned his back, "What you said was unwarranted and unneeded. Talia sacrificed herself for us. Not I nor anyone led her to such a choice. Do not tarnish her act by using her name in your petty anger," Azrael sighed, "Isidora, there have been and still are things I do vigilantly to protect you. There are so many things I have endured, so many deplorable acts I enacted, all in the name of your safety. All I ask for is your trust."

Isidora took a few steps and raised a hand towards his shoulder, as if to turn him, but dropped it to her side, "D'ni, I do trust you. But even with that trust, I will always have questions. This you have taught me, never trust blindly, and to always question, gather information, trust but verify. You give me so little; the things you do which seem clear as day and perfectly logical seem insane to me for the mere fact that I do not understand the actions themselves or the reasoning behind them. How does involving yourself in the politics of the Evening Lands protect me? What does any of this have to do with me?"

Azrael turned and removed his hood. For a moment Lear'Za saw it. The daemoness held her breath; briefly, she saw his mirrored eyes start to crack. *Say it, Seer'kaat!* She leaned forward.

Azrael took a step forward. His mouth almost formed the beginnings of a real smile; instead, it twisted to a cynical smirk. Lear'Za sighed, and her back fell against the wall.

"Isidora, I have survived the millennia by making the right choices. I have been second-guessed by people far more intelligent and wise than you only to prove them wrong time and time again. You must trust me and my choices and know they are for the best. You did not consult me on becoming a summoner. You just did it and asked for my help after the fact. You did not consult me about getting married; you went ahead and expected me to be blind to it like some imbecile. You do nothing but insult my intelligence. Not once did you consider the ramifications of such actions. You are just as impetuous now as you were as a child."

Her face contorted into a grimace. Her brows creased and her hands clenched, "You speak to me like a parent, D'ni. You are not my father! You are my teacher, and nothing more!" For a split second Azrael flinched but just as quickly he was composed. Lear'Za had seen enough. She lowered her head with a shake.

Azrael chuckled, "If it is any condolence, your father will arrive by the morn to accompany me to the Spokes. Let us hope he does not muck this up."

Isidora growled and rolled her eyes, "You are incorrigible. Have you no decency? The man is my father and a knight!"

"The man is a consistent meddler, one who believes himself more intelligent than he is, and a professional oaf!" Azrael shouted.

Isidora shook her head in disbelief, "At least that oaf knew how to be caring and made me feel like I mattered."

Azrael narrowed his eyes, "Perhaps that is for the best. However, if only to put an end to this tantrum, one day soon we are going to have an extensive discussion on the questions you have. I can assure you, at that time I will be completely forthright and honest."

Isidora's anger faded away into complete, cold calm. She replaced her hood, "I will not hold my breath, D'ni. As far as I am concerned from this day forth, we have nothing left to discuss. When you are done with this mission, you do not even have to bother to come say goodbye," She turned and walked out the room.

How long can he keep this up? Lear'Za floated over to Azrael, her arms crossed, "Was any of that necessary? Any of it at all?"

"Am I now to be guided by my student? She expects me to stay out of her choices, but she wants to dictate mine?"

"She is a mage employed by Castellamar. It has been her home and duty for the past five years. As you already know, Gideon is her husband and nephew to the king. She is both mage and a Lady here. She feels you once again taking away her agency to make choices and to lead. It is the whole reason she left your tower!"

"So what was I to do Lear'Za? Hmm? Nothing? Let this kingdom make another confounding mistake that affects the lives of thousands of innocents? I cannot, will not, in good conscious sit by and let things happen!"

"But you have no problem trampling her in the process. You disappoint me, Seer'kaat."

Azrael paused and bowed his head. His voice came out as a raspy whisper, "It is my curse to disappoint anyone close to me. I have accepted this."

The next morning found the companions well-rested yet restless. The tension was palpable at the breakfast table. Isidora seated herself with Gideon as far as possible from Azrael and had looked at the Archmage. They broke their fast with Lord Sulik and Gideon's father, Sir Falco. Gideon and his father spoke in low tones catching up.

"What do you make of all this, father?"

Falco eyed the room; his long mustachios swaying, "Something is amiss, my son. I do not trust my younger brother and never have. The fact is we have been attacked. We may have no other choice but to act."

"I am trying to keep hope this mission can bring peace and not war. I do not know if we can trust Azrael as well. I am not comfortable with him playing a large role in the parlay."

Falco sipped from his cup. He stared at Gideon for a moment and placed his hand on his son's, "You have more to fear from those in this room who claim loyalty to the Kingdom."

Gideon gave his father a confused look.

A page announced the arrival of Sir Shadowbane, interrupting their conversation. Before the page could even finish his sentence, Griffon Shadowbane burst into the room, his arms outstretched, and with a booming voice interrupted the page's introduction.

"Where is my little girl!"

Griffon Shadowbane was wearing his full plate. Dented and tarnished, the enameled yellow and black griffon, the sigil of House Shadowbane screamed in defiance. If he was not seven feet tall, he was close enough. His once auburn hair was streaked with gray and hung unkempt at shoulder length. Brown and gray stubble outlined the faint wrinkles on his face.

At the sound of her father's voice, Isidora yelped and ran to hug him, "Father! I am so glad to see you!"

Isidora placed her arm through her father's elbow and led him to the table, "I am so sorry I have not been in touch. I have been extremely occupied lately, but I was making plans to come visit you and mother after these affairs have been settled."

Griffon gave a sizeable toothy smile and patted her hand, "It is fine, my girl. You have grown into a woman, a woman with responsibilities, and your own life to live. Now, where is this son-in-law of mine?"

Gideon rose and shook hands with Griffon, "Sir Shadowbane, it is indeed an honor and a great joy to see you once again. Isidora cares for you deeply. This places you within my thoughts, as well."

Griffon clapped a hand on Gideon's shoulder, "Sir Gideon Stormcaller, the pleasure is mine my boy. She could not have picked a better man,"

Lord Sulik rose and extended his hand to Griffon, "Sir Shadowbane, I thank you again for coming at such short notice," Sulik bore his eyes into the large man. Griffon's expression hardened for a moment as he shook the Realm Regent's hand. He then smiled.

"It is my honor and duty to serve the Kingdom, Lord Sulik. I do so with no regret or dismay. Your missive was brief, so perhaps you can fill me in some more," Sulik nodded at Griffon and they all seated themselves.

Griffon settled his eyes on the Archmage when Sulik mentioned Azrael's name. His eyes were dark, "Archmage, I see you are well."

Azrael's mirrored eyes stared back, "I am, Sir Griffon. The years seem to be treating you...well."

Griffon's mouth screwed up into a snarl, "I am just a man, Archmage, and I age as a man. Unlike the unnatural state of your kind. I may not be the youthful self I was those years back when you stole my daughter from me, but I can assure you I am every bit the man I was then."

"Undoubtedly and unfortunately."

Griffon's hand clenched, and he opened his mouth to retort. Sulik began to quickly explain the situation, stopping him, "Nonetheless, we have a mission. The Kingdom's safety depends on the outcome of this. Per the Archmage's request, his companions Lear'Za and Jozef Shaddam will be accompanying him to the Spokes and you, Sir Griffon, will be their escort."

Azrael spoke without turning his head, "And as an escort, it is imperative that you remain silent during the talks with Lord Hollister."

Sulik smiled and once again spoke before Griffon could speak, "Sir Griffon is well aware of his duties, Archmagus. He knows his role in this mission," Sulik gave Griffon a nod, and the knight nodded back.

"For his sake, I certainly hope so," Isidora gave a start, and Gideon held her back with a pat on her hand. Azrael continued unfettered, "We have little time to waste. If we are to depart let us do so."

Griffon snorted, "I would like to spend at least a few minutes with my daughter, Archmage."

Azrael had already risen from the table and was making his way out. He did not turn as he spoke his parting words, "If this is how dutiful and honor-bound you are to the Kingdom,

I would hate to see those who are your lesser. It will take me fifteen minutes to prepare my horse. If you are not present by then, I will depart without you."

With a chuckle and shake of her head, Lear'Za rose and, followed by Jozef, headed for the door. She leaned over Sir Griffon as she passed by, "He isn't kidding," Her hips swayed as she walked away, leaving Sir Griffon red-faced in anger.

CHAPTER 36

Azrael held true to his word. Along with Jozef and Lear'Za, he rode out of the castle fifteen minutes later. Sir Griffon was still packing his horse as they disappeared through the gate and had to put his horse into a gallop to catch up with them. The rest of the ride was entirely silent.

The well-paved KingsMarch ran from San'Seban though Castle Pass and out into the Riverlands. From there, it continued straight south to the gates of the Spokes. The first thing Azrael noted was the lack of any sentries or scouts. For a land supposedly on the brink of war, one would think the road would be rife with Owl Men. Instead, it was eerily empty all the way south for two days until they were in close vicinity to the Spokes.

Although not far apart, one could tell the difference between Castellamar and the Riverlands. While valleys and vineyards, keeps and strongholds surrounded San'Seban, the Riverlands were more pedestrian. It consisted mostly of farms and plains.

Although the Riverlands had its lords and knights, the Riverfolk were simpler people.

It was shortly after the morning of the third day that they saw the imposing structure that was the Spokes rise on the horizon. Unlike San'Seban with its stone buildings, the Spokes architecture consisted of wood, but it was not any less imposing. The entire structure, true to its name, was seated on the intersection of four rivers looking like the central hub of a wheel that was circular looking; like a giant barrel. The vertical timbers that made the outer ring of the structure were composed of red ironwood from the foothills of the Castellian Mountains. The giant pillars were at least three feet in diameter each and stood nearly a hundred feet tall. At strategic intervals, giant metal bands encircled the timbers to hold them all together. It had stood the test of time and did not appear to be faltering.

As they neared the Spokes, the drawbridge came down, and a contingent of Hollister knights rode out to meet them. The one in the lead called his men to halt, and he drew up his horse before the envoy group.

"It is a nice day for a stroll, gentlemen, and lady. However, it seems your direction takes you to the Spokes. May I inquire your intent?" The knight's tone was polite yet stern.

Azrael lowered his hood and gave a slight smile, "Indeed it is, sir knight. You are correct; our travel does have a purpose. I wish to parley with Lord Hollister on behalf of the Kingdom of Castellamar."

The knight nodded, "Well, this is an odd sight," he eyed each of them, "Lord Hollister is a busy man. I am his nephew Sir Rodrick Hollister, commander of the Knights of the Spokes. I assume this has to do with Granary. We heard of its tragedy. We also know it was done under our banners. I do not know what treachery is at play, but this was not Hollister work."

Azrael raised an eyebrow, "I must say I did not expect this response. While it is a pleasure to make your acquaintance, Sir Rodrick, these are things of dire importance to discuss. I can assure you; this is an envoy of peaceful intent despite my Castellarian escort. I have no loyalty to the Kingdom or any kingdom. I am an independent third party unbiased in my regard. My name is Azrael, Archmagus of the black robes."

Sir Rodrick scanned the group over for a moment, then clucked his tongue, "Very well, I shall take you to my uncle. Please do not find me presumptuous, but your weapons will be left at the gate. If this is a mission of peace, I am sure you will not need them, and I can assure you we will not give you a reason to think you do. Follow me," Sir Rodrick dropped his visor and reared his horse around, back towards the Spokes. Azrael and his contingent followed him down the KingsMarch and through the massive gates of the Spokes.

The differences between San'Seban, with its halls of gilded stone, the wooden keep of the Spokes were even more apparent when they entered. The gates opened up to an immense courtyard littered with buildings. Like the outer walls, the buildings were also made of hearty wood a few with some stone as a foundation, but mostly wood nonetheless.

The intersection of the rivers met at the center of the courtyard. It was indeed a spectacle to behold and was the reason for the immense structure that was the Spokes. At the center was a vortex, which swirled as eddies and currents of the rivers crashed into each other. This confluence created a large violent lake housed within the gargantuan structure that powered various watermills. Azrael noted another structural section that seemed to have no purpose; four massive chains ran from high up the outer timber walls into the rivers themselves. He had visited the Spokes many times during his long life, and they had always been there since his first visit. No one had ever explained to him the purpose of those chains; he vowed to find out one day. At the center of the courtyard, elevated above the vortex intersection by tall standing poles stood a large building with a high roof that was five times as long as it was wide. Curiously, another large chain came out from the bottom of the building, dropping down into the vortex.

This was the well-known Mead Hall. It served as royal housing, meeting chambers, feasting hall, and audience chamber for Lord Hollister. Sir Rodrick led them up a winding staircase to the Mead Hall and escorted them in. In the center of the building ran an immensely long and thick table that looked large enough to seat every Owl Knight, the royal family, guests, dignitaries, and still leave room for more. The large chain they saw coming from beneath the building came up through the center of the table and up into the high ceiling through the roof. A stairway led up to a second story that had all the sleeping rooms on one end for guests and senior ranking members of House Hollister and on the other end the royal family suites.

Sir Rodrick pointed at the stairs, "There are readily prepared suites on this level for you. Make yourselves at home as guests when ready. My uncle is occupied at the moment but will return for dinner. Our staff will attend to any of your needs until then, and I will have them bring refreshments as well. Welcome to the Spokes," Rodrick gave a bow and briskly walked away.

Lear'Za chuckled. "Curt and polite fellow isn't he."

Jozef patted her on the back, "The Riverfolk have long been known for their hospitality, so I've been told. It is a good omen, yes?"

Lear'Za grunted and slumped into a chair that curiously rose off the ground and hovered before her back end was seated. She crossed her legs and dropped her chins into her hands, "I'm losing it. The man didn't even so much as a glance in my direction. I'm half-naked!"

"Don't let them fool you. They are a crafty lot. No doubt Lord Hollister is meeting with his war advisors as we speak, plotting another attack on the Kingdom," Sir Griffon grumbled as a staff member brought in a pitcher of mead and a decanter of wine.

Azrael gave a short snort, "Do you not think the sight of a Castellarian envoy escorted by a Castellarian knight would have given them some pause?" He casually walked over to a window and pulled aside a curtain and looked down at the comings and goings in the courtyard, "No, this is not the camp of a war-hungry campaign. It is far too relaxed and calm. With Roderick's comment claiming the Spokes has nothing to do with the attack, they believe their honor in this matter will be observed," Azrael dropped the curtain and turned with his arms folded in his sleeves, "Again, Sir Griffon, I advise you to keep your comments to yourself when we meet with Lord Hollister. If your first impression just now is any indication, your powers of observation are not to be admired."

Sir Griffon removed his gauntlets and threw them down on a table, "My loyalty is to the Kingdom, Azrael, and shall always be! Yours, on the other hand, has always been dubious at best, and for the most part, self-serving. Just like when you stole my daughter!"

"Seriously, Shadowbane, this old argument again? You know as well as I that your daughter came with the full consent yourself and your Lady. Even you cannot argue it was not in her best interest. You have no understanding of the Art. Keep your wits about you, knight. For all you doubting my motives, I seem to be the only one with his mind on the task at hand. Stop whining about an event decades ago and concentrate on the present!"

Jozef came between the two, a smile on his face as he handed them each a filled tankard, "Please, friends. Let us not argue.

We are all here for the same reason, yes? Drink. Relax. The day is ours. Let us enjoy it before we attend to serious matters."

Lear'Za gave an annoyed sigh and stood up, "You can all sit here if you want. I'm going to go get some fresh air and mingle," She flashed a wicked grin, showing the slight points of her teeth.

Azrael gave her a stern look, "Lear'Za."

Lear'Za rolled her eyes and waved her hand about, "Yes, yes, Seer'kaat. I know," She pinched her nose to mock Azrael's whispery voice, "No maiming, killing, dismembering, or harm of any kind to anyone. Basically, Lear'Za, you can have no fun at all," She released her nose and smiled, "Fear not, Seer'kaat. I only intend to find more pedestrian fun that ends up with everyone smiling and alive and well. As much as that bores me, it is better than nothing." Lear'Za gave a curt and mocking bow and left the room.

The three men watched her leave then sat at the table. Jozef took a deep swing from his tankard, then let out a loud *ahh* as he leaned back, "So, here we are, Friends. It is indeed amazing where one's journey can take one unexpectedly," Jozef smiled and looked over at Sir Griffon, "Sir Griffon, you are Isidora's father, yes? May I say, despite your disagreements with the Archmagus, I must say that you have a very well-minded and good-hearted daughter. I admire her. You should be proud."

Sir Griffon beamed, "Thank you, Master Shaddam. Mara and I tried our best to instill values in Isidora. While she spent much of her time in that infernal tower, the summers were ours, and we taught her about life where Azrael could not."

"You have no idea what I taught her, Sir Griffon, so please do not try and pretend to even grasp it. I'll allow that her time away did do her good, if only so that she might expend her childish energies elsewhere, so she could dedicate her time at the tower to her studies."

Sir Griffon drained his tankard and slammed it down, "I am going to take a nap, I tire of this company," Griffon stood and left the room to retire to his own suite.

Jozef sighed and looked at Azrael pleadingly, "Is the animosity necessary? To what end does it serve us?"

Azrael lifted his chin, "I have reasons for everything I do. You do not know that man like I do. There is history," He looked away. *You have no idea what he has done and what I have prevented him from doing.* "What you do not see is that I am testing him. His every thought is trained on his hatred of me, and I do not like it. Not because I care for his feelings about me in the slightest, but because I fear his reasons for being here are not as pure as we were meant to believe. I do not see his play yet, but we must keep a close eye on good Sir Griffon."

Jozef spread his hands, "As you wish, Beduiin. Who am I to argue your logic?" Jozef rose, "I shall also retire. Although healed, my leg is still somewhat sore and could use some rest. If you have a need, call on me, and I shall be ready at a moment's notice," Jozef gave a flourishing bow and left the room.

Azrael sat silent, mulling over everything he had seen and heard since they left San'Seban.

CHAPTER 37

Isidora watched from a window as her father and her teacher left San'Seban together. She did not go out to give them a farewell; she couldn't. Her thoughts, feelings, her everything was in conflict. This did give her some time alone with Gideon since they first departed for the Isle of Winds. He walked over to her by the window and placed his hands on her shoulders.

"A copper piece for your thoughts?" He murmured.

"This thing between my father and Azrael has always hovered over us since I can remember," She said dejectedly.

"While House Shadowbane has been on hard times the last few generations, I don't ever recall anyone in San'Seban speaking ill of Sir Griffon. He's gruff, but I like the man. It is more than I can say for Azrael."

Her eyes glazed over as she stared out the window, "I only saw him a month or two a year since I was five. I don't even remember my life before then. That is all the memories I have of him. He gave me anything I ever wanted. I remember one Yule when I was eight, I cried and cried for a Yule wreath made of hyacinths. I had no idea how expensive they were as a child.

I learned later from mother he sold one of his swords to get it for me," She paused and smiled, "But more importantly, he gave me love."

"Well that sounds wonderful and everything a father should be."

"It does. Except it was only for a month or two a year. That means by the time I took the trials, I had spent less than two years with my family in total. Every time I visited him and mother, she would tell the horrible bouts of melancholy he had. She always kept a stiff upper lip, my mother. Always smiling no matter what," She walked away from the window and sat on the bed, her hands rubbing her thighs, "But there had always been one thing missing. I could never discuss my magic with him. Anytime I brought up the new things I learned with Azrael, his face would turn dark and venomous, so much so that it would frighten me. *Not in this house, Isidora! Never speak of that here do you understand me* he would say, and instantly I would lower my head and stop. I would cry inside. For all the love he gave me, I could not share the thing I loved most, my magic. That was the one thing Azrael was always there for me. Without fail."

"Do you blame him, though? The magic and Azrael are what took you away from him for most of your life."

Isidora shook her head, "You still don't understand magi, Gideon. It is not something we just like doing. It is a part of us, a part of our soul. It was as if I had to deny my true self at home, forget that I was a talented and skilled mage and pretend to be nothing more than a knight's daughter. I always resented this, and it left a void between my father and me. Many times I felt that, despite all the love and caring I received, I did not belong there; that something just wasn't right."

Gideon frowned and sat on the bed beside her, "From what you've told me, it's not like living with Azrael was any comfort.

I'd imagine at least those precious moments at home would be a comfort."

"Oh no, Azrael gave me nary a kind word, a hug, or even a pat on the back. He was a taskmaster. Always vigilant, always diligent, the only discussions he would entertain were on the Art or history. But he always praised me when I accomplished a task or goal in my studies. I could feel his pride; it is something I held dear and was my life's goal. There definitely were times I felt my only friend was the Art. I am grateful for the fact I also had Lear'Za and Talia," She paused as she thought of her lost friend and swallowed a lump in her throat, "Lear'Za was my surrogate mother and Talia like a sister. They, at the end of it all, were my family."

"And that gave you the comfort you needed," Gideon nodded in understanding.

"There was definitely more. Nothing else mattered when I practiced," Her eyes glimmered, "By the gods, I marveled at the wonders I learned from him. He has shown me things and opened my eyes to a world, unlike any other; a world of power and beautiful majesty. He uncovered my true nature. He allowed me to be who I was and pushed me further. Just when I thought I had reached the limits of my abilities, he would give one more nudge, revealing that I was more powerful than I imagined. I owe him everything; all that I am now was because of his teachings, his encouragement, his devotion, and belief in me."

"I am glad you are telling me all this Isi. I mean, you have told me plenty since we fell in love, but this is the most open and vulnerable you've been about your life. It helps me understand better. Be better," He lowered his head and shuffled his feet, "Be better in the event I am ever a father."

The man wanted children. She smiled at the thought but never fully wrapped her mind around the idea. How could she be a mother when she was so devoted to her Art? Loving

Gideon came easy because he asked nothing of her except to be by her side. But a child! *A child would depend on me for everything, all my time and energy; all my devotion. Azrael was right, there was a reason true magi did not marry.*

She gave a weak smile and stood, "You do realize that my devotion to the Art and my successes as a Summoner will not end? There is no end game in my career; it is a lifelong devotion."

His face was crestfallen, "I know Isi. It was just a thought."

She turned and looked at herself in the mirror. Her raven curls, her violet eyes, so unlike Mara and Griffon, so unlike anyone she knew. *Who am I?* She thought. Was she the vibrant young girl that looked nothing like her parents, a girl that wanted to run and play and love? Or was she the dark, brooding black robe mage, a protégé, and duplicate of the cold teacher she owed everything to? Recently she had become a third person, a wife, a caring soul who found love, but did she give Gideon what he deserved? Since they had been married, everything, all their plans had been driven by her wishes, her desire to become a Summoner. Beautiful, wonderful Gideon; he never complained. He followed her willingly and eagerly as long as she was happy. But is that what he deserved? She didn't realize she was crying until she looked up at the mirror again. She wiped the tears in a huff and turned away.

She took a deep breath and composed herself. *Foolish girl! Wake up!* Azrael's voice rang in her head and despite the fact she knew the voice was right it, angered her more. Shaking her head, she turned to him, "I am not saying no. You would be an amazing father. I just, I can't think about that right now."

Gideon stood and cleared his throat, "I understand love. Speaking of current responsibilities, Lord Sulik asked for us to meet him at Sparta's Tower before mid-day. We should make our way there."

She had composed herself and gave Gideon a broad smile and a kiss. He smiled back and held her at arm's length to look at her.

"By the Gods, you are more beautiful every day, Isi. Why the gods decided to bless me so I will never know."

A pang of pain hit Isidora in the chest, but she did not let it show. She placed a hand on his cheek, "No, my love, it is I who is blessed. Come now, no more of this doting, your uncle waits for us."

Arm in arm, they walked together towards Sparta's Tower. They spoke idly as they walked. Gideon told her that Kethis had spoken to the Guardian and a regiment of Elvan archers was making its way to them; they would meet them at Castle Pass, and then they would depart for the Spokes to find out the result of Azrael's mission. The elves did not stand on ceremony like the Kingdom did. They pushed back a threat of attack and will present a show of force. Although they hoped his mission would result in a peaceful solution, they had to be prepared for the possibility of war. Sulik's dire warnings did not make things any better. In the meantime, Kethis was briefing the knights on elvan battle tactics, and together they were trying to find the best way to fight alongside one another, should it come to that.

They arrived at Sparta's Tower and walked up the winding staircase to Lord Sulik's chambers. They knocked on the door, and Lord Sulik answered and waved them in with a flourish.

"Thank you for coming so quickly. Please, please, have a seat. I have some chilled wine and fresh fruit. Make yourselves at home," Sulik smiled, seated himself as well, and crossed his legs, "I do apologize for how contentious it has been. I did not wish it so, nor did I mean in any way to insult your teacher, Lady Isidora."

Isidora gave a slight smile, "Azrael is quite...unique, Lord Sulik. Insult is not the way I would put it. It is more of a game of wills with him. He will never let anyone have the upper hand."

Sulik gave a broad smile, "Yes, I can see that. As a lover of the game of chess, I can appreciate his demeanor. in fact, I find it entertaining."

Isidora chuckled, "Lord Sulik, I respect your intelligence and will, but Azrael is not a man to be played with."

Sulik nodded, "I think you misinterpret my meaning, Lady Isidora, but that is neither here nor there. I did not bring you here to discuss your teacher. I am on a peacekeeping mission of my own."

Gideon furrowed his eyebrows, "What do you mean, uncle?"

Sulik stood and put his hands behind his back, "Nephew, it can easily be said that our relationship has not been of the closest of family ties. I abhor that fact. We are family, and by extension, your wife is as well. Perhaps it has been solely my fault. I dedicate myself to my post and to the well-being of the Kingdom so single-mindedly that at times, I forget the more important things."

Gideon nodded, "Go on."

Sulik scratched his chin, "You see, there are certain things about me you may not know. I am a pious man. I have kept that fact to myself to protect myself from my enemies, but my faith supports me and buoys me through the storms of life. It helps me with hard decisions and guides my hand. In these difficult times, it has also taught me that family is of the utmost importance. I see you growing into a man in your own right, as well as an important part of the Kingdom's future. I also see how important Lady Isidora is to you and would like to include her in that future. She needs a family here if she is to be your wife and a part of the royal family. I can provide that."

Gideon gave a halfhearted smile, "So can my father."

Isidora cocked an eyebrow and placed a hand on top of Gideon's, "Gideon, let us hear your uncle out. Your father is indeed a wonderful man but so devoted to his post that he rarely engages others. If your uncle is offering us this, perhaps we should think about it."

Sulik smiled even more, "Thank you, Lady Isidora. There is more, though. As I said, I am a pious man, and I would also like to introduce you to another family, a religious one. It has helped make me the man I am today. Allows me to be free to be who I am, unashamed and unabashed, surrounded by people who accept me for who I am, and care for me steadfastly."

Isidora sat forward, "I understand that want, Lord Sulik. More than you know."

"I am glad to hear that, my Lady. Let me show you," Sulik walked over to his hidden bookcase and unlocked it with the hidden switch. It swung open, revealing his alter to Leto. Isidora gasped. Both of them rubbed their arms on the tattoo of the runes. Gideon frowned. *We already made an oath to preserve balance, and this prophecy involves Leto.*

Sulik crossed his arms behind his back, "I know for someone as orderly as myself, for any Castellarian, the worship of Leto seems...odd."

"Odd is not the word, uncle," Gideon said.

Isidora had a hand over her mouth, not knowing what to say. Then slowly, she spoke, "Leto? But why, Lord Sulik? I do not understand. Artio of Order has always been revered in Castellamar. The god of chaos seems out of place, for one such as you."

Sulik made his way back to the table and took Isidora's hand in his, "It is the chaos, my Lady," Sulik's eyes shone brighter, his voice passionate, "Chaos is not all about complete anarchy, as many wish to believe. It is about being free! It is about being set free from the confines of this life to be who you want to be. Without judgment, without fear. It is everything I had dreamed of for the Kingdom and what all my work has been for. To make the Kingdom free from restraints of other nations and races."

Isidora stammered, "Leto...Leto gave Azrael those mirrored eyes as a curse. Everything I have learned from Azrael was that Leto is a spiteful and vengeful God."

Sulik gripped her hand tighter, "That is what the unfaithful and hateful wish us to believe, my Lady, but it is not true. I respect your teacher in his wisdom and age, but do you believe he knows better than a god? Who is to say why Leto cursed him so? Do you know why? Has he ever told you?" Isidora slowly shook her head, "I thought not. Only one who is ashamed would not explain something so grievous. Leto is a god, my Lady! His actions should not be questioned. As much as I understand Azrael to be significant to you, he can err, even if it is a rarity. There would be no betrayal of your teacher if you joined in the worship of Leto. Azrael's mistakes are his, not yours."

Her eyes were wide, darting back and forth. Gideon's mind went back to Azrael's words, *the oath is not to me. You owe me no allegiance. The only allegiance that mark holds you to is your own conscious of what is right.* Gideon shook his head in doubt. His father's words from when they arrived came to the forefront of his mind. *You have more to fear from those in this room who claim loyalty to the Kingdom.* He saw vipers in every shadow and needed time to think. He grasped Isidora's hand and helped her stand, "That is enough for now, uncle. Thank you for your concern. But I don't think..."

Isidora pulled away slightly, "No, Gideon, he may be right. I do not know."

Gideon furrowed his brows, and she pursed her lips. He tapped his arm where the tattoo was, "At least take some time to think about things before making any rash decision, my love. You know whatever you decide in life, I will be there and support you."

Sulik patted Isidora on her shoulder, "My nephew is right, my Lady. Take some time and think about it. Either way, I am here for you as family. Same goes for you, nephew. This offer was not only for your wife but for you as well."

Isidora wrung her hands. Gideon saw this and held her close. "Thank you, uncle. We will be in touch. Let's go, Isi," Isidora gave him a weak nod and let him lead her out the door.

Sulik watched them leave with a concerned look on his face. But when they had exited, he smiled. He made his way to the altar and knelt before it, his face rapt in devotion, "My Lord Leto, thank you for your guidance. When I thought of this course of action so quickly, I knew it could not be a coincidence but divine intervention. It only shows me nothing can stop you or your plan. I am forever your humble servant." Sulik gave a quiet and quick prayer and closed the altar. He beamed and grabbed an apple and took a hearty bite.

CHAPTER 38

As the sun settled low on the horizon Azrael and his contingent met down below in the main room of the Mead Hall. They had expected to meet with Lord Hollister in private, but to their surprise, the Hall was filled with knights and members of House Hollister. At the very head of the large table sat Lord Damian Hollister. When he saw his guests walk down the stairs he took a sip from his flagon and waved them over.

The seats nearest Lord Hollister were empty, reserved for Azrael and his company, except for the chair to his right which was occupied by his nephew, Sir Rodrick. Lord Hollister was a bear of a man. He was broad of shoulder and stood well over six feet tall, with a beard that was long and thick, dark brown with streaks of gray. Unlike Castellarians and their full plate armor, his frame was clothed more casual wear of Riverfolk. He had on a brown cuir-bouilli chest piece and gauntlets. The chest piece was branded with the stygian owl insignia of House Hollister and at his side was a massive two-handed claymore, another owl upon the pommel. Although not obese, he had some girth upon him and large red cheeks that shone beneath the facial hair.

When they neared the table, Lord Hollister stood and smiled with his arms outstretched, "Welcome, good guests, to the Spokes and the grand Mead Hall! Come, sit and break bread with us and share our ale!" They took their seats at the table and instantly buxom serving women came over and slammed down foaming flagons of ale before them. Jozef, although more partial to wine, was intrigued by the dark frothy drink and heartily took a sip. Lear'Za, on the other hand, grimaced and pushed the flagon away with a finger. With a snap, she conjured her usual long-stemmed glass full of dark red wine. A pockmarked knight across the table and down a few seats paused gnawing at a pieced of roasted duck long enough to wink at her, wiping grease from his chin. Lear'Za grimaced more, then gave a half-hearted smile back, "The abyss be damned, I need to be more selective of my romping partners," she whispered under her breath to herself. Griffon drank his ale as well, but his eyes were dark and brooding, darting around the room. Azrael ignored his flagon, watching Griffon instead, but then turned his attention to Lord Hollister.

"Thank you, Lord Hollister. We certainly appreciate your hospitality. I am sure Sir Rodrick has told you I am the Archmage Azrael, and these are my companions, Jozef Shaddam, Lear'Za, and Sir Griffon Shadowbane, who is our escort," Azrael spoke in his most formal tone.

Lord Hollister took a swig of his ale and leaned back, "Yes, Azrael. I have heard your name spoken throughout the lands. Your reputation precedes you. Please let us dispense with these formal titles. Call me, Damian. I deplore all of that 'lord' business," Lord Hollister drained his flagon and waved a girl over for a refill. After she'd poured, he slapped her on the rump as she departed and laughed. He turned back to his company, "So, my nephew here tells me you have some important matters to discuss. Judging from your escort, I am sure it has something to do with our neighbors to the north."

Azrael gave a thin-lipped smile, "Indeed it does, Damian. There have been some disturbing events at your mutual border with the Kingdom. Sir Roderick has noted the Spokes are aware of these events."

Lord Hollister shook his head as he bit off a chunk of bread. With a full mouth, he replied, "This has nothing to do with the Spokes."

Griffon slammed down his flagon and shouted, "Lies!"

Damian stood up with his hand resting on the pommel of his claymore. Azrael shot the knight a glare with his mirrored eyes and then slowly turned back to Lord Hollister and motioned him to sit. The Riverlord gave a slight snarl and seated himself, "There better be a good reason I am swallowing such insult at my table, Azrael."

Azrael nodded, "I apologize for my escort. He speaks out of turn," Azrael shot the knight one more look then returned his attention to the Riverlord, "You must understand that the attack on Granary, the decimation of House Marken, and the failed attack upon the Elvan kingdom, have all been done by men under the Owl banner and colors. This comes from multiple sources. By all accounts, the Spokes has attacked the Kingdom.

A sneer played across his visage, "I can assure you, Azrael, that none of what you speak of was ordered by me. We have had peace with the Kingdom for years and years. I have no reason to break that peace," Abruptly the Riverlord stood and in one step lifted himself up onto the tabletop. He unsheathed his claymore and slammed its tip upon the table, impaling it in the wood. Everyone in the Hall turned their attention to their lord. He rested his hands upon the pommel, and his deep voice boomed through the hall, "I have received some disturbing news! Is there any man here that has partaken in or who knows of any unsanctioned attack against the Kingdom and the elves?" The Riverlord looked around the room as no one spoke up and shook their heads. With a grunt, he pulled his claymore from the table, sheathed it, and then hopped down and seated himself, "There you have it Azrael. Whoever has committed these deeds are imposters and not Owl Men. The only person unaccounted for is my cousin Sir Harlow. He departed the Spokes a few weeks ago with two of his friends on a hunting trip. Unfortunately, and to our dismay, he has not returned. We have sent scouts and found neither hide nor hair of him. But three knights hardly make an attack force to overtake Granary. And let alone attempt an assault on the elves," The Riverlord shrugged and took a heaping bite of his roasted pork.

He is telling the truth. His cousin is also missing; this cannot be a coincidence. Damian Hollister was unfazed as he continued to eat his pork and drink his ale. Azrael removed his hood, his countenance firm, "Damian, I would not dismiss this so casually. A regiment of Castellarian Knights along with an Elvan contingent is already marching to the Spokes. They will arrive in three days. They plan for war if there is no resolution to this matter or at least some clarity to the identity of the invaders."

Damian Hollister laughed and emptied his flagon, "Let them come! No one has ever taken the Spokes and no one ever will! We are innocent in this fiasco. If Granary was occupied by my men, why should I deny it? It is on them to prove my guilt, not mine to defend my honor!"

Griffon rose from his seat and tore off his gauntlets, "Liar, murderer, and heathen! What reason does anyone have to dress up like half-rate southron knights?"

Damian gave a wild roar and stood up so quickly all his food and flagon went flying from the table. He drew his claymore, held before him at the ready. The room erupted in shouts, and everyone stood and drew weapons.

Azrael gnashed his teeth and stood up. He spoke a few words in the spidery language of the Art, and a ball of flame erupted in the room high above their heads silencing everyone.

"Enough!" he shouted. He turned his head towards Griffon, "Shadowbane, I warned you multiple times to keep your mouth shut lest you complicate matters further, and you have proven me right! You are here as an escort, nothing more! Kindly remove yourself from this table and to your quarters!" Griffon snatched up his gauntlets and stormed up the stairs to his suite.

Sir Rodrick grabbed his uncle by the arm and motioned him to sheath his sword, "I think this got a little out of hand. I am sure it is not what the Archmage had intended, my Lord. Perhaps we should continue this discussion on the morn when hopefully cooler heads prevail."

Damian snorted along with a glaring look at Griffon and sheathed his claymore, "Heh, you are right my nephew. I will not let this northron dog prompt me to sully my honor by killing an unarmed man," He wiped grease and pieces of meat off of his breast piece and sighed, "We will continue this discussion tomorrow morning in privacy, Azrael. However, I want that knight to remain in his room for the remainder of his time here. While you are not a Castellarian or a member of the Kingdom, I will hold you responsible for any actions or dishonor against House Hollister.

Azrael nodded his head, "Of course, Damian. I understand. We will let you finish your feast and finish our discussion in the morning. I offer my apologies again."

Damian gave an understanding nod, "My quarrel is not with you, Archmage. I hold you with no breach of etiquette or honor, "Feel free to remain and finish your dinner as well."

The rest of the night passed in pleasant conversation and hearty laughter. Azrael gave polite nods and smiles as Lear'Za, and Jozef entertained the conversation. His mind was elsewhere. His mirrored eyes watched the room, Damian, Sir Rodrick, the Hollister knights, thoughts to the man sequestered in his room. *I am standing at the precipice of a cliff looking down at the rocks below.* He saw all the pieces on the game board; he understood where they could move as well as all the possible moves ahead. His only problem was his opponent was a god and could move anywhere on the board he wished with any piece should he chose to. Right now, that piece was Sir Griffon, and Azrael could not see where Leto was going to place him. The sad part was the man didn't even know he was a pawn.

After a few hours, Azrael gave his goodnights and retired to his suite. Jozef and Lear'Za seemed to be enjoying themselves; he left them to it. Tonight could be one of the last nights of peace and enjoyment they had for a while. Azrael took to his bed and spent most of the night pondering everything.

The next morning, Azrael woke to the sound of knights practicing in the courtyard even though the sun had risen less than an hour prior. It was still summer, but fall was fast approaching and the mornings began to carry a chill. He rose from his bed and looked out his window on the courtyard. The knights' breath was visible as they parried and swung at faux enemies. Azrael wondered if they knew how close to war they were and that in less than two days they could be facing real combatants and real death if he was not successful today.

A Page had come to his room and informed him that Lord Hollister and Sir Rodrick were awaiting his presence in the Mead Hall, alone this time. He splashed some water on his face and washed up and put on a clean set of black robes. When he exited his room, Lear'Za and Jozef were already in the hallway waiting for him.

"Good morning, Seer'kaat. How do you plan this day to go? I grow tired of these cock measuring contests."

"As do I. One day, a leader will place logic over their ego and pride. Let's hope that day is today," Azrael retorted. He continued his pace to the stairway and Jozef, and Lear'Za followed.

Lord Hollister and Sir Rodrick waited for them in the Mead Hall. Damian smiled when he saw them, "I know it is early, but I figured it best to get these matters concluded as soon as possible."

"I am an early riser, at any rate. I had already been out of bed for some time when your page knocked on my door. Let us not waste any time," Azrael seated himself at the table and thanked the serving girl for the fresh juice she brought him, "It is safe to assume you do not want war, then."

Damian let out a roar and slapped his chest, "Azrael, if it was war I wanted, not only would I have taken Granary but I would have been at Castle Pass the next day, leading the charge myself. I am still a Riverlord and a Hollister. I have never shied from battle or a challenge, so if it war they want, it is war I shall give them."

Jozef laughed and spread his hands, "If I may, Lord Hollister, I have prided myself for being an excellent judge of character. From our time last night I found that, although you are bold and boisterous, you are not rash. Let us enter this with an open mind even if others are closed, yes?"

Azrael nodded in agreement, "Jozef is right. It will be catastrophic if you are as impetuous and foolish as our escort."

Damian opened his mouth to speak and was halted by a touch on his arm from Sir Rodrick, "Excuse me, uncle, but I have an idea," Damian waved his hand to let Rodrick speak, "Thank you. These invaders still have Granary occupied, yes? The answer is simple. As a token of goodwill, when the Castellarian and Elvan contingent arrives, we will offer to send our best knights to join them on the field of battle, to liberate Granary and bring justice to the murderers of House Marken. Now, I know they may fear betrayal on our part that we might seek to trap them between our forces here and those supposedly in Granary. To ease their worries, I will volunteer to lead this force. They will know you will not abide by any treachery when my own life is in their hands."

Damian sighed and shook his head, "Rodrick, while I admire your bravery, I cannot risk you in this. You will be a hostage. I have no sons, and you are the heir to the Spokes and House Hollister."

Without them knowing it, Leto, there are those who oppose your chaos. Azrael smiled at Rodrick, "Damian, your nephew is more than brave; he is brilliant. Two of my companions will be leading this Castellarian force, Kethis Kitharii of the Elves and Sir Gideon Stormcaller, your sister's son. Who would have thought when the unlikely marriage between Sir Falco and Lady Renna happened that its fruit could very well prevent a cataclysm? Kethis and Gideon are good men and reasonable. If Sir Rodrick and I give them this proposal, I can assure you it will be listened to and that Rodrick will be safe."

"Then why is my nephew not here?" The Riverlord questioned.

"The Realm Regent found it prudent to keep the king's nephew out of possible harm's way if there was resistance met here. Not a decision I agree with, but a decision I had no control over."

Damian gave a big sigh and rubbed his beard. After a moment he looked up at the Archmage, "You are assuring his safety then, Azrael? I will hold you personally responsible should anything go wrong. This is the price of my trust."

Azrael's mirrored eyes flashed, "Lord Hollister, I have been held accountable for things longer than your House has been in existence. I have far more dangerous entities who wish to see me dead. I can assure you that I will do everything in my power to assure Sir Rodrick's safety. That includes placing myself in harm's way."

Damian shot his large hand out, and Azrael grasped Damian's by the wrist, "Very well then, Azrael. Let us hope you are right," Damian gave him a stern look and then clapped a hand on Rodrick's back, "Well, my boy, it looks like you have a mission. They feared for Gideon sending him here. Let's show the Kingdom we are not afraid to do what they would not. I have every confidence in your abilities. When this is done, we will have a feast to remember! The ale will flow, the wenches will squeal, and with any luck, I will awake the next morn tired, sore, hungover, and not able to remember any of it with a smile."

Azrael's mind worked over a few details, and he tapped a finger on the table, "There is one more thing, Damian. I would contact your bannermen and the other Riverlords. Make them aware of the situation. If there is one thing you can ill afford, it is to lose your allies."

Damian stood and nodded his head, "I already sent messengers last night. I may be a drunkard, but I am not stupid," Damian gave him a wink, "There is nothing left to do but wait. You and your companions have leave to enjoy the hospitality of the Spokes, except your ignorant escort, of course. By your account, they should arrive tomorrow morning, noon by the latest. I intend to enjoy myself until then; I suggest you do the same." Damian turned to leave but called Azrael over to him. He spoke to the mage in hushed tones. "Oh, and speaking of enjoyment. Your one friend there, Lear'Za, could I ask you a few things?" Damian gave a broad smile.

Azrael rolled his eyes and lifted his hand, "Damian, that is not somewhere you wish to go, trust me on that. I am sure there are plenty of distractions that are homegrown unless you wish Rodrick to come by his inheritance sooner than you had planned," Damian gave a confused look. Azrael sighed, "Just trust me on this one."

Azrael turned and left the company. He glanced up the stairs at Sir Griffon's room, and his eyes narrowed. *All is in place, but why do I still feel uneasy?*

CHAPTER 39

"Good show!" Kethis screamed. A sparing sword slashed overhead as he ducked and rolled.

"Thank you! Not so bad yourself!" Gideon yelled back. He parried an attack by two opponents at once. He tilted his sword horizontally and caught the two poles coming down at him with a smack. With a heave, he pushed them on their heels and spun around three hundred and sixty degrees, smashing his sparing sword into both their heads and sending them reeling. He put his hands on his hips and grinned, "But then again, I am facing two."

Kethis laughed, "I am merely getting warmed up, my friend," Kethis urged on the six men in front of him. They shrugged and advanced. The elf backed up deftly, pointing his sparing sword at them and using his other hand for balance, "You see, dear Gideon, it is not always about brute strength. His head craned back, scanning the area around him. He gave a smile and darted towards a wall with the six men chasing after him. Grabbing a rigging rope, part of a pulley system connected to the ramparts just as the men caught up with him. He dove for the ground and, as two swords swung over his head, just missing him, he drew his dagger. With a deft movement, he sliced through the rope and held on as the weight on the other end of the pulley plummeted downward, sending the elf flying upward. The weight — a plank holding replacement braces — came crashing down on the heads of the six knights that were chasing him, knocking them to the ground. Kethis laughed as he reached the rampart and landed smoothly. He dropped to one knee and looked over the side, "There are times one must use his wits and brain, my friend."

Gideon returned the laughter and looked up, shielding his eyes from the sun with his hand, "You cheated and used a blade, elf!"

Kethis saluted, "Are you saying every opponent you will face will fight fairly, Gideon? Please tell me you are not so naïve," Kethis grabbed on to a pole and slid down to the ground to his friend's side and clasped his wrist, "At any rate, you think they are ready?"

Gideon looked around and nodded his head, "I would say so. We do have some green knights, but there are veterans enough of goblin campaigns. I think we will be fine, should it come to that."

Kethis brushed the dust from his jerkin and led Gideon away from the wall, "So you think this still a ruse and not the act of the Spokes?"

"I don't know. All I know is we must look at every possibility before acting," Gideon looked up at the windows and spotted Isidora watching the courtyard. A moment later she dropped the curtains and disappeared into the room.

Kethis' eyes followed Gideon's. He looked back to his friend, his brows creased in concern, "How is she doing?"

Gideon frowned and shook his head, "Better, I guess but still not right. It is like she is battling the forces of all she's been taught to believe and the unknown. I don't know what to do."

Kethis frowned back, "What did Lord Sulik say to her to cause such melancholy?"

Gideon sighed, "I'd rather not talk about it," He glanced up at the curtained window for another moment, "I am sure she will be fine. She is a strong woman, stronger than most I know."

Kethis looked over his shoulder, "Speak of the devil, here comes your uncle now."

Sulik came over to them at a brisk pace and a broad smile on his face, "Tomorrow gentlemen! Tomorrow, one way or another, those who dared challenge the Kingdom will pay for their crimes," He slapped them each on the back, and then left his arms draped around their shoulders, "Things are well, I take it?"

"As well as they can be, uncle. The knights are ready. We will ride tomorrow for the Spokes and hopefully find out who is behind this treachery," Gideon replied. He spotted his father enter the courtyard, who was eyeing them intently.

Sulik smiled widely, "I believe we may be able to shed light on that sooner than expected, regardless of the outcome of Azrael's meeting. Ah, here he comes now."

They looked where he pointed and saw a huffing and puffing Lord Medici running over to them with parchment in hand, waving it over his head. When he caught up, they gave the fat man a moment to catch his breath.

"Breathe, Filobane, breathe man!" Sulik patted him on the back.

"Thank…you. Thank you…my Lord," Filobane said between heavy breaths. Standing straight, he took one deep breath, exhaled and wiped his sweating bald pate, "I have word from my nephew, Sir Tollen, on his covert mission, Lord Regent."

Gideon raised an eyebrow, "Covert mission? What mission is this?"

Sulik smiled, "We sent Sir Tollen to Granary to investigate the situation."

Gideon frowned, "Uncle, we agreed we would not march anywhere towards Granary until we received the outcome of Azrael's envoy."

Sulik chuckled, "Gideon there are times when some actions must be taken that are beyond discussion. Fear not. Sir Tollen was instructed not to lay siege upon Granary and only to engage if he is attacked. But I do believe Lord Medici has news."

Filobane wobbled his head, affirmatively, "Indeed I do, Lord Regent. It seems they were engaged by the enemy. Sir Tollen liberated Granary! He rides to meet us on the Asgerd Plains. He says he carries proof of the identity of the invaders."

"And he does not say anymore?" Sulik asked.

The fat man shook his head, "I am afraid not. However, we will know by the time we arrive at the Spokes."

"Well, this is good news, indeed! I have reports to prepare, if you would excuse me, gentlemen," Sulik gave them one last pat on the backs and sprinted towards Sparta's Tower. Lord Medici shrugged and smiled, then wobbled his way back the way he had come.

Kethis and Gideon watched them leave. Gideon rubbed his chin, "I don't like this, Kethis."

"Nor do I, my friend. But let the politicians handle the politics. We are warriors. Let us ready for our trip."

Gideon looked over to the other side of the courtyard and watched his father stride over to where they stood. Falco's countenance was sullen, "What was that about?" He said, concerned.

"Lord Medici just informed us of Sir Tollen's mission to Granary."

"Mission? What mission?" Falco interrupted quickly.

Gideon looked at Kethis. The elf shrugged. He furrowed his brow and returned to his father, "Uncle told us Sir Tollen was sent to Granary to gather information on the situation. We were just informed they were able to recapture Granary and have proof of the Hollister's involvement. Were you not notified of this mission? You are privy to all the Council's meetings."

His father's face grew grave, "There was no meeting. Which means the king may be unaware as well. And now that they have conveniently won the day by recapturing Granary and have proof of Hollister involvement, bringing to light the secrecy of this so-called mission in inopportune."

"Then Azrael's mission is in vain," Gideon's jaw tightened.

Falco's forehead furrowed, "His mission was doomed before he even left," He signed deeply, "My son, not everything in the Kingdom is as honorable as it seems. Sulik is my brother, but I do not trust him. I have no proof of anything, but I know him well. His motives can be murky."

Gideon screwed his face in thought, "He has been helpful with Isidora and has shown sincere concern for her and has even offered her some peace and salvation through faith. I never knew he worshipped Leto though."

Falco's eyes grew wide, "Leto?" A knight on the other end of the courtyard called for Falco. He turned quickly and waved. He returned his attention to his son, "I must go, I am in charge of the troop assignment for the regiment you will be leading," He grabbed Gideon by the shoulders, "Keep your eyes and wits about you when dealing with your uncle, Gideon," He gripped his shoulders firmly and then took his leave.

Kethis looked at the tattoo on his arm and ran his fingers over it, "Azrael said we are to do what we know is right. There are so many shades of grey in this fog that one cannot tell the difference anymore."

Gideon watched his father's figure recede into the passage leaving the courtyard, "You are correct, my friend. Too correct."

The next morning, as promised, all was ready. Outside the gates of San'Seban stood an entire regiment, one thousand men, two hundred of which were knights on their mounts. The sun gleamed off their polished armor even as the chill of the oncoming fall turned their breaths to clouds in the morning air. Isidora sat on her horse and watched Gideon ride up and down the lines, shouting orders and commands to prepare for their march southward. She managed a weak smile.

Since Lord Sulik had invited her to join the faith of Leto, her mind had been in a whirlwind of confusion. She rebelled at first, thinking it the apparent effects of chaos working on her mind. But after some time, the realization that it was her own inner turmoil dawned on her. It had caught her off guard completely, and she could not understand why she let it affect her so. She had felt so weak since then, unable to really speak. All she could do was turn the thoughts round and round in her head, and at every turn, she seemed to face some sort of betrayal. *Go to Leto, and I betray Azrael. Become all that my D'ni expects of me, and I betray Gideon and my family. Stay as I am, and I betray myself.*

Nothing was simple any longer. Instead of the easy black and white, everything had turned to a mottled shade of gray. Azrael was right about one thing—the only constant, the only thing she could trust not to confuse or mislead her was the Art. She gazed down at her arm, at the two tattoos that marked her avatars and the third of the Sidhe runes. She cocked her head and ran a finger along the lines of the tattoos. *Well, my friends, if the Art is my guide than what am I to do?* Her fingers then ran over the runes. *And how do the Souls of Magic's Dawn play into this? Which side of the scale needs tipping to maintain balance?*

She was shaken from her musing by a trumpet blare. She shot her head up, and she saw Gideon galloping towards her, Kethis at his side. They pulled up alongside her.

"Let us be off, my love. We ride at the vanguard along with my father and uncle," Gideon spurred his horse on, and Isidora followed.

"Your uncle joins us? I know he is Realm Regent, but he was never a knight," Isidora said.

Gideon lifted his visor, "He awaits word from Sir Tollen, who is to meet us on the Asgerd Plains. He may not be a knight, but he is trained in swordplay, just like all noblemen. He can defend himself if it comes to that. Let us pray that it does not. From what my father has told me, it may be best if Lord Sulik is within our view."

Isidora lifted her eyebrow questioningly. Her thoughts were interrupted by trumpet calls; the regiment was on the move. By midmorning, they had crossed Castle Pass and were on their way down KingsMarch towards the Asgerd Plains and the Spokes.

The first day of the trip was pleasant, but as they arose the next morning the sky was dark and gloomy, with storm clouds forming to the southeast. Autumn did not seem to want to wait for its sibling's demise. No rain had begun to fall, but the winds had picked up significantly, and the temperature dropped sharply. Many had taken out traveling cloaks to wrap around them as they rode.

Isidora had not engaged in many conversations during the trip but instead kept thinking of the doubts and turmoil in her own mind. She flinched at a bright flash of lightening ahead, followed by a loud low rumble of thunder in the distance. She smirked. *The heavens match the tumult in my own mind.*

Her uneasiness began to grow. She could not pinpoint it, but her stomach started to do somersaults, and she worried her breakfast would not wish to stay in her stomach. *Does Azrael feel this way, as well?* She wondered. He had to have felt it; it was similar to the smell of water in the air and the rumble of thunder heralding a massive storm. She chuckled to herself. *Of course, he feels it. He always is two steps ahead of everyone. But I would wager his stomach is the epitome of calm. I'm frightened by what I see, but somehow I know there is much more to come. I cannot be immobilized by my fears. How does he do it? How does he shut it all out? These truths drive me to madness but how does he stop it all and will it all away?*

They crested a hill, and an intensely bright flash of lightning flashed in the sky, temporarily blinding her. She shielded her eyes, and the massive thunderclap followed almost immediately. She blinked away the spots and looked forward. A few hundred yards ahead of them was a neat line of Hollister knights and behind them the Spokes. They had arrived. To her left, a small group of riders carrying Castellarian battle standards rode at a steady gallop towards them. The one in the lead carried a brown sack. It could only be Sir Tollen.

They had been awoken by trumpet calls just as the sun broke the horizon. Azrael blinked away his sleep and looked out his window. Lord Hollister and Sir Rodrick were already in their armor and gathering their knights to meet the Castellarian contingent that was no doubt near. Without wasting time, Azrael dressed and met up with Lear'Za and Jozef. Together, they made their way to the massive courtyard. Their horses were already saddled and ready for them. They mounted and cantered over to Damian Hollister.

"Good morning, Azrael. A scout reported a few hours ago that the Castellarians are less than a league away. It appears the time has come," Lightning flashed, followed by a thunder boom. Damian looked up at the gray skies, "It also seems autumn has come with them."

Azrael narrowed his eyes and looked up at the skies. *You all feel it don't you? What are you going to do, oh gods of Tinil'Gan, if you dare do anything?* "Have you released Sir Griffon from his sequester?" he asked, "It would not do well to appear before them with our escort under lock and key."

Damian grunted, "As much as I would rather see him rotting in my dungeon, I agree with your sentiment. My men have him by the gate. He will be given his horse and sword when we pass through."

Azrael nodded, "Thank you. I will go speak to him," Azrael turned his horse and trotted over to the gate where a very disgruntled Sir Griffon stood with Owl Knights on either side of him. He looked up at the Archmage with a scowl on his face.

"This is an outrage, and an insult, Azrael," Griffon roared, "You can trust Lord Sulik will hear of this after this business is ended."

Azrael studied the man intensely, "Not only do I expect it, Sir Griffon, but I also await it," Azrael leaned forward on his pommel, "What role are you playing, Griffon? Why are you here? You know well within your heart of the things I know about you. Things my silence has offered you protection from shame."

Griffon gave a mocking laugh, "What good it has done me," He spat on the ground, "I am here to escort your sorry arse, mage. But more importantly, to protect the Kingdom and bring honor to my house, which I intend to do."

Azrael raised an eyebrow, "Protect the Kingdom, honor to your House? What do you mean? How?" Azrael was cut off by another trumpet blast, and he looked up as the massive gates began to swing open. Damian and Rodrick galloped up to him with Lear'Za and Jozef in tow. When he looked back down at Griffon, the Owl Knights were already dragging him out the gates, "Wait!" Azrael yelled, but it was too late.

Damian steadied his horse beside Azrael's and lowered his visor, "It is time, Azrael. Let us not waste any time."

Another flash of lightning and a thunderclap. Azrael looked up again; the clouds were getting thick and darker. *This isn't right. Which piece? Where is it moving? Everything appears in place, but something does not feel right.* Azrael pulled down his hood to block the cold winds and followed Damian and Rodrick out of the gates and onto the Asgerd Plains.

They lined up on the plains with an entire regiment. In the vanguard, Azrael stood with Lord Hollister and Sir Rodrick to his right. To his left were Lear'Za and Jozef. They had been waiting uneasily for a few minutes when a very bright flash of lightning burned the sky. When his eyesight cleared, he could make out the Castellarian regiment a few hundred yards ahead, cresting a hill. He narrowed his eyes to make it out.

At the Castellarian vanguard, he could make out Gideon and Kethis, along with the robed figure of his student Isidora. He raised an eyebrow when he saw riders dashing from the northeast, towards the Castellarian vanguard. *What is this? They cannot be scouts; scouts would be riding from the south.* Azrael's horse kicked and shifted restlessly. He looked over and saw Sir Griffon's horse wedging its way in between Azrael and Rodrick. Azrael gave a grunt, "For the love of the gods, Griffon, what are you doing?"

Before the knight had a chance to answer, Lear'Za broke in, "Seer'kaat, who are those riders? The one in the lead is carrying something."

Azrael looked over and saw the riders meet up with Gideon and Sulik. *Sulik? What is he doing here; he is no knight.* Again Azrael's horse shifted and neighed as Sir Griffon's horse pushed its way forward, "Griffon, please! Go to the other side of Jozef."

Lear'Za shook her head, "Something doesn't seem right here."

Azrael, annoyed, removed his hood, "Yes, Lear'Za. I know. Quiet please," Azrael squinted in the dim light to see what was happening. He saw the bag being opened and something removed from it. His eyes grew wide: it was a human head. Griffon's horse pushed its way in again, nearly unseating Azrael, "Damn you, Griffon! What are you doing?"

Azrael's voice was drowned out by the brightest lightning flash he had ever seen and a thunderclap so loud it made his ears ring. The horses kicked and neighed loudly. He struggled with the reins to keep control while his eyes attempted to make sense of the spots in his vision. Then, out of the corner of his eye, he saw a flash. His vision was still blurry, but he made out the object. It was a dagger in Sir Griffon's hand. *Too fast! Why couldn't I foresee this!*

Azrael saw the dagger dart out, towards Sir Rodrick's unprotected side as the knight struggled with his own horse, unaware of the danger. He shouted, but the thunder was still rolling, and the horses screaming. No one could hear him. Damian finally saw the danger and cried as well, but his horse kicked wildly, throwing him to the ground.

The mage did the only thing he knew would work. He muttered in the spidery language of the Art, and his own small, magical lightning bolt shot out his hands at Sir Griffon, knocking him from his horse just as his dagger dug into the joint of Rodrick armor. Both knights fell. Rodrick screamed in pain as the blade sank into his side. Smoke rose from Sir Griffon, and the smell of charred flesh filled the air. The skies opened up, and the rain began to fall heavily.

On the other side of the plains, Isidora looked at the Hollister vanguard. She spotted Azrael, Lear'Za, and Jozef. *Where is father?* She furrowed her eyebrows at the thought but was distracted as Sir Tollen approached them. The older knight reared his horse and saluted.

Lord Sulik gave a happy shout and cantered over on his horse, "Sir Tollen! You have arrived just in time. I would like to congratulate you on your heroic deeds at Granary. No one expected the town to be liberated. The kingdom owes you a debt of gratitude."

Gideon also intrigued, brought his horse over. Isidora watched in confused. *What is in that sack?* She glanced over at the Hollister line and made out her father attempting to bring his horse next to Azrael's. She shook her head. *Azrael, for once in your life don't be an arse. Let the man in.* Her thoughts and attention were brought back to Sir Tollen as the knight spoke.

"Thank you, Lord Regent. I must say, as per our orders, we had no intention of engaging the enemy, only to gather intelligence and report back to San'Seban. However, the scum came riding out of Granary and attacked us. The battle was hard but swift, and we found ourselves victorious and the gates of Granary open to us," Sir Tollen said solemnly.

Sulik placed his hand over his heart, "I am glad to hear the good news, Sir Tollen. We hear you have then discovered the true identity of the attackers?"

Isidora listened to the exchange, but her eyes kept glancing over at the Hollister vanguard. *Azrael, why aren't you letting my father's horse in? What is the matter with you, D'ni?*

Sir Tollen's voice was low, Isidora strained to hear him, "Yes, Lord Regent, we did find out. It is as we first thought. Our enemy stands before us now upon this field," Sir Tollen raised the sack up and stuck his hand inside. He pulled out the object, and a gasp ran through the lines. He held a human head, "This is the head of Sir Harlow Hollister, cousin to Lord Hollister himself!"

As if to accentuate Sir Tollen's words, a dramatic and brilliant flash of lightning broke across the sky with a deafening thunderclap. Isidora clapped her hands over her ears and shut her eyes from the brightness. Through the ringing in her ears, she heard horses scream and neigh. Her own horse reared up in fear, dumping her to the ground. She fell with a thump. Dizzy, she looked up across the plain through spotted vision and saw another flash of light, this one smaller but also very recognizable. She knew a lightning spell when she saw one. Her eyes grew wide as she watched the scene unfold before her. Azrael reached his hands up and blasted her father in the chest with the spell, knocking him from the horse.

The world went silent for a moment. Only the loud thumping of her heart pounding in her ears was audible. She watched her father slide from his horse and fall limply to the ground. A scream escaped from her throat; the sounds of the world returned. She stood wearily; her tear stricken face contorting in anger. *He killed him. He killed my father.*

No. No, no. No!" With a tortured shout, she dove deep within herself and the Art. She stood, arms outstretched and tears streaming down her face. The anger and the pain within her grew to a deafening crescendo between her ears and deep in her chest. With a fierce yell, a violet aura of magical energy enveloped her. Her violet eyes glowed with the same power. A glyph of the same shade appeared on the ground before her, and the form of the Hammer materialized upon it, his immense warhammer resting on his shoulder. She looked at the body of her father charred and burned on the ground. Through her flowing tears, she screamed, and the Hammer nodded.

His hulking ethereal form turned and bounded across the plains of Asgerd towards the Hollisters. Isidora's entire focus, all of her thoughts bent on the destruction of those that killed her father. Her eyes flickered as she looked towards Azrael as the Hammer closed the gap between the lines. His hand was the one that had slain her father. *It should be him that suffers the first blow. Why? There has to be a reason he did this. I can't.* Her breath came heavy, and she shrieked in agony. With more tears, she looked away, towards the right flank of the Hollisters and the Hammer diverted his course towards them. Someone had to pay.

"Isidora!" Gideon shouted and forced his horse through the crowd to where she stood and jumped down before her.

Her head swam, and her eyes darted around. All she wanted was revenge. *He's dead.* Her eyes were locked on her avatar causing devastation. She could feel the power, the connection she had with the Hammer. *It is so easy now. Summoning Lelani took so much effort. Why is this so easy?* Her eyes grew hard; a smile of ecstasy played on her lips.

Gideon grabbed her by the shoulders. "Isidora, please! Stop, call him back!"

Her eyes snapped to Gideon as if coming out of a trance. Her face dropped, and she began weeping. She let go of the magic, and in the distance, the Hammer stopped, lowered his hammer, and vanished. She fell into his arms. The great and powerful magic she commanded when she summoned the Hammer flew from her, leaving her exhausted.

"Gideon! You must sound the charge! We know it was the Hollisters and your friends have seen fit to join them. Azrael just killed Sir Griffon! Sound the charge!" Sulik screamed.

Gideon looked around in confusion, "There must be a reason! I can't just...what about Isidora?"

She looked up at him. *What had I seen? Did he really kill my father?* Limp in Gideon's arms, she looked up weakly and saw Lord Sulik on his horse.

Sulik jumped down from his horse and took her from Gideon, "I have her, nephew. Now go and defend the Kingdom. You know what must be done."

Gideon hesitated for a moment and looked back and forth from Sulik to Isidora and then to Kethis. The elf lord looked at him with a sad expression. Gideon bowed his head for a moment, and then looked up and lowered his visor. He leaped onto his horse and shouted, "Kethis, ready your archers. Send your first volley when we have cleared half the distance to their vanguard,"

Gideon's jaw was set firm, and he led his horse before the assembled knights. He looked at each of them, the hardened veteran, the young squire, and all in between. He lifted his sword, and all eyes turned to him. "Knights of the Kingdom! All of us have made a vow, an oath to the Measure. A promise to defend the Kingdom. Fate is now calling our names my brothers! We are the shining hope of the Evening Lands, we are the *Saoirse Le Vey*!" He trotted his horse back and forth along the front line, "Do not let fear still your hearts, for I know them to be hearts full of honor and fortitude.

"Think of the faces of the people that you defend; your wives, your children, your kin. They will provide you with all the courage you require. When this day is over the heavens shall remember the souls upon these plains, with noble acts those brave souls endure the heart's remains. Ride with me Knights of the Valley, the Stars of Castellemar, and let us hope that children of a newer day might remember and avoid our fate!"

The regiment erupted in a cacophony of shouts and hoots all around Isidora. She heard the sounds of hooves and of booted feet running all around her towards the Hollister lines. It was all a haze to her. She laid listlessly in Lord Sulik's arms, her eyes half open as if just waking from sleep. She looked up and saw Gideon ride away on his horse at the vanguard of the attack. She smiled weakly and dropped her head onto Sulik's chest. Through dry lips, she spoke.

"Lord Sulik, I have thought about your offer. I would like to talk about it more."

Sulik smiled, "Indeed, my Lady. Indeed. I will give you whatever guidance I can once we return to San'Seban. I have a feeling today shall be a glorious day."

The skies opened up, and the rains fell down on the Asgerd Plains.

CHAPTER 40

The field erupted into chaos. The rains fell down hard, and Azrael looked down at the fallen knights in disbelief. He felt the magic emanate from Isidora. His eyes grew wide when the avatar they had just helped her acquire less than a week ago charge at them, at him. He quickly put up a spell around him and those closest to him. *Her power grows, as I knew it would.* He braced himself for the coming attack, and suddenly the avatar veered off to the far end of the line and began striking at the Hollister men. In a short period, he killed and injured several men. Then, just as suddenly as he charged, the Hammer disappeared. Azrael glanced back at the other side and saw Isidora fall into Gideon's arms. He let out a sigh of relief. *She saw what happened. This was a product of her rage.*

With the immediate threat gone, he jumped from his horse and grabbed Griffon's arm to turn him over. The knight was still breathing, though labored. His steel armor had been blasted open at the chest, and a black burn marked his chest. Azrael knew it was fatal. He had been forced to act quickly, and a lightning spell was the fastest spell he had. Even that was not fast enough. Griffon's dagger had still found its mark. Would that wound be fatal as well? He stared into Griffon's eyes, and the knight gave him a smile.

Azrael gritted his teeth and grabbed the knight by the collar and pulled his face close to his own, "Why Griffon? Why!"

Griffon laughed and then choked. He spit out some blood and took a breath. His voice was weak and raspy, "Why? Why, you ask? The almighty Azrael couldn't figure this one out? He knew you would be the one to stop me. He knew you would be watching and would be the first to act," Griffon let out a choking laugh and coughed up some more blood, "He knew!"

Azrael looked the knight up and down and shook his head slowly, "You have doomed us all, you damned fool. You have single-handedly started a war that will kill thousands."

Griffon gave a weak smile. His eyes began glazing over, "No, Archmage. I didn't. You did. Look at that battlefield. The kingdom charges and they are coming for your head. When he came to me, I gladly accepted, knowing it was suicide. But I will die happy knowing my daughter will finally be free of you when your head is upon a Castellarian pike. She will be free, married to a Castellarian royal, and my House will be raised up once again. Sir Griffon, the hero of the Battle of Asgerd!" Griffon gave one more choked laugh.

Azrael ground his teeth and yelled, shaking the knight, "Who, Griffon! Who was it! Tell me!" But was too late. The knight had died. Azrael dropped him and stood. Rodrick lay on the ground nearby with his uncle hovering over him. Damian was shouting orders for a cot. He turned towards the Archmage, his face red with anger.

"I warned you if anything happened to Rodrick I would hold you responsible!" the Riverlord shouted.

"He still lives, Damian. If anything, I saved his life," Azrael said coolly, "There is still time. You must sound the retreat and explain the situation to the Kingdom."

Damian watched as two knights carried Rodrick to the back of their lines on a stretcher, then mounted his horse once again and looked down at the Archmage, "There is no retreat, Azrael. Somehow the bastards have my cousin's head. No doubt they are saying he led the attack on Granary. I am sure Sir Griffon did not act alone but on orders. There is no retreat now. It was a war they wanted, and it is war they shall get!"

"Damian, please wait and listen!" Azrael shouted, his eyes wide.

The Riverlord reared his horse and shouted the command to charge the oncoming Castellarian Knights. He also ordered Azrael to be detained.

Quickly, Lear'Za and Jozef jumped in front of the Archmage, their swords out, "Seer'kaat, I suggest we make a hasty exit!"

Azrael stood in the rain, clenching his fists. *They are fools! Every last one of them! Why are they so blind!* His thoughts were cut short as Lear'Za grabbed hold of him to heave him up onto her horse. Lear'Za and Jozef rode away hard to the south, apart from the battle as the sounds of war erupted across the Plains of Asgerd. Steel clashed against steel as the two sides finally met and engaged in combat. Horses kicked up clumps of mud, and the quickly forming puddles from the torrential rain began to turn red from the first drops of blood in the war. No one followed them. War had come to the Evening Lands.

They rode hard and fast, to place as much distance between them and the battle as possible. After an hour at breakneck speed, they found an outcropping and decided to stop and rest the horses. Lear'Za attempted to help Azrael down from the horse, but he pushed off her hand angrily and jumped down.

She sighed, "Seer'kaat, all is not yet lost!"

Azrael paced back and forth in a fury. Tendrils of blue lightning arced across his mirrored eyes and crackled audibly, "Do you not see, daemoness? Are you as blind as the rest of them? This is what he wanted! This war was his doing! It will not stop here. Oh no, war will spread across the Evening Lands like a plague. Chaos will reign, and his strength will grow! Is it not bad enough my nemesis is a god? Must I allow him to gain strength as well? How could I have been that foolish to not see the signs? Who did Leto send to manipulate Griffon Shadowbane, of all people!"

"Despite protestations from your own ego, you are not infallible! You made a mistake! It happens, damn you!" Lear'Za shouted but with a tone of pleading.

"I cannot afford mistakes, daemoness. Neither can Tinil'Gan or Isidora. My mistakes have ramifications that are far-reaching. She cannot become the Harbinger of Chaos!"

The Archmage stormed away from them. Jozef made a move to follow, but Lear'Za stopped him and shook her head. He sighed and acquiesced.

Azrael paced back and forth alone behind the outcropping; his breath came hard and fast. His long white hair hung about him and stuck to his face and head, wet and slick from the rain. His mind raced as he stalked the ground like a caged lion. *This is the only way to save you, and Tilene knew I was the only one capable of it.* **He could hear Talia's final words as if she stood before him.** *Despite protestations from your own ego you are not infallible!* He stopped his pacing and laughed. It ran through his body manically as his mind cleared and his purpose once again aligned itself. He looked up at the sky and screamed.

"Leto! You think you have won? This is not over! You have orchestrated your own undoing!" he shouted to the heavens.

The sky crackled with lightning and struck the ground near Azrael, sending mud flying. He shielded his eyes, and when he looked up he saw the shimmering gold form. He laughed.

The form glowed brightly. A booming voice erupted from it, "I won long before your birth, Sidhe. I will always win. I am a god. My will is divine."

Azrael smirked and folded his hands in his sleeves, "A personal visit, Leto? I am honored. Last time you graced the world with your presence, you gave me these wonderful eyes of mine."

"A lesson you apparently still have not learned, Sidhe. Give up, Azrael. It is over. Go back to your tower, and I will consider letting you live. Leave now before I give you something worse than those eyes," the God said.

Azrael's eyes narrowed to mere slits as tendrils of blue lightning arced between the mirrored orbs, "I long ago stopped thinking of these eyes as a curse. In fact, they have given me true vision; they allow me to see through your petty schemes and the lies of your agents."

The god laughed, his voice echoing like a storm, "When will you realize you cannot win, Azrael? I am divine! I take what I wish when I wish it. I helped create this world! It is mine to rule. Your endeavors are in vain, mage; a mere pebble in the river that will not alter its course."

Azrael paused and lowered his head for a moment, "Never. This is far from over," He chuckled and raised his head, "You have won nothing. When will you realize that? Malystrix was not enough for you? My eyes? Now you take Talia? The countless mortals that will die in this war? How many shall perish and suffer in your name just for your own personal vanity and power-lust? Oh, but I have seen the light! Lear'Za's and Talia's words opened my eyes, and I realize I am fallible. I will err and stumble. At first, I thought this a weakness that would consume me and hand you your victory, but then it became clear! I only thought this because, despite my own words on the fallibility of the gods, I had fooled myself somehow into believing you were not! Talia proved that you are fallible! A pixie, Leto, a pixie beat you! You can try, Leto. I know you will not stop until you have what you want. I will not allow that. You cannot, will not, have Isidora!"

The golden form of Leto pulsed, "She is already mine, Azrael. You have been a gnat buzzing around my head for far too long. Perhaps it is finally time to end this pathetic diversion."

Azrael tore open the front of his robes, revealing his bare chest. Through gritted teeth, he replied, "Then do it! Stand by the courage of your conviction, Leto!"

The golden form shimmered brighter, and a golden arm rose up and pointed at Azrael. Suddenly three other forms materialized between the two. Before Leto stood his siblings, Cerridwen, Caillech, and Blancheflor.

The stag that was Cerridwen stepped forward, "Do not do anything foolish, my brother."

Leto gave a low growl, "Remove yourself, Cerridwen. This does not concern you."

The stag snorted, "Oh, but it does my brother. Did we not create this world together? You know as well as I that you must let this play out on its own. If you are meant to succeed, then it will come to pass."

"Not if, brother. I will succeed," Leto said confidently.

Cerridwen shook his antlers, "Then what do you have to worry about, brother? If you are so confident, then go home and let the prophecy play itself out."

The golden form shimmered even brighter, "Cerridwen, you meddle in your better's affairs far too often. Do not forget your place," Leto lowered his arm, "I tire of this. I have many things to prepare. You can have your mage, for what it is worth. There is nothing he can do to stop me," Leto's form gave one last bright pulse, then winked out.

The three gods turned and faced Azrael, "Well Lord Azrael you certainly know how to get our brother's blood boiling" Cerridwen said, "I am glad we arrived when we did."

Azrael closed his robes and gave Cerridwen a cynical smirk, "I did not require your assistance, Cerridwen, or that of any of the gods. Leto would not have killed me. Could not have, not with his own hand at least. If he could have, he would have done it eons ago. He is just as trapped by the prophecy as I am."

Cerridwen snorted, "Nonetheless Azrael, be grateful you have some divine powers willing to aid you. Now that this course has been set, there seems to be no diverging from it. Call upon us should you require anything. If it is within our power and scope to assist, we will do what we can."

Azrael replaced his hood, "Do not count on it."

Cerridwen laughed, "We will be watching, Azrael," The three gods disappeared just as suddenly as they appeared. Azrael turned to walk away and was stopped by another voice. This, though, he was sure, was mortal.

"Did I not tell you! What more proof do you need! Stop Azrael this instant!" the voice shouted.

Azrael closed his eyes and sighed. He recognized the voice. Without turning, he spoke, "What are you doing here, Diarmuid?"

"He is not alone, Azrael," another voice spoke.

Azrael raised an eyebrow and spun around, "Berilil?" Azrael saw the mage, and looked at the others also assembled, "Judica? Hestion? What are you all doing here? What is the meaning of this?"

Berilil stepped forward and sighed, "Diarmuid brought some grievous charges against you to the Conclave, Azrael.

Charges we came to investigate. And from the outburst we just saw, the war you started, I hate to say he seems correct."

Azrael rolled his eyes, "This must be a joke. Go back to the tower, Berilil. I can handle myself."

Berilil frowned, "Have you lost your mind? You are standing in the rain alone, talking to the gods, and threatening them? How far do you intend to take this insane plan of yours?"

Azrael laughed, "You know full well I was not alone," Azrael paused and shook his head, "No, wait, you do not know, do you? You did not see them. Of course, you didn't."

Berilil looked confused, "Saw who Azrael?"

Azrael sighed, "Never mind, Berilil. Just go home."

Diarmuid stepped forward, "I'm afraid that is impossible, Archmage. You are to return with us to the Tower of Elizar, to stand trial."

Azrael looked up at the sky and smirked. *As if dealing with petty gods wasn't enough.* He looked back at Diarmuid and narrowed his eyes, "That is not going to happen."

Diarmuid snarled, "You will come with us Azrael peacefully. Do not prompt our hand to take you by force."

Azrael's mirrored eyes flashed, "By force, Diarmuid? Do you think that is even remotely possible?"

Diarmuid grinned, "You may be powerful, Azrael, but you are one, and we are many."

"Are you sure that is a gamble you are willing to take Diarmuid?" He looked up at the sky and smiled. A loud roar split the heavens. The assembled magi gasped and stepped back hastily. The large flapping wings buffeted their robes and Cirrah landed with a thud behind Azrael, "Not that the dragon is necessary for defeating you. He is my ride," Azrael smirked widely.

Cirrah harrumphed, "Seriously, Archmagus, I am not a horse."

Jozef and Lear'Za came running around the corner when they spotted the dragon. They shouted and laughed as Cirrah lowered a wing to allow them to mount his back. Azrael turned away from the magi and climbed up as well.

Diarmuid nearly frothed at the mouth, "Azrael, this course of action is subject to expulsion from the Conclave! Be reasonable!"

Azrael leaned forward and smiled, "Then expel me. Ban me, curse me, do what you will. None of it matters. I am Sidhe, and magic is my birthright. I do not practice the Art, I *am* the *Art*. I survived just fine before the Conclave and will survive without it. All I ask is that none of you stand in my way again. Cirrah, if you will."

The dragon roared and sent the magi reeling, "Of course, Archmagus," He flapped his wings hard three times and broke free of the ground and into the air.

Lear'Za shouted into the wind, "Seer'kaat, where are we going?"

Azrael shouted back, "I am now a fugitive, Lear'Za, wanted by the Kingdom, The Hollisters, and the Conclave. We are going to the only place we can go for now. The Morning Lands."

Lear'Za gave a look of surprise, "Well then, Morning Lands it is! What about Isidora?"

His eyes narrowed, "My talk with her will have to be postponed, it seems. After what just happened, I doubt she wants anything to do with me, short of killing me. I must give this time. For the moment, war has come, and there are battles to be fought. Battles in which Isidora, along with her husband, will undoubtedly fight. You said she is a grown woman, Lear'Za. It is time I understand that and let her make her choices, for good or for ill. She has her mother's heart, and I believe that in the end, that will prevail. The oaths made in the name of the Souls of Magic's Dawn will come to fruition. Some may come later than others. However, these are not our battles, I realize this now. This game of chess has advanced, and I must now move to the next piece. That piece lies to the east," Azrael patted the dragon and shouted, "To the Morning Lands, Cirrah!"

The gold dragon gave a mighty roar and veered east towards the continent across the sea.

CHAPTER 41

The stag made its way down the slight slope of the end of the forest and emerged from the trees; before him stood the shoreline of the ocean. He raised his mighty antlered head to the sky and looked at the sun. Casually he clomped down and across the sand towards the water, and a slight breeze picked up, ruffling the short hairs of his pelt.

When he reached the water, he gave a snort from the saltwater spraying over his nose. The wind picked up, tossing sand and making the waves crash a harder. A few feet to his left, the wind swirled into a vortex and coalesced into the figure of a man, shaped from sand and blowing debris. At the same time, as the waves lapped at the stag's hooves, a second figure rose out of the water and began walking towards them. This one was a woman. Her hair was long, curly, and seafoam green, her eyes the same color. Her gown was of a similar shade, and although she stepped out of the water, she appeared dry. She stopped before the man made of wind and the great stag.

"Well that was interesting," Blancheflor said in a melodious voice.

The stag kicked at the sand and whinnied, "More or less, I suppose. Have either of you heard from our elder siblings, Artio and Astraea"

"Not I," Caillech replied.

"Nor I. You know as well as I that they have long left the world in our hands. They believe Leto will honor their agreement. They believe there will always be balance and continue to slumber," Blancheflor answered with a tilt of her head.

Cerridwen lowered his antlered head in sadness, "Then it is as I have feared. Recent events made me suspect, but Artio and Astraea's silence coupled with what we witnessed leaves very little doubt. The time of the prophecy is upon us."

Blancheflor gave a sad look, "You still believe in the validity of that prophecy, Cerridwen? You really believe our brother capable of that kind of treachery?"

Cerridwen raised his head and held his antlers high, "Do you really believe he is not capable after all we know of him, after what he did millennia ago? Are you in such blind denial as Artio and Astraea?"

The sea goddess wrung her hands together, "I had always held hope. He is still our brother."

"I met with the Archmage before this unfortunate turn of fate," Cerridwen said, unmoved, "Everything is falling into place as the prophecy has prescribed."

Caillech's form twisted and shifted like the ever-changing winds he presided over, "Why did you not tell us of this sooner, brother?"

"I had to be sure. Now I am," Cerridwen snorted, his stag nostrils flared, "Either way, Artio and Astraea will not intervene. Once again it is up to us to make the difference where they stubbornly refuse, even though they played a part in all of this from the start, with Azrael and the Sidhe."

Blancheflor's face fell, "You know we are prohibited from interfering in the affairs of the Three."

Cerridwen shook his antlers in frustration, "The coming days will be perilous for Tinil'Gan, and for our pantheon. I am not saying we should interfere directly. But perhaps we should be present, to give a nudge here and there should it be needed. We are gods. It is about time we started acting like it. I can assure you, Leto will not be as faithful to the rules as you want to be. He has already broken them and because of this one of Tilene's children has perished."

Caillech gave a sigh, and the wind picked up. He looked over at Blancheflor, and they both nodded. He turned his featureless face back to Cerridwen, "Although hesitant and cautious, we are as ever with you, my brother. I only caution you to not interfere more than is urgently needed. We must let events take their natural course and only act if Leto makes a move to try and change it."

Cerridwen puffed his chest, "You have my word. Then we are concluded for now."

The three gods nodded to each other in understanding and parted ways. Blancheflor seemed to melt back into the seas and Caillech's wind form dissipated as if never there. Cerridwen's more pedestrian and corporeal form simply walked back into the forest. The beach was left quiet as if a meeting of three of the world's gods had never happened.

CHAPTER 42

The battle was indeed bloody, but the Kingdom drove the Hollisters back into the Spokes. They knew the war would not be won on this day on the Asgerd Plains. What remained of the Castellarian regiment withdrew as well. With Granary back under the banner of the Kingdom, Sir Gideon led the regiment to the small stronghold to encamp. Sir Tollen was grateful for this. He had much on his mind, much more on his mind since Granary was first overrun. He tried to get some sleep when they arrived but found he was plagued with dreams of that fateful day that started this war.

They stole away during the night. The plan was sound, as sound as any. They departed with two hundred men. One hundred set off west towards the Distillar and the elvish encampments just west of the river. Tollen gave command of that force to Sir Jasper. He was capable enough. The antagonizing of the elves was crucial, but not as critical as his mission. *It will take Jasper a*

fortnight at least to complete his task and return. My work will be over by the next morn. Sir Tollen Medici sighed and took a swig of ale in the comfort of his command tent. It was only a few hours before dawn, but he couldn't sleep.

Although sound, he didn't like the taste of this plan. He had been charged this task by his uncle Filobar, so he was duty-bound to obey. It was not knightly; there was no honor in it. But he was a Medici. A great house, yes, but always had they been known as the *shadow knights*. All kingdoms, all kings for that matter, knew that in war and politics there were always unsavory deeds that were necessary for the greater good. These tasks had ever fallen upon House Medici. He would have to take comfort in the greater honor and glory of the Kingdom to soothe his own misgivings. He downed his ale and poured another as he stared at the armor that hung in the corner of his tent. It was enameled in viridian and turquoise, bearing trappings of a stygian owl at rest upon a tree branch. Hollister colors. *Dark deeds, greater glory.* He glanced at a nearby mirror and studied his aged face. *When did I become so old?* He saw the lines of age, the graying stubble on his square jaw, the slight sagging of his jowls. He grunted and knocked the mirror over. All of his men, as well as Jasper's, carried such armor and trappings. In a few weeks, all would know of the deeds done in the name of House Hollister.

He ruminated for the remainder of the dark hours before dawn, and when the herald blew the horn for the camp to rise, he began donning the armor. Their destination was not far. Just over the next rise of hills sat the sleepy township of Granary, lorded by Lord Sethus Marken, a lessor lord of Castellamar. Although the Castellian Mountains were the official border between the Kingdom and the Riverlands there were many towns and holdings that sat at the southern foothills that fell under the banners of Castellamar. When the peace agreement after the rebellion was signed, it was agreed the tract of land for ten leagues south of the mountain should remain under Kingdom control as a buffer between the Riverlands and Castle Pass. Those lands would be the Riverlords downfall. *Dark deeds, greater glory.* Lord Marken had been made aware of the fate of his small folk were to suffer; even he knew it would serve him better in the long run.

Sir Tollen exited his tent and was greeted by a smack of slight chill to his face. Although late summer, early mornings near the mountains carried the cold of autumn and winter to come. His men were disciplined. When he approached the lines, ranks were already forming in their colors of viridian and turquoise. *Most of Granary is just rising, womenfolk preparing their families to break their fast, children rubbing their sleepy eyes.* His squire had already prepared his horse. Sir Tollen mounted up and placed his helm upon his head lowering the visor. He cantered over to the ranks of mounted men. He raised his sword and addressed them.

"Those colors you wear are what you are today," *Dark deeds, greater glory,* "Whatever inglorious feelings and dishonor placed on your soul are not yours to bear. Know that what you do, you do for the glory and prosperity of the Kingdom. In the eyes of the Kingdom, you are and always shall be its honored Castellarian Knights. Follow me, my men, and let us do our duty. For the Kingdom!"

A hundred voices echoed the call, and as one they spurred their horses after their commander. They rode over the hill, spraying sod and dirt. When they reached the crest Sir Tollen gave the signal to halt. He looked down upon Granary. He spotted the smoke from chimneys as breakfasts were being prepared. He heaved a sigh and gave the signal to charge. A hundred horses charged down the hill to the unsuspecting township.

As he suspected they met little resistance. Many of the townspeople were put to the sword before they even knew what was happening. Sir Tollen had firmly ordered his men to commit no baser actions such as rape or the murder of children. He knew those deeds would please the Lords back in San'Seban for it would make The Spokes seem even more menacing. They would have to deal with what he gave them. He was still a knight. The contingent made its way up to the Lord's keep. He was glad for one thing; they had run through the township and had taken control without having to face fellow knights. Granary was only guarded by a local militia. It would have weighed heavily on him if he had to take the life of a Castellarian Knight. He approached the gates and hailed. Two guards looked down from the parapets.

"In the name of House Hollister and The Spokes, I call out for your Lord Liege to surrender!" Sir Tollen shouted up.

"The Kingdom does not bow to the likes of a Riverlord! By what rights to you disturb our lands?"

"I will not parley with a gate guard, good sir. Send out your Lord Liege."

The guard retreated. A few moments later the gates opened and the stooped Lord Marken strolled toward Sir Tollen.

"I'd never thought I'd live to see the day a Riverlord would challenge the Kingdom," Marken spat. Sir Tollen could see the glint in his eye as if to ask, *am I playing the part well enough?* "By what rights does Lord Damien Hollister lay claim to my lands, lands of the Kingdom of Castellamar?"

Sir Tollen paused and looked at the sad-looking man. *He only wanted to please his King and the Council of Lords. Dark deeds, greater glory,* "He claims by this right," Sir Tollen unsheathed his sword and in one motion decapitated the Lord of Granary. He watched the head roll down the sloped gangway to the gates and bump into the hoof of one of his men's horses. The decapitated head had a look of surprise on its face. *He didn't expect that.* He reared his horse around.

"No Marken lives this day. Slay them all. Place Lord Sethus' head upon a pike for all to see. The Spokes!"

Sir Tollen woke with a start, sweat covering his body. What he had done was too much, even for a Medici, even for a shadow knight. He got up and splashed his face with some water from the washbasin. *What Marken called this room theirs,* he wondered. He looked up at the mirror and stared at his reflection. *I must correct this. Even if it means my disgrace and death.* He took a deep breath to calm his nerves and got dressed and made his way out of the room. After a few quick turns he arrived at the room he was looking for. He rapped his knuckles on the worn wood. After a moment the door opened.

Lord Sulik swung the door open, angrily, "Tollen? What do you want? It is the middle of the night."

"We need to talk," He said flatly.

"Can't this wait until the morning? We just fought a battle today?"

You never unsheathed your sword, Sulik. "That is not an option unless you'd like to shout about it right here in the hallway."

Sulik sneered, "Of course not, get in," Sulik opened the door wider and let Tollen pass. He glanced up and down the hall to see if anyone had witnessed his arrival. Satisfied, he shut the door, "Now, what do you want Tollen."

The knight sat down at the small table in Sulik's room and was tapping his finger on it, "This went too far Sulik. Too far. What happened here at Granary should not have happened."

Sulik smiled and walked over to an end table where a wine decanter was placed. He filled a mug as he talked over his shoulder, "You did what was required of you for the greater glory and safety of the Kingdom. Nothing more."

Tollen dropped his head in his hands, "We did not have to kill everyone. Women, children; they did not all have to die," he raised his head in a start when Sulik slammed the mug down on the table in front of him.

"Drink. It will calm your nerves," Sulik sat down gracefully across from him, "You should understand more than anyone, especially being a shadow knight."

Tollen shook his head, "No. There is always a line. We crossed it, Sulik. You crossed it when you extorted my uncle. We have to correct this. We have to tell the king what happened."

Sulik laughed, "Tell the king what exactly? That you decided to slaughter the entire city of Granary pretending to be Hollisters? To what end Tollen? What purpose will it serve?"

"I decided? It was you, Sulik! It was all your plan!" Tollen's voice cracked. He felt a tightness in his throat and found he could no longer speak. In fact, it was becoming difficult to breathe. Choking, he grabbed his throat and fell to the ground. *No, not like this. This cannot be how it ends.*

As he lay on the floor, struggling to breathe, he heard Sulik shuffle and stand. The Realm Regent walked over to him, and Tollen looked up and could see him looking down at him. A cynical smirk on his lips.

"I wouldn't struggle Tollen. It makes it far more painful. The poison will kill you shortly, which is certain. But you left me no choice really. I am disappointed. I have enough trouble with the Cardigans and Montefroys. My daughter is married to your cousin!" Sulik gave him a swift kick to the ribs. Tollen tried to scream out in pain, but his constricting throat and the fluid he could feel filling his lungs made it impossible, "Of course it was my plan. It was my plan to put your fat uncle on the Council. It was my plan to replace most of my father's people in the Council with ones that I knew owed their prosperity to me. I came up with the attack on Granary and the attack on the elves which forced them to ally with us. And now thanks to me, we have reason to take the Spokes and the rest of the Riverlands and bring the Kingdom back to its former glory. A glory I will make sure your family benefits from, despite this display of disloyalty."

Tollen's eyes grew cloudy. He was having a difficult time being able to see the gloating and treacherous face that hovered over him. *At least I tried. I tried to make it right.* His body contorted; with one last gasp, his body finally gave up the battle.

Sulik eyed the dead knight for a moment and smiled. Once he was sure he was dead, he cleared his throat and prepared himself. He walked over to his door and opened it, "Help! Someone help! Sir Tollen has had a heart attack! Send the healers, someone please!" Knights wearily awoke and ran to the distressed call.

CHAPTER 43

Isidora read over the tomes carefully. She had time to plan this time and did not want to make her next quest for an avatar as dangerous as the first. Lately, time was all she seemed to have on her hands.

It had been over a month since that tumultuous day when the war began, her father was murdered, and her new faith began. She had returned back to San'Seban with Sulik for her safety.

My safety. She snorted at the thought. She could defend herself better than most knights with swords. The power and control she had when she summoned the Hammer still played in her mind and made her heart race. But afterward, she was as weak as a babe. The combination of using more power than she ever had with witnessing the death of her father overcame her. She cursed herself every day for that weakness. She should have done something: brought Azrael to justice, joined her husband on the battlefield, something. The sting faded in time, but she promised herself she would never be that weak again, and with her newfound faith, she never would be.

In silence, she had wept for her father. His body had been brought back to San'Seban and given a noble burial in the royal crypts. He was dubbed *Hero of the Battle of Asgerd*. Sulik proclaimed during the services that his sacrifice should never be forgotten, that Sir Griffon was a true son of the Kingdom. As Gideon's wife, she shared his pride in the Kingdom. Although only living here for 5 years, it had become her home. Isidora smiled as she put down the tome and looked out her window. The sun was setting casting its orange glow on the valley.

Gideon and Kethis were still in the field. He had sent her messages letting her know the status of the war. They now lay siege on the mighty fortress. The Spokes would not fall quickly, and he hoped his supplies would last. The elves held true to their word and joined the Kingdom in the siege.

Isidora longed to be by her husband's side, to give her power to the cause, but Sulik insisted she remain in San'Seban to heal her emotional wounds first. He had baptized her into the faith and told her to become strong in will and soul. When she was ready, she could return to the battle and assist Gideon. She agreed and busied herself with learning her faith and making plans for another avatar after the war ended. She looked down at the rune tattoo on her arm. She had not forgotten her oath. Azrael had said the promise was not to him, but to the balance and what was right. This felt right, as right as war can feel.

She wrapped her robes around her more tightly. Fall had firmly set in, and the nights were severely cold with prevalent rains. She drew the thick curtains over the window and walked over to the hearth to stoke the fire a little more. As the flames sprouted higher, she gasped as a shadow hovered against the wall. She spun around the words of magic on her tongue. Leaning against the wall was Lear'Za, a playful smile on her lips.

"How dare you come here, daemoness! Where is Azrael?" Isidora ground her teeth.

Lear'Za pushed herself off the wall and floated close to Isidora, "He is not here, child. Please calm yourself. I know what you saw, and it is not as it seems."

Isidora laughed, "Not as it seems? He killed my father. You watched him do it and then fled with him. Oh, it is exactly as it seems."

Lear'Za frowned, "I know it is hard to believe, Isidora, but you must trust me. I have little time. The portal I opened will only last a few moments, and Azrael does not know I am here. I promised him I would not tell you anything, to let him handle it, but this has gotten out of hand, and you need to know."

Isidora lifted her eyebrows in confusion, "What are you talking about?"

Lear'Za looked back at her portal, and it flickered. She turned back to Isidora hastily and grabbed her by the shoulders, "I must leave. Take this and read it," Lear'Za pulled out a rolled parchment and shoved it into her hands, "Think back on the story of creation Azrael told us when we first departed on our journey. Think hard on it. They say Malystrix had the most vibrant violet eyes," Lear'Za held her gaze firmly as Isidora looked back in confusion. She turned and floated fast towards the quickly degrading portal. She stepped a leg through and turned back to Isidora one final time, "I know he doesn't show it, but he cares for you, deeply," Lear'Za turned her head and went into the portal as it closed shut behind her and the room went quiet.

Confused, Isidora unrolled the parchment and read it.

Hark the coming times I define
A Harbinger of Chaos
Blood of Magic and the Divine.
With this power Chaos consumes
The Holy Trinity becomes One
The Order of life no longer resumes.

> *A forest child's great sacrifice*
> *Souls of the undead she calls to her*
> *One tiny soul to begin the fall is all to suffice.*
> *With this act, the herald's trumpet blows*
> *In the voice of a God, it comes*
> *Shaking many to their souls*
> *The time of reckoning draws nigh*
> *When power of magic draws forth*
> *The spirits of fallen heroes ride high.*
> *A great war ensues encompassing all*
> *Old foes of East, West, North, and South battle*
> *A hero of Man shall fall*
> *In the cave of waters deep*
> *The doorway shall open*
> *Here the fate of Tinil'Gan shall keep*
> *A female it shall be*
> *A golden light shines forth*
> *Upon the Magus great tragedy.*
> *Fallen angels at her feet*
> *Evil whispers in her ear*
> *Bringing death before her eyes.*
> *A God beckons her, shall she give in*
> *Upon her birth shall it begin.*
> *Forsaking all he holds dear*
> *The Magus rises to meet the end.*

Isidora's eyes grew wide as she read. It was the prophecy, the one that had been hinted upon many times but never fully explained. She read it over and over and tried to decipher its meaning. It was terrifying and confusing at the same time. She looked up at her reflection in the mirror, her mind awash with questions. *This is insane. A harbinger of chaos? Blood of magic and the divine—does this imply a child of the gods? What does this all mean?* Her reflection looked back at her, her violet eyes bright in the firelight. Isidora's eyes went wide.

Violet eyes. She dropped the parchment and gasped and placed her hand over her mouth.

EPILOGUE

The river of time flows ever on
Its twists and turns change the view
However, not the course it bears.
For a pebble thrown into its waters
Creates beautiful ripples and eddies.
However, the mighty river flows ever on.
All hope one day to be the one.
Who can alter, reverse, or stop its rapids?
Until that day, the river flows ever on.

A loud steady clap interrupted Malystrix's gentle singing, abruptly ceasing her melody and the click-clack of the knitting needles. Usually, such an intrusion would be welcome to someone like her, who had lived in utter solitude for over three millennia. This one made her brow furrow slightly. There was only one being that could successfully enter the empty realm she resided in. A vast landscape of nothingness: the sky and land of muted amber indistinguishable from each other save the small cottage that was her home. It was the one being that she held the most contempt and hatred for; the god of chaos Leto.

"Such a memorizing and scintillating hymn, my dear. It nearly stilled my eternal heart." The disembodied, sardonic voice echoed in the quaint wooden home. The air before Malystrix shimmered briefly, and the golden outline in the shape of a man stood before her. The center of the figure was translucent, she could make out the wall and the cupboard through it, but its shade was black as night. It almost seemed as if all the universe was held within spinning violently, screaming for release from the void. A feeling she understood intimately. She resumed her knitting and swaying in the creaky rocking chair; her long auburn hair fell softly around her round and youthful face.

"Why, thank you, my Lord. I am eternally grateful for such praise. I will make sure it comforts me during these next millennia of exile you have so generously bestowed upon me."

The golden outline flared in anger, "You dare mock me? Insubordination such as this put you in this predicament."

Her hands clenched momentarily, but her voice remained even. Calm, "I am still at a loss to understand how refusing your advances is considered insubordination. You cannot and will not force me to love you, Leto."

The arm of the god shot outward and grabbed her by the throat. Struggling, Malystrix was wrenched from the chair, the thin piece of furniture fell and clattered to the floor. Her body was forcibly thrown to the far wall, held against it by the god's hand, "You are a minor goddess, Malystrix, and as such you are under my command. I do not know why I bother. It seems three thousand years has still not rid you of the filth of mortal affection."

Although pinned against the wall, her face remained passive. Her hands gripped the wrist of the god, "Even our siblings disagree with this," The words fell from her lips like venom, the only sign she gave of her hidden rage.

The outline of the god's head and shoulders shook, as in silent laughter, "Disagree they may, however they know that by Divine Law they cannot stop me. I am well within my rights. You disgraced us all with your heretical dalliance," His last sentence was uttered in a whisper of condescension.

"Love is not a dalliance, my Lord. Perhaps if you understood that you could have won my heart long before. The other gods understand this, and that is why I suffer my exile gladly knowing my love still exists in other forms."

Leto's hold on Malystrix loosened allowing her to slump to the floor, the boards beneath her groaning under the sudden weight, "Ahh. You speak of your half-breed child. You should thank me for allowing that abomination to survive."

"Your brother and sister allowed it, not you," She said as her eyes narrowed and she rubbed her throat.

"How wrong you are my dear. Your river of time has sped up dramatically, Malystrix. Even in mortal reckoning, the time of the Prophecy is at hand. As we speak, events transpire on the mortal realm that is leading to my inevitable victory," He turned from her and looked out the window at the dull landscape, "Your half-breed is unknowingly playing the part I had intended all along."

She stood up, smiled, and smoothed out her rumpled lavender dress. With a sigh, she lifted the rocking chair upright, sat back down, and reached for the fallen knitting needles, "He will stop you."

The golden outline flared once again, and he spun around not in anger but in remarkable hubris, "He cannot stop me. The fool is but a pebble in your river, Malystrix. He is trapped in the prophecy, and soon enough he will realize that he, too, is trapped, playing a part that will lead to his unraveling and my ultimate triumph. The next time I return, my dear will be in victory. And then you can choose to finally see my greatness or rot in this emptiness for all eternity!"

The god suddenly disappeared. Malystrix's steady hands lifted the blanket. The corner of her mouth dropped, and she made a clicking sound. She dropped a stitch, "He will stop you," She smiled in satisfaction, unraveling it as she had done now countless times over 3000 years, with the same soft ball of violet yarn. The only sound in the small cottage, amidst the void of nothingness, was the creaking of the rocking chair. She resumed humming the hymn she started before the unwanted interruption, with more determination.

To be continued in the next installment
of the Covenant of Souls.

About the Author

G.A. Lungaro is a writer and author of the new novel Souls of Magic's Dawn. He hails from the diverse city of Chicago, Illinois along with his partner Amanda and their three fur babies Caramon, Leo, and Ghost. He is also the father of three adult children and step-father to Amanda's young son.

He has been an avid reader and lover of the fantasy genre ever since he read it for the first time at 15. Inspired by such authors as Tolkein, George RR Martin, and Anne Rice, he has chosen to add his voice to the fantastic world-building done in the genre.

When he is not writing, you might find him entertaining himself with comic books as well as such hobbies as leather tooling and woodworking for his other passion: steampunk.

www.galungaro.com

Lightning Source UK Ltd.
Milton Keynes UK
UKHW012354130220
358691UK00003B/39